Standing in an alien darkened street, accomplice to assault and battery and so utterly, totally *alone*, he started to shake with the kind of real, gut-chilling fear that doesn't frighten as much as it numbs all reality. His thoughts fixated on a single, simple, all-consuming dread.

> I'm never going to get out of this alive.
> I'm going to die here.
> I want to go HOME!

Then a more distant fear finally began to return him to normal. If something could bring a great evil from his own world into this one, why could not that same maleficent force reverse the channel one day and thrust some similar unmentionable horror on his own unsuspecting world?

Somewhere in this world a terror beyond his imagining swelled and prepared. There was no place for him to run!

Books by
ALAN DEAN FOSTER

Alien
Clash of the Titans
Outland
Krull

The Spellsinger Series:
Spellsinger
The Hour of the Gate
The Day of the Dissonance
The Moment of the Magician
The Paths of the Perambulator

The I Inside
Shadowkeep
Starman
Pale Rider

Published by
WARNER BOOKS

ALAN DEAN FOSTER
SPELLSINGER

WARNER BOOKS

A Warner Communications Company

PROLOGUE

Discontent ruled the stars, and there were portents in the heavens.

On the fourth day of Eluria, which follows the Feast of Consanguinity, a great comet was seen in the night sky. It crossed east to west over the Tree and lasted for half a fortnight. It left a black scar on the flesh of existence, a scar that glowed and lingered.

Faces formed within the timescar. Only a very few were capable of discerning their existence. None understood their implication. The faces danced and leered and mocked their ignorant observers. Frustrated or simply terrified, the few who could see turned away or deliberately placed a calming interpretation on what had troubled their minds.

One did not. He could not, for those visions haunted his sleep and tormented his days. He dropped words from formulae, bollixed simple conjurations, stuttered in his reading and rhyming studies.

A great evil was afoot in the world, an evil encountered twice before in the wizard's own long lifetime. But never before had it seemed so potent in its anticipation of coming death and destruction. Its core remained just beyond perception; but he knew it was something he did not understand, something fresh and threatening which shattered all the rules known to commonsense magic. It was rank, alien, shudderingly devoid of emotion and meaning. It horrified him.

Of one thing only was he certain. He would need assistance this time—only another attuned to the same unknown could understand it. Only another could save the world from the horror that threatened to engulf it.

For those who know the secret ways, the tunnels between realities, the crossings between universes are no more difficult to pass than the barriers that separate one individual from another. But such passages are of rare occasion, and once the proper formula is invoked, it can rarely be repeated.

Yet it was time to take the risk.

So the wizard heaved and strained, threw out the request carefully roped to his consciousness. It sailed out into the void of space-time, propelled by a mind of great if aging power. It sought another who could help him understand this fresh darkness that threatened his world. Dimensions slid aside, cleaving around the searching thought and giving it passage.

The wizard trembled with the massive effort. Sentient winds howled about his Tree, plucking dangerously at the thin lifeline within. It had to happen quickly, he knew, or the link would fade without attaching to an ally. And this was a link he might not hope to generate again.

Yet still the void yielded nothing and no one. The . . . the writhing tentacle of wizardness caught a mind, a few thoughts, an identity. Uncertain but unable to hunt further, he plunged inward. Surprisingly, the mind was pliable and open, receptive to invasion and manifestation. It almost seemed to welcome being grasped, accepting the tug with a contented indifference that appalled the wizard, but which he was grateful for nonetheless. This mind was detached, drifting. It would be easy to draw it back.

Easy save for the aged enchanter's waning strength. He locked and pulled, heaved with every ounce of power in him. But despite the subject's lack of resistance the materialization was not clean. At the last instant, the link snapped.

No, no . . . ! But the energy faded, was lost. An infrequent but damaging senility crept in and imposed sleep on that great but exhausted mind. . . .

And while he slumbered, the contented evil festered and planned and schemed, and a shadow began to spread over the souls of the innocent. . . .

The citizens of Pelligrew laughed at the invaders. Though they lived nearest of all the civilized folk to the Greendowns, they feared not the terrible inhabitants of those lands. Their town was walled and hugged the jagged face of a mountain. The only approach was up a single narrow path which could be defended against attack, it was said, by five old women and a brace of infants.

So when the leader of the absurdly small raiding party asked for their surrender, they laughed and threw garbage and night soil down on him.

"Go home!" they urged him. "Go back to your stinking homes and your shit-eating mothers before we decorate the face of our mountain with your blood!"

Curiously, this did not enrage the leader of the raiders. A few within the town remarked on this and worried, but everyone else continued to laugh.

The leader made his way back through the tents of his troops, his dignity unimpaired. He knew what was promised to him.

Eventually he reached a tent larger and darker than any of the others. Here his courage faltered, for he did not enjoy speaking to the one who dwelt within. Nevertheless, it was his place to do so. He entered.

It was black inside, though it was mid-morning without, black and heavy with the stench of unwholesome things and the nearness of death. In the back of the tent was the wizard, awash in attendants. In back of him stood the Font of Evil.

"Your pardon, Master," the leader of the soldiers began, and proceeded to tell of his disdainful reception at the hands of the Pelligrewers.

When he had finished, the hunched form in the dark of the tent said, "Return to your soldiers, good Captain, and wait."

The leader left hurriedly, glad to be out of that unclean place and back among his troops. But it was hard to just wait there, helpless before the unscalable wall and restrained by command, while the inhabitants of the town mocked and laughed and exposed their backsides to his angry soldiers.

Suddenly, a darkening turned the sky the color of lead. There was a thunder, yet there were no clouds. Then the great wall of Pelligrew vanished, turned to dust along with many of its shocked defenders. For an instant his own warriors were paralyzed. Then the blood lust renewed them and they swarmed into the naked town, shrieking in gleeful anticipation.

The slaughter was thorough. Not a soul was left alive. Those who disdained meat relaxed and sipped the pooled blood of the still living.

There was some question as to whether or not to keep the children of the town alive for breeding. Upon consideration, the captain declined. He did not wish to convoy a noisy, bawling lot of infants back to Cugluch. Besides, his soldiers deserved a reward for the patience they had displayed beneath the barrage of verbal and physical refuse the annihilated townsfolk had heaped on them. So he gave his assent for a general butchering of the young.

That night the fire was put to Pelligrew while her children made the soldiers a fine supper. The wood of the houses and the thatch of the roofs burned all night and into the following morning.

The captain watched the last of the flames die out, nodding approvingly as recently dressed meat was loaded for the journey back home. He sucked the marrow from a small arm as he addressed the flier.

"Take the swiftest currents of the air, Herald," he instructed the winged soldier. "Go quickly to the capital. Inform everyone that taunting Pelligrew, thorn in our side for a thousand years, is no more. Tell the people and the court that

14

this first small success is complete and that all the softness of the Warmlands westward shall soon be ours, and soon all the worlds beyond that!''

The flier saluted and rose into the mountain air. The captain turned, saw the occupants of the dark tent packing their own noisome supplies. He watched as the wizard supervised the careful loading of the awful apparition which had destroyed Pelligrew, and shuddered as he turned away from it.

On the strength of that vileness and the wizard's knowledge they might truly march to mastery over the entire Universe, if the wizard was to be believed. But as for himself, he was personally inclined to stay as far away from it as possible.

He loved anything which could find new ways to kill, but this had a reach that spanned worlds. . . .

I

Size and attire alone would have made the giant otter worthy of notice, even if he hadn't tripped over Meriweather's feet. Sprawled whiskers down in the grass, the creature was barely a foot shorter than the lanky youth's own six feet two.

It was by far the largest otter Jon Meriweather had ever seen. Although he was a student of history and not zoology, he was still willing to bet that five and a half feet was somewhat more than otters normally reached. Despite the haze still fogging his brain, he was also fairly certain that they didn't run around in green felt peaked hats, snakeskin vests, or maroon velveteen pants puffed at the ankles. Very deliberately, Jon rose, regarded the stub of the joint he held tightly in his right hand, and flicked it distastefully away. The problem of the moment was not the existence of the utterly impossible otter, but of what his friend Shelly had cut the weed with.

Nevertheless, Jon couldn't take his eyes off the creature as it rolled over onto its rump. The velveteen pantaloons impressed on him a fact he'd never had much reason to consider before: otters have very low waistlines.

This one tugged its feathered cap down firmly over cookie-shaped ears and commenced gathering up the arrows that had spilled from the quiver slung across his back. The task was complicated by the short sword and scabbard strapped across his chest, which kept getting in the way whenever he bent over. An occasional murderous stare directed toward Jon gave him the feeling that the animal would enjoy putting one of the foot-long shafts into him.

That was no reason for concern. He swayed and relished the hallucination. Cannabis had never generated hallucinations in him before, but there was always a first time. What *had* Shelly been cutting their stash with?

Proof that it was cut with something powerful was stumbling about the grass before him, muttering under its breath and gathering arrows.

Doubtless his overtaxed brain was suffering from the long hours of study he'd been putting in lately, coupled with his working from nine at night until three in the morning. The work was necessary. Finals were due in seven weeks, and then presentation of his master's thesis. He savored the title once more: *Manifestations and prefiguring of democratic government in the Americas, as exemplified by the noble–sun king relationships of the Inca, 1248–1350*. It was a great title, he felt, and in presenting a thesis a good title was half the fight. No matter how brilliant the research or the writing, you were doomed without a title.

Having placed the last arrow in its quiver, the otter was carefully sliding it around to his back. This done, he gazed across the meadow. His sharp black eyes took in every tree and bush. Eventually the alert gaze came around to rest on the dreamy figure of Jon Meriweather.

Since the vision appeared to be waiting for some sort of comment, the good-natured graduate student said, "What can I do for you, offspring of my nighttime daydreaming?"

By way of reply the animal again directed its attention across the meadow, searched briefly, then pointed to a far copse. Jon lazily followed the otter's gesture.

Disappearing beneath a mossy boulder the size and shape of a demolished Volkswagen was a bright yellow lizard slightly larger than a chicken. It darted along on its hind legs, the long whiplike tail extended out behind for balance. Once

17

it stared back over its shoulder, revealing a double row of pink dots running down its throat and chest. Then it was gone into the safety of its burrow.

Reality began to rear its ugly head. Jon was slowly taking note of his surroundings. His bed and room, the rows of books on concrete-block-supported shelves, the pinups, the battered TV, had been replaced by an encircling forest of oaks, sycamores, birch, and pine. Tuliplike flowers gleamed nearby, rising above thick grass and clover, some of which was blue. A faint tinkling, as of temple bells, sounded from the distant trees.

Jon held both hands to his head. Lucidity continued to flee laughingly just ahead of his thoughts. He remembered a pain, a pulling that threatened to tear his brain out of his skull. Then he'd been drifting, a different drift from the usual relaxing stupor that enveloped him during an evening of hard study and heavy smoking. His head throbbed.

"Well?" asked the otter unexpectedly, in a high-pitched but not really squeaky voice.

"Well what?" Soon, he told himself frantically, soon I'll wake up and find myself asleep on the bed, with the rest of the Mexia *History of All the Roman Emperors* still to be finished. Not hash, he thought. Something stronger. God, my head.

"You asked what you could do for me." The otter gestured again, a quick, rapid movement in the general direction of the boulder at the edge of the woods. "As your damned great foot caused me t' fall and lose the granbit, you can bloody well go and dig it out for me."

"What for? Were you going to eat it?"

"Nay." The otter's tone was bitterly sarcastic. "I were goin' t' tie the bloody two-legs 'round me neck and wear it as a bloody pendant, I was." His whiskers quivered with his rage. "Try t' play the smartyarse with me, will you? I suppose you be thinkin' your size will protect you?"

Casually adjusting his bow across his back and chest, the

animal drew his short sword and approached Jon, who did not back away. How could he, being deep asleep?

"I know what happens now." He shifted his feet, almost fell. "You'll kill me, and I'll wake up. It's about time. I've got a whole damn book to finish."

"Be you daft!" The otter's head cocked nervously to one side and a furry paw scratched a cheek. "'Cor, I believe you are." He looked around warily. "I know not what influences are bein' brought t' bear in this place, but it's cost me a granbit. I'm for leavin'. Will you not at least apologize?"

"You mean for tripping you?" Jon considered. "I didn't do a damn thing. I'm asleep, remember?"

"You're a damn sight worse than asleep, man. The granbit choke you and make you throw up your bowels, if you be lucky enough t' catch it. I'm finished with it, if it means encounterin' the likes o' you. And if you follow me, I'll slit you from mouth to arse and hasten the process. Keep your damned apology then, and take this parting gift in return."

So saying, he jabbed the dream sword at Jon. It sliced his shirt and knicked his left side just above the belt holding up his jeans. A blinding pain exploded in his side, dampened only slightly by the lingering effects of the evening's smoking. His mouth opened to form a small "O" of surprise. Both hands went to his ribs.

The otter withdrew his sword, the tip now stained red, and slipped it back in its scabbard after cleaning it with tall grass. He turned and started away, muttering obscenities. Jon watched it waddle off across the grass, heading toward the trees.

The pain in his side intensified. Red stained his blue T-shirt. A warm wetness trickled cloyingly down inside his underwear and started down the left leg of his jeans. Superficial wounds bleed way out of proportion to their seriousness, he told himself. But it hurts, he thought despairingly.

I hope to God I wake up soon.

But if he was asleep . . . the pain was too real, far more so than trees or otter. Blood staining the grass, he limped after his assailant.

"Wait a minute . . . please, wait!" The words were thick in his dry throat, and he was ravenously hungry. Holding his wounded side with his left hand and waving his right, he stumbled after the otter. Clover broke fragrantly under his sandals and small flying things erupted in panic from the grass under his feet, to conceal themselves quickly in other pockets of protective green.

Bright sunlight filled the meadow. Birds sang strange songs. Butterflies with stained-glass wings crowned the tulips.

Having reached the outer rank of trees the otter hesitated under an umber sycamore and half drew his sword. "I'm not afeared o' you, daemon-man. Come closer and I'll stick you again." But even while he uttered this brave challenge the animal was backing slowly into the woods, looking to left and right for an avenue of escape.

"I don't want to hurt you," Jon whispered, as much from the agony in his side as from a desire not to panic the creature. "I just want to wake up, that's all." Tears started from his eyes. "Please let me wake up. I want to leave this dream and get back to work. I'll never take another toke, honest to God. It hurts."

He looked back over his shoulder, praying for the sight of his dumpy, cramped room with its cracked ceiling and dirty windows. Instead, he saw only more trees, tulip things, glass butterflies. A narrow brook ran where his bed should have been.

Turning back to the otter he took a step forward, tripped over a rock, and fell, weakened by loss of blood. Peppermint and heather smells filled his nostrils.

Please God, don't let me die in a dream. . . .

Details drifted back to him when he reopened his eyes. It was light out. He'd fallen asleep on his bed and slept the whole night, leaving the Mexia unread. And with an eight o'clock class in Brazilian government to attend.

Judging from the intensity of the light, he'd barely have enough time to pull himself together, gather up his books and notes, and make it to campus. And he'd have words with Shelly for not warning him about the unexpected potency of the pot he'd sold him.

And it was odd how his side hurt him.

"Got to get up," he mumbled dizzily.

" 'Ere now, guv'nor," said a voice that was not his own, not Shelly's, but was nonetheless familiar. "You take 'er easy for a spell. That was a bad knock you took when you fell."

Jon's eyelids rolled up like cracked plastic blinds. A bristled, furry face framing dancing black eyes stared down at him from beneath the rim of a bright green, peaked cap. Jon's own eyes widened. Details of dream slammed into his thoughts. The animal face moved away.

"Now don't you go tryin' any of your daemonic tricks on me . . . if you 'ave any."

"I"—Jon couldn't decide whether to pay attention to the bump on his head or the pain in his side—"I'm not a daemon."

The otter made a satisfied chittering sound. "Ah! Never did think you were. Knew it all along, I did. First off, a daemon wouldn't let hisself be cut as easy as you did and second, they don't fall flat on their puss when they be in pursuit of daemonic prey. Worst attempt at levitation ever I saw.

"Thinkin' I might 'ave misjudged you, for bein' upset over losin' me supper, I bandaged up that little nick I gifted you with. Guess you're naught but a man, what? No hard feelin's, mate?"

Jon looked down at himself. His shirt had been pulled up. A crude dressing of some fibrous material was tied around his waist with a snakeskin thong. A dull ache came from the bandaged region. He felt as though he'd been used as a tackling dummy.

Sitting up very slowly, he again noted his surroundings. He

was not in his apartment, a tiny hovel which now seemed as desirable and unattainable as heaven.

Dream trees continued to shade dream flowers. Grass and blue clover formed a springy mattress beneath him. Dream birds sang in the branches overhead, only they were not birds. They had teeth, and scales, and claws on their wings. As he watched, a glass butterfly lit on his knee. It fanned him with sapphire wings, fluttered away when he reached tentatively toward it.

Sinewy muscles tensed beneath his armpits as the otter got behind him and lifted. "You're a big one . . . give us a 'and now, will you, mate?"

With the otter's aid, Jon soon found himself standing. He tottered a little, but the fog was lifting from his brain.

"Where's my room? Where's the school?" He turned a circle, was met by trees on all sides and not a hint of a building projecting above them. The tears started again, surprising because Jon had always prided himself on his emotional self-control. But he was badly, almost dangerously disoriented. "Where am I? What . . . who are you?"

"All good questions, man." This is a funny bloke, the otter thought. Watch yourself, now. "As to your room and school, I can't guess. As to where we are, that be simple enough to say. These be the Bellwoods, as any fool knows. We're a couple days' walk out o' Lynchbany Towne, and my name be Mudge. What might yours be, sor, if you 'ave a name?"

Jon answered numbly, "Meriweather. Jonathan Thomas Meriweather."

"Well then, Jnthin Tos Miwath . . . Joneth Omaz Morwoth . . . see 'ere, man, this simply won't do! That's not a proper name. The sayin' of it ud give one time enough to dance twice widdershins 'round the slick thighs o' the smooth-furred Felice, who's said t've teased more males than there be bureaucrats in Polastrindu. I'll call you Jon-Tom, if you don't mind, and if you will insist on havin' more than one name.

22

But I'll not give you three. That clatters indecently on the ears.''

"Bellwoods," the lanky, disoriented youth was babbling. "Lynchbany . . . Lynchbany . . . is that near Culver City? It's got to be in the South Bay somewhere.''

The otter put both hands on Jon-Tom's wrists, and squeezed. Hard. "Look 'ere, lad," he said solemnly, "I know not whether you be balmy or bewitched, but you'd best get hold of yourself. I've not the time t' solve your problems or wipe away those baby-bottom tears you're spillin'. You're as real as you feel, as real as I, and if you don't start lookin' up for yourself you'll be a real corpse, with real maggots feedin' on you who won't give a snake fart for where you hailed from. You hearin' me, lad?''

Jon-Tom stopped snuffling, suddenly seemed his proper age. Easy, he told himself. Take this at face value and puzzle it through, whatever it is. Adhere to the internal logic and pray to wake up even if it's in a hospital bed. Whether this animal before you is real or dream, it's all you've got now. No need to make even an imaginary asshole of yourself.

"That's better." The otter let loose of the man's tingling wrists. "You mumble names I ain't never heard o'." Suddenly he slapped small paws together, gave a delighted spring into the air. "O' course! Bugger me for a rat-headed fool for not thinkin' of it afore! This 'as t' be Clothahump's work. The old sot's been meddlin' with the forces of nature again.'' His attitude was instantly sympathetic, whiskers quivering as he nodded knowingly at the gaping Jon-Tom.

" 'Tis all clear enough now, you poor blighter. It's no wonder you're as puzzled and dazed as you appear, and that I couldn't fathom you a'tall.'' He kicked at the dirt, boot sending flowers flying. "You've been magicked here.''

"Magicked?''

"Aye! Oh, don't look like that, guv'nor. I don't expect it's fatal. Old Clothahump's a decent docent and wily enough wizard when he's sober and sane, but the troublemaker o' the

23

ages when he lapses into senility, as 'e's wont t' do these days. Sometimes it's 'ard to tell when 'e's rightside in. Not that it be 'is fault for turnin' old and dotty. 'appens t' us all eventually, I expect.

"I stay away from 'is place, I do. As do any folk with brains enough. Never know what kind o' crazed incantation you might get sucked up in."

"He's a wizard, then," Jon-Tom mumbled. Trees, grass, the otter before him assumed the clarity of a fire alarm. "It's all real, then."

"I told you so. There be nothin' wrong with your ears, lad. No need t' repeat what I've already said. You sound dumb enough as it is."

"Dumb? Now look," Jon-Tom said with some heat, "I am confused. I am worried. I'll confess to being terrified out of my wits." One hand dropped reflexively to his injured side. "But I'm not dumb."

The otter sniffed disdainfully.

"Do you know who was president of Paraguay from 1936 to 1941?"

"No." Mudge's nose wiggled. "Do you know 'ow many pins can dance on the 'ead of an angel?"

"No, and"—Jon-Tom hesitated; his gaze narrowed—"it's 'how many angels can dance on the head of a pin.'"

Mudge let out a disgusted whistle. "Think we're smart, do we. I can't do fire, but I'm not even an apprentice and I can pindance."

His paw drew five small, silvery pins from a vest pocket. Each was about a quarter of an inch long. The otter mumbled something indistinct and made a pass or two over the metal splinters. The pins rose and commenced a very respectable cakewalk in his open palm.

"Allemande left," the otter commanded. The pins complied, the odd one out having some trouble working itself into the pattern of the dance.

"Never can get that fifth pin right. If only we 'ad the 'ead o' an angel."

"That's very interesting," Jon-Tom observed quietly. Then he fainted. . . .

"You keep that up, guv, and the back o' your nog's goin' to be as rough as the hills of Kilkapny Claw. Not t'mention what it's doin' t' your fur."

"My fur?" Jon-Tom rolled to his knees, took several deep breaths before rising. "Oh." Self-consciously he smoothed back his shoulder-length locks, leaned against the helpful otter.

"Little enough as you 'umans got, I'd think you'd take better care o' it." Mudge let loose of the man's arm. "Furless, naked skin . . . I'd rather 'ave a pox."

"I have to get back," Jon-Tom murmured tiredly. "I can't stay here any longer. I've got a job, and classes, and a date Friday night, and I've got to . . ."

"Your otherworldly concerns are of no matter to me." Mudge gestured at the sticky bandage below the man's ribs. "I didn't spear you bad. You ought t' be able to run if you 'ave t'. If it's 'ome you want, we'd best go call on Clothahump. I'll leave you t' 'im. I've work of me own t' do. Can you walk?"

"I can walk to meet this . . . wizard. You called him Clothahump?"

"Aye, that's it, lad. The fornicating troublemakin' blighter, muckin' about with forces 'e can't no longer control. No doubt in my mind t' it, mate. Your bein' 'ere is 'is doin'. 'E be bound to send you back to where you belong before you get 'urt."

I can take care of myself." Jon-Tom had traveled extensively for his age. He prided himself on his ability to adapt to exotic locales. Objectively considered, this land he now found himself in was no more alien-appearing than Amazonian Peru, and considerably less so than Manhattan. "Let's go and find this wizard."

"That's the spirit, guv'nor!" Privately Mudge still thought the tall youth a whining, runny-nosed baby. "We'll 'ave this 'ere situation put right in no time, wot?"

Oak and pine dominated the forest, rising above the sycamore and birch. In addition, Jon-Tom thought he recognized an occasional spruce. All coexisted in a botanistic nightmare, though Jon-Tom wasn't knowledgeable enough to realize the incongruity of the landscape.

Epiphytic bushes abounded, as did gigantic mushrooms and other fungi. Scattered clumps of brown and green vines dripped black berries, or scarlet, or peridot green. There were saplings that looked like elms, save for their iridescent blue bark.

The glass butterflies were everywhere. Their wings sent isolated shafts of rainbow light through the branches. Yet everything seemed to belong, seemed natural, even to the bells formed by the leaves of some unknown tree, which rang in the wind and gave substance to the name of this forest.

The cool woods, with its invigorating tang of mint ever present, had become almost familiar when he finally had his first close view of a "bird." It lit on a low-hanging vine nearby and eyed the marchers curiously.

Bird resemblance ended with the feathers. A short snout revealed tiny sharp teeth and a long, forked tongue. The wings sprouted from a scaly yellow body. Having loosened its clawed feet from the vine, the feathered reptile (or scaly bird?) circled once or twice above their heads. It uttered a charming trill that reminded the astonished Jon-Tom of a mockingbird. Yet it bore closer resemblance to the creature he'd seen scamper beneath the boulder in the meadow than to any bird, and was sooner cousin to a viper than a finch.

A small rock whizzed through the air. With an outraged squawk the feathered apparition wheeled and vanished into the sheltering trees.

"Why'd you do that, Mudge?"

"It were circlin' above us, sor." The otter shook his head

sadly. "Not entirely bright you are. Or don't the flyers o' your own world ever vent their excrement upon unwary travelers? Or is it that you 'ave magicked reasons o' your own for wishin' t' be shat upon?"

"No." He tried to regain some of the otter's respect. "I've had to dodge birds several times."

The confession produced a reaction different from what he'd hoped for.

"BIRDS?" The otter's expression was full of disbelief, the thin whiskers twitching nervously. "No self-respectin' bird would dare do an insult like that. Why, 'ed be up afore council in less time than it takes t' gut a snake. D'you think we're uncivilized monsters 'ere, like the Plated Folk?"

"Sorry." Jon-Tom sounded contrite, though still puzzled.

"Mind you watch your language 'ere, lad, or you'll find someone who'll prick you a mite more seriously than did I."

They continued through the trees. Though low and bandy-legged like all his kind, the otter made up for his slight stride with inexhaustible energy. Jon-Tom had to break into an occasional jog to keep pace with him.

Seeds within belltree leaves generated fresh music with every varying breeze, now sounding like Christmas chimes, now like a dozen angry tambourines. A pair of honeybees buzzed by them. They seemed so achingly normal, so homey in this mad world that Jon-Tom felt a powerful desire to follow them all the way to their hive, if only to assure himself it was not equipped with miniature windows and doors.

Mudge assured him it was not. "But there be them who are related to such who be anything but normal, lad." He pointed warningly eastward. "Many leagues that way, past grand Polastrindu and the source o' the River Tailaroam, far beyond the Swordsward, on the other side o' great Zaryt's Teeth, lies a land no warmblood has visited and returned to tell o' it. A land not to look after, a country in'abited by stinks and suppurations and malodorous creatures who are o' a vileness that shames the good earth. A land where those who are not animal as us rule. A place called Cugluch.''

"I don't think of myself as animal," Jon-Tom commented, momentarily forgetting the bees and wondering at what would inspire such loathing and obvious fear in so confident a creature as Mudge.

"You're not much of a human, either." Mudge let out a high-pitched whistle of amusement. "But I forget myself. You're a stranger 'ere, plucked unwillingly from some poor benighted land o' magic. Unwillingly snookered you've been, an' I ought by right not t' make sport o' you." Suddenly his face contorted and he missed a step. He eyed his taller companion uncertainly.

"You 'ave the right look 'bout you, and you feel right, but with magic one can never be sure. You *do* 'ave warm blood, don't you, mate?"

Jon-Tom winced, listed to his left. A powerful arm steadied him. "Thanks," he told the otter. "You should know. You spilled enough of it."

"Aye, it did seem warm enough, though my thoughts were on other matters at the time." He shrugged. "You've proved yourself harmless enough, anyway. Clothahump will know what he's called you for."

What could this wizard want with me, Jon-Tom wondered? Why is this being done to me? Why not Shelly, or Professor Stanhope, or anyone else? Why me? He noticed that they'd stopped.

"We're there?" He looked around, expecting maybe a quaint thatched cottage. There was no cottage in sight, no house of any kind. Then his eyes touched on the dull-paned windows in the flanks of the massive old oak, the wisp of smoke rising lazily from the chimney that split the thick subtrunks high up, and the modest door scrunched in between a pair of huge, gnarly roots.

They started for the doorway, and Jon-Tom's attention was drawn upward.

"Now what?" wondered Mudge, aware that his entranced companion was no longer listening attentively to his description of Clothahump's growing catalog of peculiarities.

"It's a bird. A real one, this time."

Mudge glanced indifferently skyward. "O' course it's a bird. What, now, did you expect?"

"One of those hybrid lizard things like those we passed in the forest. This looks like a true bird."

"You're bloody right it is, and better be glad this one can't 'ear you talkin' like that."

It was a robin, for all that it had a wingspan of nearly a yard. It wore a vest of kelly green satin, a cap not unlike Mudge's, and a red and puce kilt. A sack was slung and strapped across its chest. It also sported a translucent eyeshade lettered in unknown script.

Three stories above ground a doweled landing post projected from the massive tree. Braking neatly, the robin touched down on this. With surprisingly agile wing tips it reached into the chest sack, fumbled around, and withdrew several small cylinders. They might have been scrolls.

These the bird shoved into a dark recess, a notch or small window showing in the side of the tree. It warbled twice, piercingly, sounding very much like the robins who frequented the acacia tree outside Kinsey Hall back on campus.

Leaning toward the notch, it cupped a wing tip to its beak and was heard to shout distinctly, "Hey, stupid! Get off your fat ass and pick up your mail! You've got three days' worth moldering up here, and if I come by tomorrow and it's still piled up I'll use it for nest lining!" There followed a string of obscenities much out of keeping with the bird's coloring and otherwise gentle demeanor. It turned from the notch with a gruff chirp, grumbling under its breath.

"Horace!" shouted the otter. The bird looked downward and dropped off the perch to circle above them.

"Mudge? Whatcha doin'?" The voice reminded Jon of one he'd heard frequently during a journey to another exotic section of the real world, a realm known as Brooklyn. "Ain't seen ya around town much lately."

"Been out 'untin', I 'ave."

"Where'd ya pick up the funny-looking bozo?"

"Long story, mate. Did I 'ear you right when you said the old geezer hain't been 'ome in three days?"

"Oh, he's inside, all right," replied the bird. "Mixing and sorcering as usual. I can tell because there's a different stink blowing out that mail drop every time I fly in. You wouldn't happen to have worm on ya, would ya?"

"Sorry, mate. Crayfish and oysters run more t' my taste."

"Yeah, I know. No harm in asking." He cocked a hopeful eye at Jon-Tom. "How 'bout you, buddy?"

"Afraid not." Anxious to please, he fumbled in his jeans' pockets. "How about a Juicyfruit?"

"Thanks, but I've had all the berries I can stand for now. I'm up to my ass feathers in berries." He stared at Jon a moment longer, then bid them a civil good-bye.

"Always did envy them birds." Mudge looked envious. "Wings are so much faster than feet."

"I think I'd rather have real feet and hands."

Mudge grunted. "That's a point t' reckon with, guv'nor." They moved to the doorway. "'Ere goes now. Mind," he whispered, "you be on your best behavior, Jon-Tom. Old Clothahump's got the reputation o' bein' fair-tempered for a wizard, but they're a cranky group. Just as soon turn you into a dung beetle as look at you. It ain't good policy t' provoke one, 'specially one as powerful and senile as Clothynose 'ere."

The otter knocked on the door, nervously repeated it when no reply was forthcoming. Jon-Tom noted the animal's tenseness, decided that for all his joking and name-calling he was deeply fearful of wizards or anything having to do with them. He twitched and shifted his feet constantly while they waited. It occurred to Jon-Tom that at no time had he actually seen the otter standing motionless. Trying to ignore the pain pounding in his side he struggled to stand straight and presentable.

In a moment the door would creak inward and he would be standing face to face with what was, at least to Mudge's mind, a genuine magic-making wizard. It was easy enough to visualize him: six and a half feet tall, he would be garbed in flowing purple robes enscribed with mystic symbols. A bestarred pointy hat would crown the majestic head. His face would be wrinkled and stern—what wasn't hidden beneath a flowing white beard—and he would very likely be wearing thick glasses.

The door opened inward. It creaked portentously. "Good morning," he began, "we . . ."

The rest of the carefully rehearsed greeting shattered in his throat as he stumbled backward in panic, tripped, and fell. Something tore in his side and he sensed dampness there. He wondered how much longer he could tolerate the wound without having it properly treated, and if he might die in this falsely cheerful place, as far from home as anyone could be. The monstrosity that had filled the open doorway drifted toward him as he tried to crawl, to scramble away. . . .

II

Mudge stared disgustedly down at his charge, sounded both angry and embarrassed. "Now wot the bloody 'ell's the matter with you? It's only Pog."

"P-p-pog?" Jon-Tom was unable to move his eyes from the hovering horror.

"Clothahump's famulus, you colossal twit! He . . ."

"Never mind," rumbled the gigantic black bat. "I don't mind." His wing tips scraped the jambs as he fluttered back into the portal. Oversized pink ears and four sharp fangs caught the light. His voice was incredibly rough, echoing from a deep gravel mine. "I know I'm not pretty. But I never knocked anyone down because of it." He flew out now to hover nearer Jon.

"You're not very handsome yourself, man."

"Go easy on 'im, Pog." Mudge tried to sound conciliatory. "'E's been magicked from 'is world into ours, and 'e's wounded besides." The otter diplomatically avoided mentioning that he'd been the cause of the injury.

Jon-Tom struggled unsteadily to his feet. Claret ran from the left leg of his pants, thick and warm.

"Clothahump been workin' up any otherworldly invokings?"

"He is soberer dan usual, if dat's what you mean." The bat let loose a derisive snort.

A rich, throaty voice called from the depths of the tree, an

32

impressive if slightly wavering voice that Jon-Tom instinctively knew belonged to the master sorcerer. "Who's there, Pog?"

"Mudge, da otter hunter, Master. And some damaged, dopey-looking human."

"Human, you say?" There was an excited edge to the question. "In then, bring them in."

"Come on," ordered Pog curtly. "His nibs'll see you." The bat vanished into the tree, wings larger than the robin's barely clearing the entrance.

"You all right, mate?" Mudge watched the swaying form of his unwanted companion. "Why'd you 'ave a fit like that? Pog be no uglier than any other bat."

"It wasn't . . . wasn't his countenance that upset me. It was his size. Most of the bats where I'm from don't grow that big."

"Pog be about average, I'd say." Mudge let the thought slide. "Come on, now, and try not to bleed too much on the floor."

Refusing the otter's support, Jon-Tom staggered after him. The hallway was a shock. It was far too long to fit inside the oak, despite its considerable diameter. Then they entered a single chamber at least twenty-five feet high. Bookshelves lined the walls, filled with tomes of evident age and all sizes and bindings. Incense rose from half a dozen burners, though they could not entirely obliterate the nose-nipping miasma which filled the room.

Scattered among books lay oddly stained pans and bowls, glass vials, jars filled with noisome objects, and other unwholesome paraphernalia. Skulls variously treated and decorated were secured on the walls. To Jon-Tom's horror, they included a brace that were obviously human.

Windows offered ingress to topaz light. This colored the high chamber amber and gold and made live things of the dust motes pirouetting in the noxious air. The floor was of wood chips. A few pieces of well-used furniture made of heavy wood and reptile skin dominated the center of the room.

Two doors ajar led to dimly glimpsed other rooms.

"This is impossible," he said to Mudge in a dull whisper. "The whole tree isn't wide enough to permit this one room, let alone others and the hallway we just came through."

"Aye, guv'nor, 'tis a neat trick it is." The otter sounded impressed but not awed. "Sure solves the space problem, don't it? I've seen it in towns in a few wealthy places. Believe me, the initial spell costs plenty, not t'mention the frequent renewals. Permanently locked hyperdimensional vortical expansions don't come cheap, wot?"

"Why don't they?" Jon-Tom asked blankly, unable to think of a more sensible comment in the face of spatial absurdity.

Mudge looked up at him conspiratorially. "Inflation."

They looked around to see Pog returning from another room. "He says he'll be along in a minute or two."

"What kind of mood is he in?" Jon-Tom looked hopefully at the bat.

"Comprehensible." Keeping his balance in midair, the bat reached with a tiny clawed hand set halfway along his left wing into a pouch strapped to his chest. It was much smaller than the robin's. He withdrew a small cigar. "Gotta light?"

"I'm out o' flints, mate."

"Just a second." Jon-Tom fumbled excitedly in his jeans. "I do." He showed them his cheap disposable lighter.

Mudge studied it. "Interestin'."

"Yeah." Pog fluttered close. Jon-Tom forced himself to ignore the proximity of those gleaming, razor-sharp fangs. "Never saw a firemaker like it." He swung the tiny cigar around in his mouth.

Jon-Tom flipped the wheel. Pog lit the cigar, puffed contentedly.

"Let's 'ave a look, lad." Jon-Tom handed the lighter over. The otter turned it around in his paws. "'Ow's it work?"

"Like this." Jon-Tom took it back, spun the wheel. Sparks, but no flame. He studied the transparent base. "Out of fluid."

"Got stuck wid a bum spell?" Pog sounded sympathetic. "Never mind. And thanks for da light." He opened his mouth, blew smoke squares.

"It has nothing to do with spells," Jon-Tom protested. "It words on lighter fluid."

"Get my money back if I were you," advised the otter.

"I'd rather get me back." Jon-Tom studied his wrist. "My watch has stopped, too. Battery needs replacing." He held up a hand. "And I don't want to hear anything more about spells." Mudge shrugged, favoring Jon-Tom with the look one would bestow on an idiot relation. "Now where's this lazy old so-called wizard of yours?" Jon-Tom asked Pog.

"OVER HERE!" a powerful voice thundered.

Shaking lest his discourteous remark had been overheard, Jon turned slowly to confront the renowned Clothahump.

There were no flowing robes or white beard, no peaked hat or cryptically marked robe. But the horn-rimmed glasses were present. Somehow they remained fixed above a broad, rounded beak, just above tiny nostrils. The glasses did not have arms extended back and behind ears, since a turtle's ears are almost invisible.

A thick book clutched in one stubby-fingered hand, Clothahump waddled over to join them. He stood a good foot shorter than Mudge.

"I mean no disrespect, sir," Jon had the presence of mind to say. "I didn't know you were in the room and I'm a stranger here and I . . ."

"Tosh, boy." Clothahump smiled and waved away the coming apology. His voice had dropped to normal, the wizardly thunder vanished. "I'm not easily offended. If I were I wouldn't be able to put up with *him*." He jerked a thumb in Pog's direction. "Just a moment, please."

He looked down at himself. Jon followed the gaze, noticing a number of small knobs protruding from the wizard's plastron. Clothahump tugged several, revealing tiny drawers built into his front. He hunted around for something, mumbling apologies.

"Only way I can keep from losing the really important powders and liquids," he explained.

"But how can you . . . I mean, doesn't that hurt?"

"Oh heavens no, boy." He let loose an infectious chuckle. "I employ the same technique that enables me to enlarge the inside of my tree without enlarging the outside."

"Bragging," grumped Pog, "when da poor lad's obviously in pain."

"Hold your tongue!" The bat whirled around in tight cirlces, but went silent. "I have to watch his impertinence." Clothahump winked. "Last time I fixed him so he could only sleep right side up. You should have seen him, trying to hang from his ears." He chuckled again.

"But I don't like to lose my temper in front of guests. I cultivate a reputation for mildness. Now then," he said with a professional air, "let's have a look at your side."

Jon-Tom watched as the turtle gently eased aside the crude bandage concocted by Mudge. Stubby fingers probed the glistening, stained flesh, and the youth winced.

"Sorry. You'd best sit down."

"Thank you, sir." They moved to a nearby couch, whose legs were formerly attached to some live creature of unimaginable shape. He lowered himself carefully, since the cushions were barely half a foot off the floor, at a level designed to accomodate the turtle's low backside.

"Stab wound." Clothahump regarded the ugly puncture thoughtfully. "Shallow, though. We'll soon have you fixed."

"'Ere now, your wizardship," Mudge broke in. "Beggin'

your pardon, but I've always 'eard tell 'twas sorceral procedure to seek payment for magicking services in advance.''

"That's not a problem here . . . what did you say your name was?"

"I didn't, but it's Mudge."

"Um. As I said, payment will be no problem for this lad. We'll simply consider this little repair as an advance against his services."

"Services?" Jon-Tom looked wary. "What services?"

"He ain't much good for anything, from what I've seen," Mudge piped up.

"I would not expect a mere scavanger such as yourself, Mr. Mudge, to understand." The wizard adjusted his glasses haughtily. "There have been forces at work in the world only I could fully comprehend, and only I am properly equipped to deal with them. The presence of this lad is but a small piece of a dangerously complex puzzle."

There, Mudge thought triumphantly. Knew he'd been muckin' about.

"It is obvious he is the one I was casting for last night. You see, he is a wizard himself."

"Who . . . 'im?" Mudge laughed in the manner of others, high and squeaky, like the laughter of wise children. "You're jokin', mate."

"I do not joke in matters of such grave import." Clothahump spoke somberly.

"Yeah, but '*im* . . . a wizard? He couldn't even put a new spell on 'is firemaker."

The turtle sighed, spoke slowly. "Coming as he does from a world, from a universe, other than our own, it is to be expected that some of his magic would differ from ours. I doubt I would be able to make use of my own formidable talents in his world. But there is an awesome interdimensional magic abroad in the world, Mudge. To cope successfully with it we require the aid and knowledge of one accustomed to its workings.'' He looked troubled, as though burdened by some hidden weight he chose to keep hidden from his listeners.

"He is the magician I sought. I used many new and unproven words, many intergrams and formulae rare and difficult to blend. I cast for hours, under great strain. I had given up hope of locating anyone, and then chanced upon this drifting spirit, so accessible and free.''

Jon-Tom thought back to what he'd been smoking; he'd been drifting, no doubt of that. But what was all this about him being a wizard-magician?

Sharp eyes were staring into his own from behind thick lenses. "Tell me, boy. Are not the wizards and magicians of your world known by the word En'geeniar?''

"En'gee . . . engineer?''

"Yes, that is the proper sounding of it, I think.''

"I guess that's as good an analogy as any.''

"You see?'' He turned knowingly back to Mudge. "And it is through his service he will pay us back.''

"Uh, sir . . . ?'' But Clothahump had disappeared behind a towering stack of books. Clinking noises sounded.

Mudge was now convinced he'd have been much better off had he never tracked that granbit or set eyes on this particular gangling young human. He studied the slumping form of the injured youth. Jon-Tom was spritely enough of word . . . but a wizard? Still, one could never be certain of anything, least of all appearances, when dealing with wizardly doings. Common folk did well to avoid such.

How could anyone explain a wizard who could not spell a simple firemaker, much less fix an injury to himself? The lad's disorientation and fear were real enough, and neither spoke of the nature of wizards. Best to wait, perhaps, and see what concealed abilities this Jon-Tom might yet reveal. Should such abilities suddenly surface, it might also be best to insure that he forgot who put the hole in his ribs.

"Now lad, don't pay no mind t' what Clothahump says

about payments and such. No matter what the final cost, we'll see it's taken care of. I feel sort o' responsible t' make certain o' that.''

"That's good of you, Mudge.''

"Aye, I know. Best not even t' mention money to 'is nibs.''

Laden with bottles and odd containers fashioned of ceramic, the turtle waddled back toward them. He arranged the collection neatly on the wood chips in front of the couch. Chosing from several, he mixed their contents in a small brass bowl set between Jon-Tom's legs. A yellow powder was added to a murky pool in the bowl and was followed by a barely audible mumbling. Mudge and Jon-Tom clutched suddenly at their nostrils. The paste was now emitting an odor awful in the extreme.

Clothahump added a last pinch of blue powder, stirred the mixture, and then began plastering it directly on the open wound. Thoughts of infection faded when it became clear to Jon that the paste was having a soothing effect on the pain.

"Pog!" Clothahump snapped short fingers. "Bring a small crucible. The one with the sun symbols engraved on the sides.''

Jon-Tom thought he might have heard the bat mumble, "Why don't ya get it yourself, ya lazy fat cousin to a clam.'' But he couldn't be sure.

In any case, Pog did not speak when he returned with the requested crucible. He deposited it between Jon-Tom and the wizard, then flapped back out of the way.

Clothahump measured the paste into the crucible, added a vile-smelling liquid from a tall, waspish black bottle, then a pinch of something puce from a drawer near his right arm. Jon-Tom wondered if the wizard's built-in compartments ever itched.

"What the devil did I do with that wand . . . ah!'' Using a small ebony staff inlaid with silver and amethyst, he stirred the mixture, muttering continuously.

Within the crucible the paste had gained the consistency of a thick soup. It began to glow a rich emerald green. Tiny explosions broke its surface, were reflected in Jon-Tom's wide eyes. The mixture now smelled of cinnamon instead of swamp gas.

Using the wand, the wizard dipped out some of the liquid and tasted it. Finding it satisfactory, he gripped the wand at either end with two fingers of each hand and began passing it in low swoops over the boiling crucible. The sparks on the liquid's surface increased in intensity and frequency.

> "Terra bacteria,
> Red for muscle, blue for blood,
> Ruination, agglutination, confrontation,
> Knit Superior.
> Pyroxine for nerves, Penicillin for curds.
> Surgical wisps, solvent site, I bid you complete
>   your unquent fight!"

Jon-Tom listened in utter bewilderment. There was no deep-throated invocation of tail of newt, eye of bat. No spider's blood or ox eyes, though he remained ignorant of the powders and fluids the wizard had employed. Clothahump's mystic singsong chatter of pyroxine and agglutinating and such sounded suspiciously like the sort of thing a practicing physician might write to amuse himself in a moment of irrepressible nonsense.

As soon as the recital had been completed, Jon-Tom asked about the words.

"Those are the magic words and symbols, boy."

"But they actually mean something. I mean, they refer to real things."

"Of course they do." Clothahump stared at him as if concerned more about his sanity than his wound. "What is more real than the components of magic?" He nodded at the watch. "I do not recognize your timepiece, yet I accept that it keeps true time."

"That's not magical, though."

"No? Explain to me exactly how it works."

"It's a quartz-crystal. The electrons flow through . . . I mean . . ." He gave up. "It's not my specialty. But it runs on electricity, not magic formulae."

"Really? I know many electric formulae."

"But dammit, it runs on a battery!"

"And what is inside this thing you call a battery?"

"Stored electric power."

"And is there no formula to explain that?"

"Of course there is. But it's a mathematical formula, not a magic one."

"You say mathematics is not magic? What kind of wizard are you?"

"I keep trying to tell you, I'm . . ." But Clothahump raised a hand for silence, leaving a frustrated Jon-Tom to fume silently at the turtle's obstinacy.

Jon-Tom began to consider what the wizard had just said and grew steadily more confused.

In addition to the firefly explosions dancing on its surface, the paste-brew had changed from green to yellow and was pulsing steadily. Clothahump laid his wand aside ceremoniously. Lifting the crucible, he offered it to the four corners of the compass. Then he tilted it and drained the contents.

"Pog." He wiped paste from his beak.

"Yes, Master." The bat's voice was subservient now.

Clothahump passed him the crucible, then the brass bowl. "Scullery work." The bat hefted both containers, flapped off toward a distant kitchen.

"How's that now, my boy?" Clothahump eyed him sympathetically. "Feel better?"

"You mean . . . that's it? You're finished?" Jon-Tom thought to look down at himself. The ugly wound had vanished completely. The flesh was smooth and unbroken, the sole

41

difference between it and the surrounding skin being that it wasn't suntanned like the rest of his torso. It occurred to him that the pain had also left him.

Tentatively he pressed the formerly bleeding region. Nothing. He turned an open-mouthed stare of amazement on the turtle.

"Please." Clothahump turned away. "Naked adulation embarrasses me."

"But how . . . ?"

"Oh, the incantations healed you, boy."

"Then what was the purpose of the stuff in the bowl?"

"That? Oh, that was my breakfast." He grinned as much as his beak would allow. "It also served nicely to distract you while you healed. Some patients get upset if they see their own bodies healing . . . sometimes it can be messy to look upon. So I had the choice of putting you to sleep or distracting you. The latter was safer and simpler. Besides, I was hungry.

"And now I think it time we touch on the matter of why I drew you into this world from your own. You know, I went to considerable trouble, not to mention danger, of opening the portals between dimensions and bending space-time. But first it is necessary to seal this room. Move over there, please."

Still wordless at his astonishing recovery, Jon-Tom obediently stepped back against a bookcase. Mudge joined him. So did the returning Pog.

"Scrubbing crucibles," the bat muttered under his breath. Clothahump had picked up his wand and was waving it through the air, mumbling cryptically. "Dat's all I ever do around here; wash da dishes, fetch da books, clean da dirt."

"If you're so disgusted, why stick around?" Jon-Tom regarded the bat sympathetically. He'd almost grown used to its hideousness. "Do you want to be a wizard so badly?"

"Shit, no!" Pog's gruffness gave way to agitation. "Wizarding's mighty dangerous stuff." He fluttered nearer. "I've indentured myself to da old wreck in return for a major, permanent transmogrification. I only gots ta stick it out another few years . . . I tink . . . before I can demand payment.''

"What kind o' change you got in mind, mate?''

Pog turned to face the otter. ''Y'know da section o' town at da end of da Avenue o' da Pacers? Da big old building dere dat's built above da stables?''

"Cor, wot be you doin' thereabouts? You don't rate that kind o' trade. That's a high-rent district, that is.'' The otter was grinning hugely under his whiskers.

"I know, I know,'' confessed the disconsolate Pog. ''I've a friend who made a killing on da races who took me dere one night ta celebrate. He knows Madam Scorianza, who runs da house for arboreals. Dere's a girl who works up dere, not much more dan a fledgling, a full flagon o' falcon if ever dere one was. Her name's Uleimee and she is,'' he fairly danced in the air as he reminisced, ''da most exquisite creature on wings. Such grace, such color and power, Mudge! I thought I'd die of ecstasy.'' The excitement of the memory trembled in the air.

"But she won't have a thing ta do wid me unless I pay like everyone else. She dotes on a wealthy old osprey who runs a law practice over in Knotsmidge Hollow. Me she won't do much more dan loop da loop wid, but whenever dis guy flicks a feather at her she's ready ta fly round da world wid him.''

"Forget 'er then, mate,'' Mudge advised him. ''There be other birds and some of 'em are pretty good-lookin' bats. One flyin' fox I've seen around town can wrap 'er wings 'round me any time.''

"Mudge, you've never been in love, have ya?''

"Sure I 'ave . . . lots o' times.''

"I thought dat much. Den I can't expect ya ta understand.''

"I do.'' Jon-Tom nodded knowingly. ''You want Clothahump to transform you into the biggest, fastest falcon around, right?''

"Wid da biggest beak,'' Pog added. ''Dat's da only reason why I hang around dis hole waitin' wing and foot on da doddering old curmudgeon. I could never afford ta pay for a permanent transmogrification. I got ta slave it out.''

Jon-Tom's gaze returned to the center of the room. Having miraculously cured the stab wound, the doddering old curmudgeon was beckoning for them to rejoin him. The windows were dimming rapidly.

''Come close, my friends.'' Mudge and Jon-Tom did so. Pog hung himself from the upper rim of a nearby bookcase.

''A great crisis threatens to burst upon us,'' the wizard said solemnly. It continued to darken inside the tree. ''I can feel it in the movement of worms in the earth, in the way the breezes whisper among themselves when they think no one else is listening. I sense it in the pattern formed by raindrops, in the early flight of leaves this past autumn, in the call of reluctant winter seedlings and in the nervous belly crawl of the snake. The clouds collide overhead, so intent are they on the events shaping themselves below, and the earth itself sometimes skips a heartbeat.

''It is a crisis of our world, but its crux, its center, comes from another . . . from *yours*,'' and he stabbed a stubby finger at a shocked Jon-Tom.

''Be calm, boy. You yourself have naught to do with it.'' It was dark as night inside the tree now. Jon-Tom thought he could feel the darkness as a perceptible weight on his neck. Or were the other things crowding invisibly near, fighting to hear through the protective cloak the sorcerer had drawn tight about the tree?

''A vast malevolence has succeeded in turning the laws of magic and reason inside out, to bring spells of terrible power from your world into ours, to threaten our peaceful land.

''It lies beyond my meager skills to determine what this power is, or to cope with it. Only a great en'geeneer-magician from your own world might supply the key to this menace. Woeful difficult it be to open the portal between dimensions, yet I had to cast out for such a person. It can be done only once or twice in a year's time, so great is the strain on parts of the mind. That is why you are come among us now, my young friend.''

''But I've been trying to tell you. I'm not an engineer.''

Clothahump looked shaken. ''That is not possible. The portals would open *only* to permit the entrance of an en'geneer.''

''I'm truly sorry,'' Jon-Tom spread his hands in a gesture of helplessness. ''I'm only a prelaw student and would-be musician.''

''It can't be . . . at least, I don't think it can.'' Clothahump abruptly looked very old indeed.

''Wot's the nature o' this 'ere bloomin' crisis?'' the irrepressible Mudge demanded to know.

''I don't precisely know. I know for certain only that it is centered around some powerful magic drawn from this lad's world-time.'' A horny hand slammed a counter, rocking jars and cannisters. Thunder flooded the room.

''The conjuration could not have worked save for an en'geneer. I was casting blind and was tired, but I cannot be wrong in this.'' He took a deep breath. ''Lad, you say you are a student?''

''That's right.''

''A student en'geneer, perhaps?''

''Sorry. Prelaw. And I don't think amateur electric guitar qualifies me, either. I also work part time as a janitor at . . . wait a minute, now.'' He looked worried. ''My official title is *sanitation engineer*.''

Clothahump let out a groan of despair, sank back on the couch. ''So ends civilization.''

Pog let loose of the bookcase shelf and flew high above them, growling delightedly. ''Wonderful, wonderful! A wizard of garbage!'' He dove sharply, braked to hover in front of Jon. ''Welcome oh welcome, wizard most high! Stay and help me make all da dirt in dis dump disappear!''

''BEGONE!'' Clothahump thundered in a tone more suited to the throat of a mountain than a turtle. Jon-Tom and Mudge shook as that unnatural roar filled the room, while Pog was

..p against the far side of the tree. He tumbled
...y to the floor before he could right himself and get
..aky wings working again. He whipped out through a side
passage.

"Blasphemer of truth." The turtle's normal voice had
returned. "I don't know why I retain him. . . ." He sighed,
adjusted his spectacles, and looked sadly at Jon-Tom.

" 'Tis clear enough now what happened, lad. I was not
precise enough in defining the parameters of the spell. I am
an old turtle, and very tired. Sloppy work has earned its just
reward.

"Months it took me to prepare the conjuration. Four
months' careful rune reading, compiling the requisite materials and injunctives, a full cauldron of boiled subatomic
particles and such—and I end up with you."

Jon-Tom felt guilty despite his innocence.

"Not to trouble yourself with it, lad. There's nothing you
can do now. I'll simply have to begin again."

"What happens if you don't succeed in time, sir? If you
don't get the help you think you'll need?"

"We'll probably all die. But it's a small matter in the
universal scheme of things.

"That's all?" asked Jon-Tom sarcastically. "Well, I do
have work to get back to. I'm really sorry I'm not what you
expected, and I do thank you for fixing my side, but I'd
really appreciate it if you could send me back home."

"I don't think that's possible, lad."

Jon-Tom tried not to sound panicked. "If you open this
portal or whatever for me, maybe I could find you the
engineer you want. Any kind of engineer. My university's
full of them."

"I am sure of that," said Clothahump benignly. "Otherwise the portal would not have impinged on the fabric of your
world at the place and time it did. I was in the proper fishing
ground. I simply hooked the wrong subject.

"Sending you back is not a question of choice, but of time

and preparation. Remember that I told you it takes months to prepare such a conjuration, and I must rest as near to a year as possible before I risk the effort once more. And when I do so, I fear it must be for more important things than sending you back. I hope you understand, but it will not matter if you do not."

"What about another wizard?" Jon-Tom asked hopefully.

Clothahump sounded proud. "I venture to say no other in all the world could manipulate the necessary incantations and physical distortings. Rest assured I will send you back as soon as I am able." He patted Jon-Tom paternally with one hand and wagged a cautionary finger at him with the other.

"Never fear. We will send you back. I only hope," he added regretfully, "I am able to do so before the crisis breaks and we are all slaughtered." He whispered some words, absently waved his wand.

> "Dissemination vanish,
> Solar execration banish.
> Wormwood high, cone-form low,
> Molecules resume thy flow."

Light returned, rich and welcome, to the dimensionally distorted interior of the tree. With the darkness went the feeling of unclean things crawling about Jon-Tom's back. Lizard songs sounded again from the branches outside.

"If you don't mind my saying so, your magic isn't at all what I expected," Jon-Tom ventured.

"What did you expect, lad?"

"Where I come from, magic formulae are always done up with potions made from things like spiders' legs and rabbits' feet and . . . oh, I don't know. Mystic verbs from Latin and other old languages."

Mudge snorted derisively while Pog, peering out from a doorway, allowed himself a squeaky chuckle. Clothahump merely eyed the pair disapprovingly.

"As for spiders' legs, lad, the little ones underfoot are no

47

good for much of anything. The greater ones, on the other hand . . . but I've never been to Gossameringue, and never expect to.'' Clothahump gestured, indicating spiders as long as his arm, and Jon-Tom held off inquiring about Gossameringue, not to mention the whereabouts of spiders of such magnitude.

''As for the rabbits' feet, I'd expect any self-respecting rabbit to cut me up and use me for a washbasin if I so much as broached the idea. Words are time-proven by experimentation, and agreed upon during meetings of the sorcerer's grand council.''

''But what do you use then to open a passage from another dimension?''

Clothahump edged conspiratorially close. ''I'm not supposed to give away any Society secrets, you understand, but I don't think you'd even remember. You need some germanium crystals, a pinch of molybdenum, a teaspoon of californium . . . and working with those short-lived superheavies is a royal pain, I'll tell you. Some regular radioactives and one or two transuranics, the acquisition of which is a task in itself.''

''How can you locate . . . ?''

''That's other formulae. There are other ingredients, which I definitely can't mention to a noninitiate. You put the whole concatenation into the largest cauldron you've got, stir well, dance three times moonwise around the nearest deposit of nickel-zinc and . . . but enough secrets, lad.''

''Funny sort of magic. Almost sounds like real science.''

Clothahump looked disappointed in him. ''Didn't I already explain that to you? Magic's pretty much the same no matter what world or dimension you exist in. Only the incantations and the formulae are different.''

''You said that a rabbit would resist giving up a foot. Are rabbits intelligent also?''

''Lad, lad.'' Clothahump settled tiredly into the couch, which creaked beneath him. ''All the warm-blooded are intelligent. That is as it should be. Has been as far back as history goes. All except the four-foot herbivores: cattle, horses, antelopes, and the like." He shook his head sadly. "Poor creatures never developed useful hands from those hooves, and the development of intelligence is concurrent with digital dexterity.

"The rest have it, though. Along with the birds. None of the reptiles save us turtles, for some reason. And the inhabitants of Gossameringue and the Greendowns, of course. The less spoken about them, the better." He studied Jon-Tom.

"Now since we can't send you home, lad, what are we going to do with you . . . ?"

III

Clothahump considered several moments longer. "We can't just abandon you in a strange world, I suppose. I do feel somewhat responsible. You'll need some money and a guide to explain things to you. You, otter, Mudge!"

The otter was intent on a huge tome Pog was avidly displaying. "Both of you get away from the sex incantations. You wouldn't have the patience to invoke the proper spirits anyhow. Serve you both right if I let you make off with a formula or two and you messed it up right clever and turned yourselves neuter."

Mudge shut the book while Pog busied himself dusting second-story windows.

"What d'you want o' me, your wizardness?" an unhappy Mudge asked worriedly, cursing himself for becoming involved.

"That deferential tone doesn't fool me, Mudge." Clothahump eyed him warningly. "I know your opinion of me. No matter, though." Turning back to Jon-Tom he examined the young man's attire: the poorly engraved leather belt, the scuffed sandals, the T-shirt with the picture of a hirsute human wielding a smoking instrument, the faded blue jeans.

"Obviously you can't go tramping around Lynchbany Towne or anywhere else looking like that. Someone is likely to challenge you. It could be dangerous."

"Aye. They might die alaughin'," suggested Mudge.

"We can do without your miserable witticisms, offspring

of a spastic muskrat. What is amusing to you is a serious matter to this boy.''

''Begging your pardon, sir,'' Jon-Tom put in firmly, ''but I'm twenty-four. Hardly a boy.''

''I'm two hundred and thirty-six, lad. It's all relative. Now, we must do something about those clothes. And a guide.'' He stared meaningfully at Mudge.

''Now wait a minim, guv'nor. It were your bloomin' portal 'e stumbled through. I can't 'elp it if you pinched the wrong chap.''

''Nevertheless, you are familiar with him. You will therefore assume charge of him and see that he comes to no harm until such time as I can make other arrangements for him.''

Mudge jerked a furry thumb at the watching youth. ''Not that I don't feel sorry for 'im, your wizardship. I'd feel the same way toward any 'alf mad creature . . . let alone a poor, furless human. But t' make me responsible for seein' after 'im, sor? I'm a 'unter by trade, not a bloody fairy godmother.''

''You're a roustabout by trade, and a drunkard and lecher by avocation,'' countered Clothahump with considerable certitude. ''You're far from the ideal guardian for the lad, but I know of no scholars to substitute, feeble intellectual community that Lynchbany is. So . . . you're elected.''

''And if I refuse?''

Clothahump rolled up nonexistent sleeves. ''I'll turn *you* into a human. I'll shrink your whiskers and whiten your nose, I'll thin your legs and squash your face. Your fur will fall out and you'll run around the rest of your life with bare flesh showing.''

Poor Mudge appeared genuinely frightened, his bravado completely gone. ''No, no, your sorcererness! If it's destined I take the lad in care, I ain't the one t' challenge destiny.''

''A wise and prosaic decision.'' Clothahump settled down. ''I do not like to threaten. Now that the matter of a guide is settled, the need of money remains.''

"That's so." Mudge brightened. "Can't send an innocent stranger out into a cruel world penniless as well as ignorant."

"Mind you, Mudge, what I give the lad is not to be squandered in wining and wenching."

"Oh, no, no, no, sor. I'll see the lad properly dressed and put up at a comfortable inn in Lynchbany that accepts humans."

Jon-Tom sounded excited and pleased. "There are people like me in this town, then?"

Mudge eyed him narrowly. "Of course there are people in Lynchbany Towne, mate. There are also a few humans. None your size, though."

Clothahump was rummaging through a stack of scrolls. "Now then, where is that incantation for gold?"

"'Ere, guv'nor," said Mudge brightly. "Let me 'elp you look."

The wizard nudged him aside. "I can manage by myself." He squinted at the mound of paper.

"Geese . . . gibbering . . . gifts . . . gneechees . . . *gold*, there we are."

Potions and powders were once more brought into use, placed in a shallow pan instead of a bowl. They were heaped atop a single gold coin that Clothahump had removed from a drawer in his plastron. He noticed Mudge avidly following the procedure.

"Forget it, otter. You'd never get the inflection right. And this coin is old and special. If I could make gold all the time, I wouldn't need to charge for my services. This is a special occasion, though. Think what would happen if just any animal could wander about making gold."

"It would ruin your monetary system," said Jon-Tom.

"Bless my shell, lad, that's so. You have some learning after all."

"Economics are more in my line."

The wizard waved the wand over the pan.

"Postulate, postulate, postulate.
Heavy metal integrate.
Emulate a goldecule,
Pile it high, shape it round,
I call you from the ground.
Metal weary, metal sound, formulate thy wondrous
   round!"

There was a flash, a brief smell of ozone. The powders vanished from the pan. In their place was a pile of shining coins.

"Now, that's a right proper trick," Mudge whispered to Jon-Tom, "that I'd give a lot to know."

"Come help yourself, lad." Clothahump wiped a hand across his forehead. "That's a short spell, but a rough one."

Jon-Tom scooped up a handful of coins. He was about to slip them into a pocket when their unusual lightness struck him. He juggled them experimentally.

"They seem awfully light to be gold, sir. Meaning no disrespect, but . . ."

Mudge reached out, grabbed a coin. "Light's not the word, mate. It looks like gold, but 'tis not."

A frowning Clothahump chose a golden disk. "Um. Seems to be a fine edge running the circumference of the coin."

"On these also, sir." Jon-Tom picked at the edge. A thick gold foil peeled away, to reveal a darker material underneath. High above, Pog was swimming air circles and cackling hysterically.

"I don't understand." Clothahump finished peeling the foil from his own specimen. He recognized it at the same time as Jon-Tom took an experimental bite.

"Chocolate. Not bad chocolate, either."

Clothahump looked downcast. "Damn. I must have mixed my breakfast formula with the transmuter."

"Well," said the starving youth as he peeled another, "you may make poor gold, sir, but you make very good chocolate."

"Some wizard!" Pog shouted from a sheltered window recess. "Gets chocolate instead of gold! Did I mention da time he tried ta conjure a water nymph? Had his room all laid out like a beaver's lair, he did. Incense and perfume and mirrors. Got his water nymph all right. Only it was a Cugluch dragonfly nymph dat nearly tore his arm off before . . ."

Clothahump jabbed a finger in Pog's direction. A tiny bolt of lightning shot from it, searing the wood where the bat had been only seconds before.

"His aim's always been lousy," taunted the bat.

Another bolt missed the famulus by a greater margin than the first, shattered a row of glass containers on a high shelf. They fell crashing, tinkling to the wood-chip floor as the bat dodged and skittered clear of the fragments.

Clothahump turned away, fiddling with his glasses. "Got to conjure some new lenses," he grumbled. Reaching into his lower plastron, he drew out a handful of small silvery coins, and handed them to Jon-Tom. "Here you are, lad."

"Sir . . . wouldn't it have been simpler to give me these in the first place?"

"I like to keep in practice. One of these days I'll get that gold spell down pat."

"Why not make the lad a new set of clothes?" asked Mudge.

Clothahump turned from trying to refocus a finger on the jeering famulus and glanced angrily at the otter. "I'm a wizard, not a tailor. Mundane details such as that I leave to your care. And remember: no care, no fur."

"Relax, guv'nor. Let's go, Jon-Tom. 'Tis a long walk if we're to make much distance before dark."

They left Clothahump blasting jars and vials, pictures and shelving in a vain attempts to incinerate his insulting assistant.

"Interesting character, your sorcerer," said Jon-Tom conversationally as they turned down a well-trod path into the woods.

"Not my sorcerer, mate." A brightly feathered lizard

pecked at some bananalike fruit dangling from a nearby tree. "''Ave another chocolate coin?''

"No thanks."

"Speakin' o' coins, that little sack o' silver he gave you might as well be turned over t' me for safe keepin', since you're under me protection."

"That's all right." Jon-Tom patted the pocket in which the coins reposed. "It's safe enough with me, I think. Besides, my pockets are a lot higher than yours. Harder to pick."

Instead of being insulted, the otter laughed uproariously. He clapped a furry paw on Jon-Tom's lower back. "Maybe you're less the fool than you seem, mate. Frost me if I don't think we'll make a decent animal out o' you yet!"

They waded a brook hauntingly like the one that ran through the botanical gardens back on campus. Jon-Tom fought to keep his mind from melancholy reminiscence. "Aren't you the least bit curious about this great crisis Clothahump was referring to?" he asked.

"Bosh, that's probably just a figment o' 'is sorceral imagination. I've heard tell plenty about what such chaps drink and smoke when they feels the mood. They calls it wizardly speculatin'. Me, I calls it gettin' well stoked. Besides, why dwell on crises real or imagined when one can 'ave so much fun from day t' day?"

"You should learn to study the thread of history."

Mudge shook his head. "You talk like that in Lynchbany and you *will* 'ave trouble, mate. Thread o' 'Istory now, is it? Sure you won't trust me with that silver?" Jon-Tom simply smiled. "Ah well, then."

Any last lingering thoughts that it might all still be a nightmare from which he'd soon awake were forever dispelled when they'd come within a mile of Lynchbany, following several days' march. Jon-Tom couldn't see it yet. It lay over another rise and beyond a dense grove of pines. But he could clearly smell it. The aroma of hundreds of animal bodies basking in the warmth of mid-morning could not be mistaken.

"Something wrong, mate?" Mudge stretched away the last of his previous night's rest. "You look a touch bilious."

"That odor . . ."

"We're near Lynchbany, like I promised."

"You mean that stench is normal?"

Mudge's black nose frisked the air. "No . . . I'd call 'er a mite weak today. Wait until noontime, when the sun's at its 'ighest. Then it'll be normal."

"You have great wizards like Clothahump. Haven't any of them discovered the formula for deodorant?"

Mudge looked confused. "What's that, mate? Another o' your incomprehensible otherworldly devices?"

"It keeps you from smelling offensive," said Jon-Tom with becoming dignity.

"Now you do 'ave some queer notions in the other worlds. How are you t' know your enemies if you can't smell 'em? And no friend can smell offensive. That be a contradiction, do it not? If 'e was offensive, 'e wouldn't be a friend. O' course you 'umans," and he sniffed scornfully. " 'ave always been pretty scent-poor. I suppose you'd think it good if people 'ad no scent a'tall?"

"It wouldn't be such a bad idea."

"Well, don't go propoundin' your bizarre religious beliefs in Lynchbany, guv'nor, or even with me t' defend you you won't last out the day."

They continued along the path. This near to town it showed the prints of many feet.

"No scent," Mudge was muttering to himself. "No more sweet perfumes o' friends and ladies t' enjoy. Cor, I'd rather be blind than unable t' smell, mate. What senses do they use in your world, anyway?"

"The usual ones. Sight, hearing, touch, taste . . . and smell."

"And you'd wish away a fifth o' all your perception o' the universe for some crazed theological theory?"

"It has nothing to do with theology," Jon-Tom countered, beginning to wonder if his views on the matter weren't sounding silly even to himself. "It's a question of etiquette."

"Piss on your etiquette. No greetin' smells." The otter sounded thoroughly disgusted. "I don't think I'd care t' visit long in your world, Jon-Tom. But we're almost there. Mind you keep control o' your expressions." He still couldn't grasp the notion that anyone could find the odor of another friendly creature offensive.

"You 'old your nose to someone and they'll likely spill your guts for you."

Jon-Tom nodded reluctantly. Take a few deep breaths, told himself. He'd heard that somewhere. Just take a deep breaths and you'll soon be used to it.

They topped the little hill and were suddenly gazing across treetops at the town. At the same time the full ripeness of struck him. The thick musk was like a barnyard sweltering a swamp. He was hard pressed not to heave the contents his stomach out the wrong orifice.

"'Ere now, don't you go be sick all over me!" Mudge took a few hasty steps backward. "Brace up, lad. You'll soon be enjoyin' it!"

They started down the hill, the otter trotting easily, Jon-Tom staggering and trying to keep his face blank. Shortly they encountered a sight which simultaneously shoved all thought of vomiting aside while reminding him this was dangerous, barely civilized world he'd been dragged into.

It was a body similar to but different from Mudge's. It had its paws tied behind its back and its legs strapped together. The head hung at an angle signifying a neatly snapped neck. It was quite naked. Odd how quickly the idea of clothing on an animal grew in one's mind, Jon-Tom thought.

Some kind of liquid resin or plastic completely encased the body. The eyes were mercifully closed and the expression not pleasant to look upon. A sign lettered in strange script was mounted on a post driven into the ground beneath the dangling, preserved corpse. He turned questioningly to Mudge.

"That's the founder o' the town," came the reply.

Jon-Tom's eyes clung to the grotesque monument as they strolled around it. "Do they always hang the founders of towns around here?"

"Not usually. Only under special circumstances. That's the corpse o' old Tilo Bany. Ought t' be gettin' on a couple 'undred years old now."

"That body's been hanging there like that for hundreds of years?"

"Oh, 'e's well preserved, 'e is. Local wizard embalmed 'im nice and proper."

"That's barbaric."

"Want to hear the details?" asked Mudge. John-Tom nodded.

"As it goes, old Tilo there, 'e's a ferret you see—and they come o' no good line t' start with—'e was a confidence man. Fleeced farmers 'ereabouts for years and years, takin' their money most o' the time and their daughters on occasion.

"Well, a bunch of 'em finally gets onto 'im. 'E'd been buyin' grain from one farmer, sellin' it t' another, borrowin' the money, and buyin' more. It finally came t' a 'ead when a couple o' 'is former customers found out that a lot o' the grain they'd been buyin' afore'and existed only in Tilo's 'ead.

"They gets together, cornerin' 'im in this 'ere grove, and strings 'im up neat. At that point a couple o' travelin' craftsmen . . . woodworker and a silversmith, I think, or maybe one was a cobbler . . . decided that this 'ere valley with its easy water would be a nice place t' start a craft's guild, and the town sort o' grew up around it.

"When folks from elsewhere wanted t' locate the craftsmen, everyone around told 'em t' go t' the place where they'd lynched Tilo Bany, the confidence ferret. And if you 'aven't noticed yet, guv, you're breathin' right easy now."

Much to his surprise, the queasiness had receded. The

smell no longer seemed so overpowering. "You're right. It's not so bad anymore."

"That's good. You stick near t' me, mate, and watch yourself. Some o' the local bully-boys like t' toy with strangers, and you're stranger than most. Not that I'd be afraid t' remonstrate with any of 'em, mind now."

They were leaving the shade of the forest. Mudge gestured ahead. His voice was full of provincial pride.

"There she be, Jon-Tom. Lynchbany Towne."

IV

No fairy spires or slick and shiny pennant-studded towers here, Jon-Tom mused as he gazed at the village. No rainbow battlements, no thin cloud-piercing turrets inlaid with gold, silver, and precious gems. Lynchbany was a community built to be lived in, not looked at. Clearly, its inhabitants knew no more of moorish palaces and peacock-patrolled gardens than did Jon-Tom.

Hemmed in by forest on both sides, the buildings and streets meandered down a narrow valley. A stream barely a yard wide trickled through the town center. It divided the main street, which, like most of the side streets he could see, was paved with cobblestones shifted here from some distant riverbed. Only the narrow creek channel itself was unpaved.

They continued down the path, whch turned to cobblestone as it came abreast of the rushing water. Despite his determination to keep his true feelings inside, the fresh nausea that greeted him as they reached the first buildings generated unwholesome wrinkles on his face. It was evident that the little stream served as community sewer as well as the likely source of potable water. He reminded himself firmly not to drink anything in Lynchbany unless it was bottled or boiled.

Around them rose houses three, sometimes four stories tall. Sharp-peaked roofs were plated with huge foot-square shingles of wood or gray slate. Windows turned translucent eyes on the street from second and third floors. An occasional balcony projected out over the street.

Fourth floors and still higher attics displayed rounded entrances open to the air. Thick logs were set below each circular doorway. Round windows framed many of these aerial portals. They were obviously home to the arboreal inhabitants of the town, cousins of the red-breasted, foul-mouthed public servant they had met delivering mail to Clothahump's tree several days ago.

The little canyon was neither very deep nor particularly narrow, but the houses still crowded together like children in a dark room. The reason was economic; it's simpler and cheaper to build a common wall for two separate structures.

A few flew pennants from poles set in their street-facing sides, or from the crests of sharply gabled rooftops. They could have been family crests, or signals, or advertisements; Jon-Tom had no idea. More readily identifiable banners in the form of some extraordinary washing hung from lines strung over narrow alleyways. He tried to identify the shape of the owners from the position and length of the arms and legs, but was defeated by the variety.

At the moment furry arms and hands were working from upper-floor windows, hastily pulling laundry off the lines amid much muttering and grumbling. Thunder rumbled through the town, echoing off the cobblestone streets and the damp walls of cut rock and thick wooden beams. Each building was constructed for solidity, a small home put together as strongly as a castle.

Shutters clapped hollowly against bracings as dwellers sealed their residences against the approaching storm. Smoke, ashy and pungent, borne by an occasional confused gust of wet wind, drifted down to the man and otter. Another rumble bounced through the streets. A glance overhead showed dark clouds clotting like black cream. First raindrops slapped at his skin.

Mudge increased his pace and Jon-Tom hurried to keep up.

He was too fascinated by the town to ask where they were rushing to, sufficiently absorbed in his surroundings not to notice the isolated stares of other hurrying pedestrians.

After another couple of blocks, he finally grew aware of the attention they were drawing.

"It's your size, mate," Mudge told him.

As they hurried on, Jon-Tom took time to look back at the citizens staring at him. None stood taller than Mudge. Most were between four and five feet tall. It did not make him feel superior. Instead, he felt incredibly awkward and out of place.

He drew equally curious stares from the occasional human he passed. All the locals were similarly clad, allowing for personal differences in taste and station. Silk, wool, cotton, and leather appeared to be the principal materials. Shirts, blouses, vests, and pants were often decorated with beads and feathers. An astonishing variety of hats were worn, from wide-brimmed seventeenth-century-style feathered to tiny, simple berets, to feathered peaked caps like Mudge's. Boots alternated with sandals on feet of varying size. He later learned one had a choice between warm, filthy boots or chilly but easily cleanable sandals.

Keeping clean could be a full-time trial. They crossed the main street just in time to avoid a prestorm deluge when an irritable and whitened old possum dumped out a bucket of slops from a second-floor porch into the central stream, barely missing the pair below.

"Hey . . . watch it!" Jon-Tom shouted upward at the closing shutters.

"Now wot?"

"That wasn't very considerate," Jon-Tom mumbled, his nose twisting at the odor.

Mudge frowned at him. "Stranger and stranger sound your customs, guv. Now wot else is she supposed t' do with the 'ouse'old night soil?" With a hand he traced the winding course of the steady stream that flowed through the center of the street.

"This time o' year it rains 'ere nigh every day. The rain washes the soil into the central flue 'ere and the stream packs it off right proper."

Jon-Tom let out fervent thanks he hadn't appeared in this land in summertime. "It wasn't her action I was yelling about. It was her aim. Damned if I don't think she was trying to hit us."

Mudge smiled. "Now that be a thought, mate. But when you're as dried up and 'ousebound as that faded old sow, I expect you grab at every chance for amusement you can."

"What about common courtesy?" Jon-Tom muttered, shaking slop from his shoes.

"Rely on it if you wants t' die young, says I."

Shouts sounded from ahead. They moved to one side of the street and leaned up against a shuttered storefront. A huge double wagon was coming toward them, one trailing behind another. The vehicle required nearly the entire width of the street for passage.

Jon-Tom regarded it with interst. The haggard, dripping driver was a margay. The little tiger cat's bright eyes flashed beneath the wide-brimmed floppy felt hat he wore. Behind him, riding the second half of the wagon, was a cursing squirrel no more than three feet tall. His tail was curled over his head, providing extra protection from the now steadily falling rain. He was struggling to tug heavy canvas or leather sheets over the cargo of fruits and vegetables.

Four broad-shouldered lizards pulled the double wagon. They were colored iridescent blue and green, and in the gloom their startlingly pink eyes shone like motorcycle taillights. They swayed constantly from side to side, demanding unvarying attention from their yowling, hissing driver, who manipulated them as much with insults as with cracks from his long thin whip.

Momentarily generating a louder rumble than the isolated

bursts of thunder, the enormous wagon slid on past and turned a difficult far corner.

"I've no sympathy for the chap who doesn't know 'is business," snorted Mudge as they continued on their way, hugging the sides of buildings in search of some protection from the downpour. "That lot ought long since to 'ave been under cover."

It was raining quite heavily now. Most of the windows had been closed or shuttered. The darkness made the buildings appear to be leaning over the street.

From above and behind came a distant, sharp chirping. Jon-Tom glanced over a shoulder, thought he saw a stellar jay clad in yellow-purple kilt and vest alight on one of the fourth-floor landing posts and squeeze through an opening. There was a faint thump as the circular door was slammed behind him.

They hurried on, sprinting from one rickety wooden porch covering to the next. Once they paused in the sheltering lee of what might have been a bookstore. Scrollstore, rather, since it was filled with ceiling-high wooden shelves punched out like a massive wine rack. Each hole held its thick roll of paper.

As Mudge had indicated, the rain was washing the filth from the cobblestones and the now swollen central creek carried it efficiently away.

The front moved through and the thunder faded. Instead of the heavy, driving rain the clouds settled down to shedding a steady drizzle. The temperature had dropped, and Jon-Tom shivered in his drenched T-shirt and jeans.

"Begging your pardon, sir."

Jon-Tom uncrossed his arms. "What?" He looked to his right. The source of the voice was in a narrow alley barely large enough to allow two people to pass without turning sideways.

A gibbon lay huddled beneath a slight overhang, curled protectively against several large wooden barrels filled with trash. His fuzzy face was shielded by several large scraps of wrapping paper that had been wound together and tied with a knot beneath his chin. This crude hat hung limp in the rain. Badly ripped trousers of some thin cotton material covered the hairy legs. He had no shirt. Long arms enfolded the shivering chest, and large circular sores showed where the hair had fallen out. One eye socket was a dark little hollow.

A delicately fingered hand extended hopefully in Jon-Tom's direction. "A silverpiece, sir. For one unlucky in war and unluckier still in peacetime? It was a bad upbringing and a misinformed judiciary that cost me this eye, sir. Now I exist only on the sufferance of others." Jon-Tom stood and gaped at the pitiful creature.

"A few coppers then, sir, if you've no silver to give?" The gibbon's voice was harsh with infection.

Suddenly he shrank back, falling against the protective trashcans. One fell over, spilling shreds of paper, bones, and other recognizable detritus into the alley. Dimensional dislocation does not eliminate the universality of garbage.

"Nay, sir, nay!" An arm shook as the simian held it across his face. "I meant no harm."

Mudge stood alongside Jon-Tom. The otter's sword was halfway clear of its chest scabbard. "I'll not 'ave you botherin' this gentleman while 'e's in my care!" He took another step toward the ruined anthropoid. "Maybe you mean no 'arm and maybe you do, but you'll do none while I'm about."

"Take it easy," murmured Jon-Tom, eyeing the cowering gibbon sympathetically. "Can't you see he's sick?"

"Sick be the word, aright. D'you not know 'ow to treat beggars, mate?" He pulled on his sword. The gibbon let out a low moan.

"I do." Jon-Tom reached into his pocket, felt for the small linen purse Clothahump had given him. He withdrew a small coin, tossed it to the gibbon. The simian scrambled among the stones and trash for it.

"Blessings on you, sir! Heaven kiss you!"

Mudge turned away, disgustedly sliding his sword back in place. "Waste o' money." He put a hand on Jon-Tom's arm. "Come on, then. Let's get you t' the shop I 'ave in mind before you spend yourself broke. It's a hard world, mate, and you'd better learn that soonest. You never saw the blighter's knife, I take it?"

"Knife?" Jon-Tom looked back toward the alley entrance. "What knife?" He felt queasy.

"Aye, wot knife indeed." He let out a sharp squeak. "If I 'adn't of been with you you'd 'ave found out wot knife. But I guess you can't 'elp yourself. Your brains bein' up that 'igh, I expect they thin along with the air, wot? 'Wot knife'...pfagh!" He stopped, glared up at the dazed Jon-Tom.

"Now if 'twere just up t' me, mate, I'd let you make as much the idiot of yourself as you seem to 'ave a mind t'. But I can't risk offendin' 'is wizardship, see? So until I've seen you safely set up in the world and on your own way t' where I think you might be able t' take some care for yourself, you'll do me the courtesy from now on o' takin' me advice. And if you'll not think o' yourself, then 'ave some pity for me. Mind the threats that Clothahump put on me." He shook his head, turned, and started on down the street again. "Me! Who was unlucky enough to trip over you when you tripped into my day."

"Yeah? What about me, then? You think I like it here? You think I like you, you fuzz-faced little fart?"

To Jon-Tom's dismay, Mudge smiled instead of going for his sword. "Now that's more like it, mate! That's a better attitude than givin' away your money." He spat back in the direction of the alley. "God-rotted stinkin' layabout trash as soon split your gut as piss on you. D'you wonder I like it better in the forest, mate?"

They turned off the main street into a side avenue that was not as small as an alley, not impressive enough to be a genuine street. It boasted half a dozen shopfronts huddled together in the throat of a long cul-de-sac. A single tall oil lamp illuminated the street. Cloth awnings almost met over the street, shutting out much of the lamplight as well as the rain. A miniature version of the central stream sprang from a stone fountain at the end of the cul-de-sac.

Jon-Tom shook water from his hands, and squeezed it from his long hair as he ducked under the cover of one awning. It was not designed to shield someone of his height. He stared at the sign over the large front window of the shop. It was almost comprehensible. Perhaps the longer he spent here the more acclimated his brain became. In any case, he did not have to understand the lettering to know what kind of shop this was. The window was filled with vests and shirts, elaborately stitched pantaloons, and a pair of trousers with bells running the length of the seams. Some lay on the window counter, others fitted dressmaker dummies that sometimes boasted ears and usually had tails.

A bell chimed brightly as Mudge pushed open the door. "Mind your 'ead now, Jon-Tom." His tall companion took note of the warning, and bowed under the eave.

The interior of the shop had the smell of leather and lavender. There was no one in sight. Several chairs with curved seats and backs were arranged neatly near the center of the floor. Long poles supported cross-racks from which clothing had been draped.

"Hoy, Proprietor!" Mudged whooped. "Show yourself and your work!"

"And work you shall have, my dear whoever-you-ares." The reply issued from the back of the shop. "Work only of the finest quality and best stitchery, of the toughest materials and prettiest . . ." The voice trailed off quickly.

The fox had come to a halt and was staring past Mudge at the dripping, lanky shape of Jon-Tom. Silk slippers clad the owner's feet. He wore a silk dressing gown with four matching ribbons of bright aquamarine. They ran around his tail in intersecting loops to meet in a bow at the white tip. He also wore a more practical-looking belt from which protruded rulers, marking sticks, several pieces of dark green stone, and various other instruments of the tailor's craft. He spoke very deliberately.

"What . . . is *that*?" He gestured hesitantly at Jon-Tom.

"That's the work we're chattin' about, and a job it's goin' t' be, I'd wager." Mudge flopped down in one of the low-slung chairs with complete disregard for the upholstery and the fact that he was dripping wet. He put both short legs over one arm of the chair and pushed his feathered cap back on his forehead. "Off to it now, that's a good fellow."

The fox put both paws on hips and stared intently at the otter. "I do *not* clothe monsters! I have created attire for some of the best-dressed citizens of Lynchbany, and beyond. I have made clothing for Madam Scorianza and her best girls, for the banker Flaustyn Wolfe, for members of the town council, and for our most prominent merchants and craftsmen, but I do *not* clothe monsters."

Mudge leaned over in the chair and helped himself to a long thin stick from a nearby tall glass filled with them. "Look on it as a challenge, mate." He used a tiny flinted sparker to light the stick.

"Listen," said Jon-Tom, "I don't want to cause any trouble." The fox took a wary step backward as that towering form moved nearer. "Mudge here thinks that . . . that . . ." He was indicating the otter, who was puffing contentedly on the thin stick. Smoke filled the room with a delightfully familiar aroma.

"Say," said Jon-Tom, "do you suppose I could have one of those, uh, sticks?"

"For the convenience o' the customers, lad." Mudge magnanimously passed over a stick along with his sparker. Jon-Tom couldn't see how it worked, but at this point was more than willing to believe it had been treated with a good fire spell.

Several long puffs on the glowing stick more than relaxed him. Not everything in this world was as horrible as it seemed, he decided. It was smoking that had made him accessible to the questing thoughts of Clothahump. Perhaps smoking would let something send him home.

Ten minutes later, he no longer cared. Reassured by both Mudge and the giant's dreamy responses, the grumbling fox was measuring Jon-Tom as the latter lay quite contentedly on the carpeted floor. Mudge lay next to him, the two of them considerably higher mentally than physically. The tailor, whose name was Carlemot, did not object to their puffing, which indicated either an ample supply of the powerful smokesticks or a fine sense of public relations, or both.

He left them eventually, returning several hours later to find otter and man totally bombed. They still lay on the floor, and were currently speculating with great interest on the intricacies of the wormholes in the wooden ceiling.

It was only later that Jon-Tom had recovered sufficiently for a dressing. When he finally saw himself in the mirror, the shock shoved aside quite a bit of the haze.

The indigo silk shirt felt like cool mist against his skin. It was tucked neatly into straight-legged pants which were a cross between denim and flannel. Both pants and shirt were secured with matching buttons of black leather. The jet leather vest was fringed around the bottom and decorated with glass beadwork. The cuffs of the pants were likewise fringed, though he couldn't tell this at first because they were stuffed into calf-high black leather boots with rolled tops. At first it seemed surprising that the tailor had managed to find any footgear at all to fit him, considering how much larger he was than the average local human. Then it occurred to him that many of the inhabitants were likely to have feet larger in proportion to their bodies than did men.

A belt of metal links, silver or pewter, held up the pants, shone in sharp contrast to the beautifully iridescent hip-length cape of some green lizard leather. A pair of delicate but functional silver clips held the cape together at the collar. Despite Mudge's insistence, however, he categorically refused to don the orange tricornered cap. "I just don't like hats."

"Such a pity." Carlemot's attitude had shifted from one of distress to one of considerable pride. "It really is necessary to complete the overall effect, which, if I may be permitted to say so, is striking as well as unique."

Jon-Tom turned, watched the scales of the cape flare even in the dim light. "Sure as hell would turn heads in L.A."

"Not bad," Mudge conceded. "Almost worth the price."

"'Almost' indeed!" The fox was pacing round Jon-Tom, inspecting the costume for any defects or tears. Once he paused to snip a loose thread from a sleeve of the shirt. "It is subdued yet flashy, attention-gathering without being obtrusive." He smiled, displaying sharp teeth in a long narrow snout.

"The man looks like a noble, or better still, a banker. When one is confronted with so much territory to cover, the task is at first daunting. However, the more one has to work with, the more gratifying the end results. Never mind this plebian, my tall friend," the fox continued, gazing up possessively at Jon-Tom, "what is your opinion?"

"I like it. Especially the cape." He spun a small circle, nearly fell down but recovered poise and balance nicely. "I always wanted to wear a cape."

"I am pleased." The tailor appeared to be waiting for something, coughed delicately.

"Crikey, mate," snapped Mudge, "pay the fellow."

Some good-natured haggling followed, with Mudge's task made the more difficult by the fact that Jon-Tom kept siding with the tailor. A reasonable balance was still struck, since Carlemot's natural tendency to drive a hard bargain was somewhat muted by the pleasure he'd received from accomplishing so difficult a job.

That did not keep Mudge from chastising Jon-Tom as they left the shop behind. The drizzle had become a heavy mist around them.

"Mate, I can't save you much if you're goin' t' take the side of the shopkeeper."

"Don't worry about it." For the first time in a long while, he was feeling almost happy. Between the lingering effects of the smoke session and the gallant appearance he was positive his new attire gave him, his mood was downright expansive. "It was a tough task for him and he did a helluva job. I don't begrudge him the money. Besides," he jingled the purse in his pocket, "we still have some left."

"That's good, because we've one more stop t' make."

"Another?" Jon-Tom frowned. "I don't need any more clothing."

"That so?" Far as I'm concerned, mate, you're walkin' around bloody naked." He turned right. They passed four or five storefronts on the wide street, crossed the cobblestones and a little bridge arcing over the central stream, and entered another shop.

It possessed an entirely different ambiance from the warm tailor shop they'd just left. While the fox's establishment had been spotless, soft-looking, and comfortable as an old den, this one was chill with an air of distasteful business.

One entire wall was speckled with devices designed for throwing. There were dozens of knives; ellipsoidal, stiletto, triangular, with or without blood gutters grooved nastily in their flanks, gem-encrusted little pig-stickers for argumentative ladies, trick knives concealed in eyeglass cases or boot soles . . . all the deadly variety of which the honer was capable.

Throwing stars shone in the lamplight like decorations plucked from the devil's Christmas tree. A spiked bolo hung from an intricate halberd. Maces and nunchaku alternated wall space with spears and shields, pikes and war axes. Near the back of the shop were the finer weapons, long bows and swords with more variety of handle (to fit many different size and shape of hand) than of blade. One particularly ugly half-sword looked more like a double scythe. It was easy to envision the damage it could do when wielded by a knowledgeable arm. That of a gibbon with a deceptive reach, for example.

Some of the swords and throwing knives had grooved or hollow handles. Jon-Tom was at a loss to imagine what sort of creature they'd been designed for until he remembered the birds. A hand would not make much use of such grips, but they were perfect for, say, a flexible wing tip.

For a few high moments he'd managed to forget that this was a world of established violence and quick death. He leaned over the counter barring the back of the shop from the front and studied something that resembled a razor-edged frisbee. He shuddered, and looked around for Mudge.

The otter had moved around the counter and had vanished behind a bamboolike screen. When Jon-Tom thought to call to him, he was already returning, chatting with the owner. The squat, muscular raccoon wore only an apron, sandals, and a red headband with two feathers sticking downward past his left ear. He smelled, as did the back of the shop, of coalsmoke and steel.

"So this is the one who wants the mayhem?" The raccoon pursued his lips, looked over a black nose at Jon-Tom.

"Mudge, I don't know about this. I've always been a talker, not a fighter."

"I understand, mate," said the otter amiably. "But there are weighty arguments and there are weighty arguments." He hefted a large mace to further illustrate his point. "Leastways, you don't have to employ none of these tickle-me-tights, but you bloody well better show something or you'll mark yourself an easy target.

"Now, can you use any of these toys?"

Jon-Tom examined the bewildering array of dismembering machinery. "I don't . . ." he shook his head, looking confused.

The armorer stepped in. " 'Tis plain to see he's no experience." His tone was reproving but patient. "Let me see, now. With his size and reach . . ." He moved thoughtfully to a wall where pikes and spears grew like iron wheat from the floor, each set in its individual socket in the wooden planks. His right paw rubbed at his nose.

With both hands he removed an ax with a blade the size of his head. "Where skill and subtlety are absent, mayhap it would be best to make use of the other extremes. No combat or weapons training at all, young lad?"

Jon-Tom shook his head, looked unencouraging.

"What about sports?"

"I'm not bad at basketball. Pretty good jump shot, and I can—"

"Shit!" Mudge kicked at the floor. "What the devil's arse is that? Does it perhaps involve some hittin'?" he asked hopefully.

"Not much," Jon-Tom admitted. "Mostly running and jumping, quick movements. . . ."

"Well, that be something," Mudge faced the armorer. "Something less bull-bright than that meat cleaver you're holdin', then. What would you recommend?"

"A fast retreat." The armorer turned dourly to another rack, preening his whiskers. "Though if the man can lay honest claim to some nimbleness, there ought to be something." He put up the massive ax. "Mayhap we can give him some help."

He removed what looked like a simple spear, made from the polished limb of a tree. But instead of a spearpoint, the upper end widened into a thick wooden knob with bumps and dull points. It was taller than Mudge and reached Jon-Tom's ears, the shaft some two inches in diameter.

"Just a club?" Mudge studied the weapon uncertainly.

" 'Tis the longest thing I've got in the shop." The armorer dragged a clipped nail down the shaft. "This is ramwood. It won't snap in a fight. With your friend's long reach, he can use it to fend an opponent off if he's not much interested in properly disposing of him. And if things get tight and he's still blood-shy, why, a good clop on the head with the business end of this will make someone just as dead as if you'd split his skull. Not as messy as the ax, but just as effective.'' He handed it to the reluctant Jon-Tom.

"It'll make you a fine walking stick, too, man. And there's something else. I mentioned giving you some help." He pointed at the middle of the staff. Halfway up the shaft were two bands of inlaid silver three inches apart. The space between was decorated with four silver studs.

"Press any one of those, man."

Jon-Tom did so. There was a click, and the staff instantly grew another foot. Twelve inches of steel spike now projected from the base of the staff. Jon-Tom was so surprised he almost dropped the weapon, but Mudge danced about like a kid in a candy shop.

"Bugger me mother if that ain't a proper surprise for any discourteous dumb-butt you might meet in the street. A little rub from that'll cure 'em right quick, I venture!"

"Aye," agreed the armorer with pride . "Just tap 'em on the toe and press your release and I guarantee you'll see one fine wide-eyed expression." Both raccoon and otter shook with amusement.

Jon-Tom pushed down on the shaft and the spear-spike retracted like a cats-claw up inside the staff. Another experimental grip on the studs, and it shot out once more. It was clever, but certainly not amusing.

"Listen, I'd rather not fool with this thing at all, but if you insist . . ."

"I do." Mudge stopped laughing, wiped tears from his eyes. "I do insist. Like the master armorer 'ere says, you don't 'ave t' use that toe-chopper if you've no mind t', but there'll likely be times when you'll want t' keep some sword-swingin' sot a fair few feet from your guts. So take claim to it and be glad."

Jon-Tom hefted the shaft, but he wasn't glad. Merely having possession of the deceptive weapon was depressing him.

Outside they examined the contents of the little purse. It

was nearly empty. A few small silver coins gleamed forlornly like fish in a dark tank from the bottom of the sack. Jon-Tom wondered if he hadn't been slightly profligate with Clothahump's generosity.

Mudge appraised the remnants of their fortune. Mist continued to dampen them, softening the lamplight that buttered the street and shopfronts. With the easing of the rain, other pedestrians had reappeared. Animal shadow-shapes moved dimly through the fog.

"Hungry, mate?" asked the otter finally, black eyes shining in the light.

"Starving!" He was abruptly aware he hadn't had a thing to eat all day. Mudge's store of jerked meat had given out the previous evening.

"I also." He clapped Jon-Tom on his cape. "Now you looks almost like a real person." He leaned conspiratorially close. "Now I know a place where the silver we 'ave left will bring us as fat a feast as a pregnant hare could wish. Maybe even enough t' fill your attenuated belly-hollow!" He winked. "Maybe some entertainment besides. You and I 'ave done our duty for the day, we 'ave."

As they strolled further into town, they encountered more pedestrians. An occasional wagon jounced down the street, and individuals on saddled riding lizards hopped or ran past. Long pushbrooms came into play as shopkeepers swept water from porches and storefronts. Shutters snapped open. For the first time Jon-Tom heard the wails of children. Cubs would be the better term, he corrected himself.

Two young squirrels scampered by. One finally tackled the other. They tumbled to the cobblestones, rolling over and over, punching and kicking while a small mob of other youngsters gathered around and urged them on. To Jon-Tom's dismay their initial cuteness was muted by the manner in which they gouged and scratched at each other. Not that his own hometown was devoid of violence, but it seemed to be a way of life here. One cub finally got the other down and was assiduously making pulp of his face. His peers applauded enthusiastically, offering suggestions for further disfigurement.

"A way of life, mate?" Mudge said thoughtfully when Jon-Tom broached his thoughts. "I wouldn't know. I'm no philosopher, now. But I know this. You can be polite and dead or respected and breathin'." He shrugged. "Now you can make your own choice. Just don't be too ready to put aside that nice new toy you've bought."

Jon-Tom made sure he had a good grip on the staff. The increasing crowd and lifting of the fog brought fresh stares. Mudge assured him it was only on account of his unusual size. If anything, he was now clad far better than the average citizen of Lynchbany Towne.

Five minutes later he was no longer simply hungry, he was ravenous.

"Not much longer, mate." They turned down a winding side street. There was an almost hidden entrance on their left, into which Mudge urged him. Once again he had to bend nearly double to clear the overhang.

Then he was able to stand. The ceiling inside was a good two feet above his head, for which he was more than slightly grateful.

"The Pearl Possum," said Mudge, with considerably more enthusiasm than he'd displayed toward anything else so far. "Me, I'm for somethin' liquid now. This way, mate. 'Ware the lamps."

Jon-Tom followed the otter into the bowels of the restaurant, elbowing his way through the shoving, tightly packed crowd and keeping a lookout for the occasional hanging lamps Mudge had warned him about. From outside there was no hint of the considerable, sweaty mob milling inside.

Eight feet inside the entrance, the ceiling curved upward like a circus tent. It peaked a good two and a half stories above the floor. Beneath this central height was a circular counter dispensing food and brew. It was manned by a small battalion of cooks and mixologists. A couple were weasels.

There was also a single, nattily dressed rabbit and one scroungy-looking bat, smaller and even uglier than Pog. Not surprisingly, the bat spent most of his time delivering food and drink to various tables. Jon-Tom knew of other restaurants which would have been glad of an arboreal waiter.

What tables there were spotted the floor like fat toadstools in no particular order. On the far side of the Pearl Possum were partially enclosed booths designed for discussion or dalliance, depending on the inclination of the inhabitants.

They continued to make their way through the noisy, malodorous crowd. Isolated ponds of liquor littered the floor, along with several splinters from smashed wooden mugs. The owners had sensibly disdained the use of glass. Numerous drains pockmarked the wooden planking underfoot. Occasionally someone would appear with a bucket of water to wash down a section of floor too slippery with booze, sometimes of the partially digested variety.

He was easily the tallest man—the tallest animal—in the room, though there were a couple of large wolves and cats who were built more massively. It made him feel only a little more confident.

" 'Ere lad, over 'ere!" Following the triumphant shout Jon-Tom felt himself yanked down to a small but abandoned table. His knees pressed up toward his chest—the chairs were much too low for comfortable seating.

Furry bodies pressed close on all sides, filling his nostrils with the stink of liquor and musk. Supporting the table was the sculpted plaster figure of a coquettishly posed female opossum. It had been scratched and engraved with so many lewd comments that the sheen was almost gone.

Somehow a waiter noticed that their hands and table were empty, shoved his way through to them. Like the armorer he was wearing an apron, only this one was filthy beyond recognition, the pattern beneath obliterated by grease and other stains. Like the armorer he was a black-masked raccoon. One ear was badly mangled, and a white scar ran

77

boldly from the ear down the side of his head, just past the eye, and on through the muzzle, but particularly noticeable where it crossed the black mask.

Jon-Tom was too busy observing the life and action swirling around them to notice that Mudge had already ordered.

"Not t' worry, mate. I ordered for you."

"I hope you ordered food, as well as liquor. I'm hungrier than ever."

"That I 'ave, mate. Any fool knows 'tis not good t' drink on an empty belly. 'Ere you, watch yourself." He jabbed an elbow into the ribs of the drunken ocelot who'd stumbled into him.

The animal spun, waving his mug and sending liquor spilling toward the otter. Mudge dodged the drink with exceptional speed. The feline made a few yowling comments about the rib jab, but was too sloshed to pick a serious fight. It lurched helplessly off into the crowd. Jon-Tom followed the pointy, weaving ears until their owner was out of sight.

Two large wooden mugs of something highly carbonated and smelling of alcohol arrived. The hardwood mug looked oversized in Mudge's tiny hand, but it was just the right size for Jon-Tom. He tried a sip of the black liquid within, found it to be a powerful fermented brew something like a highly alcoholic malt liquor. He determined to treat it respectfully.

The waiter's other hand deposited a large platter covered by a badly dented and scratched metal dome. When the dome was removed, Jon-Tom's nose was assailed by a wonderfully rich aroma. On the platter were all kinds of vegetables. Among strange shapes were comfortingly familiar carrots, radishes, celery, and tiny onions. A raft of potatoes supported a huge cylindrical roast. A single center bone showed at either end. It was burnt black outside and shaded to pink near the bone.

He hunted in vain for silverware. Mudge pointed out that the restaurant would hardly provide instruments for its patrons to use on one another. The otter had a hunting knife out. It was short and triangular like the tooth of a white shark and went easily through the meat.

"Rare, medium, or well burnt?" was the question.

"Anything." Jon-Tom fought to keep the saliva inside his mouth. Mudge sliced off two respectable discs of meat, passed one to his companion.

They ate as quietly as smacking fingers and gravy-slick lips would permit. Jon-Tom struggled to keep the juice off his freshly cut clothes. Mudge was not nearly so fastidious. Gravy ran down his furry chin onto his vest, was sopped up by vest and chest fur.

They were halfway full when a partially sated Jon-Tom relaxed long enough to notice that in addition to the center bone running through the roast, there were thin, curving ribs running from the bone to meet like the points of calipers near the bottom.

"Mudge, what kind of meat is this?"

"Not tasty enough, mate?" wondered the otter around a mouthful of vegetables.

"It's delicious, but I don't recognize the cut or the flavor. It's not any kind of steak, is it? I mean, beef?"

"Beef? You mean, cattle?" Mudge shook his head. "They may not be smart, but we're not cannibals 'ere, we're not." He chewed appraisingly. "'O' course, it ain't king snake. Python. Reticulated, I'd say."

"Wonderful." Why be squeamish in the face of good taste, Jon-Tom mused. There was no reason to be. He never had understood the phobia some folk had about eating reptile, though he'd never had the opportunity to try it before. After all, meat was meat. It was all muscle fiber to the tooth.

He did not think he'd care to meet a snake of that size away from the dinner plate, however.

They were dismembering the last of the roast when the waiter, unbidden, appeared with a small tray of some fat puff pastries seared black across their crowns. Though he was no longer hungry, Jon-Tom sampled one, soon found himself shoveling them in as fast as possible. Despite their heavy appearance they were light and airy inside, full of honey and chopped nuts and encrusted with burnt cinnamon.

Later he leaned back in the short chair and picked at his teeth with a splinter of the table, as he'd seen some of the other patrons doing.

"Well, that may take the last of our money, but that's the best meal I've had in years."

"Aye, not bad." Mudge had his short legs up on the table, the boot heels resting indifferently in the pastry tray.

A band had begun playing somewhere. The music was at once light and brassy. Jon-Tom took a brief professional interest in it. Since he couldn't see the players, he had to be satisfied with deciding that they employed one or two string instruments, drums, chimes, and a couple of oddly deep flutes.

Mudge was leaning across the table, feeling warm and serious. He put a cautionary paw on Jon-Tom's wrist. "Sorry t' shatter your contentment, mate, but we've somethin' else t' talk on. Clothahump charged me with seein' t' your well-bein' and I've a mind t' see the job through t' the end.

"If you want t' continue eatin' like that, we're goin' to 'ave t' find you some way t' make a living, wot ... ?"

V

Reality churned in Jon-Tom's stomach, mixed unpleasantly with the pastry. "Uh, can't we just go back to Clothahump?" He'd decided he was beginning to like this world.

Mudge shook his head slowly. "Not if 'e don't get that gold spell aright. Keep in mind that as nice and kindly as the old bugger seemed a few days ago, wizards can be god-rotted temperamental. If we go back already and pester 'im for money, 'e's not going t' feel much proud o' you. Not to mention wot 'is opinion o' *me* would be. You want to keep the old twit feelin' responsible for wot 'e's done t' you, mate.

"Oh, 'e might 'ave a fair supply of silver tucked away neat and pretty somewhere. But 'is supply of silver's bound to be limited. So long as 'e's got 'is feeble old mind set on this dotty crisis of 'is, 'e's not goin' to be doin' much business. No business, no silver. No silver, no 'andouts, right? I'm afraid you're goin' t' 'ave t' go t' work."

"I see." Jon-Tom stared morosely into his empty mug. "What about working with you, Mudge?"

"Now don't get me wrong, mate. I'm just gettin' t' where I can tol'rate your company."

"Thanks," said Jon-Tom tartly.

"That's all right, it is. But huntin's a solitary profession. I don't think I could do much for you there. You don't strike me as the type o' chap who knows 'is way 'round a woods. You'd as soon trip over a trap as set one, I think."

"I won't deny that I feel more at home around books, or a basketball court."

"Otherworldly sports won't do you ant's piss good 'round 'ere, lad. As far as the learnin' part of it . . . wot was it then you were acquiring?"

"I'm into prelaw, Mudge."

"Ah, a barrister-t'-be, is it? Never 'ad much use for the species meself," he added, not caring what Jon-Tom might think of his detrimental opinions of the legal profession. "Wot did you study besides the law itself, for the laws 'ere as you might imagine are likely a mite different from those o' your own."

"History, government . . . I don't guess they'd be much use here either."

"I suppose we might get you apprenticed to some local barrister," Mudge considered. He scratched the inside of one ear, moved around to work on the back. "I don't know, mate. You certain there's nothin' else? You ever work a forge, build furniture? Do metalwork, build a house, cure meat . . . anythin' *useful*?"

"Not really." Jon-Tom felt uncomfortable.

"Huh!" The otter let loose a contemptuous whistle. "Fine life you've led for a so-called wizard."

"That's Clothahump's mistake," Jon-Tom protested. "I never claimed to be that. I've never claimed to be anything other than what I am."

"Which don't appear to be much, as far as placin' you's concerned. Nothin' more in the way of skills, is it?"

"Well . . ." Another ambition flooded through him. With it came the laughs of his friends and the condemnations and horrified protests of his family. Then they were drowned by a vision of himself with a guitar and by the memories of all the groups, all the performances he'd collected and mimicked in his less intellectual, more emotional moments of introspection. Memories and sounds of Zepplin and Harum, of Deep Purple and Tangerine Dream and Moody Blues and a thousand others. Electric melodies tingled in his fingertips. Logic and reason vanished. Once more good sense and truth clashed within him.

Only here good sense did not serve. Heart's desire again took control of him.

"I play a g . . . an electric bass. It's a kind of a stringed instrument. It's only a hobby. I thought once I *might* try to make a career out of it, only . . ."

"So you're a musician then!" Consternation vanished as understanding filled the otter. He pushed back his chair, let his feet down on the floor, and stared with new interest at his companion. "A minstrel. I'll be bloody be-damned. Aye, there might be a way there for you t' make some coppers, maybe even some silver. You'd be a novelty, anyways. Let me 'ear you sing something."

"Right here?" Jon-Tom looked around nervously.

"Aye. No one's goin' to 'ear you anyway. Not between the babble and band."

"I don't know." Jon-Tom considered. "I need to warm up. And I don't have my guitar with me."

"A pox on your bleedin' instrument," growled the otter. " 'Ow do you expect t' act a proper minstrel if you can't sing on demand, when someone requires it o' you? Now don't mind me, mate. Get on with it." He sat expectantly, looked genuinely intrigued.

Jon-Tom cleared his throat self-consciously and looked around. No one was paying him the least attention. He took a fortifying swallow from Mudge's mug and considered. Damn silly, he thought. Oh well, best try an old favorite, and he began "Eleanor Rigby." Am I one of all the lonely people now? he thought as he voiced the song.

When he'd finished, he looked anxiously at the otter. Mudge's expression was fixed.

"Well?" How was I?"

Mudge leaned back in his seat, smiled faintly. "Maybe you were right, Jon-Tom. Maybe it 'twould be better with some instrumental accompaniment. Interestin' words, I'll grant you that. I once knew a chap who kept several faces in jars, though 'e didn't 'ave 'em up by 'is door.''

Jon-Tom tried not to show his disappointment, though why he should have expected a different reaction from the otter than from previous audiences he couldn't imagine.

"I'm really much more of an instrumentalist. As far as voice goes," he added defensively, "maybe I'm not smooth, but I'm enthusiastic.''

"That's so, mate, but I'm not so sure your listeners would be. I'll try t' think on what else you might do. But for now, I think maybe it would be a kindness t' forget about any minstrelin'.''

"Well, I'm not helpless." Jon-Tom gestured around them. "I don't want to keep imposing on you, Mudge. Take this place. I'm not afraid of hard work. There must be hundreds of mugs and platters to wash and floors to be mopped down, tables to be cleaned, drains to be scoured. There's a helluva lot of work here. I could . . .''

Mudge reached across the table and had both paws digging into Jon-Tom's indigo shirt. He stared up into the other's surprise and whispered intently.

"You can't do that! That's work for mice and rats. Don't let anyone 'ear you talk like that, Jon-Tom.'' He let go of the silk and sat back in his chair.

"Come on now," Jon-Tom protested softly. "Work is work.''

"Think you that now?" Mudge pointed to his right.

Two tables away from theirs was a rat about three feet tall. He was dressed in overalls sewn from some heavy, thick material that was badly stained and darkened. Thick gloves covered tiny paws, and knee-high boots rested on the floor as the rodent scrubbed at the planking.

The others nearby completely ignored his presence, dropping bones or other garbage nearby or sometimes onto his back. As Jon-Tom watched, the rodent accidentally stumbled across the leg of a drunken gull hunting a table with perches to accommodate ornithological clients. The big bird cocked a glazed eye at him and snapped once with its beak, more taunting than threatening.

Stumbling clear, the rat fell backward, tripped over his own feet, and brought his bucket of trash and goo down on himself. It ran down his boots and over the protective overalls. For a moment he lay stunned in the heap of garbage. Then he slowly struggled to his knees and began silently gathering it up again, ignoring but not necessarily oblivious to the catcalls and insults the patrons heaped on him. A thick bone bounced off his neck, and he gathered it up along with the rest of the debris. Soon the watchers grew bored with the momentary diversion and returned to their drinking, eating, and arguing.

"Only rats and mice do that kind of work?" Jon-Tom inquired. "I used to do something like it all the time. Remember, that's what confused Clothahump into bringing me here in the first place."

"What you do elsewhere you'd best not try 'ere, mate. Any self-respectin' animal would sooner starve before doin' that, or go t' beggin' like our sticker-hiding friend, the gibbon."

"I don't understand any of this, Mudge."

"Don't try t', mate. Just roll with the waves, wot? Besides, those types are naturally lazy and dumb. They'd rather lie about and guzzle cheese all day than do any honest work, they would. Spend all their time when not eatin' in indiscriminate screwing, though you wouldn't think they'd 'ave enough brains t' know which end to work with."

Jon-Tom was fighting to control his temper. "There's nothing wrong with doing menial work. It doesn't make those who do it menial-minded. I . . ." He sighed, wondered at the hopelessness of it all. "I guess I just thought things would be different here, as far as that kind of thing goes. It's my fault. I was imagining a world that doesn't exist."

Mudge laughed. "Little while back I recall you insistin' that this one didn't exist."

"Oh, it exists all right." His fists rubbed angrily on the table as he watched the subservient rat suddenly go down on his chest. A turtle with a disposition considerably less refined than Clothahump's had stuck out a stubby leg and tripped the unfortunate rodent. Once more the laboriously gathered garbage went flying while a new burst of merriment flared from the onlookers.

"Why discrimination like that here?" Jon-Tom muttered. "Why here too?"

"Discrimination?" Mudge seemed confused. "Nobody discriminates against 'em. That's all they're good for. Can't argue with natural law, mate."

Jon-Tom had expected more from Mudge, though he'd no real reason to. From what he'd already seen, the otter was no worse than the average inhabitant of this stinking, backward nonparadise.

There were a number of humans scattered throughout the restaurant. None came near approaching Jon-Tom in height. Nearby a single older gentleman was drinking and playing cards with a spider monkey dressed in black shot through with silver thread. They paired off against a larger simian Jon-Tom couldn't identify and a three-foot-tall pocket gopher wearing a crimson jumpsuit and the darkest sunglasses Jon-Tom had ever seen.

No doubt they were as prejudiced and bigoted as the others. And where did he come off setting himself up as arbiter of another world's morals?

"There ain't nothin' you can do about it, mate. Why would anyone want t' change things? Cor now, moppin' and sweepin' and such are out, unless you want t' lose all respect due a regular citizen. Politickin' you're also qualified for, but that o' course ranks even lower than janitorial-type drudgeryin'. I'd hope you won't 'ave t' fall back on your abilities for minstrelin'.'' His tone changed to one of hope mixed with curiosity.

"Now ol' Clothahump, 'e was bloody well sure you were some sort of sorcerer, 'e was. You sure you can't work no magic? I 'eard you questioning 'is wizard-wart's own special words.''

"That was just curiosity, Mudge. Some of the words were familiar. But not in the way he used them. Even you did the business with the dancing pins. Does everyone practice magic around here?''

"Oh, everyone practices, all right.'' Mudge swilled down a snootful of black brew. "But few get good enough at it to do much more than a trick or two. Pins are my limit, I'm afraid. Wish to 'ell I knew 'is gold spell.'' His gaze suddenly moved left and he grinned broadly.

"Course now, when the situation arises I ain't too bad at certain forms o' levitation.'' His right hand moved with the speed of which only otters are capable.

How the saucily dressed and heavily made up chipmunk managed to keep from dumping the contents of the six tankards she was maneuvering through the crowd was a bit of magic in itself, Jon-Tom thought as he ducked to avoid the few flying suds.

She turned an outraged look on the innocent-seeming Mudge. "You keep your hands to yourself, you shit-eating son of a mud worm! Next time you'll get one of these up your furry backside!'' She threatened him with a tankard.

"Now Lily,'' Mudge protested, '' 'aven't you always told me you're always 'untin' for a way t' move up in the world?''

She started to swing an armful of liquor at him and he cowered away in mock fear, covering his face with his paws and still smiling. Then she thought better of wasting the brew. Turning from their table she marched away, elbowing a path through the crowd. Her tail switched prettily from side to side, the short dress barely reaching from waist to knee. It was gold with a gray lining that neatly set off her own attractive russet and black and white striping.

"What did I tell you, mate?" Mudge grinned over his mug at Jon-Tom.

He tried to smile back, aware that the otter was trying to break the glum mood into which Jon-Tom had fallen. So he forced himself to continue the joke.

"Mighty short levitation, Mudge. I don't see how it does her any good."

"Who said anything about her?" The otter jabbed himself in the chest with a thumb. "It's *me* the levitatin' benefits!" He clasped both furry arms around his chest and roared at his own humor, threatening to upset table and self.

Wooden shades were rolled down to cover the two windows, and someone dimmed the oil lamps. Jon-Tom started to rise, felt a restraining paw on his wrist.

"Nay, guv, 'tis nothing t' be concerned about." His eyes were sparkling. "Quite the contrary. Did I not promise you some entertainment?" He pointed to the circular serving counter and up.

What looked like an upside-down tree was slowly descending from a gap in the center of the peaked ceiling. It was green with fresh growth, only the foilage had been tacked on and doubtless was periodically renewed. The still unseen band segued into an entirely new tune. The percussionist was doing most of the work now, Jon-Tom noted. The beat was heavy, slow, and sensuous.

The yelling and shouting that filled the establishment changed also. Barely organized chaos faded to a murmur of anticipation spotted with occasional roars of comment, usually lewd in nature.

Mudge had shifted his seat, now sat close to Jon-Tom. His eyes were on the fake tree as he elbowed his companion repeatedly in the ribs.

"Eyes at the alert now, mate. There's not a fairer nor more supple sight in all Lynchbany."

An animal appeared at the dark opening in the ceiling, prompting a bellow from the crowd. It vanished, then teasingly reappeared. It was slight, slim, and made its way very slowly from the hidden chamber above down into the branches of the ersatz conifer. About three and a half feet in length, it displayed another half foot of active tail and was completely, almost blindingly covered in snow-white fur save for a few inches of black at the tip of the tail.

Its costume, if such so lithe a wrapping could be called, consisted of many layers of black veils of some chiffonlike material through which the brilliant white fur showed faintly. Its face was streaked with red painted on in intricate curlicues and patterns that ran from face and snout down onto shoulders, chest, and back before vanishing beneath the airy folds. A turban of matching black was studded with jewels. The final touch, Jon-Tom noted with fascination, were long false eyelashes.

So absorbing was this glittering mammalian vision that for several moments identification escaped him. That slim form and muscular torso could only belong to some member of the weasel family. When the apparition smiled and displayed tiny sharp teeth he was certain of it. This was an ermine, still in full winter-white coat. That confirmed the time of year he'd arrived, though he hadn't thought to ask anyone. About the creature's femininity he had no doubt whatsoever.

A hush of interspecies expectancy had settled over the crowd. All attention was focused overhead as the ermine ecdysiast began to toy with the clasps securing one veil. She unsnapped one, then its companion. Cries of appreciation started to rise from the patrons, an amazing assortment of hoots, whistles, squeaks, yowls, and barks. She began to uncoil the first veil with snakelike motions.

Jon-Tom had never had occasion to imagine an animal executing anything as erotic as a striptease. After all, beneath any clothing lay another layer of solid fur and not the bare flesh of a human.

But eroticism has little to do with nudity, as he soon discovered. It was the movement of the creature, a supple twisting and turning that no human female could possibly match, that was stimulating. He found himself thoroughly engrossed by the mechanics of the dance alone.

To rising cries of appreciation from the crowd one veil followed another. The cool indifference Jon-Tom had intended to affect had long since given way to a distinct tingling. He was no more immune to beauty than any other animal. The ermine executed a series of movements beyond the grasp of the most talented double-jointed human, and did so with the grace and demeanor of a countess.

There was also the manner in which she oozed around the branches and leaves of the tree, caressing them with hands and body in a way only a chunk of cold granite could have ignored. The room was heavy with musk now, the suggestiveness of motion and gesture affecting every male within sight.

The last veil dropped free, floated featherlike to the floor. The music was moving almost as fast as the performer. That white-furred derrière had become a gravity-defying metronome, a passionate pendulum sometimes concealed, sometimes revealed by the position of the twitching tail, all vibrating in time to the music.

The music rose to a climax as the ermine, hanging by her arms from the lowermost branches, executed an absolutely impossible series of movements which incidentally revealed to Jon-Tom the reason for the circular, central nature of the main serving counter. It served now as fortress wall behind which the heavily armed cooks and bartenders were able to fend off the hysterical advances of the overheated patrons.

One long-eared rabbit which Jon-Tom supposed to be a jack actually managed to grab a handful of black-tipped tail which was coyly but firmly pulled out of reach. A burly bobcat dumped the rabbit back among the surging patrons as the ermine blew a last kiss to her audience. Then she slithered back through branches and leaves to disappear inside the ceiling with a last fluid bump and grind.

Shades and tree were promptly rolled up. Conversation resumed and normality returned to the restaurant. Waitresses and waiters continued to wend their way through the crowd like oxygen in the bloodstream.

"D'you see now wot I mean, mate?" Mudge said with the contentment of one who'd just cashed a very large check, "when I say that there's no one who—" He stopped, stared strangely across the table.

"What's wrong?" asked Jon-Tom uncomfortably.

"'Ave me for breakfast," was the startled reply, "if you ain't blushin'! You 'umans . . ."

"Bull," muttered Jon-Tom, turning angrily away.

"Nope." The otter leaned over the table, peering closely at Jon-Tom despite his attempts to keep his face concealed. "Blimey but it's true . . . you're as red as a baboon's behind, lad." He nodded upward, toward the peak of the roof. "'Ave you ne'er seen such a performance before, then?"

"Of course I have." He turned forcefully back to face his guardian, rocked a little unsteadily. It seeped into his brain that he might have become a little bit tipsy. How much of that black booze had he downed?

"That is, I have . . . on film."

"What be that?"

"A magic apparition," Jon-Tom explained facilely.

"Well if you've gazed upon such, though not, I dare to say," and he gazed admiringly ceilingward, "of such elegance and skill, then why the red face?"

"It's just that," he searched for the right words to explain his confusion, "I shouldn't find the actions of . . ." How could he say, "another animal" without offending his companion? Desperately he hunted for an alternate explanation.

"I've never seen anything done with quite that . . . well, with quite that degree of perverse dexterity."

"Ah, I understand now. Though perverse I wouldn't call it. Crikey, but that was a thing of great beauty."

"If you say so, I guess it was." Jon-Tom was grateful for the out.

"Aye." Mudge growled softly and smiled. "And if I could once get my paws on that supple little mother-dear, I'd show '*er* a thing of beauty."

The thick, warm atmosphere of the restaurant had combined with the rich food and drink to make Jon-Tom decidedly woozy. He was determined not to pass out. Mudge already did not think much of him, and Clothahump's warnings or no, he wasn't ready to bet that the otter would stay with him if he made a total ass of himself.

Determinedly he shoved the mug away, rose, and glanced around.

"What be you searchin' for now, mate?"

"Some of my own kind." His eyes scanned the crowd for the sight of bare flesh.

"What, 'umans?" The otter shrugged. "Aw well, never 'ave I understood your peculiar affinity for each other's company, but you're free enough to choose your own. Espy some, do you?"

Jon-Tom's gaze settled on a pair of familiar bald faces in a booth near the rear of the room. "There's a couple over that way. Two men, I think."

"As you will, then."

He turned his attention down to the otter. "It's not that I'm not enjoying your companionship, Mudge. It's just that I'd like one of my own kind to talk to for a while."

His worries were groundless. Mudge was in entirely too good a mood to be offended by anything.

"Wotever you like, mate. We'll go and 'ave a chat then, if that's wot you want. But don't forget we've still the little matter o' settlin' you on some proper course o' employment." He shook his head more to clear it than to indicate displeasure.

"Minstrel . . . I don't know. There might still be the novelty factor." He scratched the fur just under his chin. "Tell you what. Give us another song and then we'll go over and see if we can't make the acquaintance o' those chaps."

"I thought you'd heard enough the first time."

"Never go on first appearances, mate. Besides, 'twas a damn blue and gloomy tune you let out with. Try somethin' different. Many's the minstrel who well mangles one type o' tune yet can warble clearly another."

Jon-Tom sat down again, linked his fingers, and considered. "I don't know. What would you like to hear? Classical, pop, blues, jazz?" He tried to sound enthusiastic. "I know some classical, but what I really always wanted to do was sing rock. It's a form of popular music back where I come from."

"I don't know either, mate. 'Ow 'bout ballads? Everyone likes ballads."

"Sure." He was warming again to his true love. "I know a number of 'em. What subject do you like best?"

"Let me think on it a minute." Actually, it was only a matter of seconds before a gleam returned to the black eyes, along with a smile.

"Never mine," Jon-Tom said hastily. "I'll think of something."

He thought, but it was hard to settle on any one song. Maybe it was the noise and smell swirling around them, maybe the aftereffects of the meal, but words and notes flitted in and out of his brain like gnats, never pausing long enough for him to get a grip on any single memory. Besides, he felt unnatural singing without his trusty, worn Grundig slung over his shoulder and across his stomach. If he only had something, even a harmonica. But he couldn't play that and sing simultaneously.

"Come on now, mate," Mudge urged him. "Surely you can think o' something?"

"I'll try," and he did, launching into a cracked rendition of "Strawberry Fair," but the delicate harmonies were drowned in the bellowing and hooting and whistling that filled the air of the restaurant.

Nonetheless, he was unprepared for the sharp blow that struck him between the shoulderblades and sent him sprawling chest-down across the table.

Angry and confused, he turned to find himself staring into a ferocious dark brown face set on a stocky, muscular body as tall as Mudge's but more than twice as broad. . . .

VI

The snakeskin beret and red bandana did nothing to lessen the wolverine's intimidating appearance.

"Sorry," Jon-Tom mumbled, uncertain of what else to say.

The face glared down at him, powerful jaws parting to reveal sharp teeth as the lips curled back. "You ban not sorry enough, I think!" the creature rumbled hollowly. "I ban pretty sorry for your mother, she having much to listen to a voice like that. You upset my friends and my meal."

"I was just practicing." He was beginning to feel a mite indignant at the insults. The warmth of the roast was still with him. He failed to notice the queasy expression that had come over Mudge's face. "It's difficult to sing without any music to accompany me."

"Yah, well, you ban practice no more, you hear? It ban hurt my ears."

Mudge was trying and failing to gain Jon-Tom's attention. Jon-Tom rose from his seat to tower over the shorter but more massive animal. It made him feel better, giving proof once again to the old adage about the higher, the mightier. Or as the old philosopher said, witness the pigeon's tactical advantage over man.

However the wolverine was not impressed. He gazed appraisingly up and down Jon-Tom's length. "All that voice tube and no voice. Maybe you ban better at singing in harmony, yah? So maybe I put one half neck here and the other half across the table," and powerful clawed hands reached for Jon-Tom's face.

Dodging nimbly, Jon-Tom slipped around the table, brought up his staff, and swung the straight end down in a whistling arc. Having had plenty to consume himself, the wolverine reacted more slowly than usual. He did not quite get both hands up in time to defend himself, and the staff smacked sharply over one set of knuckles. The creature roared in pain.

"Look, I don't want any trouble."

"You stick up for your rights, mate!" Mudge urged him, beginning a precipitous retreat from the vicinity of the table. "I'll watch and make sure it be a fair fight."

"Like hell you will!" He held the staff tightly, trying to divide his attention between the wolverine and the otter. "You remember what Clothahump said."

"Screw that!" But Mudge hesitated, his hand fumbling in the vicinity of his chest sword. Clearly he was sizing up the tense triangle that had formed around the table and debating whether or not he stood a better chance of surviving Clothahump's vengeful spell-making than the wolverine and his friends. The latter consisted of a tall marten and a chunky armadillo who displayed a sword hanging from each hip belt. Of course, carrying weapons and knowing how to use them were two different matters.

They were rising and moving to flank the wolverine and gazing at Jon-Tom in a decidedly unfriendly manner. The wolverine himself had regained his composure and was sliding an ugly-looking mace from the loop on his own belt.

"Steady on, mate," the otter urged his companion, sword out and committed now.

The wolverine was bouncing the spiked iron head of the mace up and down in one palm, gripping the handle with the other. "Maybe I ban wrong about that harmony." He eyed the man's throat. "Maybe I ban eliminate that voice altogether, yah?" He started forward, encountered a waiter who started to curse him, then saw the mace and fled into the crowd.

"Is too crowded in here though. I tink I meet you outside, hokay?"

"Hokay," said Jon-Tom readily. He moved as if to leave, got his right hand under the edge of the table, and heaved. Table, drinks, remnants of their greasy meal and platterware showered down on the wolverine, his companions, and several unsuspecting occupants of other tables. The innocent by-standers took exception to the barrage. One of the wolverine's associates side-stepped the flying table and jabbed his sword at the otter's face. Mudge ducked under the marten's thrust and kept his sword ready to challenge the emerging armadillo while neatly kicking the bellicose marten in the nuts. The stricken animal grabbed himself and went to his knees.

Among those who had received the dubious decorations proferred by Jon-Tom's action were a pair of female coatis whose delicacy of shape and flash of eye were matched by the outrage in their voices. They had drawn slim rapiers and were struggling to join the fray.

Jon-Tom had moved backward and to his left, this being the only space still not filled with potential combatants, and was quickly joined by Mudge. They continued backing until they upset another table and its patrons. This instituted a chain reaction which led with astonishing rapidity to a general mayhem that threatened to involve every one in the establishment.

Only the chefs and bartenders kept their calm. They remained invulnerable behind their protective circular counter, defending liquor and food as assiduously as they had the honor and person of their gleaming white star performer. Only when some stumbling battler intruded on their territorial circle did their heavy clubs come into play. Waiters and waitresses huddled behind this front line of defense, casually making book on the outcome of the fight or downing drinks intended for otherwise occupied patrons.

The fight whirlpooled around this central bastion of calm as the room was filled with yelps and meows, squeaks and squeals and chirps of pain and outrage.

It was an arboreal that almost got Jon-Tom. He was effectively if unartistically using his long staff to fend off the short sword thrusts of an outraged pika when Mudge yelled, "Jon-Tom . . . duck!"

As it was, the bola-wielding mallard missed his neck but got his weapon entangled in the club end of Jon-Tom's staff. He shoved down hard on it. In order to remain airborne the fowl had to surrender his weapon, but not without dropping instead a stream of insults on the tall human. Jon-Tom had time to note the duck's kilt of orange and green. He wondered if the different kilt colors signified species or some sort of genus-spanning clan equivalent.

There was little time for sociological contemplation. The marten had recovered from Mudge's low blow and was moving to put the sharp edge of his blade through Jon-Tom's midsection. Instinctively he tilted the staff crosswise. The club end came over and around. It missed the agile marten, but the entangled bird's bola caught around the weasel's neck.

Dropping his sword, he pulled the device free of the staff and stumbled away, fighting to free his neck from the strangling cord. Jon-Tom, momentarily clear of attackers, hunted through the crowd for his companion.

Mudge was close by, kicking furniture in the way of potential assailants, throwing mugs and other eating utensils at them whenever possible, avoiding hand-to-hand combat wherever he could.

Jon-Tom took no pride, felt no pleasure in his newfound capacity for violent self-defense. If he could only get out of this dangerous madhouse and back home to the peace and quiet of his little apartment! But that distant, familiar haven had receded ever farther into memory, had reached the point where it existed only as misty history compared to the all too real blood and fury surrounding him.

Thank God, he thought frantically, fending off another attacker, for Clothahump's ministrations. Even a well-bandaged wound would have broken open again by now, but he felt nothing in his formerly injured side. He was well and truly healed.

That would not save him if one of many sword or pike thrusts punctured him anew. The indiscriminate nature of the fighting was more frightening than anything else now. It was impossible to tell potential friend from foe.

In vain he looked across the milling crest of the fight for the entrance. It was seemingly at least a mile away across an ocean of battling fur and steel. A desperate examination of the room seemed to show no other exit save via the central bastion of the bar and food counter, whose defenders were not admitting refugees. That left only the windows, an idea the panting Mudge quickly quashed.

"Blimey, mate, you must be daft! That glass be 'alf an inch thick in places and thicker where 'tis beveled. I'd sooner take a sword thrust than slice meself t' bloody ribbons on that.

"There be an alley out back. Let's make our way in that direction."

"I don't see any doors there," said Jon-Tom, straining to see past the rear booths.

"Surely there's a service entryway. I'll settle now meself for a garbage chute."

Sure enough, they eventually discovered a single low doorway hidden by stacks of crates and piles of garbage. The close-packed mob made progress difficult, but they forced their way slowly toward the promise of freedom and safety. Only Jon-Tom's overbearing height enabled them to keep their goal in view. To the other brawlers he must have looked like an ambling lighthouse.

Already his shining snakeskin cape was torn and blood-stained. Better it than me, he thought gratefully. It was not a pretty riot. The only rules were those of survival.

He passed one squirrel prone on the floor, tail sodden and matted with blood. His left leg was missing below the knee. So much blood and spilled drink and food had accumulated on the floor, in fact, that one of the greatest dangers was losing one's footing on the increasingly treacherous planking.

Jon-Tom watched as a cape-clad coyote picked over the unconscious form of a badly bleeding fox. While his attention was thus temporarily diverted, someone grabbed his left arm. He turned to swing the staff one-handed or jab as was required. So far he hadn't been forced to utilize the concealed spearpoint and hoped he'd never have to.

The figure that had grabbed him was completely swathed in maroon and blue material. He could discern little of the figure save that the mostly hidden face seemed to be human. The short figure tugged hard and urged him back behind a temporary wall formed by a trio of fat porcupines, who, for self-evident reasons, were having little trouble fending off any combatant foolish enough to come close.

He decided there was time later for questions, since the figure was pulling him toward the haven promised by the back door, and that was his intended destination anyway.

"Hurry it up!" Though muffled by fabric the voice was definitely human. "The cops have been called and should be here any second." There was a decided undertone of real fear in that warning, the reason for which Jon-Tom was to discover soon enough.

Visions of hundreds of furry police swarming through the crowd filled his thoughts. From the size and breadth of the conflict he guessed it would take at least that number several more hours to quell the fighting. He was reckoning without the ingenuity of Lynchbany law enforcement.

Mudge, upon hearing of the incipient arrival of the gendarmes, acted genuinely terrified.

"That's fair warnin', mate," he yelled above the din, "and

we'd best get out or die trying." He redoubled his efforts to clear a path to the door.

"Why? What will they do?" He swung his staff in a short arc, brought it up beneath the chin of a small but gamely threatening muskrat who was swinging at Jon-Tom's ankles with a weapon like a scythe. Fortunately, he'd only nicked one trouser leg before Jon-Tom knocked him out. "Do they kill people here for fighting in public?"

"Worse than that." Mudge was nearly at the back door, fighting to keep potential antagonists out of sword range and the invulnerable porcupines between himself and the rest of the mob. Then he shouted frantically.

"Quickly—quick now, for your lives!" Jon-Tom thought it peculiar the otter had not sought the identity of their concealed compatriot. "They're here!"

From his position head-and-shoulders high above the crowd Jon-Tom could see across to the now distant main entrance. He also noted with concern that the chefs and bartenders and waiters had vanished, abandoning their stock to the crowd.

Four or five figures of indeterminate furry cast stood inside the entryway now. They wore leathern bonnets decorated with flashing ovals of metal. Emblems on shoulder vests glinted in the light from the remaining intact lamps and the windows. There was a crash, and he saw that unmindful of the danger Mudge had outlined, the appearance of the police had actually frightened one of the fighters into following a chair out through a thick window pane. Jon-Tom wondered what horrible fate was in store for the rest of the still battling mob.

Then he was following the strange figure and Mudge out through the door. As they turned to slam and bar it with barrels behind them he had a last glimpse across the room as the police took action against the combatants within. This was accompanied by a whiff of something awful beyond imagining and concentrated beyond the power of man or beast to endure.

It weakened him so badly that he barely had strength enough to heave his not-yet-digested dinner all over the far wall. It helped his pride if not his stomach to see that the momentary smell had produced the same effect on Mudge and the maroon-clad stranger. As he knelt in the alley and emptied his nausea-squeezed guts, the pattern he'd glimpsed on the arriving police came back to him.

Then they were all up and stumbling, running down the cobblestoned alley, the mist still dense around them and the smell of garbage like perfume compared to that which was fading with merciful speed behind them.

"Very . . . efficient, though I'm not so sure I'd call it humane, even if no one is killed." He clung tightly to his staff, using it for support as they slowed a little.

"Aye, mate." Mudge jogged steadily alongside him, behind the long-legged stranger. Occasionally he gave a worried, disgusted glance back over a shoulder to check for possible pursuit. None materialized.

"Indecent it is. You only *wish* you were dead. It be that way in every town, though. 'Tis clean and there's no after caterwaulerin' about accidental death or police brutalness and such. There's worse things than takin' an occasional sword in the side, though. Like puking to death.

"Makes it a good thing for the skunks, though. I've never seen a one of those black and white offal that lacked a good job in any township. 'Tis a brother and sisterhood sort of comradeship they 'ave, which is well for 'em, since none o' the common folk care for their companionship. They keep the peace, I suppose, and keep t' themselves." He shuddered. "And keep in mind, mate, that we were clean across the room from 'em. Those by the front will likely not touch food for days." Several small lizards left their claimed bit of rotting meat, skittered into a hole in the wall while the refugees hurried past, then returned to their scavaging.

"Never could stand 'em myself, either. I don't like cops and I cannot abide anyone who fights with 'is rear end."

Noises reached them from the far end of the alley and vestiges of that ghastly odor materialized to stab at Jon-Tom's nostrils and stomach.

"They're followin'," said a worried Mudge. "Save us from that. I'd far rather be cut."

"This way!" urged the cloaked figure. They turned up a branch of the alleyway. Mist covered everything, slickened walls and cobblestones and trash underfoot. They plunged onward, heedless of falling.

Gradually the smell began to recede once more. Jon-Tom was grateful for the time he'd spent on the basketball court, and for the unusual stride that enabled him to keep up with the hyperactive Mudge and their racing and still identityless savior.

"They took the main passage," said that voice. "This should be safe enough."

They had emerged on a small side street. Dim will-o'-the-wisp glows came from the warm globes of the street lamps overhead. It was quite dark otherwise, and though the mist curtained the sky Jon-Tom was certain that sunset had come and gone while they'd been dining in the restaurant.

The stranger unwrapped the muffler covering face and neck and let it hang across shoulders and back. Cloak, shirt, and pants were made of the same maroon material touched with silver thread. The material was neither leather nor cotton but some mysterious organic hybrid. Pants, boots, and blouse had further delicate designs of copper thread worked through them, as did the high, almost Napoleonic collar.

A slim blade, half foil, half saber, was slung neatly from the waist. She stood nearly as tall as Mudge's five foot six, which Jon-Tom had been given to understand was tall for a human woman hereabouts. She turned, still panting from the run, to study them. He was glad of the opportunity to reciprocate.

The maroon clothing fit snugly without binding and the face above it, though expectedly petite, was hard and sharp-featured. The green eyes were more like Mudge's than his own. They moved with almost equal rapidity over street and alleyway, never ceasing. Her shoulder-length curls were flamered. Not the red-orange of most redheads but a fiery, flashing crimson that looked in the lamplight like kinky blood.

Save for her coloring and the absence of fur and whiskers she displayed all the qualities of an active otter. Only the pale green eyes softened the savage image she presented, standing there nervously by the side of a building that seemed to swoop winglike above them in the mist.

As for the rest of her, he had the damndest feeling he was seeing a cylindrical candy bar well packed with peanuts. Her voice was full of hints of clove and pepper, as active as her eyes and her body.

"Thought I'd never get you out of there." She was talking to Mudge. "I tried to get you separated but," she glanced curiously up at Jon-Tom, "this great gangling boy was always between us."

"I'd appreciate it," said Jon-Tom politely, "if you wouldn't refer to me as a 'boy'." He stared unblinkingly at her. "You don't look any older than me."

"I'll change my tune," she shot back, "when you've demonstrated the difference to my satisfaction, though I hope more time isn't required. Still, I have to admit that you handled yourself well enough inside the Possum. Clumsy, but efficient. Size can make up for a helluva lot."

Clove and pepper, he thought. Each word was snapped off sharply in the air like a string of firecrackers.

She turned distastefully away from his indelicate stare and asked Mudge with disarming candor, "How soon can we be rid of it?" She jerked a thumb in Jon-Tom's bemused direction.

"I'm afraid we can't, m'love. Clothahump 'imself 'as entrusted 'im t' me tender care."

"Clothahump, the wizard of the Tree?" Again she looked curiously at Jon-Tom.

"Aye. It seems 'e was castin' about for an otherworldly

wizard type and 'e came up with this chap Jon-Tom instead. As I said, because I 'appened t' be unlucky enough to stumble into this manifestation, I've been ordered t' take care of 'im. At least until e' can take better care of 'imself.'' Mudge raised a paw.

"On penalty o' curses too 'orrible t' explain, luv. But it 'ain't been too bad. 'E's a good enough lad, if a trifle naïve.''

Jon-Tom was beginning to feel a resurgence of the volatility that had set off the riot in the Pearl Possum. "Hey now, people, I'm getting a little tired of everyone continually running off my list of disabilities.''

"Shut up and do as you're told,'' said the woman.

"Fuck you, sister,'' he spat back angrily. "How'd you like your backside the same color as your hair?''

Her right hand suddenly sported a sixth finger. The knife gleamed in the dim light. It was no longer than her middle finger but twice as broad and displayed an unusual double blade.

"And how'd you like to sing about three octaves higher?''

"Please now, Talea.'' Mudge hurriedly interposed himself between them. "Think of me, if naught else. 'E's me responsibility. If any 'arm comes to 'im while 'e's in my care, Clothahump'll 'ave me 'ide. As to 'is singin' I've 'ad more than enough for one night. That's wot started the trouble in the Possum in the first place.''

"More's the pity for you then, Mudge.'' But the blade disappeared with a twist of the wrist, vanishing back inside her right sleeve. "I'll truce on it for you . . . for now.''

"I'm not taking any orders from her,'' Jon-Tom said belligerently.

"Now, now, mate.'' Mudge made placating gestures. "No one's said that you must. But you're willin' to accept advice, ain't you? That's what I'm 'ere for, after all.''

"That's true,'' Jon-Tom admitted. But he couldn't keep his eyes off the lethal little lady Mudge had called Talea. Her temper had considerably mitigated his first feelings toward her. She was no less beautiful for their argument, but it had become the beauty of a rose sealed in glass. Delicacy and attractiveness were still there, but there was no fragrance, and both were untouchable.

"That's the second time tonight you've shown concern for me, luv." Mudge looked at her uncertainly. "First by 'elpin' us flee that unfortunate altercation back in the Pearl Possum and now again by respectin' me wishes and makin' peace with the lad. I've never known you t' be so solicitous o' my 'ealth or anyone else's exceptin' your precious own. So wot's behind the sudden nursmaidin'?"

"You're right about the first, Mudge. Most of the time you can find your own way to hell for all I care." Her voice finally mellowed, and for the first time she sounded vulnerable and human.

"Truth is that I needed some help, fast. The Pearl Possum was the nearest and most likely place in which to find it. You were the first one I saw that I knew, and considering what was going on in there I didn't have a whole hell of a lot of time to be picky. I do need your help." She looked hesitantly past him at Jon-Tom. "And so I guess I have to put up with him, too." She walked over to Jon-Tom, looked him over sharply.

"In truth, he's an impressive physical speciman." Jon-Tom stood a little taller. "What I need now are strong backs, not brains." He lost an inch.

"I knew you were needin' something, dear," said Mudge knowledgeably. "I couldn't see you givin' yourself over t' philanthropy. Jon-Tom, meet Talea. And widdershins likewise."

"Charmed," said Jon-Tom curtly.

"Yeah, me too." She paused thoughtfully. "So the old magic bugger-in-the-shell was looking around for an otherworld wizard and got you instead. I can imagine what his reaction must have been."

"I don't need this." Jon-Tom turned away, spoke almost

cheerfully. "I don't need this at all. I'll make my own damn way!"

" 'Old on now, mate," said Mudge desperately. "You think o' me, too. Everyone think o' poor old Mudge for a change."

"When did you ever think of anything else?" snorted Talea.

"Please, luv. Go easy on the poor lad. 'Tis right that you owe 'im nothing and likewise meself. But consider, 'e's a whole new world t' try and cope with, and you're not makin' it any easier."

"What have his problems to do with me?" she replied indifferently, but for a change left off adding any additional insults.

"You said that you needed our help," Jon-Tom reminded her. "And I suppose we owe you a favor for helping us out of that mess back there." He jerked a hand back toward the now distant restaurant. "Or at least for warning us about the police. You can have the use of my back without my affection. At least I can use that without running my mouth."

She almost smiled, flipping away hair from her eyes. The oil lamps set her curls on fire. "That's fair enough. We've wasted enough time here, and I suppose I've wasted most of it. Follow me. . . ."

They trailed her down the street. No strollers were out this time on so miserable a night. Rain dripped off tile and wood roofs, trickled metallically down drainpipes and into gutters. Sometimes they passed a sharper, richer echo where dripwater plunged into a collection barrel.

They'd walked several blocks before she turned into another alleyway. Several yards into the narrow passage he began to hear a strange yet somehow familiar snuffling noise. It sounded like a drunk hog.

Almost stumbling over something firm and heavy, he looked down and saw to his considerable dismay that it was an arm, badly decomposed and with the fur falling from forearm and paw. Nude bone projected like soap from one end.

Mudge and Talea were just ahead. The otter was bending over and examining something on the stones. Jon-Tom hurried to join them.

Two bodies lay sprawled awkwardly across the damp paving, necklaced by puddles of rainwater. One was that of a squirrel he assumed by attire to be female. She was richly dressed in a pleated gown puffed up like a cloud by a series of lace petticoats. Long ruffled sleeves covered each gray-furred arm. Nearby lay a feathered, broad-rimmed hat, torn and broken. She was half a foot shorter than Talea and her carefully applied face powder and paint were smeared like mud across her cheeks.

Nearby was a fat furry form that he at first thought might be a small beaver but that turned out to be another muskrat. An oddly creased tricornered hat still rested on the motionless head, though it was tilted over the hidden eyes. A pair of cracked pince-nez spectacles, much like those worn by Clothahump, reflected the still, small pools between the cobblestones. The iridescent blue silk suit he wore was rich enough to shine even in the dim light of the alley.

One boot had come off and lay limply near a naked foot. Its rhinestone-inlaid mate lay up against the far wall. Talea ignored it as she rechecked the body with professional speed.

"Blimey, luv, what's all this now?" Mudge's attention was directed nervously back toward the narrow plank of light from the street. "I ain't so sure we want to be compromisin' ourselves with business of this disreputable nature."

"Shit, you're compromised just by standing there." Talea heaved at the thick silk jacket. "Not that your reputation would suffer. Who are you lying to, Mudge; yourself, me, or him?" and she nodded briefly toward the self-conscious Jon-Tom. "You know what the cops will do if they find you standing here flapping your whiskers."

"Now Talea, luv—" he began.

"I think we've exchanged enough pleasantries, otter. I need you for muscle, not platitudes.

"Now I don't object to an occasional mugging, especially when the apple stands around begging to be plucked." She was pulling gold buttons off the comatose muskrat's trousers. "But murder's not my style. This fat little twerp decided to show off and resist, and I'll be damned if that fuzzy harridan he was with didn't try to help him. Between the two of them I didn't have much time to get selective with the hilt of my sword. So I bashed him proper and then she just sort of fainted."

Mudge moved over to study the fallen lady. While John-Tom watched, the otter knelt and moved her head. There was a dark stain on the stones and a matching one at the back of the furry skull.

"This one's still bleedin', you know."

"I didn't mean to hurt anyone." Talea did not sound particularly contrite. "I was just trying to keep them off. I told you, she fainted. What the hell was I supposed to do, dive underneath and break her fall?"

Mudge moved away and performed a similar examination of the muskrat. "Now why would you 'ave t' do that, luv, when these gentle rocks 'ave done such a neat job of it for you?" he said sardonically. His paws moved over the muskrat's face. "Still breathin', the two of 'em. Bloody lucky you are." He looked up at her.

"Right then. What is it you want of us?"

She finally finished her scavenging, gestured back toward the street. "I've got a wagon tied around the corner on Sorbarlio Close. If I'd left it alley-opposite it would've blocked traffic and worse, drawn attention to this little drama. Besides, it's too wide to fit in the alley entrance.

"Now, I can't carry that fat little bugger by myself. By the time I could drag the two of them to the Close some nosy-body's sure to notice me and ask questions I couldn't

109

answer. Even if I got lucky I'm not sure I could heave these two bloated pumpkins up into the wagon.''

Mudge nodded sagely. ''That's for us, then. Jon-Tom?''

Jon-Tom's head had finally cleared of smoke and drink, but plenty of confusion still remained. Things had happened awfully fast and his thoughts were running into one another.

''I don't know.'' He was also worriedly watching the street. Foul-fighting police might appear at any minute, and what Talea had told Mudge about them being guilty by their mere presence at the scene of the crime had a transworldly ring of truth to it.

''I'm not sure this is what Clothahump had in mind when he asked you to educate me.''

'' 'Tis a fine innocent you are, mate. As you of all people ought t' know, life's incidents are dictated by fate and not neat plannin'. We can't stay 'ere jabberin' all night, lest some idle patrol stumble on us. If you think the copfolk were hard on those poor innocent brawlers, consider wot they're likely t' do t' those they think 'ave assaulted respectable citizens. Or be it then so much different where you come from?''

''No,'' he replied, ''I think they'd react about the same as here.''

Mudge had moved to slip an arm around the waist of the unconscious squirrelquette, then flipped her with a whistle over his shoulders. ''I'll take charge o' this one,'' he said, stumbling.

''Thought you might,'' snorted Talea. ''Here, let me help.'' She caught the lady's legs just as the overburdened Mudge was about to lose his balance completely, then looked back at Jon-Tom.

''Don't just stand there gawking like a kid at a treepeep nook. Put that great gangling self of yours to work.''

Jon-Tom nodded, knelt, and managed to get his arms underneath the snoring, bubbling muskrat shape. The creature was as heavy as he appeared, and the weight made Jon-Tom stagger. Working the mass around he finally got the rotund burden in a fireman's carry.

"Truth, 'tis muscles the lad 'as, if not yet overmuch common sense," Mudge observed. "Does 'e not, lass?"

"Let's get on with it," she said curtly.

On reaching the end of the alley they hesitated. Talea studied the street to the right while Mudge cautiously checked out the other end. Nothing was visible in the nebulous lamplight save cobblestones and lonely clumps of garbage. The night mist had thickened somewhat from earlier in the evening and bestowed on the fugitives a blessing beyond price.

Jon-Tom hurried out after them, the globular body of the muskrat bouncing slightly on his shoulders. He felt something warm on his cheek. At first he thought it was blood, but it turned out to be only saliva dripping from the victim's gaping mouth. He pushed the drooling head farther aside and concentrated on keeping close enough to the others to insure he wouldn't lose track of them in the fog.

His feet were carrying him along a course of events he seemed powerless to alter. As he jogged up the street, he considered his present condition.

In the short time he'd been in Lynchbany he'd nearly been assaulted by a beggar, had taken part in a distressingly violent riot, and was presently serving as an accessory to assault, robbery, and possibly murder. He decided firmly that as soon as circumstances permitted he would have to make his way back to Clothahump's Tree, with or without Mudge's assistance. There he would plead with the wizard to try sending him home, no matter the cost. He could not stand another day of this.

But though he did not know it, he was destined to spend rather more time than that. Forces far greater than anything he could imagine continued to gather, the little sounds his boots made in the street puddles faint echoes of the thunder to come. . . .

VII

Eventually they turned a corner onto another street. Mudge and Talea heaved the motionless form of the squirrelquette onto the back of a low-slung buckboard. Clicking sounds like thick wire brushing against glass came to them. They froze, waited in damp silence. But the wagon they heard did not turn down their street.

"Hurry up!" Talea urged Jon-Tom. She turned and snapped at Mudge, "Quit that and let's get out of here."

Mudge removed his hand from beneath the squirrelquette's dress as Jon-Tom bent his head and shoulders to dump the muskrat. That unfortunate landed with a dull thump in the wagon. Despite Mudge's insistence that both victims were still alive and breathing, the muskrat felt very dead to the worried Jon-Tom.

That was now a major concern. He thought he might be able to talk his way out of being in the same wagon with a couple of robbery victims, but if either one of them died and they were stopped by the police he doubted even Clothahump would be able to help him.

Talea was rapidly pulling a thick blanket of some woven gray material over the bodies. Then the three of them were running around to the front seat of the wagon.

There wasn't enough room there for all of them on the down-sized platform. Talea had grabbed the reins and Mudge had already mounted alongside her, so Jon-Tom had no choice but to vault the wagon rail and sit in the bed behind them.

" 'Tis best anyway, mate." Mudge smiled sympathetically. "I know the wood's 'ard, but as big as you are we don't want to draw any more attention than we can get away with. Snuggle yourself down low and we won't."

Talea gave a flip of the reins and shouted a soft "Hup!" and they were on their way. Just in time, too. As they rumbled down the street another rider passed them close.

Despite his exhaustion and confusion Jon-Tom's interest was aroused. He barely had time for a glance at the mist-shrouded rider.

A white-faced, leather-clad rabbit was mounted on a slim lizard traveling on all fours. The reptile had a long snout with two short tusks protruding upward from just back of the nostrils. Its eyes were searchlight bright and yellow with black slit pupils.

The rider sat in a saddle that was securely attached by multiple straps to the lizard's neck and belly, the extra ties necessary because of the animal's peculiar twisting, side-to-side method of travel. It gave a snakelike appearance to the motion. The long tail was curled up in a spiral and fastened to the reptilian rear with a decorative silver scroll. Blunt claws appeared to have been trimmed close to the quick.

As he watched them vanish down the street, he thought that the rider must be getting a smoother ride than any horse could provide, since all the movement was from side to side instead of up and down.

That inspired him to inspect their own team. Shifting around on the wood and trying to avoid kicking the terribly still forms beneath the gray blanket, he peered ahead beneath the raised wagon seat.

The pair of creatures pulling the wagon were also reptilian, but as different from the rabbit's mount as he was from Mudge. Harnessed in tandem to the wagon, they were shorter and bulkier than the single mount he'd just seen. They had blunt muzzles and less intelligent appearances, though that evaluation was probably due more to his unfamiliarity with the local reptilian life than to any actual physiologic difference.

They trudged more slowly over the cobblestones. Their stride was deliberate and straightforward instead of the unusual twisting, side-to-side movement of the other. Stumpy legs also covered less ground, and leathery stomach folds almost scraped the pavement. Obviously they were intended for pulling heavy loads rather than for comfort or speed.

Despite their bovine expressions they were intelligent enough to respond to Talea's occasional tugs on the reins. He studied the process of steering with interest, for there was no telling when such knowledge might prove useful. He was a good observer, one of the hallmarks of both lawyer and musician, and despite his discouragement about his surroundings he instinctively continued to soak up local information.

The reins, for example, were not attached to bits set in the lizard's mouths. Those thick jaws could have bitten through steel. Instead, they were joined to rings punched through each nostril. Gentle tugs at these sensitive areas were sufficient to guide the course of the lumbering dray.

His attention shifted to a much closer and more intriguing figure. From his slouched position he could see only flaming curls and the silver-threaded shape of her blouse and pants, the latter curving deliciously over the back edge of the wooden seat.

Whether she felt his eyes or not he couldn't tell, but once she glanced sharply back down at him. Instead of turning embarrassedly away he met her stare. For a moment they were eye to eye. That was all. No insults this time. When he stepped further with a slight smile, more from instinct than intent, she simply turned away. She had not smiled back, but neither had that acid tongue heaped further abuse on him.

He settled back against the wooden side of the wagon, trying to rest. She was under a lot of pressure, he told himself. Enough to make anyone edgy and impolite. No doubt in less dangerous surroundings she was cosiderably less antagonistic.

He wondered whether that was likely or if he was simply rationalizing away behavior that upset him. It was admittedly difficult to attribute such bellicosity to such a beautiful lady. Not to mention the fact that it was bad for a delicate male ego.

Shut up, he told himself. You've got more important things to worry about. Think with your head instead of your gonads. What are you going to tell Clothahump when you see him again? It might be best to . . .

He wondered how old she actually was. Her diminutive size was the norm among local humans and hinted at nothing. He already knew her age to be close to his own because she hadn't contradicted his earlier comment about it. She seemed quite mature, but that could be a normal consequence of a life clearly somewhat tougher than his own. He also wondered what she would look like naked, and had reason to question his own maturity.

Think of your surroundings, Meriweather. You're trapped, tired, alone, and in real danger.

Alone . . . well, he would try his best to be friends with her, if she'd permit it. It was absurd to deny he found her attractive, though every time she opened her mouth she succeeded in stifling any serious thoughts he might be developing about extending that hoped-for friendship.

They *had* to become friends. She was human, and that in itself was enough to make him homesick and desperate. Maybe when they'd deposited the bodies at whatever location they were rolling toward she would relax a little.

That prompted him to wonder and worry about just where they *were* taking their injured cargo, and what was going to be done with it when they got there.

A moan came from beneath the blanket behind him, light and hesitant. He thought it came from the squirrelquette, though he couldn't be certain.

"There's a doctor out on the edge of town," Talea said in response to his expression of concern.

"Glad to hear it." So there was at least a shred of soul to complement the beauty. Good. He watched in silence as a delicately wrought two-wheeled buggy clop-clopped past their wagon. The two moon-eyed wallabies in the cab were far too engrossed in each other to so much as glance at the occupants of the wagon, much less at the lumpy cargo it carried.

Half conscious now, the little squirrel was beginning to kick and roll in counterpoint to her low moans. If she reawakened fully, things would become awkward. He resolved that in spite of his desire to make friends with Talea, he would bolt from the wagon rather than help her inflict any more harm. But after several minutes the movement subsided, and the unfortunate victim relapsed into silence.

They'd been traveling for half an hour and were still among buildings. Despite their plodding pace, it hinted that Lynchbany was a good-sized community. In fact, it might be even larger than he supposed, since he didn't know if they'd started from the city center or its outskirts.

A two-story thatched-roof structure of stone and crisscrossed wooden support beams loomed off to their left. It leaned as if for support up against a much larger brooding stone building. Several smaller structures that had to be individual homes stretched off into the distance. A few showed lamps over their doorways, but most slept peacefully in the clinging mist.

No light showed in the two thick windows of the thatched building as Talea edged their wagon over close to it and brought it to a halt. The street was quite empty. The only movement was from the mouths and nostrils of lizards and passengers, where the increasing chill turned their exhalations to momentarily thicker, tired fog. He wondered again at the reptiles. Maybe they were hybrids with warm blood; if not, they were being extremely active for cold-blooded creatures on such a cold night.

He climbed out of the back of the wagon and looked at the

doorway close by. An engraved sign hung from two hooks over the portal. Letters painted in white declaimed:

NILANTHOS—PHYSICIAN AND APOTHECARY

A smaller sign in the near window listed the ailments that could be treated by the doctor. Some of them were unfamiliar to Jon-Tom, who knew a little of common disease but nothing whatsoever of veterinary medicine.

Mudge and Talea were both whispering urgently at him. He moved out of the street and joined them by the door.

It was recessed into the building, roofed over and concealed from the street. They were hidden from casual view as Talea knocked once, twice, and then harder a third time on the milky bubble-glass set into the upper part of the door. She ignored the louder bellpull.

The waited nervously but no one answered. At least no one passed them in the street, but an occasional distinct groan was now issuing from the back of the wagon.

" 'E's not in, 'e ain't." Mudge looked worried. "I know a Doctor Paleetha. 'E's clear across town, though, and I can't say 'ow trustworthy 'e be, but if we've no one else t' turn t'..."

There were sounds of movement inside and a low complaining voice coming closer. It was at that point that Jon-Tom became really scared for the first time since he'd materialized in this world. His first reactions had been more disbelief and confusion than fear, and later ones were tied to homesickness and terror of the unknown.

But now, standing in an alien darkened street, accomplice to assault and battery and so utterly, totally *alone*, he started to shake. It was the kind of real, gut-chilling fear that doesn't frighten as much as it numbs all reality. The whole soul and body just turn stone cold—cold as the water at the bottom of a country well—and thoughts are fixated on a single, simple, all-consuming thought.

I'm never going to get out of this alive.
I'm going to die here.
I want to go HOME!

Oddly enough, it was a more distant fear that finally began to return him to normal. The assault of paranoia began to fade as he considered his surroundings. A dark street not unlike many others, pavement, mist chill inside his nose; no fear in any of those. And what of his companions? A scintillating if irascible redhead and an oversized but intelligent otter, both of whom were allies and not enemies. Better to worry about Clothahump's tale of coming evil than his own miserable but hardly deadly situation.

"What's the matter, mate?" Mudge stared at him with genuine concern. "You're not goin' t' faint on me again, are you?"

"Just queasy," said Talea sharply, though not nearly as sharply as before. "It's a nasty business, this."

"No." Jon-Tom shook away the last clinging rags of fear. They vanished into the night. "It's not that. I'm fine, thanks." His true thoughts he kept to himself.

She looked at him uncertainly a moment longer, then turned back to the door as Mudge said, "I 'ear somethin'."

Footsteps sounded faintly from just inside. There was a rattling at the doorknob. Inside, someone cursed a faulty lock.

Their attention directed away from him, Jon-Tom dissected the fragment of Clothahump's warning whose import had just occured to him.

If something could bring a great evil from his own world into this one, an evil which none here including Clothahump could understand, why could not that same maleficent force reverse the channel one day and thrust some similar unmentionable horror on his own unsuspecting world? Preoccupied as it was with petty politics and intertribal squabbles between nations, could it survive a powerful assault of incomprehensible and destructive magic from this world? No one would believe what was happening, just as he hadn't believed his first encounters with Clothahump's magic.

According to the aged wizard, an evil was abroad in this

place and time that would make the minions of Nazism look like Sunday school kids. Would an evil like that be content at consuming this world alone, or would it reach out for further and perhaps simpler conquests?

As a student of history that was one answer he knew. The appetite of evil far exceeds that of the benign. Success fed rather than sated its appetite for destruction. That was a truth that had plagued mankind throughout its entire history. What he had seen around him since coming here did not lead him to think it would be otherwise with the force Clothahump so feared.

Somewhere in this world a terror beyond his imagining swelled and prepared. He pictured Clothahump again: the squat, almost comical turtle shape with its plastron compartments; the hexagonal little glasses; the absentminded way of speaking; and he forced himself to consider him beyond the mere physical image. He remembered the glimpses of Clothahump's real power. For all the insults Pog and Mudge levied at the wizard, they were always tinged with respect.

So on those rounded—indeed, nonexistent—shoulders rested possibly not only the destiny of one, but of two worlds: this, and his own, the latter dreaming innocently along in a universe of predictable physics.

He looked down at his watch, no longer ticking, remembered his lighter, which had flared efficiently one last time before running out of fuel. The laws of science functioned here as they did at home. Mudge had been unfamiliar with the "spell," the physics, which had operated his watch and lighter. Research here had taken a divergent path. Science in his own, magic in this one. The words were similar, but not the methodology of application.

Would not evil spells as well as benign ones operate to bewildering effect in his own world?

He took a deep breath. If such was the case, then he no longer had a safe place to run to.

If that was true, what was he doing here? He ought to

be back at the Tree, not pleading to be sent home but offering what little help he could, if only his size and strength, to Clothahump. For if the turtle was not senile, if he was correct about the menace that Jon-Tom now saw threatened him anywhere, then there was a good chance he would die, and his parents, and his brother in Seattle, and . . .

The enormity of it was too much. Jon-Tom was no world-shaker. One thing at a time, boy, he told himself. You can't save worlds if you're locked up in a filthy local jail, puking your lunch all over yourself because the local cops don't play by the rules. As you surely will if you don't listen to Mudge and help this lovely lady.

"I'm all right now," he muttered softly. "We'll take things easy, pursue the internal logic. Just like researching a test case for class."

"Wot's that, mate?"

"Nothing." The otter eyed him a moment longer, then turned back to the door.

Life is a series of tests, Jon-Tom reminded himself. Where had he read that? Not in the laws of ancient Peru, or in Basic Torts or California Contracts. But he was ready for it now, for whatever sudden turns and twists life might throw at him.

Feeling considerably more at peace with himself and the universe, he stood facing the entrance and waited to be told what to do next.

The stubborn knob finally turned. A shape stood inside, staring back at them. Once it had been massively proportioned, but the flesh had sagged with age. The arms were nearly as long as the otter's whole body. One held a lantern high enough to shower light down even on Jon-Tom's head.

The old orangutan's whiskers shaded from russet to gray. His glasses were round and familiar, with golden metal rims. Jon-Tom decided that either wizardly spells for improving eyesight were unknown or else local magic had not progressed that far.

A flowing nightgown of silk and lace and a decidedly

feminine cast clad that simian shape. Jon-Tom was careful not to snicker. Nothing surprised him anymore.

"Weel, what ees eet at thees howar?" He had a voice like a rusty lawnmower. Then he was squinting over the top rims of the glasses at Talea. "You. Don't I know you?"

"You should," she replied quickly. "Talea of the High Winds and Moonflame. I did a favor for you once."

Nilanthos continued to stare at her, then nodded slowly. "Ah yes. I reemeember you now. 'Taleea off thee poleece records and thee dubeeous reeputation,'" he said with a mocking smile.

Talea was not upset. "Then along with my reputation you'll recall those six vials of drugs I got for you. The ones whose possession is frowned upon by the sorceral societies, an exclusion extended even to," she coughed delicately, "physicians."

"Yees, yees, off course I reemeember." He sighed resignedly. "A deebt ees a deebt. What ees your probleem that you must call mee op from sleep so late?"

"We have two problems, actually." She started for the wagon. "Keep the door open."

Jon-Tom and Mudge joined her. Hastily they threw aside the blanket and wrestled out the two unlucky victims of Talea's nighttime activities. The muskrat was now snoring noisily and healthily, much to Jon-Tom's relief.

Nilanthos stood aside, holding the lamp aloft while the grisly delivery was hauled inside. He peered anxiously out into the street.

"Surgeree ees een back."

"I . . . remember." Talea grunted under her half of squirrel-quette burden. Blood dripped occasionally onto the tiled floor. "You offered me a free 'examination,' remember?"

The doctor closed and locked the door, made nervous quieting motions. "Sssh, pleese. If you wakeen thee wife, I weel not bee able to canceel my half off thee deebt. And no talk off exameenations."

"Quit trembling. I just like to see you sweat a little, that's all."

Nilanthos followed them, his attention now on the limp form slung over Jon-Tom's shoulders. "Eef eether off theese pair are dead, wee weel all sweat a leetle." Then his eyes widened as he apparently recognized the blubbering muskrat.

"Good God, eet's Counceelman Avelleeum! Couldn't you have peeked a leess dangerous veecteem? He could have us all drawn and quarteered."

"He won't," she insisted. "I'm depending on you to see to that."

"You and your good nature." Nilanthos closed the door behind them, moved to spark the oil lamps lining the surgery. "You might have been beetter off leeting theem die."

"And what if they hadn't? What if they'd lived and remembered who attacked them? It was dark, but I can't be sure they'd never recognize me again."

"Yees, yees, I see what you mean," he said thoughtfully. He stood at a nearby sink and was washing long-fingered hands carefully.

"Weel then, what story should I geeve theem wheen they are brought around?" He was pulling on gloves and returning to the large central table on which the two patients had been deposited.

Jon-Tom leaned back against a wall and watched with interest. Mudge paced the surgery and looked bored. Actually, he was keeping one eye on Nilanthos while searching for anything he might be able to swipe undetected.

With a more personal interest in the welfare of the two victims, Talea stood close to the table as Nilanthos commenced his preliminary examination.

"Tell them they had an accident," she instructed him.

"What kind off acceedent?"

"They ran into something." He looked over at her skeptically and she shrugged. "My fist. And the iron chain I had wrapped around it. And maybe a wall. Look, you're a doctor.

Think of something reasonable, convince them. Some passersby found them and brought them to you.''

He shook his head dolefully. ''Why a primate as attracteeve as yourseelf would eendulge een such neefarious doings ees more than I can fathom, Taleea.''

She moved back from the table. ''You fix them up, and let me take care of me.''

Several minutes passed and the examination continued. ''Thee Counceelman weel bee fine. Hee has onlee a mild concussion and minor cuts and bruises. I know. I weel make arrangements to have heem deeposited on hees front doorstep by a couple off rats I know who weel do that sort off work weethout letting cureeosity get een their way.'' He turned his gaze on the squirrelquette, long fingers moving carefully through her hair.

''Theese one ees not as good. There ees a chance off a skull fracture.'' He looked up at Talea. ''That means posseeble eenternal eenjuries.'' The subject of the examination moaned softly.

''She seems lively enough,'' Talea commented.

''Appeerances can deeceive, eespecially weeth head eenjuriees.'' He was applying disinfectant and then bandaging to the wound. The bandage promptly began to show a dark stain. ''I'll just have to watch her carefullee. Do you by any chance know her?'' Talea shook her head.

''Neither do I. The Counceelman's lady for thee evening. Probably lady *off* thee eevening, too. Shee'll bee angry when shee regains consciousness, but no dangeer. I'll see to that, too.''

''Good.'' Talea started for the exit, hesitated, put a hand on the orang's broad shoulder. ''Thanks, Nilanthos. You've more than canceled out our debt. Now I owe you. Call on me if you need *my* services.''

The physician replied with a wide simian leer.

''Professionally, I mean.'' The leer broadened. ''You are impossible, Nilanthos!'' She feigned a swing at him.

"Do not strike thee doctor while hee ees een thee process off performing hees heeling duties."

"That's a laugh! But I still owe you."

"Honor among theeves, ees that eet?" He looked seriously down at the squirrelquette and the now badly stained bandage wrapped around her skull. "Veree weel. For now eet's best eef you all geet out off heer." He said it while staring at Mudge.

The otter nodded, moved away from the slipcatch-latched drug-and-narcotics case where he'd been idling the past several minutes.

"What's the hurry?" Jon-Tom wanted to know.

Mudge put a hand on his arm, pulled him along. "Be you daft, mate? We've got t' get out o' town."

"But I don't . . . I thought . . ." He barely remembered to duck as they exited the surgery. "If Doctor Nilanthos is going to take care of things as he said, why do we have to run?"

"Cor, he can take away the worries as far as those two in there be concerned, but someone else might 'ave seen us. They might even now be reportin' us t' the police. Your size makes us too conspicuous, lad. We 'ave t' leave, especially after that fight in the Pearl Possum."

"But I still don't see . . ."

"Not *now,* mate." Mudge was insistent. They were out in the dark street again.

"Come on, Jon-Tom," said Talea. "Don't make trouble."

He halted, stared open-mouthed at her. "*Me* make trouble? I've been the innocent victim of trouble ever since I set foot in this stinking, lousy excuse for a world."

"Easy now, mate." Mudge looked sideways at him. "Don't be sayin' somethin' you may be sorry for later."

Jon-Tom's carefully constructed calm had lasted about ten minutes. His voice rose unreasonably, echoing in the mist. "I don't regret anything I have to say!" Talea was looking back toward town, clearly upset. "I want to see some of the goodness, the kindness that this world should have."

"Should 'ave?" Mudge looked confused. "By who's determination?"

"By the . . ." His voice trailed off. What could he say? By rights of legend. What legend? By logic? Mudge was right.

"Oh, never mind." The anger and frustration which had flared inside faded quickly. "So we're fugitives. So I make us conspicuous. That's the way it is." He nodded at nothing in particular. "Let's get going, then."

He vaulted into the back of the wagon. Mudge climbed into the front seat, caught Talea's questioning glance, and could only shrug blankly. She hefted the reins and let out a vibrant whistle. The somnolent lizards came awake, leaned forward into their reins. The wagon resumed its steady forward motion, the thick feet of its team sounding like sacks of flour landing on the damp pavement.

Jon-Tom noted that they were headed out of town, as Mudge had insisted they must. Houses decorated with little gardens slipped past. No lights showed in their windows at this stygian hour.

They passed the last street lamp. Here the road turned from cobblestone to gravel. Even that gave way to a muddy track only a little while later. All light had vanished behind them.

It was deep night of early morning now. The mist continued to dog them, keeping them wet and chilled. Never is the winter so cloying as at night.

Among the occupants of the wagon only Jon-Tom had a lingering concern for the greater night that threatened to do more to the world than chill it. Talea and Mudge are creatures of the moment, he thought. They cannot grasp the significance of Clothahump's visions. He huddled deeper under the gray blanket, ignoring the persistent aroma of the squirrelquette's perfume. It clashed with the smell of dried blood.

Thunder crossed the sky overhead, oral signatory to the last distant vestiges of the night storm. It helped them bid farewell to Lynchbany. He was not sorry to leave.

Soon they were in the woods. Oaks and elms showed

familiar silhouettes against the more melodious boles of belltree and coronet vine. The latter generated an oboesque sob as if pleading for the advent of day and the refreshing heat of the sun.

For hours they plodded steadily on. The road wound like a stream around the hills, taking advantage of the lowest route, never cresting more than an occasional rise. Small lakes and ponds sometimes flanked the trail. They were inhabited by a vast assortment of aquatic lizards who meeped and gibbered in place of frogs. Each glowed a different color, some green, others red or pink, still others a rich azure. Each bubble of sound was accompanied by an increase in light. The ponds were full of chirping searchlights that drifted from branch to bank.

Jon-Tom watched the water and its luminescent reptilians fade behind them. The ponds became a brook which ran fast and friendly alongside the rutted wagon track. Unlike the other travelers it was indifferent to who might overhear its conversation, and it gurgled merrily while teasing their wheels.

Resignation gave way once more to his natural curiosity.

"Well, we're long out of town." He spoke to Talea. "Where are we going?" Rising to his knees he reached out a hand to steady himself in the jouncing wagon. It gave an unexpected lurch to the right, and he caught her side instead of the back of the seat. Hastily he moved his fingers, but she had neither moved away nor protested.

"Somewhere where we can't be trapped," she replied. "For God knows even a blithering Lynchbany cop could piss and track the ruts of this wagon at the same time. Like any other creature we retreat to a lair and we don't fight unless we're cornered. And where we're going not even the police will dare come."

"I ain't sure I'd agree to that." Mudge sounded more hopeful than assured. " 'Tis more of an uneasy truce."

"Nonetheless," she countered, "we're far more likely to

be safe there than anyplace else." Jon-Tom still gazed questioningly at her.

"We're going to the local branch of the intracounty association of disadvantaged self-employed artisans and underachievers," she explained.

"Thieves' Hall," Mudge grunted. . . .

VIII

They spent the rest of the night curled beneath the thick blanket in the back of the wagon. Mudge and Talea were soon as motionless as her former victims, but Jon-Tom was too keyed up to sleep. Talea was silent as a stone, but a steady snoring in the form of a high-pitched whistle came from the gray-clad lump that was Mudge.

Jon-Tom lay on his back and studied the night sky, framed by the overhanging branches of the trees. Some of the constellations overhead were familiar, though out of place. Location as well as season was different here. It was a great comfort, however, to see the easily recognizable shape of Orion standing stalwart as ever against the interstellar vastness.

Once something with ghostly gray fluorescent wings passed between him and the moon, a delicate crinoid shape that might have been a reptile, or bird, or something unimaginable. It trailed thin yellow streamers behind it, and for an instant it glittered in the sky.

Then it was gone behind the trees. A low hiccoughing came from some concealed arboreal thing.

Tiny feet sounded like twigs on the road. Their owner paused to sniff at the wagon wheels before skittering onward. Sycamores and gingkos conversed in low philosophical wood-tones. They lulled him finally into a deep, dreamless sleep. . . .

He awoke to a welcome sun filtering down through the leaves and a weight on his left shoulder. Turning his head, he saw Talea snuggled up against him. She was sleeping on her side, resting on his shoulder, one arm thrown limply across his chest. He had mixed feelings about disturbing the sculpture.

However . . . they had a destination. He moved a little. Her eyes fluttered, body stirred. She blinked, simultaneously taking note of both him and proximity. As she pulled away, she rubbed sleep from her eyes.

"Easy night," she murmured thickly, "though I've had softer beds."

"Me too." To his surprise he saw that Mudge was already wide awake. He had no idea how long the otter had lain there watching them.

"Best we be on about our business," the otter said brightly. "The Lynchbany lockups ain't particularly persistent, but if it was a slow night a few ambitious types might've elected to come follow." He stood up, gestured back down the road.

"Personally I think we're well clear of 'em, but you never can be sure."

"Right." She was climbing into the driver's seat. "Best never to take chances with a skunk."

Shortly they were trundling once more down a road that had become hardly more than a trail. They'd turned off, he noted, on a branch that was almost devoid of wagon ruts. Their absence was compensated for by large rocks that did nothing to help his kidneys.

They paused later for a Spartan breakfast of bread, jerky, and a kind of dried fruit that resembled lime but tasted much better. Then off again.

It was noon when Talea indicated they'd arrived. Jon-Tom peered ahead between her and the otter. "I don't see anything."

"What did you think?" she asked archly. "That a place like the local branch of the intracounty . . . a place like Thieves' Hall would announce itself with flying banners and a brass band?"

They turned down a still narrower path and penetrated as deeply into the dense woods as trees would allow. After a half-mile walk they came to a crude corral filled with an astonishing assortment of reptilian mounts. Several hundred yards off to the right of this open-air stable Talea located a metal doorway. It lay half hidden beneath the roots of several massive oaks and was set directly into the rock face of a low-browed cliff.

She rapped hard on the metal three times with her open palm, waited, then repeated the knock.

Presently a small window opened in the top of the door. No face showed itself. It was easy enough for whoever was within to see outside without placing an eye invitingly near a possible knife thrust.

"Succor and surcease, comfort and respite to those who know how to live," said a voice from within.

"T' practice usury without interference," Mudge responded promptly. "T' get one's fair share. T' never givin' a sucker an even break."

There was a pause and then the door swung outward on rusty hinges. Talea entered first, followed by Mudge. Jon-Tom had to bend almost double to clear the ceiling.

Inside they confronted a muscular otter a couple of inches taller than Mudge. He inspected them cautiously, reserving particular attention for Jon-Tom.

"That one I don't know."

" 'E's a friend." Mudge smiled as he spoke. "An acquaintance from a far province, wot?" He did not elaborate on that, nor did he mention Clothahump.

The other otter blew his nose on the floor and turned perfunctorily away. They followed. Before long they passed a series of interlocking tunnels. These all seemed to devolve into a much larger central cavern. It was filled with a noisy, raunchy, squalling crowd that made the patrons of the Pearl Possum look like nursery schoolers their first day away from home.

There was enough sharpened steel in that one room to fight a small war. A fair amount of dried blood on the stone floor showed that those instruments were frequently in use. In the enclosed area the noise was close to deafening. Not to mention the odor. He'd almost come to ignore the animal smells, but in that tight, poorly ventilated chamber, populated as it was by a less than usually hygienic assembly, it was overpowering.

"What do we do now?"

"First we find the president of the local chapter," Talea explained, "and pay our protection money. That allows us to stay here. Then we find a piece of unoccupied tunnel. There are hundreds of them honeycombing this hillside. We set up temporary housekeeping and lie low until the councilman has a chance to forget what happened to him.

"Of course, he may buy Nilanthos' explanation, but I wouldn't put it past his type to check out any citizen's reports for that night. That's where we could have trouble, remember. We'll wait here a couple of weeks until it all turns to memory-mush. Then we can safely leave."

As his look of distress, Mudge said, "Don't look so ill, mate. Crikey, 'tis only for a couple o' weeks." He grinned. "Lynchbany cops 'ave mem'ries as brief as their courage. But it do behoove us t' stay out o' sight o' casual travelers for a while. None save the completely daft are likely t' come within leagues o' this spot."

Jon-Tom focused on well-used swords and knives. "I can't imagine why not," he said drily, trying to hold his breath.

As it turned out they did not utilize Thieves' Hall for two weeks. It was less than a day before Jon-Tom made his mistake. It didn't seem like a mistake at the time, and afterward he was too confused to be sorry.

There was a game. It was common in Lynchbany and well known among those who preyed upon the townsfolk. It involved the use of triangular dice and a circle. There were no hidden complexities.

A good student like Jon-Tom had no trouble picking it up, after a few hours of careful study. He was still a mite hesitant about actually participating, but Talea was off somewhere chatting with friends and Mudge had simply disappeared. Left on his own and mentally exhausted, he was both bored and irritable. A little game playing would be good for him.

Clothahump's purse still contained a few tiny copperpieces, the remnants of the Mudge-directed spending spree that had enriched several of Lynchbany's merchants. Cutting an impressive figure in his flashing green cape, Jon-Tom leaned on his club-staff and studied one of the several continuous games before finally deciding to join.

The particular game he'd selected seemed to be the largest. With the greater number of participants he would have more opportunities between throws to study the play. No one objected to or commented on his joining. It was simply a matter of taking the place of a distraught lynx when the latter ran out of money and dropped out.

Through no particular skill (the fickleness of dice being everywhere constant) he did quite well. Dutifully, he concentrated on doing still better. So intent on the game did he become that he failed to notice that he was drawing something of a crowd of onlookers.

Players angrily left and were replaced by eager newcomers, full of fresh spirit and fresh cash. There were always nine or ten throwers seated or squatting around the circle.

The rock was cold against his backside, even through the leather pants. Not quite as chilled were the well-traveled coins beginning to stack up in front of him. For the first time in a long while he was not only relaxed but enjoying himself.

Much to the delight of the crowd, which always pulls for a big winner, he hit two nines in a row. Mutterings of magic came from a few of the other players. They remained mere mutterings. An aged bat named Swal hung himself from the overhead lamps. From there he could watch all the players. His opinion was well respected, Jon-Tom could tell, and his knowledge of magic extensive though he was no wizard himself. Very poor basketball players can make very fine coaches. Swal had a detailed knowledge of magic though he couldn't work any himself.

Nevertheless, one of the other players tried to turn the tide in his own favor, attempting to magic the dice before his turn to throw came up. Neither Jon-Tom nor any of the other players or onlookers caught the unnatural vibration, but the outraged Swal noticed it immediately.

"He muttered it softly, but I tasted the end of it," Swal explained to the crowd.

At that point Jon-Tom had a sampling of thieves' justice in a world where normal justice was not known for its temperance. A group of angry spectators hauled the screaming, protesting gopher out of sight. This was followed by a brief pause, then a single nerve-twisting screech. Wiping their paws and looking grimly satisfied, the vigilantes soon returned.

Another member of the game was throwing, and Jon-Tom had time to turn and ask an onlooker what had happened.

The tall rabbit leaned low on his shoulder. "Swal say that one mutter it softly. You no cheat in Thieves' Hall. Like cheat you brother, you know? I expect they make punishment fit the crime." Jon-Tom continued to stare questioningly up at the other.

The rabbit shrugged. "Since he whisper the formula, others probably cut out his tongue. If he done divinations with his hands, they would have cut them off. Same for eye, and so on."

"Isn't that kind of extreme? It's only a friendly game."

Oddly milky pink eyes looked down at him. "This an extreme business we all in, man. You know that. Difficult enough to get by without having to cope with cheating courts and sly lawyers. We can't stand backstabbingers among own family. Fair punishments like that," and he jerked a thumb back toward the region of the scream, "make sure fairness good sense. You stay healthy, hear; that one was lucky. What line you in?"

"Sorry . . . my dice," Jon-Tom said quickly.

The game continued. Sometimes he lost, more often he won. Now the continued absence of Talea and Mudge was making him nervous. He wondered if he dare take his winnings and drop out. Might not one of the game's big losers have a friend or associate in the crowd, ready to stick a small knife in Jon-Tom's back or accuse him of magic in order to protect his friend or boss?

But the tall rabbit remained close by, reassuring and urging him on. That was only natural, since he was betting along with Jon-Tom's rolls. Yet Jon-Tom's thoughts kept returning to that horrible scream, kept imagining the knife coming down, the blood spurting. . . .

Swal the bat kept his post. Occasionally he would shift his perch on the hanging lamps or tug at the green-feathered cap secured by a strap to his head. His eyes roved steadily over the players.

There were no more cries of cheating. The pile of coins in front of Jon-Tom continued its steady growth.

Then there was an unexpected pause in the action. A very sleek, lupine figure stumbled into the playing circle. The players scrambled to protect their coins from uncertain feet. She seemed outraged and embarrassed, a condition not helped by the catcalls and hoots from the male and female specta-tors. The bitch replied to the insinuations with a rustle of petticoats and some choice execrations of her own.

Jon-Tom looked to his rabbit friend for an explanation.

"Sorry, man. I wasn't paying attention. But I think I see what's going on. See that fox over there?" He pointed to a tired but well-dressed thrower seated across the circle. Only two or three small silver coins lay on the stone in front of him.

"He out of money I see, but he want to stay in. You know the type. So he bet the girl."

Jon-Tom frowned. "Is she a slave?"

That prompted a mildly angry response. "What you think we are here, barbarians? Only the Plated Folk keep slaves.

No, most likely he gotten her to agree to temporary contract.'' The rabbit winked. ''Most likely a couple of nights or so.''

''She doesn't look very willing,'' said Jon-Tom critically.

''Hard to say. Maybe she is, maybe not.''

''Then why is she doing it?''

''Because she in love. Can't you see that?'' The rabbit sounded surprised at Jon-Tom's evident naïveté.

''Hey... I can't play this round.''

''Why not, man?'' Suddenly the rabbit sounded considerably less friendly.

''I just think I've had enough.'' He was starting to gather up his winnings, looking for pockets in pants and shirt to shove handfuls of coins into. The other players looked upset and there were some movements in his direction.

But there was honor among thieves here, too. For every angry grumbling from the players there were cries from the onlooker of, ''He won fair.... The man can pull out any time!...Let him leave if he wants....You can't stop him....'' and so forth. But some of the comments were accompanied by eager looks at the pile of coins in front of him. It occurred to Jon-Tom that winning the money was no assurance he'd leave with it. Of course, no one would think of making an outright attack on an honest winner. But Thieves' Hall was full of tunnels and dark cul-de-sacs.

He looked helplessly up at the rabbit, whispered, ''What should I do?''

The other's attitude softened, turned friendly once again.

''Well first thing, pay attention to you own clothing.'' He laughed and reached for Jon-Tom's throat. Jon-Tom instinctively started to pull away, but the rabbit only paused and grinned hugely at him. ''With you permission?''

Jon-Tom hesitated, then nodded. There was no reason to assume the animal had turned suddenly hostile.

Unclipping the cape while the rest of the players waited impatiently, the rabbit spread it out on the floor. ''Ah, I thought right so. Good tailor you got,'' and he pointed out the hiden stitching and buttons lining the bottom hem of the cape.

This he carefully unsnapped. With Jon-Tom's help, he filled the hidden compartment with handfuls of coins. When it was full to the snaps they sealed it tight again. Jon-Tom clipped it back around his neck. The weight was a tolerable drag.

"There," said the rabbit with satisfaction, "that be more better. No one think to pickpocket a cape. Only these few here, and I see no skilled one among them. Others who see will think only rocks in there."

"Why would I fill my cape with rocks?"

"To keep it from blow over you head and blind you in a fight, or while riding in a storm. Also to use in a fight. You may look weaponless, but what you got now is five-foot flexible club to complement long staff." He turned his gaze skyward. "That how I like to go, though. Beaten to death with somebody's money. Or perhaps..." He looked back over at Jon-Tom. "It no matter my problems."

"Maybe it does." Jon-Tom reached into the still sizable pile of coins in front of him and selected three large gold circles. "These are for your problems. And for your good advice and counsel."

The rabbit took them gratefully, slipped them in a vest pocket, and sealed it. "That kind of you, man. I take because I need the money. Under better circumstances I refuse. More advice: don't go passing around gold too much like this. You attract attention of some not so noble as I.

"Now as to what you should do, you pull out now if you really want. But you in middle of round. It be better if you finish this one go-round. Then no one can say shit to you."

"But what about the girl?" The bitch was tapping feet clad in pastel blue ballet slippers and looking quite put out.

"Well, I tell you man," and he winked significantly, "you finish out this round. I have three goldpieces you know. You have place in circle to finish. If you win, I give you back gold circle for her.'' He eyed the muscular, tawny form of the she-wolf. "Maybe two."

"Oh, all right." He looked a last time at the ring of spectators. Still no sign of Mudge or Talea.

The dice were passed as the watchers nudged one another, muttered, made side bets, or simply stared curiously. A ferret on the far side rolled a seven, moaned. Next to him was a mole wearing immensely thick dark glasses and a peaked derby. He dumped an eight, then a six, then a seven, and finally a losing three.

The dice came around to Jon-Tom. He tossed them into the circle. Two fours and a two. Then a ten. The dice went to the fisher on his right. He rolled a ten. Cries went up from the crowd, which pushed and shoved discourteously at the circle of players. Jon-Tom rolled a six. Back to the fisher, who looked confident. Over went the three dice, came up showing a one, a two, and a three. The fisher kicked dirt into the circle. The shouts were ear-shaking.

Jon-Tom had won again.

He spoke as he turned. "There you go, friend. It's time to . . ." He stopped. There was no sign of the rabbit.

Only a smartly dressed howler monkey nearby had noted the disappearance of Jon-Tom's advisor. "The tall fella? White with gray patches?" Jon-Tom nodded, and the simian gestured vaguely back down a main passage.

"He went off that way a while ago. So little golden ground squirrel came up to him . . . delicate little bit of fluff she was . . . and he went off with her."

"But I can't . . ."

A hand touched his shoulder. He turned, found himself staring across into aluminum-like eyes, glistening and penetrating. "I have not done it with many humans, man. I understand some of you are fond of strange practices." The voice was low, husky, and not altogether uninterested. "Is that true also with you?"

"Listen, I don't think you understand."

"Try me."

"No, no . . . that's not what I meant. I mean . . ." He was more flustered than at any time since they'd entered the hall. "It's just that I can't, I don't want you. Go back there." He waved across the circle. "Go back to him."

"Just what the hell are you implying, man?" Her eyes flashed and she stepped back.

The fox was suddenly standing next to her, angry at something other than his losing. "Something wrong with Wurreel? Do you think I need your charity?"

"No, it's not that at all." He slowly climbed to his feet, kept a firm grip on the staff. Around him the crowd was murmuring in an unfriendly manner. The looks he was receiving were no longer benign.

"Please," he told the bitch, "just go back to your master here, or friend, or whatever."

The fox moved nearer, jabbed a clawed finger in Jon-Tom's stomach. "Just what kind of fellow are you? Do you think I don't pay my debts? Do you think I'd renege on my obligations?"

"Screw your obligations, Mossul," said the wolf haughtily. "What about my honor?" Her tone and gaze were now anything but interested. "See how he looks at me, with disgust. I am insulted."

That brought a nasty series of cries from the crowd. "Shame, shame! . . . down with him!"

"It's not that. I just . . . don't want you."

She made an inarticulate growl, hit him in the chest with a fist. "That does it!" She looked around at the shifting circle of spectators. "Is there a male here who will defend my reputation? I demand satisfaction . . . of this kind if not the other!"

"Your reputation . . ." Jon-Tom was becoming badly tongue-tied. "I didn't insult . . . what about him?" He pointed at the fox. "He was the one selling you."

"Loaning, not selling," countered the fox with dignity. "And it was mutually agreed upon."

"That's right. I'd do anything for Mossul. Except be insulted, like this, in public." She put an affectionate arm around the fox's silk-clad shoulders.

"Turn him out, turn him out!" came the rising shouts.

"Wot's 'appening 'ere, mate. I leave you alone for a bit and you manage t' upset the 'ol 'all." Mudge was at Jon-Tom's back and Talea nearby.

"I don't understand," Jon-Tom protested. "I've been winning all day."

"That's good."

"And I just won that," and he indicated the she-wolf, "for a couple of nights."

"That's very good. So what's your problem, mate?"

"I don't want her. Don't you understand? It's not that she's unattractive or anything." The subject of that appraisal growled menacingly. "It's just that . . . I can't do it, Mudge. I'm not prejudiced. But something inside me just . . . can't."

"Easy now, mate. I understand." The otter sounded sympathetic. " 'Tis part o' your strange customs, no doubt, and you're the loser for it."

"Well, tell them that. Tell them where I'm from. Explain to them that I'm . . ."

Mudge put a hand momentarily over Jon-Tom's mouth. "Hush, lad. If they think that you're from some other land, no matter 'ow alien, you won't longer 'ave their protection. As it be, they think you're a local footpad like Talea and meself." His eyes noted the weight dragging down the hem of Jon-Tom's cape. "And judgin' from wot you've won from some 'ere, they'd be more than 'appy to see you made fair game. You wouldn't last twenty seconds." He pulled at an arm. "Come on now. Quiet and confident's the words, while they're still arguin' wot t' do."

They were bumped and even spat upon, but Mudge and Talea managed to hustle their thoroughly confused friend out of the gambling chamber, through the tunnels, and back out the iron door that sealed off the hall from the outside world.

It was mid-morning outside. Jon-Tom suddenly realized how exhausted he was. He must have played through the night. That explained why he hadn't seen Talea or Mudge. They'd been sleeping. But it was time-deceptive inside Thieves' Hall, where the lamps burned round the clock, much in keeping with the activities of the members.

"Why didn't you go with her?" Talea sounded bitter. "Now look at us! Forced out of the one refuge where we'd be impregnable." She stalked on ahead, searching the nearby corral for their team and wagon.

"I suppose I should have lost." He and Mudge had to hurry to keep pace with her. "That would have made you happy, wouldn't it?"

"It would be better than this," she snapped back. "Where do we go now? When you're turned out of Thieves' Hall, there's no place else to run to, and we haven't been in hiding near long enough. We'll still be fresh in the minds of citizens and police, if anyone noticed us. Damn it all!" She jumped the fence, kicked at the flank of an innocent riding lizard. It hissed and scuttled out of her way.

"It's too bad you weren't around, Mudge. You could have played that last round for me."

"It don't work that way, mate. You 'ad t' play it out yourself, from what I 'eard. 'Tis a pity your peculiar customs forced you t' insult that lovely lady's honor. You refused 'er. I couldn't 'ave substituted meself for you thatawise, much willin' as I would've been."

Jon-Tom stared morosely at the ground. "I can't believe she was trading herself willingly like that."

"Blimey lad, 'tis bloody ignorant you be about women. She did it for love of 'er fox-chap. Couldn't you see that?

And so when you refused 'er, you insulted 'im as well. You don't know much about the leanin's o' ladies, do you?''

''That's ridiculous. Of course I . . .'' He looked away. ''No. No, not a great deal, Mudge. My energies have been pretty much focused on intellectual pursuits. That's one reason why I wanted to be a musician so badly. Musicians don't seem to have to worry about women.''

''There not be much pleasure in ignorance, mate. You're a damnsight better off understandin' the whys and wherefores o' what's goin' on.'' He nodded ahead.

''Now 'ave a look at dear Talea there. Don't tell me you don't find 'er attractive.''

''I'd be lying if I said otherwise.''

''Well then? Close enough quarters we've been living in these past few days and I 'aven't seen you so much as lean close t' 'er. Me she knows and won't let near, but you're a new factor.''

''You've got to be kidding.'' He watched that mane of red hair bob and weave its way among the herd. ''If I so much as touched her she'd split me from brain to belly.''

''Don't be so sure, mate. You've already confessed your ignorance, you know.''

''And you're the expert, I suppose?''

''I get by on experience, yes. Not much time for that now. But think on what I've said.''

''I will. Mudge, what she said about us having no place to go, are we that desperate?''

'' 'Ard to say, mate. Depends on whether anyone reported our late-night doin's in Lynchbany. But we'd best move on t' somewhere else for a while.''

''I know where I want to go.'' He looked longingly skyward, though he knew that his world was beyond even the stars that lay hidden behind the sunlight.

Something stung the side of his face. He turned and looked in shock at Mudge.

''A long way to reach with an open palm,'' the otter said

tightly. "Now you listen well, mate. I've told you before and I don't aim to waste time on it again. These maudlin sorrowings for yourself 'ave to stop. You're 'ere. We can't get you back where you belong. Clothahump can't or won't get you back t' where you belong. That's bloody well it, and the sooner you get used t' it, the better it'll go for you. Or do you expect me t' wet-nurse you through your next sixty years?"

Jon-Tom, still stunned, didn't reply. Sixty years . . . odd how he hadn't thought of his stay here in terms of years, much less decades. There was always the thought that he could be going home tomorrow, or the next day.

But if Clothahump's genius was as erratic as Mudge insisted, he might never be going home. The wizard could die tomorrow. That night in Lynchbany outside Dr. Nilanthos' he'd reached a temporary accommodation with his situation. Maybe Mudge was right, and it was time he made that accommodation permanent.

Try to regard it like negative thinking for an exam. That way you're only satisfied if you fail, happy with a fifty, and ecstatic with a hundred. That's how you're going to have to start thinking of your life. Right now he was living a zero. The sooner he got used to it, the less disappointed he'd be if Clothahump proved unable to send him back. Back to the lazy mental meanderings of school, the casual tripe mumbled by directionless friends, the day-to-day humdrum existence he'd been leading that inaccessibility now made so tempting.

Zero, he told himself firmly. Remember the zero.

"Goddam rotten son-of-a-bitch! Shit-holes, all of 'em!"

The cry came from the other side of the corral. He and Mudge hurried through the packed animals. But Talea was not in danger. Instead she sat tiredly on a smooth rock while riding lizards of varying size and shape milled nervously around her.

"Stinking sneaky bastards," she rumbled. Jon-Tom started to say something but turned at a touch on his arm. Mudge put a finger to his whiskers, shook his head slowly.

They waited while the bile burned itself up. She finally looked up and seemed to take notice of them. Then she rose and swept an arm around the corral.

"Our wagon's gone. I've been through the whole glade and it's not here. Neither's our team. Do you know what I went through to steal that team?"

"Mossul's friends might have slipped out and run it off to help him cover 'is losses. Or it might 'ave been done as punishment for the insult we did the she-wolf," Mudge said thoughtfully, caressing his whiskers.

"I'll fry the gizzards of whoever's responsible!" She started back toward the hall. Mudge intercepted her quickly. She pushed at him, tried to dodge around, but he was as heavy as she and far faster. Eventually she just stood there, glaring at him.

"Be reasonable, luv. We barely slipped out of there without 'avin' to cut anyone. We can't go back in. Anger's no substitute for another sword. Even if we did get back in clear and free we're just guessin' as to who's responsible. We can't be sure it's Mossul or 'is friends."

The glare softened to a look of resignation. "You're right, otter. As usual." She slumped down on the mossy earth and leaned back against a fence rail. "So much, then, for 'honor among thieves.'"

"I'm sorry." Jon-Tom sat down next to her. "It was my fault. If it means anything, I'll be happy to pay you back for the cart." He jiggled the clinking hem of his cape meaningfully.

"Don't be ridiculous. I stole it. You needn't worry about paying back what you don't owe."

They considered their situation. "We could buy someone else's cart," he suggested.

Mudge looked doubtful. "Good transportation's dearer to a thief than any amount o' money. We could buy such in town, but not 'ere."

"Well then, why don't we steal some of these?"

"Now that's not a bad idea, mate. You're startin' to adapt.

Save for one little complication." He looked to his right. At first Jon-Tom saw nothing. Then he noticed the little knot of figures that had appeared outside the Hall entrance. Puffs of smoke rose from the small crowd, and he could see an occasional glance in their direction.

"But they don't know which cart or steeds are ours," Jon-Tom protested. "If we acted like we knew what we were doing, they couldn't tell we were up to anything."

Mudge smiled slightly. "On the other 'and, we don't know that we might not pick on one o' their mounts. A single shout could bring the whole o' Thieves' 'All out on us."

"A pox on this!" said Talea abruptly, springing to her feet. "So we walk, but we're going back to see this wizard of yours. He's bound to put us up for a few days. Might even be safer than the Hall. And we can even pay him." She indicated Jon-Tom's winnings.

"Now 'old on a minim, luv." Mudge looked worried. "If we return there so soon, I'll 'ave t' admit I've run into some difficulties in educatin' this lad."

"Difficulties!" Jon-Tom laughed aloud. "You've already managed to involve me in a local tavern brawl, a police matter, and you," he looked at Talea, "in a mugging and robbery. Two robberies. I suppose I have to count in the cart and team, now."

"Count it any way you like, Jon-Tom." She gestured to the west. "But we can't go to town just yet, and we can't use the hall. I'm not about to strike off into the forest toward somewhere distant like Fifeover or Timswitty. Besides, they cooperate with the Lynchbany cops."

"Be that as it may," said Mudge, folding his arms, "I'm not goin' back t' Clothahump's. The old bugger's too unpredictable for my comfort."

"Suit yourself." She looked up at Jon-Tom. "I think you know the way. You afraid of Clothahump, too?"

"You bet your ass I am," he replied promptly, "but I don't

think he's the vengeful type, and I can't think of anything else to do."

She gestured expansively. "After you, Jon-Tom."

He turned and started out of the corral, heading south and hoping his sense of direction wasn't too badly distorted by the time they'd spent riding the night. Mudge hesitated until they were nearly out of sight. Then he dropped a few choice words to the indifferent lizards and sprinted anxiously after the retreating humans. . . .

IX

Thieves' Hall was southeast of Lynchbany Towne. They had to cross the local roads carefully, for according to Talea you never knew when you might encounter a police patrol out for bandits. They also had to take time to hunt and gather food.

It was three days of hard walking before some of the forest started to look familiar to Mudge. They were standing by the side of a muddy, narrow road when Jon-Tom noticed the large sack that had been caught in the crook of a pair of boulders. There was the sparkle of sunlight on metal.

"Your eyes are good, Jon-Tom," said Talea admiringly, as they fell on the sack like three jackals on the half-gnawed carcass of a zebra.

The sack was full of trade goods. Glass beads, some semiprecious gems that might have been garnets or tourmalines, and some scrolls. Talea threw the latter angrily aside as they searched the sack for other valuables. There were more scrolls, some clothing, and several musical instruments. Jon-Tom picked up a set of pipes attached to a curved gourd, puffed experimentally at the mouth openings.

"Hell." Talea sat back against the rocks. She picked up the empty sack and threw it over her shoulder. "Double hell Even when we find some lucky, it turns out to be deceptive."

Mudge was inspecting the jewelry. "These might fetch two or three golds from a fair fence."

"How delightful," Talea said sarcastically. "You just whistle up a fair fence and we'll have a go at it." The otter let out a long, sharp whistle no human could duplicate, then shrugged.

"Never know till you try." He tucked the jewelry into the pouch at his waist, caught Talea eyeing him. "You don't trust me t' share out." He pouted.

"No, but it's not worth fighting over." She was rubbing her left calf. "My feet hurt."

Jon-Tom had set down the gourd flute and picked up the largest of the three instruments. This one had six strings running in a curve across a heart-shaped resonator. Three triangular openings were cut into the box. At the top of the curved wires were tuning knobs. Near the base of the heartbox resonator was a set of six smaller metal strings, a miniature of the larger, upper set. Twelve strings altogether.

He considered the arrangement thoughtfully. Let's see, the smaller set wouldn't be much good except for plucking the more delicate, higher notes. So the larger sextet is probably strummed. Except for the extra set of tiny strings it looked something like a plastic guitar left too long in an oven.

Talea had picked up one of the flute-things. She tried to blow a tune, produced only a few sour notes that faded quickly, and tossed it away. The second was apparently more to her liking. She finished testing it, slipped it into her belt, and started off back into the forest. Mudge followed, but Jon-Tom, absorbed in the peculiar guitar, hung behind.

Eventually she paused, turned to face him, and waited until he caught up with them. "What's holding you back, larklegs?" He smiled as though he hadn't heard her, turned his attention back to the instrument. A few notes from the small strings filled the air.

"That's a duar. Don't tell me you can play that?"

"Actually, the lad 'as made claims to bein' somethin' of a musician." Mudge studied Jon-Tom's obvious interest hopefully. "You always 'ave said that you sounded better with instrumental accompaniment, mate."

"I know. I remember." Jon-Tom ran his fingers over the

upper-level strings. The sound was much softer than he was used to. Almost lyrelike, but not very alien. He plucked once again at the lower strings. They echoed the upper, deeper tones.

The curved arm running out from the heart-shaped box was difficult to cradle. The instrument had been designed to fit around a much broader chest than his own. The short strap that ran from the top of the arm to the base of the resonator helped a little, however. Letting the instrument hang natural- ly, he found that by leaning forward he could get at both sets of strings. It hurt his back a little, but he thought he could get used to it. He used both hands, trying to strum the upper strings while plucking in counterpoint at the lower.

Talea sighed, turned away, and started off again, Mudge in tandem and Jon-Tom bringing up the rear. His heart still hurt more than his feet, but the music helped. Gradually he discovered how to swing his arm in an arc instead of straight down in order to follow the curve of bar and strings. Soon he was reproducing familiar chords, then snatches of song. As always the tranquilizing sounds made him feel better, lifting his spirits as well as his adrenaline level.

Some of the songs sounded almost right. But though he tuned and retuned until he was afraid of breaking the strings or the tuning knobs, he couldn't create the right melodies. It wasn't the delicate instrument, either, but something else. He still hadn't discovered how to tune it properly.

It was late afternoon when Talea edged closer to him, listening a while longer to the almost music he was making before inquiring, with none of her usual bitterness or sar- casm, "Jon-Tom, are you a spellsinger?"

"Hmmm?" He looked up at her. "A what?"

"A spellsinger." She nodded toward the otter, who was walking a few yards ahead of them. "Mudge says that the wizard Clothahump brought you into our world because he thought you were a wizard who could help him in sorceral matters."

"That's right. Unfortunately, I'm in prelaw."

She looked doubtful. "Wizards don't make those kinds of mistakes."

"Well, this one sure did."

"Then you're not..." She eyed him strangely. "A spellsinger is a wizard who can only make magic through music."

"That's a nice thought." He plucked at the lower strings and almost-notes danced with dust motes in the fading daylight. "I wish it were true of me." He grinned, slightly embarrassed. "I've had a few people tell me that despite my less than mesmerizing tenor, I can make a little music-magic. But not the kind you're thinking of."

"How do you know you can't? Maybe Clothahump was right all along."

"This is silly, Talea. I'm no more a magician than I am any other kind of success. Hell, I'm having a hard enough time trying to play this thing and walk at the same time, what with that long staff strapped to my back. It keeps trying to slide free and trip me.

"Besides," he ran his fingers indifferently along the upper strings, "I can't even get this to sound right. I can't play something I can't even tune."

"Have you used all the dutips?" When he looked blank, she indicated the tuning knobs. He nodded. "And what about the dudeeps?" Again the blank gaze, and this time he had a surprise.

Set into a recess in the bottom of the instrument were two knobs. He hadn't noticed them before, having been preoccupied with the strings and the "dutips," as she'd called them. He fiddled with the pair. Each somehow contracted tiny metal and wood slats inside the resonator. One adjusted crude treble, the other lowered everything a couple of octaves and corresponded very roughly to a bass modulator. He looked closely at them and then looked again. Instead of the usual "treble" and "bass," they read "tremble" and "mass."

But they definitely improved the quality of the duar's sound.

"Now you should try," she urged him.

"Try what? What kind of song would you like to hear? I've been through this with Mudge, so if you want to take the risk of listening to me. . . ."

"I'm not afraid," she replied, misunderstanding him. "Try not for the sound. Try for the magic. It's not like a wizard as great as Clothahump, even if his powers are failing, to make such a mistake."

Try for the magic, he thought. Huh . . . try for the sound. That's what the lead bass player for a very famous group had once told him. The guy had been higher than the Pope when Jon-Tom had accidentally run into him in a hall before a concert playing to twenty thousand. Stuttering, hardly able to talk to so admired a musician, he'd barely been able to mumble the usual fatuous request for "advice to a struggling young guitarist."

"Hey, man . . . you got to try for the sound. Hear? Try for the sound."

That hastily uttered parable had been sufficiently unspecific to stick in his mind. Jon-Tom had been trying for the sound for years, but he hadn't come close to finding it. Most would-be musicians never did. Maybe finding the sound was the difference between the pro and the amateur. Or maybe it was only a matter of getting too stoked to notice the difference.

Whatthehell.

He fiddled a little longer with the pseudo-treble/bass controls. They certainly improved the music. Why not play something difficult? Stretch yourself, Jon-Tom. You've nothing to lose. These two critics can't change your career one way or t'other. There was only one sound he'd ever hoped to reach for, so he reached.

"Purple haze . . ." he began, and thereafter, as always, he lost himself in the music, forgetting the watching Talea, forgetting Mudge, forgetting the place and time of where he was, forgetting everything except reaching for the sound.

He played as hard as he could on that strange curved instrument. It lifted him, juiced him with the natural high playing always brought him. As he played it seemed to him that he could hear the friendly prickling music of his own old electric guitar. His nerves quivered with the pleasure and his ears rang with the familiarity of it. He was truly happy, cradling and caressing that strange instrument, forgetting his surroundings, his troubles, his parents.

A long time later (or maybe it was only a couple of minutes) he became aware that someone was shaking him. He blinked and stopped playing, the last rough chord dying away, soaked up by the earth and trees. He blinked at Talea, and she let loose of his arms, backed away from him a little. She was looking at him strangely.

Mudge also stood nearby, staring.

"What's going on? Was I that bad?" He felt a little dizzy.

"'Tis a fine chap you are, foolin' your mate like this," said the otter with a mixture of awe and irritation. "Forgive me, lad. I'd no idea you'd been toyin' with me all this time. Don't go too harsh on me. I've only done what I thought best for you and . . ."

"Stop that, Mudge. What are you blubbering about?"

"The sounds you made . . . and something else, spellsinger." He gaped at her. "You're still trying to fool us, aren't you? Just like you fooled Clothahump. Look at your duar."

His gaze dropped and he jumped slightly. The last vestiges of a powerful violet luminescence were slowly fading from the edges of the instrument, slower still from the lambent metal strings.

"I didn't . . . I haven't done anything." He shoved at the instrument as though it might suddenly turn and bite him. The strap kept it secure around his neck and it swung back to bounce off his ribs. The club-staff rocked uncomfortably on his back.

"Try again," Talea whispered. "Reach for the magic again."

It seemed to have grown darker much too fast. Hesitantly (it was only an instrument, after all) he plucked at the lower strings and strummed again a few bars of "Purple Haze." Each time he struck a string it emitted that rich violet glow.

There was something else. The music was different. Cold as water from a mountain tarn, rough as a file's rasp. It set a fire in the head like white lightning and sent goosebumps down his arms. Bits of thought rattled around like ball bearings inside his skull.

My oh, but that was a fine sound!

He tried again, more confidently now. Out came the proper chords, with a power and thunder he hadn't expected. All the time they reverberated and echoed through the trees, and there was no amplifier in sight. That vast sound was pouring purple from the duar resting firm on his shoulder and light beneath his dancing fingers.

Is it the instrument that's transformed, he thought wildly, or something in me?

That was the key line, of course, from another song entirely. But it rationalized, if not explained, he thought, what was happening there in the forest.

"I'm not a spellsinger," he finally told them. "I'm still not sure what that is." He was surprised at the humbleness in his voice. "But I always thought I had something in me. Every would-be musician does. There's a line that goes, 'The magic's in the music and the music's in me.' Maybe you're right, Talea. Maybe Clothahump was more accurate than even he knew.

"I'm going to do what I can, though I can't imagine what that might be. So far all I know I can do is make this duar shine purple."

"Never mind 'ow you do it, mate." Mudge swelled with pride at his companion's accomplishment. "Just don't forget 'ow."

"We need to experiment." Talea's mind was working furiously. "You need to focus your abilities, Jon-Tom. Any wizard . . ."

"Don't . . . call me that."

"Any spellsinger, then, has to be able to be specific with his magic. Unspecific magic is not only useless, it's dangerous."

"I don't know any of the right words," he protested. "I don't know any songs with scientific words."

"You've got the music, Jon-Tom. That's magic enough to make the words work." She looked around the forest. Dusk was settling gently over the treetops. "What do we need?"

"Money," said Mudge without hesitation.

"Shut up, Mudge. Be serious."

"I'm always serious where money be concerned, luv."

She threw him a sour look. "We can't buy transportation where none exists. Money won't get us safely and quickly to Clothahump's Tree." She looked expectantly at Jon-Tom.

"Want to try that?".

"What? Transportation? I don't know what kind . . ." He broke off, feeling drunk. Drunk from the after effects of the music. Drunk from what it seemed he'd done with it. Drunk with the knowledge of an ability he hadn't known he'd possessed, and completely at a loss as to what to make of it.

Make of it some transportation, dummy. You heard the lady.

But what song to play to do so? Wasn't that always the problem? No matter whether you're trying to magic spirits or an audience.

Beach Boys . . . sure, that sounded right. "Little Deuce Coupe." What would Talea and Mudge make of *that*! He laughed wildly and drew concerned looks from his companions.

His hands moved toward the strings . . . and hesitated. "Little Deuce Coupe"? Now as long as we're about this, Meriweather, why fool around with small stuff? Try for some *real* transportation.

He cleared his throat self-consciously, feeling giddy, and started to sing. "She's real fine, my four-oh-nine."

In his cradling arms the duar began to vibrate and glow mightily. This time the luminescence spread from the strings to encompass the entire instrument. It was like a live thing in his hands, struggling to break free. He hung on tight while awkwardly picking out the notes. Rising chords sprang from his right fingers.

Talea and Mudge stepped back from him, their eyes wide and intent on the open grass between. A pulsing, yellow ball of light had tumbled from the duar to land on the earth. It grew and twisted, swollen with the music. Jon-Tom was facing away from it, preoccupied with his playing.

When Talea's cry finally made him turn the glowing shape had grown considerably. It was working, he told himself excitedly! The shape was beginning to assume a roughly cylindrical outline. He hoped the lemon-yellow convertible would materialize with a full tank of gas (he didn't know any songs about gasoline). Then they would continue in luxury through the forest in a vehicle the likes of which this world had never imagined.

He really was a little drunk now. Too much pride can stupify the brain as readily as alcohol. He began to improvise stanzas about AM/FM radios, CB's, racing stripes and mags and slicks. After all, as long as he was conjuring up a vehicle he might as well do it up right.

Abruptly there was a loud bang, a toy thunderbolt like a thousand capguns all going off simultaneously. It knocked him back on his butt. The duar flopped against his stomach.

There was something long and powerful where the contorting yellow cylinder had been. It did not boast slicks, but of its traction there could be no doubt. There were no racing stripes and certainly nothing electronic.

The headlights turned to look at him. They were a bright, rich red save for the black slashes in the centers. A long tongue emerged from the front and flicked questioningly at his sprawled form.

There was a noise from the "vehicle." He looked frantically over at it, and it back at him.

In contrast to his evident terror, both Talea and Mudge appeared anything but cowed. They were inspecting the vehicle casually, admiringly. That gave him the courage to sit up and take a closer look at his conjuration.

It was sight of the reins that brought understanding. There was no bit in the enormous snake's mouth. No living thing could control that single mass of muscle by pulling on its mouth. Instead, the reins were linked to the two ear openings set just in back of the eyes.

Talea moved around in front of the snake and gathered in the reins. She gave a short, sharp tug and barked a single word. Twice as thick as Jon-Tom was tall, the immense reptile turned and docilely dropped its head to the ground. Red eyes stared blankly straight ahead.

Jon-Tom had climbed to his feet and allowed himself to be pulled along by an exuberant Mudge. "Come on then, mate. 'Tis one hellaciously fine wizard you be! Sorry I am that I made fun o' you."

"Forget it." He shook himself out of his mental stupor, allowed himself to be led toward the great snake. It was at least forty feet long, though its immense bulk made it appear shorter. Four saddles were mounted on its back. They were secured not by straps around the belly as with a horse but by a peculiar suction arrangement that held the seats tight to the slick scales.

Having calmed down a little, he had to admit that the snake was quite lovely, clad as it was in alternating bands of red, blue, and bright orange that ran like tempera around its girth. This then was the "vehicle" his song had called up. The magic had worked, but translated into this world's terms. Apparently his abilities weren't quite powerful enough for the forces of magic to take his words literally.

"Is it poisonous?" was the first thing he could think to ask.

Mudge let out his high, chirping otter-laugh, urged Jon-Tom toward one of the rear saddles. "Cor, you're a funny one, mate." Talea had already taken the lead position. She was waiting impatiently for her companions to mount up.

" 'Tis a L'borean Riding Snake, and what pray tell would it need poison for t' defend itself against? 'Cept one o' its own relatives, and its teeth are plenty big enough t' 'andle that occasional family chore.''

"What the devil does something this size feed on?"

"Oh, other lizards, most. Any o' the large nonintelligent herbivores it can find in the wild."

"Even so, some of them are tamed for riding?"

Mudge shook his head at the obvious joke. "Now what were you imaginin' these were for?" He rapped the leather saddle loudly. The stirrups were a bit high for him, but strong arms pulled him to where he could get his feet into them.

"Climb aboard, then, mate, and ride."

Jon-Tom moved to the last saddle. He got a good grip on the pommel, put his right boot in the stirrup, and pulled. His left foot dragged against the side of the creature, which took no notice of the contact. It was like kicking a steel bar.

He found himself staring past Mudge at the beacon of Talea's hair. She uttered a low hiss. The snake started forward obediently, and Jon-Tom reached down and used the curved handle-pommel to steady himself.

The movement was unlike anything he'd ever experienced. Not that he'd ever ridden any animal other than the ponies who once frequented his hometown, but it still seemed incredibly gentle. He was put in mind of the stride of the lizards who had pulled their lost wagon; only having no legs, the snake produced an even smoother ride. Technically, it had no gait at all.

There was no jouncing or bouncing. The snake glided like oil over bumps and boulders. After a few minutes of vibration-free ride Jon-Tom felt confident in letting loose of the handle. He relaxed and enjoyed for a change the passing sights of the forest. It was amazing how relaxed the mind could become when one's feet no longer hurt.

He made certain the duar was secured across his belly and

his fighting staff was still tight on his back, then settled back to enjoy the ride.

The only thing difficult to get used to was the feeling of not knowing where they were headed, since the snake's slithering, rippling method of making progress was quite deceptive. Eventually he learned to keep a close eye on the reptile's head. It was more like traveling in a tacking sailboat than on a horse.

Smooth as the ride was, the constant moving from right to left in order to proceed forward was making him slightly queasy. This was solved when he directed his attention sideways instead of trying to stare straight ahead.

"I didn't mean to call this monster up, you know," he said to Mudge. "I was trying for something completely different."

"And what might that 'ave been?" A curious Mudge looked back over his shoulder, content to let Talea lead now that he'd given her a heading.

"Actually, I was sort of hoping for a Jeep Wagoneer, or maybe a Landcruiser. But I didn't know any songs—any spells—for them, so I tried to come as close as I could with what I had."

"I don't know wot the first might be," replied Mudge, meticulously preening his whiskers and face, "but a 'landcruiser' be wot we 'ave, if not just precisely the variety you'd 'oped for."

"I guess." Jon-Tom sounded thoughtful. "I suppose it's a good thing I didn't know any songs about tanks. No telling what we might have ended up with."

Mudge frowned. "Now that's a peculiar thing t' say. Wot would we 'ave needed with extra water, wot with streams aboundin' throughout this part o' the Bellwoods?"

Jon-Tom started to explain, decided instead that this was not the time to launch into a complicated explanation of otherworldly technologies. Mudge and Talea appeared quite pleased with the snake. There was no reason for him not to be equally satisfied. Certainly its ride was far smoother than any mechanized vechicle's would have been.

Idly he ran his fingers over the small strings of the duar. Delicate harplike notes sauntered through the forest air. They still possessed the inexplicable if familiar electronic twang of his old Grundig. Blue sparks shot from beneath his fingers.

He started to hum a few bars of ''Scarborough Fair,'' then thought better of it. He didn't want anything to divert them from their intended rendezvous with Clothahump. Who knew what some casually uttered words might conjure up? Possibly they might suddenly find themselves confronted with a fair, complete with food, jugglers and minstrels, and even police.

Play to amuse yourself if you must, he told himself, but keep the words to yourself. So he kept his mouth shut while he continued to play. His fingers stayed clear of the longer upper strings because no matter how softly he tried to strum those, they generated a disconcertingly vast barrage of sound. They remained linked to some mysterious magickry of amplification that he was powerless to disengage.

He'd hoped for a four-wheel drive, tried for two-wheel, and had produced a no-wheel drive that was far more efficient than anything he'd imagined. Now, what else would add to his feeling of comfort in the forest? An M-16 perhaps, or considering the size of the riding snake and its as yet unseen but possibly belligerent relatives, maybe a few Honest John Rockets.

What'd he'd likely get would be a sword or something. Better to rely on his wits and the war staff bouncing against his spine. Or he might produce the weapon in the firing stage. He would have to be very, very careful indeed if he tried to sing up anything else, he decided. Perhaps Clothahump would have some good advice.

He continued to play as they slithered on through increasing darkness. When asked about why they were continuing, Talea replied, ''We want to make as much distance as we can tonight.''

"Why the sudden rush? We're doing a helluva lot better than we did when we were walking."

She leaned to her left, looked past him, and pointed downward. "We weren't leaving this kind of trail, either." Jon-Tom looked back and noted the wake of crushed brush and grass the snake was producing. "Outriders from Thieves' Hall will surely pick it up."

"So? Why should they connect that up with us?"

"Probably they won't. But L'borean riding snakes are available only to the extremely wealthy. They'd follow any such track, especially one not leading straight for town, hoping to run down a fat prize. Their disappointment in finding us instead of some rich merchant wouldn't bode well for our futures."

"Bloody well right," agreed Mudge readily. "There's a disconcertin' and disgustin' tendency toward settlin' discontents without resortin' to words."

"Beg your pardon?" said Jon-Tom with a frown.

"Kill first and ask questions afterward."

He nodded grimly. "We have some of those where I come from, too."

He turned moodily back to the duar. It was barely visible in the intensifying night. He fiddled with the bottom controls, and the strings fluttered with blue fire as he played. Carefully he kept his lips closed, forced himself not to voice the words of the song he was playing. It was hard to remember the melody without voicing the words. A silver-dollar moon was rising in the east.

Once he caught himself softly singing words and something green was forming alongside the snake. Damn, this wasn't going to work. He needed to play something without words in order to be completely safe.

He changed the motion of his fingers on the strings. Better, he thought. Then he noticed Mudge staring at him.

"Something wrong?"

"Wot the 'ell is goin' on with you, Jon-Tom?"

"It's a Bach fugue," he replied, not understanding. "Quite a well-known piece where I come from."

" 'Ell with that, mate. I wasn't referrin' t' your music. I was referrin' t' your company."

His voice was oddly muted, neither alarmed nor relaxed. Jon-Tom looked to his right . . . and had to grab the saddle handle to keep from falling out of his seat. . . .

X

He found himself staring directly at a huge swarm of nothing. That is, it seemed that there was definitely something present. Hundreds of somethings, in fact. But when he looked at them, they weren't there.

They had moved to his left. He turned to face them, and as he did so, they moved somewhere else.

"Above you, mate . . . I think." Jon-Tom's head snapped back, just in time to espy the absence of whatever it had been. They'd moved down and to his right, behind a large gingko tree where he couldn't see them because they'd shifted their position to his left, where they no longer were and . . .

He was getting dizzy.

It was as if he were hunting a visual echo. He was left teasing his retinas; every time he turned there were the shadows of ghosts.

"I don't see a thing. I almost do, but never quite."

"Surely you do." Mudge was grinning now. "Just like meself, we're seeing them after they aren't there any more."

"But you were looking at them a moment ago," said Jon-Tom, feeling very foolish now because he knew there was definitely *something* near them in the forest. "You told me where to look, where they'd moved to."

"You're 'alf right, mate. I told you where t' look, but not where they were. You can only see where they've been, not where they are." He scratched one ear as he stared back over a furry shoulder. "It never works. You never can see 'em, but those folks who are lucky enough not t' almost see 'em never stop from tryin'. There!"

He gestured sharply to his right. Jon-Tom's head spun around so fast a nerve spasmed in his neck and he winced in pain. Visual footprints formed an afterimage in his brain.

"They're all around us," Mudge told him. "Around you, mostly."

"*What* are?" His brain was getting as twisted as his optic nerves. It was bad enough not to be able to see something you knew was present without having to try and imagine what they were. Or weren't. It was like magnets. You could get the repelling poles close to each other, but at the last possible instant, they'd always slide apart.

"Gneechees."

Jon-Tom turned sharply to his left. Again his gaze caught nothing. He was positive if he shifted his eyes just another quarter inch around he'd have whatever was there in clear focus. "What the hell are gneechees?"

"Blimey, you mean you don't 'ave 'em where you come from?"

"Where I come from we don't have a lot of the things you're used to, Mudge."

"I always thought . . ." The otter shrugged. "The gneechees be everywhere around us. Some times they're more visible than at others, or less invisible 'ud be a better way o' puttin' it. Millions and millions of 'em."

"Millions? Then why can't I see just one?"

Mudge threw up his paws. "Now that's a fine question, ain't it? I don't know. Nobody knows. Not even Clothahump, I'd wager. As to wot they be, that's another nice little mystery. 'Bout the best description I ever 'eard of 'em was that they're the things you seen when you turn your 'ead and there's nothin' there, but you're sure there was *somethin'*. Gneechees are wot you almost see out o' the corner o' your eye, and when you turn to look at it, it's gone. They're the almost-wases, the nearly theres, the maybe-couldbes. They're always with us and never there.''

Jon-Tom leaned thoughtfully back in his saddle, fighting the urge to glance constantly to right or left. "Maybe we do have them. But they seem to be just slightly more visible, just a touch more substantial here than back home." He wondered if there were millions of gneechees swarming around the university. They might be the explanation for a lot of things.

"How can you be so sure they're real, if you can never see one?"

"Oh, they're real enough, mate. You know they're real just as I do, because your noggin tells you there's somethin' there. It's foolin' your mind and not quite completely foolin' your eyes. Not that I care much 'bout 'em. My concerns are more prosaic, they are.

"'Tis mighty frustratin' t' them who worry about such things, though. See, they're immune t' magic. There's not the wizard been who could slow down a gneechee long enough t' figure exactly what one was. Not Clothahump, not Quelnor, not the legendary sorceress Kasadelma could do it.

"They be 'armless, though. I've never 'eard o' anyone bein' affected by 'em one way or t'other."

"How could you tell?" Jon-Tom wondered. "You can't see them."

"Cor, but you could sure enough see the victim, if they took a notion to go to troublin' someone."

"They give me the crawlies." He tried not to look around, and found himself hunting all the harder. It was one thing to think you were seeing things that weren't, quite another to learn for a fact that millions and millions of minute creatures of unknown aspect and intent were occupying the air around you.

"Why are they hanging around me?"

"Who knows, mate. 'Cept that I've 'eard gneechees are attracted t' worried folk. People who be frettin', or upset. Same goes for magickers. Now, you fit both categories.

'Aven't you ever noticed somethin' around you when you've been like that?''

"Naturally. You always tend to imagine more when you're upset or stressed.''

"'Cept you're not imaginin' them,'' Mudge explained. "They're 'angin' about all right. 'Tis not their fault. I expect that's just wot they're sensitive to, not t' mention the fact that your emotions and feelin's are otherworldly in nature.''

"Well, I wish they'd go away.'' He turned and shouted, "Go on, go away! All of you!'' He waved his hands as though it were a flock of flies he could shoo from his psyche. "Harmless or otherwise, I don't want you around. You're making me nervous!''

"Now that won't do, Jon-Tom.'' Talea had twisted around in her lead saddle and was staring back at him. "The more angry you become the more the gneechees will cling to your presence.''

He continued swatting sideways. "How come I can't hit one? I don't have to see one to hit one. If there's something there, surely I ought to get in a lucky swipe sooner or later.''

Mudge let out a sigh. "Crikey, lad, sometimes I think whoever set you out on the tightrope o' life forgot t' give you your balancin' pole. If the gneechees be too fast for us t' see, 'ow do you expect t' fool one with somethin' as slow as the back o' your 'and? I expect we must seem t' be swimmin' through a vat o' blackstrap molasses from their point o' view. Maybe we don't seem t' be movin' at all and they just consider us parts o' the landscape. 'Cept we're the parts that generate the emotions or forces or wotever it is that occasionally attracts 'em in big numbers. Just thank whotever sign you were born under that they *are* 'armless.''

"I don't believe in astrology.'' Maybe it was time to change the subject. Continued talk of gneechees was frustrating as well as fruitless.

"Now who said anything about astrology?'' The otter eyed him in puzzlement. "Now meself was born beneath a cobbler's sign in the riverbank community o' Rush-the-Rock. 'Ow about you?''

"I don't know . . . oh heck, I guess I was born under the sign of L.A. County General.''

"Military family, wot?''

"Never mind.'' His tone was resigned, and he was a little worn out from his experiments with his newfound abilities, not to mention the discovery that millions of not quite physical creatures found him attractive. In order to get rid of them it seemed he was going to have to cease worrying so much, relax, and stop being strange.

He would work on the first two, but he didn't know if he could do anything about the third.

He spent an uneasy night. Mudge and Talea slept quietly, save for a single incident involving a muffled curse followed by the sound of a fist striking furry flesh.

No matter how hard he tried he could not go to sleep. Trying not to think of the gneechees' presence was akin to not thinking of a certain word. What happened was that one couldn't think of anything *except* the forbidden word or, in this case, the gneechees.

His gaze hunted the dark, always aware of minuscule not-quite-luminescent sparks that darted tantalizingly just out of view. But there are parts of the mind that make their own demands. Without being aware of it, his eyes slowly grew as tired as the rest of his body and he fell into a soft, deep sleep serenaded by the dull cooing of giant walking ferns, night-flying reptiles, and a pool full of harmonizing water bugs who managed a marvelous imitation of what sounded like the journey movement from Prokofiev's Lieutenant Kije Suite.

When he woke the next morning, the bright sunlight helped push thoughts of gneechees from his mind. The reciprocal nature of their existence was instantly apparent. The more you searched for them the more of them you attracted. In contrast, the less you cared and the more you accepted their existence as normal, the less they swarmed. With practice it seemed that the honey could will away the bees.

Before afternoon the tireless riding snake was slithering uphill. They had entered a region of familiar hills and low valleys. Off to the east was something Jon-Tom had not seen on his previous march through this section of the Bellwoods. He and Mudge had not climbed quite this high.

A distant rampart of mountains ragged and rough as the Grand Tetons lay swathed in high clouds and haze. It stretched unbroken from north to south.

Mudge had taken a turn at guiding their mount, and Talea had moved in behind him. She turned as she replied to Jon-Tom's question.

"Those? Zaryt's Teeth." She was gesturing across the treetops as they began to descend again into concealing forest. "That great massif there just to the north is Brokenbone Peak, which holds up this part of the world and whose slopes are littered with the dead bones of would-be climbers."

"What's on the other side?"

There was a tremor in her reply and, startlingly for the redoubtable Talea, a hint of fear. "The Greendowns, where reside the Plated Folk."

"I've heard of them." Childishly, he pounced on the rare hint of weakness. "You sound scared of them."

She made a face, brows narrowing, and idly shook aside red hair, ran a hand through the glowing curls. "Jon-Tom," she said seriously, "you seem to me to be a brave if occasionally foolish man, but you know nothing of the Plated Folk. Do not dismiss so lightly that which you are unfamiliar with.

"Your words do not insult me because I am not afraid to confess my fear. Also, I know that you speak from ignorance, or you would not say such things. So I am not upset."

"I might say such things even if I knew." He was properly abashed. But now he stared at her openly.

"Why are you doing that?" Green eyes stared curiously at him.

"Because I want to upset you."

"I don't understand, Jon-Tom."

"Look, you've been taunting me, chiding me, and generally making fun of me ever since we met. I wanted to strike back at you. Not that I've given you much reason to think better of me. I've probably given you more ammunition than you need. The trouble I caused back at Thieves' Hall is a good example. I'm sorry about things like that, but I can only learn by experience, and if some of those experiences don't work out very well there's not a whole hell of a lot I can do about it.

"I mean you no harm, Talea. I'd like to be more than just allies. I want to be friends. If that's going to come about then I need a little more understanding and a lot less sarcasm from you. How about it?"

He relaxed in his saddle, more than a little surprised at his lengthy speech.

Talea just stared at him while the snake slid down into a meadow alive with green and pink glass butterflies and sunflowers blinking their cyclopean amber eyes.

"I thought we were already friends, Jon-Tom. If I seem to have been brusque with you it was from frustration and impatience, not from dislike."

"Then you do like me?" He couldn't repress a hopeful grin.

She almost smiled back. "If you prove as quick with your newfound magic as you are with your words, then we will be safe indeed." She turned away, and as she did so he caught a glimpse of an expression midway between amusement and genuine interest. He couldn't be certain it reflected either, for Talea's true feelings could be as not-there as the gneechees.

So he said nothing further, let the brief exchange pass. It was enough that he now felt better about their relationship, even if it was no more than an assurance she was not openly hostile to him. At the same time he discovered a surefire way for pushing thoughts of the gneechees completely from his mind. All he had to do was concentrate on the gentle, subtle rolling action of Talea's derrière on the smoothly undulating snake-saddle. . . .

Another day done. Another day of roots, nuts, berries, and the reptilian meat which proved considerably tenderer and sweeter than he had any right to expect. Skillful hunter and braggart that Mudge was, they now had lizard venison or snake fillet at every meal.

Another day done and a familiar glade came into view. The massive, ancient oak in its center seemed not to have shed a single leaf since last he saw it.

They dismounted tiredly. Talea secured the riding snake so that it could move around in a modest circle. It would not do, she explained, simply to turn it out to hunt, since without constant attention a L'borean riding snake could revert rapidly to the wild.

"Shit, you back again?" griped the black-winged shape that opened the Tree door. "You're either not very bright, man, or else just downright dumb." He looked appreciatively past Mudge and Jon-Tom. "Now who's dat? Nice lookin' dame."

"My name is Talea. And that's enough for you, slave."

"Slave? Who's a slave? I'll show ya who's a slave!"

"Easy now, Pog old chap." Mudge had moved forward to block the bat's egress by waving short arms. "She's a friend, even if her tongue be a bit tart at times. Just tell Clothahump that we're back." He cast a cautioning glance at Jon-Tom. "We've 'ad some bad luck, we 'ave, that's necessitated us returnin' a mite early."

"Bet you did," said the bat expectantly, "or ya wouldn't be here now. I bet ya fouled up real good. It gonna be interesting ta see the old bugger turn ya into a human." His gaze dropped. "You'll make a funnier lookin' one than normal, wid dose legs."

"Now is that any way t' greet a friend, Pog? Don't say such 'orrible things or you'll 'ave me befoulin' me pants and embarrassin' meself in front o' the lady. We did nothin' we couldn't avoid. Isn't that the truth, lad?" He looked concernedly back at Jon-Tom.

It took a moment of internal wrestling to go along with the statement. Maybe Mudge was something less than the most altruistic of teachers, but he'd tried. The otter was the closest thing he had in this world to a real friend, barring development of his relationship with Talea. Though he had to admit honestly to himself that if things ever got really tough he was not sure he could depend on the otter, and certainly not on Talea.

However, there was no point in detailing any of those feelings to Pog. "Yeah. We had a rough time of it in Lynchbany. And we have other reasons for coming back to see His Wizardness."

"Well, all right. Come on in. Damn fools . . . I suppose your presence will make more work for me again." He flapped on ahead, grumbling steadily in his usual broken-engine tone.

Jon-Tom stayed a step back of Mudge and the bat. "Be careful about what you say, Talea. This Clothahump's the one who brought me here, remember. He's a very powerful wizard and although I found him to be concerned and even kindly, he's obsessed with this crisis he dreams about, and I've seen him come near to frying that bat."

"Don't worry," she replied with a tight smile. "I know who he is, and what he is. He's a borderline senile who ought to have enough sense to retract into his shell and stay there. Do you think I'm an ignorant country sodder? I follow current rumors and talemongerings. I know who's in power and who's doing what, and to whom. That's how I know he's responsible for the mess he's made of your life, Jon-Tom." She frowned at him.

"You're the weirdest sorcerer I've ever encountered or

heard tell of, except *maybe* for this Clothahump. In that respect it's a good match, and I can see how in his searching he seized on you.'' The comparison startled Jon-Tom. He hadn't considered that he and the turtle might have personal affinities, or that they might be responsible for his presence here.

"That's okay," he replied readily. "You're the most interesting mugger I've ever run into."

"Better not do it on a dark street or you're liable to find out just how interesting I am," she said warningly.

"Really? I've never done it on a dark street, and I would like to find out how interesting you are."

She started to snap out a reply, looked uncertain, and then accelerated. "Oh, come on." There was exasperation in her voice and just possibly something else. "You're a funny one, Jon-Tom. I'm never quite sure about you."

And you, he thought as he watched her hurry on ahead of him, are maybe not as hopeless as I once thought.

It was quite astonishing, he thought as he followed her, how the sight of a beautiful figure teasingly wrapped in snug clothes could shove aside all worries about such picayune matters as survival. Base animal nature, he mused.

But if he was going to survive in this world, he would have to revert to basics. Wasn't that just what Clothahump and, in different ways, Mudge had both told him? Maybe by keeping his thoughts focused on those basics he could keep a firmer grip on his sanity.

All assuming that Talea didn't change her mind as fast as she seemed able to and didn't decide to shove a sword through his belly. That thought cooled his ardor, if not his long-term interest.

Slowing, he found himself standing close to her in the central chamber of the tree. Her perfume was in his nose, her presence a constant comfort in alien surroundings. Yes, they would nave to remain friends, if naught else. She was too familiar, too human for him to abandon that.

Pog directed them out of the central room and into a work area he and Mudge hadn't visited before. The bat hovered nearby while all four watched in silence as the wizard Clothahump fumbled awkwardly among bottles and vials.

Thoroughly engrossed in his work, the wizard failed to notice his visitors. After a proper pause, Pog fluttered forward and said deferentially, "Pardon da intrusion, Master, but dey have returned."

"Um . . . what? Who's returned?" He looked around and his gaze fell on Jon-Tom. "Oh yes, you. I remember you, boy."

"Not too well, it seems." It was something less than the exuberant welcome he'd hoped for.

"I have a lot on my mind, boy." He slid off the low bench and sought out the gray figure of Mudge, who was partly hidden behind Jon-Tom. "Back early, I see. Well, you lazy, foul-mouthed, slanderous mammal, what have you to say for yourself? Or is this merely a courteous visit and I should assume you've encountered no troubles?" The last sentence was spoken with false sweetness.

" 'Tis not like you're thinkin' at all, Your Worshipfulness," the otter insisted. "I was showin' the lad the ways o' Lynchbany and we ran into some unforeseen problems, we did. They weren't no more my fault than they was 'is," and he jerked a short thumb in Jon-Tom's direction.

Clothahump looked up at the tall young man. "Is what he says true, boy? That he's done his best and taken good care of you? Or is he the outright liar he looks?"

"Wot a thing to say," muttered Mudge, but not too loudly.

"It's hard to lay responsibility for what we've been through lately at anyone's feet, sir." He was aware of black otter eyes hard on his back. "On the one hand, it certainly seems as though I . . . as though we've been the victims of a really unlikely sequence of unfortunate happenings. On the other. . . ."

"No, mate," interrupted Mudge hurriedly, "there be no need t' go into such silliness now." He looked back to the wizard. "I did me best for the lad, Your Highestness. Why, I venture t' say nary a stranger's 'ad quite such fullness o' experience o' local customs as 'e 'as in these past several days."

Jon-Tom kept his expression carefully neutral. "I certainly can't argue with that, sir."

Clothahump considered while he inspected Jon-Tom. "At least the laggard has clothed you properly." He took note of the war staff and the duar. Then his attention shifted to the third member of the little group.

"And who might you be, young lady?"

She stepped proudly forward. "I am Talea of Wuver County, of the Brightberries that mature at Night, third on my mother's side, first of red hair and green eyes, and I am afraid of neither man, woman, beast . . . nor wizard."

"Hmph." Clothahump turned away from her, then suddenly seemed to slump in on himself. Sitting back down on the workbench he leaned his shell against the table. Fingers rubbed tiredly at his forehead as he smiled almost apologetically at his visitors.

"Pardon my tone, my friends. You especially, Jon-Tom. I forget common courtesy myself these days, as I forget many other things too easily. Responsible as I am for your inconveniencing, I owe you more than a curt interrogation concerning your recent activities. If I seemed brusque it was only out of worry for your welfare. But you see, things are growing worse and not better."

"The coming crisis you told us about?" Jon-Tom wondered sympathetically.

The turtle nodded. "It turns my sleep into a cauldron of black distress. I dream of nothing save darkness and death. Of an ocean of putrification about to drown the worlds."

"Ahhh, I don't see why ya worry yourself so much," said Pog from a nearby rafter. "You knockin' yourself out fer noddin', boss. Everybody else scoffs at ya, taunts ya behind your shell. Ya know some of da names dey call ya? 'Senile' is da best o' them.''

"I am aware of the local opinion." Clothahump grinned slightly. "In order for one to be affected by insults, one must have some respect for their source. I've told you that before, Pog. The comments of the rabble are of no import, even if they are the rabble one is trying to save. You'll never make a decent peregrine unless you change your attitude in such matters. Hawks and falcons are a haughty folk. You need to cultivate more mental and social independence."

"Yeah, tell me about it," the bat muttered.

Jon-Tom was fascinated by the still unspecified threat, despite his own personal problems. "So you haven't learned anything new about this evil since we left? Or about its source, or when it will come?"

The wizard shook his head dolefully. "It remains as nebulous in nature, as tenuous of touch as before, boy. Nor am ⁻ any nearer concocting a methodology to combat it with."

Jon-Tom tried to cheer the despondent turtle. "I've surprise for you, Clothahump. It was a surprise to me, also."

"What are you riddling me with, boy?"

"I think I may be able to help after all." Clothahump looked up at him curiously.

"Aye, 'tis true, Your Geniusness," said Mudge excitedly. "Why, 'twas meself who first suggested that . . ." He broke off, thinking better of the incipient lie. "No. No, dammit, I cannot take any o' the credit. The lad did it all on 'is own."

"Did *what* on his own?" asked the exasperated wizard.

"We'd been tryin' 'ard t' discover some useful skill for 'im, Your Mastership. 'Is range o' experience matches 'is youthfulness, so wasn't much in the way o' things 'e was practiced at. 'E 'as 'is natural size and reach, and some agility. At first I thought 'e might make a good mercenary. But 'e kept insistin' 'e wanted t' be either a lawyer or musician." Jon-Tom nodded in confirmation.

"Well, Your Lordship can imagine wot I thought o' *the*

first suggestion. Concernin' 'tother, while the lad's voice is o' considerable volume, it leaves somethin' t' be desired as far as carryin' the tune, if you follow me meaning. But 'is musicianship was another matter, sor. 'E 'as real enthusiasm for music . . . and as it turned out, somethin' more.

"We stumbled, literally stumbled we did, across that fine duar you see 'angin' about 'is neck. And when he got to strummin' on it, well, the most unbelievable things started a-happenin'! You would not believe it 'ad not you been there yourself. All purple and 'azy it started to shine, and its shape a shakin', and the *sounds*, sor." The otter put his hands melodramatically to his ears.

"The sounds this lad can coax out o' that little musicbox. 'E calls it music like 'e's used to playin', but 'tis of a size I never 'eard in me short but full little life."

"I don't know what happened or why, sir." Jon-Tom ran his fingers over the duar. "It vibrates a little when I play it. I think it's trying to become the kind of instrument I'm used to, and can't. As to the magic"—he shrugged—"I'm afraid I'm not very good at it. I only seem to have the vaguest kind of control over what I call up."

"He's too modest, sir," said Talea. "He's a true spellsinger.

"We were tired and worn from our long march through the woods when he started a strange song about some kind of transportation." She looked sideways at Jon-Tom. "I cannot imagine what it was he was singing about, but what he produced was a L'borean riding snake. I do not think it was specified by his song."

"Not hardly," agreed Jon-Tom.

"Nevertheless, that is what he materialized, and a fine ride it provided us, too."

"Nor be that all, sor," said Mudge. "Soon afterward, as we glide through the forest night, 'e's a-strummin' those strings and then . . . why sor, the like's o' so many gneechees was never seen in this country! I swear by me piece they were about us like fleas on a fox followin' a four-day drunk. You never saw the almost-likes o' it.''

Clothahump was silent for long moments. Then, ''So it seems you've some spellsinging abilities.'' He scratched at a loose drawer in his plastron.

''It looks that way, sir. I've heard about hidden talent, but I never expected to find any in myself.''

''All most interesting.'' The wizard rose from the bench, put both hands as far behind his back as they'd reach, and scratched at his shell. ''It would help to explain so many things. It would explain why in casting I settled upon you and passed over others.'' There was a touch of resurgent pride in his voice. ''So it may be I am not as senile as some say. I thought there was more to this than mere confusion on my part. The talent I sought has been present all along.''

''Not exactly, sir. As Talea explained, I can call for something, but I get something quite different. I don't have control over my, uh, magic. Couldn't that be awfully dangerous?''

''My boy, all wizardry is dangerous. So you think you might be able to help now? Well, if we can settle on something for you to help me against, your services will be most welcome.''

Jon-Tom shuffled his feet nervously. ''Actually, sir, I didn't mean I'd be able to help in that way. Wouldn't you still prefer a real magician, a real 'engineer' from my world to assist you?''

''I expect I would.'' Clothahump adjusted his spectacles.

''Then send me back and exchange me for another.''

''I told you before, boy, that the energies required, the preparations involved need time to . . .'' He stopped, squinted upward. ''Ah, I believe I follow your meaning now, Jon-Tom spellsinger.''

''That's it, sir.'' He could not longer restrain his excitement. ''If we both concentrate, both devote our energies to it, maybe the combination will be powerful enough to work the switch. It's not like you're shoving me back home all by yourself, or pulling a replacement here alone. We'd be complementing each other's talents, and making an exchange all at once. Only a single conjuration would be involved instead of two.''

Clothahump looked seriously at his workbench. ''It *might* be possible. There are certain shortcuts. . . .'' He glanced back at Jon-Tom. ''It involves definite risks, boy. You might find yourself stuck halfway between this world and your own. There's no future in limbo. Only eternity, and I can't think of a duller way to spend existence.''

''I'll take that chance. I'll take any chances necessary.''

''Good for you, but what about whoever you're going to be trading places with?''

''How do you mean?'' He looked uncertain.

''This eng'neer that we locate with our thoughts, Jon-Tom, will be as thrown from his familiar time and place as you were. He will likely also be trapped here for considerably longer than yourself, since I will not have the power to try and return him to his normal life for some time. He might not adapt here as well as you have, might not ever be sent home.

''Are you willing to accept the responsibility for doing that to someone else?''

''You have to take the same responsibility.''

''My entire world is at stake, possibly your own as well. I know where I stand.'' The wizard was staring unwinkingly at him.

Jon-Tom forced himself to think back, to remember what his first sight and feelings were like when he'd materialized in this world. Glass butterflies and utter disorientation. A five-foot-tall otter and bellwoods.

How might that affect an older man of forty or fifty, who might find it far harder to cope with the physical hardships of this place, not to mention the mental ones? A man with a family perhaps. Or a woman who might leave children behind?

He looked back down at Clothahump. "I'm willing to try the exchange and . . . if you're as serious about this crisis as you say, then you don't have any choice. Not if you want a real engineer."

"That is so," replied the wizard, "but I have far more important reasons for wanting to make this switch."

"My reasons are important enough to me." He turned away from the others. "I'm sorry if I don't measure up to your heroic standards."

"I expect no heroic stances from you, Jon-Tom," said Clothahump gently. "You are only a man. All I ask now is that you make the decision, and you have. That is enough for me. I will commence preparations." He turned back to his bench, leaving Jon-Tom feeling expectant, pleased, and slightly anxious.

Self-preservation, he told himself angrily. He would wish whoever was to take his place the best of luck, and could do no more than that. He'd never know who was chosen.

Besides, his erratic and possibly dangerous magic could do little to help Talea and Mudge and Clothahump's world. Probably whoever took his place would be able to, if Clothahump's perception of the danger threatening them was accurate. Rationalization or not, that was a comforting thought to cling to.

I didn't ask to be here, he told himself firmly, and if I have a chance to get home, damned if I'm not going to take it. . .

XI

The rest of the preparations took all afternoon. They were not ready until evening.

In the middle of the Tree's central chamber a circle had been painted on the wood-chip floor. It was filled with cryptographic symbols that might have been calculus and might have been nonsense. Talea, Pog, and Mudge had been directed to stay out of the way, an admonition they needed no urging to obey.

Clothahump stood on the opposite side of the circle from Jon-Tom, who tapped nervously at the wood of the duar.

"What do I do when we begin?"

"You're the spellsinger. Sing."

"Sing about what?"

"About what we're going to try and do. I wish I could help you, my boy, but I have other things to worry about. I never did have much of a voice."

"Look," said Jon-Tom worriedly, "the riding snake was an accident. I don't know how I did that. Maybe we should stop and . . ."

"Not now, boy," the wizard told him curtly. "Do the best you can. Sing naturally and the magic will follow. That's the way it is with spellsingers. You do that and I will do my part."

He slipped into a semitrance with startling speed and began to recite formulae and trace symbols in the air. There was a great deal of mumbling about time vortices, dimensional nexi, and controlled catastrophe theory.

In contrast Jon-Tom started to pluck hesitantly at the strings of the duar. They glowed blue as he furiously searched for an appropriate tune. His thoughts were confused enough without his having to recall the specifics of a song.

Eventually though he settled on one (he had to select *something*) and began. It was "California Dreamin'."

He started to feel the rhythm of the song, the deceptive power of the ballad, and his voice rose higher, the chords becoming richer as he put all his homesick feelings and desires into it: "I'd be safe and warm, if I was in L.A." It grew dark in the Tree. Brilliant yellow clouds formed in the center of the circle. They were echoed by a thick emerald fog that coalesced just above the floor.

Yellow drops of swirling energy started to spill from the clouds, while green rain rose skyward from the lazy fog. Where they met they formed a whirlpool-globe that began to swell and spin.

Jon-Tom's voice echoed around the chamber, his fingers flying over the strings. The powerful electronic mimicry thundered off the walls, blending with Clothahump's sonorous and steady chant. A deep, low ringing like the distant sound of a huge bell being played two speeds too slowly on a bad tape recorder began to fill the room. A tingling came over Jon-Tom's entire body, a glittering heat that radiated through him.

He continued to play, though it felt now as though his fingers were passing through the strings instead of striking them. Glass bottles shattered on the workbench and books tumbled from their shelves as the very heart of the Tree quivered with the sound. For all anyone inside knew, the whole forest was shaking.

The climax of the song was nearing, the end of the ballad, and he was still within the Tree. He tried to convey his helplessness to Clothahump, his uncertainty about what to do next. Perhaps the wizard understood his anxious stare. Perhaps it was just that their timing was naturally good.

A violent yellow-green explosion obliterated clouds and fog and whirlpool-globe. A great invisible fist struck Jon-Tom hard in the sternum and sent him stumbling backward. He bounced off the far wall, staggered a couple of steps, and fell to his right. Scrolls, fragments of skull, some stuffed heads mounted on the wall, wood shavings and chips, powders and bits of cloth were raining around him. Within the circle a whitish haze was beginning to dissipate.

He paid it little attention because he could see it, and he should not have been able to. Even through the shock of the explosion and his subsequent fall he knew he oughtn't to be able to see haze or Tree. He should be back home, preferably in his own room, or in class, or even flat in the middle of Wilshire traffic.

Instead he lay on his butt within the same Tree.

"It didn't work," he murmured aloud. "I didn't go back." He felt like the hero of a war movie who'd set off the magazine of his own ship and gone down with his captors.

The last of the haze was fading from the circle. He caught his breath, aware of something besides his own self-pity now.

A tall young woman just a hair short of six feet was sitting spraddle-legged in the center of the circle. Her arms were straight behind her, keeping her in a sitting position as she gazed around with an altogether appropriate air of bewilderment. Long black hair was tied in a single ponytail.

She was clad in an absurdly brief skirt with matching pantyshorts beneath, sneakers and high socks, and a long sweater with four large blue letters sewn on its front. Her face was a stunning cross between that of a Tijuana professional and a Tintoretto madonna. Jet-black eyes, black as Mudge's, and coffee skin.

Shakily she got to her feet, dusted herself off, and looked around.

With Pog's assistance Clothahump was rolling off his back.

Once on all fours he was able to stand up. He started hunting around for his glasses, which had been knocked off by the concussion. A curved dent in the Tree wall behind him showed where he'd struck.

"What happened?" Jon-Tom thought to ask, his eyes still mesmerized by the woman. "What went wrong?"

"You, obviously, did not go back," said Clothahump prosaically, "but someone else was drawn to us." He stared at the new arrival, asked solicitously, "Are you by any chance, my dear, an eng'neer? Or wizard, or sorceress, or witch, as they would be known hereabouts?"

"*Sangre de Christo*," husked the girl, taking a cautious step away from the turtle. Then she stopped. Her confusion and momentary fear were replaced by an expression of outrage.

"What is this place, huh? *Comprende tortuga?* Do you understand?" She turned slowly. "Where the hell am I?"

Her eyes narrowed as they located Jon-Tom. "You . . . don't I know you from someplace?"

"Am I correct then in assuming you are not an eng'neer?" asked Clothahump despondently.

She looked back over a shoulder at him. "Engineer, me? *Infierno,* no! I'm a theater-arts student at the University of California in Los Angeles. I was on my way to cheerleading squad practice when . . . when I suddenly find myself in a nightmare. Only . . . you are not very frightening, *tortuga*.

"So if this is no nightmare . . . what is it?" She put a hand to her forehead, staggered a little. "*Madre de dios,* have I got a headache."

Clothahump looked across the demolished circle. Jon-Tom was still staring open-mouthed at the girl, his own failure now forgotten. "You know this young lady, spellsinger?"

"I'm afraid I do, sir. Her name is Flores Quintera."

At the mention of her name the girl spun back to face him. "I thought I recognized you." She frowned. "But I still can'* place you."

"My name is Jon Meriweather." When she didn't react to that, he added, "We attend the same school."

"I still can't place you. Have we had a class together, or something?"

"I don't think so," he told her. "I'd remember if we had. I have seen—"

"Wait a minuto . . . *now* I know!" She pointed an accusatory finger at him. "I've seen you working around campus. Sweeping the halls, working the grounds at practice."

"I do that occasionally," he replied, embarrassed. "I always managed to be out gardening whenever the cheer squad had practice." He smiled hesitantly.

Loud, high-pitched feminine laughter came from behind him. Everyone turned to see Talea sitting on the wood-chip floor, holding her sides and roaring hysterically.

"I don't know you," said Flores Quintera. "What's so funny?"

"Him!" She pointed at Jon-Tom. "He was supposed to be helping Clothahump cast for an engineer to switch places with. So he was thinking back to his home, to familiar surroundings. But he couldn't keep his mind on his business. It was drifting while he was spellsinging, from engineering to something more pleasant, I think."

"I couldn't help it," Jon-Tom mumbled. "Maybe it was something about the song. I mean, I don't remember exactly what aspects of home I was concentrating on. I was too busy singing. Maybe it was the line, 'If I had to tell her. . . .'" He was more embarrassed than he'd ever been in his life.

"So you're responsible for my being here," said the raven-haired amazon, "wherever 'here' is?"

"Sort of," he mumbled. "I've kind of admired you from afar and when I should have been thinking of something else, my thoughts sort of . . . drifted," he finished helplessly.

"Sure. That clarifies everything." She fluffed her hair, looked around at man, woman, otter, turtle, bat. "So since this guy is too tongue-tied to explain, please would one of you?''

Clothahump sighed and took her by the hand. She didn't resist as he led her to a low couch and sat her down. ''It is somewhat difficult to explain, young lady.''

''Try me. When you come from the *barrio*, nothing surprises you.''

So the wizard patiently elucidated while Jon-Tom sat off to one side morose and at the same time perversely happy. If he was going to be marooned here, as it seemed he was, there were worse people to be trapped with than the voluptuous Flores Quintera.

Eventually Clothahump concluded his explanation. His intense listener rose from the couch and walked over to confront Jon-Tom.

''Then it wasn't entirely your fault. I think I understand. *El tortuga* was very enlightening.'' She turned and waved around the chamber. ''Then what are we waiting here for? We have to help these people as best we can.''

''That is most commendable of you,'' said an admiring Clothahump. ''You are a most adaptable yound lady. It is a pity you are not the eng'neer we sought, but you are bigger and stronger than most. Can you fight?''

She grinned wickedly at him, and something went all weak inside Jon-Tom. ''I have eleven brothers and sisters, Mr. Clothahump, and I'm the second youngest. The only reason I'm on the cheerleading squad is because they don't let women play on the football team. Not at the university level, anyhow. I grew up with a switchblade in my boot.''

''I am not familiar with the weapon,'' replied a pleased Clothahump, ''but I believe we can arm you adequately.''

Talea had stifled her amusement and had walked over to gaze appraisingly up at the new arrival. ''You're the biggest woman I've ever seen.''

''I'm tall even for back home,'' said Quintera. ''It's been a drawback sometimes, except in sports.'' She smiled dazzlingly down at Talea and extended a hand. "Do you shake hands here?"

"We do." Talea reached out hesitantly.

"*Bueno.* I'd like for us to be friends."

"I think I'd like that too." The two women shook, each taking the measure of the other without conceding anything.

"It's just like I've always dreamed," Quintera murmured, eyes shining.

"You mean you're not upset?" Jon-Tom gaped at her.

"Oh, maybe a little."

Pog grumbled steadily as he began cleaning up the debris created by the explosive collapse of the interdimensional vortex.

"But I've always wanted to be the heroine in shining armor, ever since I was a little girl," Quintera continued.

"No need to worry, then," said Jon-Tom firmly. "I've learned quite a bit since I've been here. I'll make sure no harm comes to you."

"Oh, don't worry about me," she replied gaily.

Pog appeared with an armful of old weapons. "Got 'em since ya left," he told the curious Jon-Tom. "Boss thought it'd be a good idea t'have a few lizard-stickers around in case his magic really got rusty."

Flores Quintera immediately knelt over the pile of destruction and began sorting through it with something other than doll-like enthusiasm. "Hoy, but I'm looking forward to this."

"It could be very dangerous." Jon-Tom had moved to stand protectively close to her.

"Well, of course it could, from what Clothaheemp... Clothahump tells me... watch your foot there, that ax is sharp." He took a couple of steps backward. "It wouldn't be any fun if it didn't have any danger," she informed him, as though addressing a complete fool.

"Oh, this looks nice," she said brightly, hefting a saw-edged short sword. "Can I have this one?" It was designed for someone Mudge's size. In her lithe hands it looked like a long, thick dagger.

She moved as if to put it in her belt, became aware she wasn't wearing one.

"I can't go marching around in this," she muttered.

"Oh God!" Mudge threw up his paws and spun away. "Not again. Please, I can't go back to Lynchbany and go through this again."

"Never mind." Talea was studying the towering female form. "If the wizard can conjure up some material, I think the two of us can make you something, Flores."

"Call me Flor, please."

"I don't know about conjuring," said Clothahump carefully, "but there are stores in the back rooms of the Tree. Pog will show you where."

"O' course he will," snorted the bat under his breath. "Don't he always?"

The two young women vanished with the bat into yet another section of the seemingly endless interior of the tree.

"I 'ave to 'and it t' you, mate." Mudge smacked Jon-Tom's back with a friendly whack from one furry paw and leered up at him. "First you make friends with Talea and now you materialize this black-maned gable o' gorgeousness. Would that I were up t' such, wot?"

"I'd rather have switched places with an engineer," Jon-Tom mumbled.

He considered Flor Quintera. Her personality somehow did not seem to match his imagining of same. "This new lady, Flor. I've seen her a lot, Mudge, but I'd always imagined her to be somewhat more, well, vulnerable."

"'Er? Vulnerable? Kiss me bum, mate, but she seems as vulnerable as an ocelot with six arms."

"I know," said Jon-Tom sadly.

Mudge was looking at the doorway through which the women had disappeared. "'Crikey but I won't mind unvulnerablin' 'er. It'd be like climbin' a bloomin' mountain. I always did 'ave a 'ankerin' t' go explorin' through the peaks and valleys of a challengin' range, wot.'' He moved away from the distraught Jon-Tom, chuckling lasciviously.

Jon-Tom shuffled across to the workbench. Clothahump sat there, inspecting his shattered apparatus and trying to locate intact bits and pieces with which to work.

"I'm really sorry, sir," he said a little dazedly. "I tried my best."

"I know you did, boy. It is not your fault." Clothahump patted Jon-Tom's leg reassuringly. "Rare is the man, wizard, warrior, or worker, who can always think with his brains instead of his balls. Not to worry. What is done is done, and we must make the best of it. At least we have added another dedicated fighter and believer to our ranks. And we still have you and your unpredictable but undeniably powerful spellsinger's abilities, and something more."

"I don't suppose we could try again."

The wizard shook his head. "Impossible. Even if I thought I could survive and control another such conjuration, the last of the necessary powders and material have been used. It would take months simply to find enough ytterbium to constitute the necessary pinch the formula requires."

"I hope you're right about my abilities," Jon-Tom mumbled. "I don't seem to be much good at anything here lately. I hope I can think of the right song when the time comes." He frowned abruptly. "You said we have my abilities and 'something more'?''

The wizard nodded, looked pleased with himself. "Sometimes a good shock is more valuable than any amount of concentration. When I was thrown against the Tree wall by the force of the transdimension dissipation, I had a brief but ice-clear image. I now know who is behind the growing evil." He gazed meaningfully up at the staring Jon-Tom.

"Tell me, then. Who and what are—"

But the turtle raised a restraining hand. "Best to wait until everyone has returned. There is ample threat to all in this, and I shall not begin to play favorites now."

So they waited while Jon-Tom watched the wizard. Clothahump sat quietly, contemplating something beyond the ken of the others.

The women returned with Pog muttering irritably behind them. Jon-Tom was a little shocked at the transformation that had come over the delicate flower of his postadolescent fantasies.

In place of the familiar cheerleader's sweater and skirt Flor Quintera was clad in pants and vest of white leatherlike material. The sharply cut vest left her arms and shoulders bare, and her dark skin stood out startlingly against the pale cream-colored clothing. A fringed black cape hung from her neck and matched fringe-topped black boots. The long dagger (or short sword) hung from a black metal belt and a double-headed mace hung from her right hand.

"What do you think?" She twirled the mace gracefully and thus indicated to Jon-Tom why she'd selected it. It was not dissimilar to the baton she was so accustomed to. The major difference was the pair of spiked steel balls at one end, lethal rather than entertaining.

"Don't you think," he said uneasily, "it's a mite extreme?"

"Look who's talking. What's the matter, not what you'd like to see?" She turned on her toes and did a mock curtsey. "Is that more ladylike?"

"Yes. No. I mean . . ."

She turned and walked over to him, laughing, and put a comforting hand on his shoulder. It burned him right through his indigo shirt and iridescent green cape.

"Relax, Jon. Or Jon-Tom, as they call you." She smiled, and his initial irritation at her appearance melted away. "I'm still the same person. You forget that you really don't know anything about me. Oh, don't feel bad . . . few people ever really do. I'm the same person I ever was, and now I've been given the chance to enjoy one of my own fantasies. I'm sorry if I don't fulfill yours.''

''But the disorientation,'' he sputtered. ''When I first arrived here I was so confused, so puzzled I could hardly think.''

''Well,'' she said, ''I guess I've read a little more of the impossible than you, or dreamed a little deeper. I feel very much at home, *compadre mio*.'' She clipped the double mace to her link belt, pushed back her cape, and sat down on the floor. Even that simple motion seemed supernaturally graceful.

''I was explaining to Jon-Tom,'' Clothahump began, ''that the shock or the combination of the shock of the explosion and the magic we were working finally showed me the source of the evil that threatens to overwhelm this world. Perhaps yours as well, young lady,'' he said to Flor, ''if it is not stopped here.''

Talea and Mudge listened respectfully, Jon-Tom uncertainly, and Flor anxiously. Jon-Tom divided his attention between the wizard's words and the girl of his dreams.

At least, she had been the girl of his dreams. Her instant adaptation to this strange existence made her seem a different person. Moreover, she seemed to welcome their incredible situation. It left him feeling very inadequate. How many days had it taken him to arrive at a mature acceptance of his fate?

The insecurity passed, to be replaced by a burst of anger at the unfairness of it all, and finally by resignation. Actually, as Mudge had indicated, his situation could have been much worse. If Flor was (as yet, he thought yearningly) no more than a friend, she was a damnsight more interesting to have around than a fifty-year-old male engineer. And he'd made a friend of Talea as well.

Decidedly, life could be worse. There was ample time for events to progress in a pleasant and satisfying fashion. He allowed himself a slight inward smile.

After all, Flor's enthusiastic acceptance of the status quo might be momentary posturing on her part. If what Clothahump believed turned out to be true things were going to become much worse. They would all have to depend on each other. He would be around when it was Flor's turn to do some depending. He accepted her as she was and turned his full attention to Clothahump.

"It is the Plated Folk," the wizard was telling them as he paced slowly back and forth before a tall rack of containers that had not been shattered. "They are gathering in all their thousands, in their tens of thousands, for a great invasion of the warmlands. Legions of them swarm through the Greendowns.

"I saw in an instant great battle-practice fields being constructed on the plains outside Cugluch. Burrows for an endless horde are being dug in anticipation of the arrival and massing of still more troops. I saw thousands of the soulless, mindless workers putting down their work tools and taking up their arms. They are preparing such an onslaught as the warmlands have never seen. I saw—"

"I saw a double-jointed margay once, in a bar in Oglagia Towne," broke in Mudge with astonishing lack of tact. For several minutes he'd been growing more and more restless. Now his frustration burst out spontaneously. "No disrespect t' these ominous foretellin's, Your Omnipotentness, but the Plated Folk 'ave attacked our lands too many times t' count. 'Tis expected that they're t' try again, but wot's the fear of it?" Talea's expression indicated that she agreed with him. "They've always been stopped in the Troom Pass behind the Jo-Troom Gate. Always they 'ave the kind o' impressive numbers you be recitin' t' us, but their strategy sucks, and what bravery they 'ave is the bravery o' the stupid. All they ever 'ave ended up doin' is fertilizin' the plants that grow in the Pass."

"That's true enough," said Talea. "I don't see that we have anything unusual to fear, so I don't understand your worry."

The wizard stared patiently at her. "Have you ever fought

the Plated Folk? Do you know the cruelties and abominations of which they are capable?''

Talea leaned back in the chair fashioned from the horns of some unknown creature and waved the question away with one tiny hand.

"Of course I've never fought 'em. Their last attack was sixty-seven years ago."

"The forty-eighth interregnum," said Clothahump. "I remember it."

"And what were the results?" she asked pointedly.

"After considerable fighting and a great loss of life to both sides, the Plated Folk armies were driven back into the Greendowns. They have not been heard from since. Until now."

"Meaning we kicked the shit out of 'em," Mudge paraphrased with satisfaction.

"You have the usual confidence of the untested," Clothahump muttered.

"What about the previous battle, and the one before that, and the thirty-fifth interregnum, which the histories say was such a Plated fiasco, and all the battles and fighting back to the beginning of the Gate's foundations?"

"All true," Clothahump admitted. "In all that time they have not so much as topped the Gate. But I fear this time will be far different. Different from anything a warmlander can imagine."

Talea leaned forward in the chair. "Why?"

"Because a new element has been introduced into the equation, my dear ignorant youngling. A profound stress presses dangerously on the fabric of fate. The balance between the Plated Folk and the warmlander has been seriously altered. I have sensed this, have felt it, for many months now, though I could not connect my unease directly to the Plated Ones. Now I have done that, and the nature of the threat at once becomes clear and thrice magnified.

"Hence my desperate casting for one who could divine and

perhaps affect this alteration. You, Jon-Tom, and now you, my dear,'' and he nodded toward a watchful Flores Quintera.

She shook black strands from her face, clasped both arms around her knees as she stared raptly at him.

"Ahhh, I can't believe it, guv'nor," Mudge said with a disdainful sniff. "The Plated Folk 'ave never made it t' the top o' the Gate as you say. If they did, why, we'd annihilate 'em there at our leisure."

"The assurance of the young," murmured Clothahump, but he let the otter have his say.

" 'Tis only because the warmlander fighters o' the past wanted some decent competition that they sallied out from behind the Gate t' meet the Plated Folk in the Pass, or there'd o' been even more unequal combat than history tells us of. I'm surprised they keep a-tryin'."

"Oh, they will keep 'a-tryin', my fuzzy friend, until they are completely obliterated, or we are."

"And you're so sure this great unknown whateveritis that you know nothin' about 'as given those smelly monstrosities an edge they've never 'ad before?"

"I am afraid that is so," said the wizard solemnly. "Yet I am admittedly no more clear as to the nature of that fresh evil now than I was before. I know only that it exists, and that it must be prepared for if not destroyed." He shook a warning finger at Talea.

"And that, my dear, raises the other important advantage the Plated Folk have, one which must immediately be countered. We of the warmlands are divided and independent, while the Plated Folk possess a unity of purpose under their ultimate leader. They have the strength of central organization, which is not magical in nature but deadly dangerous nonetheless."

"That still hasn't kept them from a thousand years of getting the shit kicked out of their common unity," she replied, unperturbed.

"True enough, but this time . . . this time I fear a terrible disaster. A disaster made worse by the centuries of complacency you have just demonstrated, my dear. A disaster that threatens to break the boundaries of time and space and spread to all continuui.

"I fear if this threat is not contained, we face not a losing fight, my friends. We face Armaggedon."

XII

It was silent within the Tree for a while. Finally Talea asked, "What word then has come out of the Greendowns to you, honorable magician?" Clothahump's warning had quieted even her usually irrepressible bravado.

"From what I have sensed," he began solemnly, "Skrritch the Eighteenth, Supreme Ruler of Cugluch, Cokmetch, Cot-a-Kruln, and of all the far reaches and lands of the Greendowns, Commander of all Plated Folk and heir to their allegiance, has called upon that allegiance. They have been building their armies for years. That and this new evil magic they have acquired has convinced them that this time they cannot fail to conquer. That self-confidence, that terrible feeling of surety, is what came through to my mind more powerfully than anything else."

"And you learned nothing more about this new magic," said Jon-Tom.

"Only one thing, my boy. That Eejakrat, master sorcerer among the Plated Ones, is behind it. That is something we could have naturally guessed, for he has been behind most of the exceptional awfulness that rumor occasionally carries to us from out of the Greendowns.

"Do not underestimate these opponents set before us, Jon-Tom." He gestured at the indifferent Talea and Mudge. "Your friends talk like cubs, through no fault of their own." He moved closer to the two tall humans.

"Let me tell you, the Plated Folk are not like us. They would as soon cut up one of us to see what's inside as we would a tree. No, I modify that. We would have more concern and respect for the tree."

"You don't have to go into details," Jon-Tom told him. "I believe you. But what can we do from here?" He flicked casual fingers across the duar. "This magic that seems to be in my music is new to me, and I can't control it very well. I don't know what my limits may be. If you can't do anything, I don't see how an ignorant novice like myself could."

"Tut, my boy, your approach is different from mine, the magic words you employ are new and unique. You may be of some use when least you expect it. Both you and your companion," he indicated the attentive Flor, "are impressive specimens. There will be times when I may be required to impress the reluctant or the doubtful."

"We can fight, too," she said readily, eyes sparkling with uncharacteristic bloodthirstiness in that sensual but childlike face.

"Restrain yourself, my dear," the wizard advised her with a fatherly smile. "There will likely be ample opportunity for slaughter. But first . . . you are quite right, Jon-Tom, in saying that there is little we can do here. We must begin to mobilize the warmlanders, to assuage their doubts and disbelief. They must prepare for the coming attack. A letter or two will not convince. Therefore we must carry the alarm in person."

"The 'ell you say," Mudge sputtered. "I'm not trippin' off t' the ends o' the earth on some 'alf-cocked crusade."

"Nor am I." Talea rose and let her left hand drop casually to the dagger at her hip. "We've our own personal business to attend to and care for."

"Children," Clothahump half whispered. Then, more audibly, "What business might that be? The business of being chased and hunted by the police of the Twelve Morgray Counties? The business of thievery and petty con schemes? I offer you instead the chance to embark upon a far grander and nobler business. One that is vital to the future of not one but two worlds. One in which all who participate will assuredly go down in the memories of all those who sing songs, for twice ten thousand years of legend!''

"Sorry," said Talea. "Not interested."

"Nor me, guv'nor," Mudge added.

"Also," said Clothahump with a tired sigh, "I will make it worth your while."

"Cor, now that be more like it, Your Imponderableness." Mudge's attitude changed radically. "Exactly 'ow worth our whiles did you 'ave in mind?"

"Sufficiently," said the wizard. "You have my word on it."

"Now I don't know as that's exactly..." Mudge's sentence floundered like a shark in a salt lake as he detected something new and dangerous and very unsenile in the wizard's expression. "Wot I mean to say, sor, is that naturally that's good enough for us. The word o' a great sorcerer like yourself, I mean." He looked anxiously at Talea. "Ain't it, luv?"

"I suppose so," she said carefully. "But why us? If you're going to need an honor guard, or body guard, or whatever, why not seek out some more amenable to your crazy notions?"

Clothahump replied instantly. "Because you two are already here, have already been exposed to my crazy notions, are familiar with the histories of these two," and he indicated Flor and Jon-Tom, "and because I have no more time to waste with others, if we are to make haste toward distant Polastrindu."

"Now, guv'nor," said Mudge reluctantly, "I've agreed I 'ave, and I'll stick by *me* word, but Polastrindu? You want that we should go...do you know 'ow far, meaning no disrespect, that be, sor?"

"Quite precisely, my good otter."

"It'd take months!" shouted an exasperated Talea.

"Yes it would...if we were to travel overland. But I am

not so foolish or so young as to consider such a cross-country hike. We must make speed, for while I know what is going to happen I do not know when; consequently I am ignorant of how much time we may have left to prepare. In such circumstances it is best to be stingy with what we may not possess.

"We shall not trudge overland but instead will make our way up the River Tailaroam."

"*Up* the river?" said Talea, eyebrows raised.

"There are ways of traveling against the current."

"To a certain point, Your Wonderness." Mudge looked skeptical. "But what 'appens when we reach the rapids o' Duggakurra? And I've 'eard many a tale o' the dangers the deep parts o' the river possess."

"All obstacles can be surmounted." Clothahump spoke with confidence if not assurance. "They matter not. Obstacle or no, we must hurry on."

"I think I'd rather go by land after all," said Talea.

"I am sorry, my dear. Tailaroam's secrets might be better concealed, but it will be the cleaner and faster route."

"Easy for you to say," she grumbled. "You'd be right at home in the water if we had any trouble."

"I have not spent more than occasional recreational time in the water for some years, my dear. While I may be physiologically adapted to an aquatic life, my preferences are for breathing and living in air. As just one example, scrolls do not hold up well at all beneath the water.

"Furthermore, we have now an excellent means for making our way to the river."

"The L'borean riding snake." Talea nodded thoughtfully. "Why not take it all the way to Polastrindu?"

"Because the river will be as steady and much faster. Perhaps our young friend Jon-Tom can conjure up an equally efficient form of water travel."

"Conjure up?" The query came from Flores Quintera, and she looked sideways at Jon-Tom. "You mean, like magic?"

"Yes, like magic." He endeavored to stand a little straighter as he held out the duar. "Clothahump was casting about for an otherworldly magician to assist him with his troubles and he got me. It turns out that my singing, coupled with my playing of this instrument, coupled with *something*—I don't know what—gives me the ability to work magic here."

"That's very impressive," she said in a voice that lit a fire high above his boots.

"Yes, it would be, except that it's kind of a shotgun effect. I fire off a song and never manage to hit exactly what I'm aiming at. I was trying for an old Dodge Charger and instead materialized the grandfather of all pythons. It turned out to be tamed to riding, though." He smiled at her. "No need to worry about it."

"I'm not worried," she replied excitedly. "I love snakes. Where is it? It's really big enough to ride?" She was heading for the door at a respectable jog.

Mudge was whispering to him. "Now you'll 'ave to do better than that, mate. That's no ordinary maiden you've brought t' yourself. Now if I were you . . ."

But Jon-Tom didn't hear the rest because he was hurrying after her. Clothahump watched them, frowning.

"I must make ready. Pog!" the wizard yelled.

"Here, Master." The bat moved tiredly to hover over the workbench, knowing what would be expected of him. Together they began assembling several large piles of potions and powders: a traveling sorcerer's work kit.

"Now 'ow did we get ourselves roped into this, luv?"

Talea looked across at the otter. "Don't trouble your furry noggin about it. We're committed. You agreed yourself."

"Yes, yes," he said softly, looking back to see if Clothahump was paying them any attention. He was not. "But it were only to keep the old bugger-nut from puttin' a spell on me. Then I'd never 'ave a chance to slip away when the proper time comes."

"It's better that we go," she told him. "I've been thinking, Mudge. If a wizard as great as Clothahump says that the danger is so great, then we must help fight it if we can.''

"I don't think you follow me thoughts, luv. This wizard Clothahump, 'e's a brilliant one, all right. But 'e 'as lapses, if you know wot I mean.'' He tapped his head with one furry fist.

"You're saying he's senile.''

"Not all the time, no. But 'e *is* two 'undred and ought odd years old. Even for a wizard o' the hard-shell, that's gettin' on a bit, wot? I'm a thinkin' 'e's overexaggeratin' this 'ere Plated danger.''

"Sorry, Mudge, I don't agree with you. I've seen and heard enough to convince me he's more sane than senile. Besides,'' she added with a disdainful air, "he was right in that we have no immediate prospects. In fact, it would do us good to get out of this area for a while. He'll pay us to do that. So we're doing right if he's mad and right if he's not.''

Mudge looked resigned. "Maybe so, luv. Maybe so. Though I wish 'e'd been a bit more specific in spellin' out just wot 'e meant by 'worth our while.' ''

"What do you mean?''

"Sorcerers 'ave the use o' words that you and I ain't privy to, luv. So it stands t' reason they could be more subtle when it comes t' the employin' o' more familiar ones.''

"Mudge! Are you saying he lied to us?''

"No. 'E couldn't do that, not and keep 'is wizardly powers. But there be direct truth and then there be spiral truth, as me sainted mother used t' tell me.''

"You had a mother?''

He took a playful swipe at her with a paw and she stepped lithely out of reach. "I always did think a lot o' you, luv. If you only 'ad a bit more body fur, at least on your chest, say.''

"No thanks.'' She edged toward the door. "We'd better go see how the others are making out.''

They started down the hallway. "I'm not worried much about the giantess,'' Mudge was saying, "but our friend

Jon-Tom still displays pangs o' loneliness. I worry that the appearance o' the girl from 'is 'ome may do him more 'arm than good, seein' as how besotted 'e is on her."

"Besotted?" Talea studied the walls. "You think so?"

They had almost reached the doorway. "'Tis in the lad's voice, in 'is manner and look. I've dodged traps that were better 'idden. But I don't think 'e'll 'ave much luck with this one. She's cheery enough, but I 'ave a 'unch 'er true love's reserved for 'er new sword. She strikes me a proper mate for a wolverine, not our Jon-Tom."

"I don't think he's besotted," Talea murmured. "A boyish attraction, certainly."

"And that be somethin' else. 'E may act boyish, but in a fight 'e's all right. Remember 'is magic, and they also say that those who can draw the gneechees in the numbers 'e can may 'ave greater powers locked within 'em than even they can imagine."

"He's already admitted he doesn't know much about his own magical capabilities," she replied. "I don't think they're so much greater than what we've seen."

"We're likely to find out on this bug-brained journey."

The riding snake would have carried the extra load with ease, but they had only four saddles. They were fashioned of the finest hides and specially worked in far-off Malderpot by the warmland's most skilled leatherworkers.

"Two of us will have to double up," said Clothahump, voicing the obvious as the last of their baggage was secured to the snake's lengthy back. "At least Pog does not present a problem."

"Thank the Design!" agreed the bat, fluttering overhead and adjusting his body and back pouches. "It going to be hard enough ta slow down ta keep up wid ya."

"Jon-Tom and Flor must have saddles to themselves," the wizard pointed out, "they being simultaneously the largest and least experienced of us. Perhaps the two of you . . . ?" He gestured at Talea and Mudge.

"Oh no." She shook her head negatively. "I'm not riding with *him*." Mudge looked hurt.

"In that case," Clothahump bowed as best he could, considering his short legs and weighty front, "you may join me."

"Fine."

"Cor, now, Talea me luv. . . ."

"Get to your own saddle, you mange-mouthed mucker. D'you honestly think I'd let you sit that close to me?"

"Talea sweets, you 'ave poor Mudge all wrong."

"Sure I do." She mounted the lead saddle, spoke down to Clothahump. "You can ride behind me. I trust your hands, and we've a shell between us."

"I can assure you, my dear," said the wizard, sounding slightly offended, "that I have no intentions in the slightest of . . ."

"Yeah, that's what they all say." She slipped both boots into her stirrups. "But come on and get aboard."

Clothahump struggled with the high seat, puffing alarmingly. His short legs and great weight rendered mounting all but impossible. Jon-Tom moved forward and got his arms and shoulders beneath the considerable bulk. It was against Clothahump's principles (not to mention his ego) to use magic to lift himself into the saddle. With Jon-Tom pushing and Talea pulling he managed to make it with a minimum of lost pride.

When they were all seated Talea tugged lightly back on the reins. Having slept all night and morning as was the habit of its kind, the snake came awake slowly. She let the reins hang loose and the snake started to move forward.

A laugh of surprise and delight came from the third saddle, where Flores Quintera sat. She was clearly enjoying the new sensation provided by an extraordinary means of locomotion. Looking back over her shoulder, she flashed a dazzling smile at Jon-Tom.

"What a wonderful way to travel! *Que magnifico!* You can

see everything without having your behind battered." She faced forward again and placed both hands on the pommel of the saddle.

"Giddy up!" Her heels kicked girlishly at the scaly sides. The snake did not notice the minuscule tapping on its flanks, but paid attention only to the steering tugs at its sensitive ears.

"Any particular route you'd like me to follow?" Talea inquired of her fellow saddle-mate.

"The shortest one to the Tailaroam," replied Clothahump. "There we will hire passage."

"What about building our own raft?"

"Impossible. Tacking upstream against the current would be difficult. At the Duggakurra rapids it would become impossible. We must engage professionals with the know-how and muscle to fight such obstacles. I think we should turn slightly to the left here, my dear."

Talea pulled gently on the reins, and the snake obediently altered its slither. "That'll take us a day longer, if I remember the land right. It's been a long time since I've been as far south as the river. Too many nasty types hole out there."

"I agree it may take us a little longer to reach our goal this way, but by doing so we will pass a certain glade. It is ringed with very old oaks and is a place of ancient power. I am going to risk a dangerous conjuration there. It is the best place for it, and will be our last chance to learn the nature of the special corruption the warmlands will have to face.

"To do this involves stretching my meager powers to the utmost, so I will require all the magical support the web of Earthforce can supply me. The web is anchored at Yul, at Koal-zin-a-Mec, at Rinamundoh, and at the Glade of Triane."

"I've never heard of the others."

"They lie far around the world and meet at the center of the earth. The affairs of all sentient beings are interwoven in the web, each individual's destiny tied to its own designated strand. I will stand on one of the four anchors of fate and make the call that I must."

"Call? Who are you going to call?"

But Clothahump's thoughts seemed to have shifted. "The glade is close enough to the river so that we may leave our riding snake before we reach it and walk the rest of the way."

"Why not ride the snake all the way to the river?"

"You do not understand." She could feel his eyes on the back of her neck. "You will not, until you see the result of what I am to attempt. Such as this," and he tapped the riding snake's back with a foot, "is but a dumb creature whose life might not survive even a near confrontation of the sort I have in mind. It is as strong as it is stupid, and in a panic could be the undoing of all of us. So we must leave it a day behind when we give it its freedom."

She shrugged. "Whatever you say. But my feet will argue with you." She urged the snake to a faster pace.

Several days of pleasant travel passed as they journeyed southward. No predator came near the massive snake, and at night they didn't even bother to set a watch.

Flores Quintera was a pleasant companion, but what troubled Jon-Tom was not her dissuasion of his hesitant attempts at intimacy so much as that the excitement of the trip seemed to make her oblivious to anything else.

"It's everything I ever dreamed of when I was a little girl." She spoke to him as they sat around the small cookfire. The flames danced in her night-eyes, prompting thoughts of obsidian spewing from the hearts of volcanoes.

"When I was little I wished I was a boy, Jon-Tom," she told him fervently. "I wanted to be an astronaut, to fly over the poles with Byrd, to sail the unexplored South Pacific with Captain Cook. I wanted to be with the English at Agincourt and with Pizzaro in Peru. Failing a change of gender, I imagined myself Amelia Earhart or Joan of Arc."

"You can't change your sex," he told her sympathetically, "and you can't go back in time, but you could have tried for the astronaut training."

She shook her head sadly. "It's not enough to have the ambition, Jon-Tom. You have to have the wherewithal. *Los cerebros.* I've got the guts but not the other.'' She looked up at him and smiled crookedly. "Then there is the other thing, the unfortunate drawback, the crippling deformity that I've had to suffer with all my life.''

He stared at her in genuine puzzlement, unable to see the slightest hint of imperfection.

"I don't follow you, Flor. You look great to me.''

"That's the deformity, Jon-Tom. My lack of one. I'm cursed with beauty. Don't misunderstand me now,'' she added quickly. "I'm not being facetious or boastful. It's something I've just had to try and live with.''

"We all have our handicaps,'' he said, not very sympathetically.

She rose, paced catlike behind the fire. Talea was stirring the other one nearby. Mudge was humming some ribald ditty about the mouse from Cantatrouse who ran around on her spouse, much to the gruff amusement of Pog. Clothahump was a silent, brooding lump somewhere off in the darkness.

"You don't understand, do you? How could you imagine what's it like to be a beautiful animal? Because that's how the world sees me, you know. I did the cheerleader thing because I was asked to.'' She paused, stared across the flames at him. "Do you know what my major is?''

"Theater Arts, right?''

"Acting.'' She nodded ruefully. "That's what everyone expected of me. Well it's easy for me, and it lets me concentrate on the harder work involved in my minor. I didn't have the math for astrophysics or tensor analysis or any of that, so I'm doing business administration. Between that and the theater arts I'm hoping I can get in on the public relations end of the space program. That's the only way I ever thought I'd have a chance of getting close to the frontiers. Even so, no one takes me seriously.''

"I take you seriously,'' he murmured.

She stared at him sharply. "*Do* you? I've heard that before. Can you really see beyond my face and body?''

"Sure." He hoped he sounded sincere. "I don't pretend that I can ignore them."

"Nobody can. Nobody!" She threw up her hands in despair. "Professors, fellow students: it's hell just trying to get through an ordinary class without having to offend someone by turning down their incessant requests for a date. And it's next to impossible to get any kind of a serious answer out of a professor when he's staring at your *tetas* instead of concentrating on your question. You can call it beauty. I call it my special deformity."

"Are you saying you'd rather have been born a hunchback? Maybe with no hair and one eye set higher than the other?"

"No." Some of the anger left her. "No, of course not. I just could have done with a little less of everything physical, I suppose."

"*Asi es la vida*," he said quietly.

"*Si, es verdad*." She sat down on the grass again, crossing her legs. "There's nothing I can do about it. But here"—and she gestured at the dark forest and the huge serpentine shape coiled nearby—"here things are different. Here my height and size are helpful and people, furry or human, seem to accept me as a person instead of a sex object."

"Don't rely on that," he warned her. "For example our otter friend Mudge seems to have no compunctions whatsoever about crossing interspecies lines. Nor do very many others, from what I've seen."

"Well, so far they've accepted me as a warrior more than a toy. If that's due to my size more than my personality, at least it's a start." She lay down and stretched langorously. The fire seemed to spread from the burning embers to Jon-Tom's loins.

"Here I have a chance to be more than what heredity seemed to have locked me into. And it's like my childhood dreams of adventure."

"People get killed here," he warned her. "This is no fairyland. You make a mistake, you die."

She rolled over. It was a warm winter night and her cape was blanket enough. "I'll take my chances. It can't be any worse than the *barrio*. Good night, Jon-Tom. Remember, when in Rome . . ."

He kicked dirt over the fire until it subsided and wished he were in Rome, or any other familiar place. All he said was, "Good night, Flor. Pleasant dreams." Then he rolled over and sought sleep. The night was pleasant, but his thoughts were troubled.

The following day found them climbing and descending much hillier terrain. Trees were still plentiful, but on the higher knolls they tended to be smaller and with more land between. Occasionally bare granite showed where the ground cover had thinned, though they were still traveling through forest.

And the gneechees were back. Even when Jon-Tom was not strumming his duar, swarms of almost-theres were clustering thickly around the little party of travelers.

He explained to Flor about gneechees. She was delighted at the concept and spent hours trying to catch one with her eyes. Talea mumbled worriedly about their inexplicable presence. Clothahump would have none of it.

"There is no room in magic for superstition, young lady," the turtle admonished her. "If you would learn more about the world you must disabuse yourself of such primitive notions."

"I've seen primitive notions kill a lot of people," she shot back knowingly. "I don't mean to question you, but I bet you'd be the last person to say that we know everything there is to know."

"That is so, child," agreed the wizard. "If the latter were true we would not be making our way to this glade." He snapped irritably at Pog. The bat was diving and swooping above their heads.

"You know you'll never catch one, Pog. You can't even see one."

"Yeah. Dey don't even react to my headseek either." He snapped at empty air where something might have been.

"Then why do you persist?"

"Gives me somethin' ta do, as opposed ta idly dancin' in da air currents. But dat's a thrill you'll never know, ain't it?"

"Do not be impertinent, Pog." The wizard directed Talea to stop. He dismounted, looked around. "We walk from now on."

Packages and supplies were doled out, stuffed into backpacks. Then they started uphill. The rise they were ascending was slight but unvarying. It grew dark, and for a while they matched strides with the mounting moon. Clouds masked its mournful silver face.

"We are close, close," Clothahump informed them much later. The moon was around toward the west now. "I have sensed things."

"Yeah, I just bet ya have, boss," the bat muttered under his breath. He snapped hungrily at a passing glass moth.

If the wizard had heard, he gave no sign. In fact, he spent the next two hours in complete silence, staring straight ahead. No conversational gambit could provoke a response from him.

A subtle tingling like the purr of a kitten began to tickle Jon-Tom's spine. Tall trees closed tight around them once again, ranks of dark green spears holding off the threatening heavens. Stars peeked through the clouds, looking dangerously near.

A glance showed Talea looking around nervously. She reacted to his gaze, nodded. "I feel it also, Jon-Tom. Clothahump was right. This is an ancient part of the world we are coming to. It stinks of power."

Clothahump moved nearer to Jon-Tom. Clouds of gneechees now dogged the climbers. "Can you feel it, my boy? Does it not tease your wizardly senses?"

Jon-Tom looked around uneasily, aware that something was playing his nerves as he would play the strings of the duar. "I feel something, sir. But whether it's magical influences or just back trouble I couldn't say.''

Clothahump looked disappointed. Somewhere an anxious night hunter was whistling to its mate. There were rustlings in the brush, and Jon-Tom noted that the hidden things were moving in the same direction: back the way the climbers had come.

"You are not fully attuned to the forces, I expect," said the wizard, unnaturally subdued, "so I suppose I should not expect more of you." He looked ahead and then gestured pridefully.

"We have arrived. One corner of the subatomic forces that bind the matter of all creatures of all the world lies here. Look and remember, Jon-Tom. The glade of Triane."

XIII

They had crested the last rise. Ahead lay an open meadow that at first glance was not particularly remarkable. But it seemed that the massive oaks and sycamores that ringed it like the white hair of an old man's balding skull drew back from that open place, shunning the grass and curves of naked stone that occasionally thrust toward the sky.

Here the moonlight fell unobstructed upon delicate blue blades. A few darker boulders poked mushroomlike heads above the uneven lawn.

"Stop here," the wizard ordered them.

They gratefully slid free of packs and weapons, piled them behind a towering tree that spread protective branches overhead.

"We have one chance to learn the nature of the great new evil the Plated Folk have acquired. I cannot penetrate all the way to Cugluch with any perceptive power. No magic I know of can do that.

"But there is another way. Uncertain, dangerous, but worthy of an attempt to utilize, I think. If naught else it could give us absolute confirmation of the Plated Folk's intentions, and we may learn something of their time schedule. That could be equally as valuable.

"You cannot help me. No matter what happens here, no matter what may happen to me, you must not go beyond this point." No one said anything. He turned, looked up into the tree. "I need you now, Pog."

"Yes, Master." The bat sounded subdued and quite unlike his usual argumentative self. He dropped free, hovered expectantly above the wizard's head as the two conversed.

"What's he going to try?" Talea wondered aloud. Her red hair turned to cinnabar in the moonlight.

"I don't know." Jon-Tom watched in fascination as Clothahump readied himself. Flor had the collar of her cape pulled tight up around her neck. Mudge's ears were cocked forward intently, one paw holding him up against the tree trunk.

From beneath the leaf-shadowed safety of the ancient oak they watched as the wizard carefully marked out a huge ellipse in the open glade. The fluorescent white powder he was using seemed to glow with a life of its own.

Employing the last of the powder, he drew a stylized sun at either end of the ellipse. Red powder was then used to make cryptic markings on the grass. These connected the two suns and formed a crude larger ellipse outside the first.

"If I didn't know better," Flor whispered to Jon-Tom, "I'd think he was laying out some complex higher equations."

"He is," Jon-Tom told her. "Magic equations." She started to object and he hushed her. "I'll explain later."

Now Clothahump and Pog were creating strange, disturbing shapes in the center of the first ellipse. The shapes were not pleasant to look upon, and they appeared to move across the grass and stone of their own volition. But the double ellipse held them in. From time to time the wizard would pause and use a small telescope to study the cloudy night sky.

It had been a windless night. Now a breeze sprang up and pushed at the huddling little knot of onlookers. It came from in front of them and mussed Jon-Tom's hair, ruffled the otter's fur. Despite the warmth of the night the breeze was cold, as though it came from deep space itself. Branches and leaves and needles blew outward, no matter where their parent trees were situated. The breeze was not coming from the east, as Jon-Tom had first thought, but from the center of the glade. It emerged from the twin ellipses and blew outward in all directions as if the wind itself were trying to escape. Normal meteorological conditions no longer existed within the glade.

Clothahump had taken a stance in the center of the near sun drawing. They could hear his voice for the first time, raised in chant and invocation. His short arms were above his head, and his fingers made mute magic-talk with the sky.

The wind strengthened with a panicky rush, and the woods were full of zephyr-gossip. These moans and warnings swirled in confusion around the watchers, who drew nearer one another without comment.

A black shape rejoined them, fighting the growing gale. Pog's eyes were as wide as his wing beats were strained.

"You're all ta stay right where ya are," he told them, raising his voice to be heard over the frightened wind. "Da Master orders it. He works his most dangerous magic." Selecting a long hanging limb, the famulus attached himself to it and tucked his wings cloaklike around his body.

"What is he going to do?" Talea asked. "How can he penetrate all the way to Cugluch through the walls of sorcery this Eejakrat must guard himself with?"

"Da Master makes magic," was all the shivering assistant would say. A wing tip pointed fretfully toward the open glade.

The wind continued to increase. Flor drew her cape tight around her bare shoulders while Mudge fought to retain possession of his feathered cap. Large branches bent outward, and occasional snapping sounds rose above the gale to hint at limbs bent beyond their strength to resist. Huge oaks groaned in protest all the way down to their roots.

"But what is he trying to *do*?" Talea persisted, huddling in the windbreak provided by the massive oak.

"He summons M'nemaxa," the terrified apprentice told her, "and I don't intend ta look upon it." He drew his wings still closer about him until his face as well as his body was concealed by the leathery cocoon.

"M'nemaxa's a legend. It don't exist," Mudge protested.

"He does, he does!" came the whimper from behind the wings. "He exist and da Master summon him, oh, he call to him even now. I will not look on it."

Jon-Tom put his lips close to Talea in order to be heard over the wind. "Who or what's this 'Oom-ne-maxa'?"

"Part of a legend, part of the legends of the old world." She leaned hard against the bark. "According to legend it's the immortal spirit of all combined in a single creature, a creature that can appear in any guise it chooses. Some tales say he/she may actually have once existed in real form. Other stories insist that the spirit is kept alive from moment to moment only by the belief all wizards and sorceresses and witches have in it.

"To touch it is said to be death, to look upon it without wizardly protection is said to invite a death slower and more painful. The first death is from burning, the second from a rotting away of the flesh and organs."

"We'll be safe, we'll be safe," insisted Pog hopefully. "If da Master says so, we'll be safe." Jon-Tom had never seen the bellicose mammal so cowed.

"But I still won't look on it," Pog continued. "Master says da formulae and time-space ellipsoids will hold him. If not . . . if dey fail and it is freed, Master says we should run or fly and we will be safe. We are not worthy of its notice, Master say, and it not likely to pursue."

A delicate gray phosphorescence had begun to creep like St. Elmo's fire up the trunks and branches of the trees ringing the glade. Argent silhouettes now glowed eerily against the black night. The glade had become a green bowl etched with silver filigree. Earth shivered beneath it.

"Can this thing tell Clothahump what he wants to know?" Jon-Tom was less skeptical of the wizard's abilities than was Pog.

"It know all Time and Space," replied the bat. "It can see what da Master wants to know, but dat don't mean it gonna tell him."

There was a hushed, awed murmur of surprise from the otter. "Cor! Would you 'ave a look at that."

"I won't, I won't!" mewed Pog, shaking behind his wings.

Clothahump still stood erect within his sun symbol. As he turned a slow circle, arms still upraised, he was reciting a litany counterpointed by the chorus of the ground. Earth answered his words though he talked to the stars.

Dark, boiling storm clouds, thick black mountains, had assembled over the glade with unnatural haste. They danced above the wind-bent trees and blotted out the friendly face of the moon. From time to time electric lava jumped from one to another as they talked the lightning-talk.

Winds born of hurricane and confusion now assaulted the ancient trees. Jon-Tom lay on the ground and clung to the arched root of the sage-oak. So did Talea and Mudge, while Pog swayed like a large black leaf above them. Flor nestled close to Jon-Tom, though neither's attention was on the other. Branches and leaves shot past them, fleeing from the glade.

None of the swirling debris struck the chanting wizard. The winds roared down into the double ellipse, then outward, but avoided the sun symbol. Above the center of the glade the billowing storm clouds jigged round and round each other in a majestic whirlpool of energy and moisture.

Lightning leapt earthward to blister the ground. No bolt struck near Clothahump, though two trees were shattered to splinters not far away.

Somehow, above the scream of wind, of too close thunder and the howling vortex that now dominated the center of the glade, they could still hear the steady voice of Clothahump. Trying to shield his eyes from flying dirt and debris, Jon-Tom clung tightly to the tree root and squinted at the turtle.

The wizard was turning easily within his proscribed symbol. He appeared completely unaffected by the violent storm raging all around him. The sun symbol was beginning to glow a deep orange.

Clothahump halted. His hands slowly lowered until they were pointing toward the small heap of powders in the center of the inner ellipse. He recited, slowly and with great care, a dozen words known only to a very few magicians and perhaps one or two physicists.

The ancient oak shuddered. Two smaller trees nearby were torn free of the earth and hurled into the sky. There was a mighty, rumbling crescendo of sound that culminated in a volcanic rumble from the glade, and a brief flash of light that fortunately no one looked at directly.

The shape that appeared out of that flash within the inner ellipse took away what little breath remained to Jon-Tom and his companions. He could not have moved his knuckles to his mouth to chew on them, nor could his vocal cords give form to the feelings surging through him.

Soft, eerie moans came from Flor and a slight, labored whistling from Mudge. All were motionless, paralyzed by the sight of M'nemaxa, whose countenance transfigures continents and whose hoofbeats can alter the orbits of worlds.

Within the inner ellipse was a ferociously burning shape. The form M'nemaxa had chosen to appear in was akin to all the horses that had ever been, and yet was not. He showed himself this time as a stallion with great wings that beat at the air more than sixty feet from tip to body. Even so the spirit shape could not be more than partially solid. It was formed of small solar prominences bound together in the form of a horse. Red-orange flames trailed from tail and mane, galloping hooves and majestic wings, to trail behind the form and flicker out in the night.

Actually the constantly shed shards of sunmeat vanished when they reached the limits imposed by the double ellipse, disappeared harmlessly into a thermonuclear void only Clothahump could understand. Though wings tore at the fabric of space and flaming hooves galloped over the plane of existence, the spirit stallion remained fixed with the boundaries of sorceral art.

There was no hint of fading. For every flaming streamer that fell and curled from the equine inferno, new fire appeared to keep the shape familiar and intact, as M'nemaxa continuously renewed his substance. A pair of fiery tusks descended from the upper jaw of the not quite perfect horse shape, and pointed teeth burned within jaws of flame.

Among all that immense length of horsehell, a living stallion sun whose breath would have incinerated Apollo, there were only two things not composed of the ever regenerating eternal fire—eyes as chillingly cold as the rest was unimaginably hot.

The eyes of the stallion-spirit M'nemaxa were dragonfly eyes, great black curving orbs that almost met atop the skull. They were far too large for a normal horse shape, but that was only natural. Through the still angry cyclone, Jon-Tom thought he could see within those all-seeing spheres of black tiny points of light; purple and red, green, blue, and purest white that stood out even against the perpetual fusion that constituted the body shape.

Though he could not know it, those eyes were fragments of the Final Universe, the greater one which holds within it our own universe as well as thousands of others. Galaxies drifted within the eyes of M'nemaxa.

Now a long snake tongue flicked out, a flare from the surface of a living horse star. It tasted of dimensions no puny creature of flesh could ever hope to sample. It arched back its massive flaming head and whinnied. It stunned the ears and minds of the tiny organic listeners. The earth itself trembled, and behind the clouds the moon drew another thousand miles away in its orbit. Rarely was so immense an eminence brought within touch of a mere single world.

"ONE WHO KNOWS THE WORDS HAS SUMMONED!" came the thunder. Great red-orange skull and galactic eyes looked down upon the squat shape of an old turtle.

But the wizard did not bend or hide his head. He remained safe within his sun symbol. His shells did not melt and crack, his flesh did not sear, and he looked upon the horse-star without fear. It dug at existence and its hooves burned time, but it moved no nearer.

"I would know the new magic that gives so much confidence to the Plated Folk of the Greendowns as they ready their next war against my peoples!" Clothahump's most sonorous sorceral tone sounded tinny beside the world-shaking whisper of the horse.

"THAT IS OF NO CONSEQUENCE TO ME."

"I know," said Clothahump with unbelievable brashness, "but it is of consequence to me. You have been summoned to answer, not to question."

"WHO DARES . . . !" Then the anger of the stallion spirit faded slightly. "YOU HAVE SPOKEN THE WORDS, MASTER OF A HUMBLE KNOWLEDGE. YOU HAVE DONE THE CALLING, AND I MUST REPLY." The spirit seemed almost to smile. "BEWARE, LEADER OF AN IGNORANT SLIME, FOR THOUGH THEY KNOW IT NOT THEMSELVES, I FORSEE THEM DESTROYING YOU WITH MIRRORS OF WHAT IS IN YOUR OWN TINY MIND."

"I don't understand," said Clothahump with a frown.

Again the whinny that frightened planets. "AND WHY SHOULD YOU, FOR YOU HAVE NOTHING TO UNDERSTAND WITH. THE DANGER TO YOU IS NOTHING TO ME, AND YOU CANNOT IMAGINE IT."

"When will this take place?"

"THEY ARE UNCERTAIN, AS I MUST BE UNCERTAIN, AS IS EVER THE FUTURE UNCERTAIN. LET ME GO NOW."

Suddenly the flaming hooves were another ten feet above the surface. Yet it was not M'nemaxa who had moved, but the earth, which had pulled away in fear at the spirit's rising fury.

"Stay!" Clothahump threw up his hands. "I am not finished."

"THEN BE QUICK, LITTLE CREATURE, OR, WORDS OR NOT, I WILL MAKE OF THIS WORLD WHITE ASHES."

"I still do not understand the Plated Folk's new magic. If

you cannot describe it to me any better, at least tell me how to counter it. Then I will let you go."

"I WILL GO ANYWAY, FOR WORDS CAN HOLD ME BUT SO LONG AND NO LONGER. I CAN TELL YOU NO MORE. I CHOSE NOT TO ARBITRATE THE FATE OF THIS WORLD, FOR I HAVE MY OWN JOURNEY TO MAKE AND YOU CANNOT STOP ME." There was a vast, roaring chuckle. "IF YOU WOULD KNOW MORE, ASK YOUR ENEMY YOURSELF!"

A violent concussion shook Jon-Tom loose from the tree root. Bark came away in his bloody fingertips. But he was blown only a few feet downslope when the wind began to fade from hurricane to mere gale force.

The thermonuclear stallion spirit vanished in an expanding ellipse of brilliant light. As the light faded, it left behind a three-dimensional residue. He saw a wavy image of some huge, sinister chamber. It was decorated with red gems, blue metal . . . and white bone.

Within the bower stood an insect shape ten feet tall. Chains of jewels and cloth and small skulls of horribly familiar design draped the chitin. The nightmare stood next to a throne with a high curving back decorated with larger jewels and skulls. Some of the skulls still had flesh on them.

It was talking to someone out of their view. Then something made it turn, and it saw them. A high, vibrating shriek filled the glade, and made Jon-Tom shiver. No dentist's drill could have made a more excruciating sound.

A far smaller flash, an echo of M'nemaxa's blinding passing, obliterated the awful sight.

And then there was no longer anything within the glade save one very tired wizard, wind, and grass.

The gale had become a breeze. As if confused by its presence, the wind-cloud vortex that had hung above the glade simply dispersed. Silver phosphorescence shimmied down trunks and branches to run like water back into the soil.

A light rain began to fall. Hesitantly, the moon peeked

through the intermittent clouds, filling the glade with healthy light.

By the time the panting Jon-Tom and the others had reached the center of the glade the ellipses and suns and arcane symbols and formulae no longer glowed against the ground. Though he sought Clothahump, Jon-Tom's mind still saw the face of the towering praying mantis, heard once more the grating scream that had issued from it just before it vanished.

Pog was hovering nervously above them. The rain was steadily washing the powders and rare essences back into the soil from which they'd been extracted. This corner of the web of the world had held.

They found Clothahump sitting on the grass, his glasses askew on his horned beak.

"Are you all right, sir?" Jon-Tom spoke with a mixture of anxiety and respect.

"Who, me? Yes, my boy, I believe I am."

"You ought not to have tried it, good wizard." Talea studied the empty ellipse warily. "There are extremes of magic which should not be touched."

He shook a finger at her. "Don't try to tell me my business, young lady. Pog, give me a wing up." The bat dipped lower, helped the wizard to his feet.

"I have learned part of what I wished to know, my friends. Though I must confess I did not expect the spirit M'nemaxa to speak in riddles."

"Actually, I don't see that we've learned that much," said Flor.

"We have something to work with, my dear, even if it is only couched as a riddle or metaphor. That is a great deal more than we had before." He sounded pleased. "And if naught else, we have given a scare to the Empress Skrritch that may make her hesitate or delay her attack, for she it was whom we saw in that final moment.

"We can continue our journey, secure now in the knowledge that this will be a full-scale war led by the Empress of all the Plated Folk herself. That should win over some of muddleheads in Polastrindu!''

"I hope we don't have to go through this many more times,'' Flor muttered. "Santa Cecilia may not have many more blessings left for me.''

"Not to worry, child,'' he assured her. "I will not attempt it again. Such a conjuration cannot be made more than once in a lifetime, and tonight I have used mine. I employed incantations I will never employ again, spoke words I may not safely speak henceforth.

"From now on, each day on earth will be one twenty-two thousandth of a day shorter than previously, for in order to draw the immortal from the far depths of his journey I had to utilize the soul-strength of the earth itself.''

Jon-Tom walked out into the inner ellipse. Every blade of grass within the marked shape had been vaporized. So had the soil. All that remained was a perfect ellipsoidal shape of melted stone. The white granite had been twisted like taffy.

"You spoke of its journey, sir, and so did it. I . . . I heard it.''

"Did you see how furiously it soared, how steadily it galloped, though it did not move beyond my confinement?'' Jon-Tom nodded.

"It was at once here with us and holding its place in its journey.'' He checked to make certain his plastron compartments were still tightly closed. "If the legends of wizards and the admonitions of necromants are correct, the spirit M'nemaxa has traveled approximately a thirtieth of its journey. The journey began at the beginning of the first life, life which in making its journey M'nemaxa strews across the worlds behind it.

"It is galloping around the circumference of the Universe. It is said that when it meets itself coming it will annihilate purpose. Then it can finally rest. 'Tis no surprise it was irritated at our interruption. With a journey of several trillion years still to make, even a little pause is unwelcome.

"Yet despite all that, the formulae worked. The ellipse held." He glowed a little bit himself, with pride. "It was contained, and It answered when It was called." He blinked and slowly sat down on the grass again. "I'm a little tired, all of a sudden."

"I think we're all a little tired," said Jon-Tom knowingly.

"Aye, I'll not argue that, mate." The afterimage of the enormous winged flame-horse still lingered on the otter's outraged retinas. "I think we could all do with a bit 'o sleep 'ere."

Everyone agreed. After a brief mutual examination to insure that no injuries had been sustained, they began to make camp. Sleep finally came to all, but fiery images alternated with visions of a tall green-black horror to provoke less than benign dreams.

Far above and away a distant pinprick of light flared briefly across the cosmos. The tiny burst faded quickly. It came from the vicinity of NGC 187, where M'nemaxa angrily kicked aside a star or two as he raced back to where he'd left off his eternal race around the infinite bowl of existence. . . .

XIV

There was panic in Cugluch Keep.

Word of the troubles seeped down from servitors to attendants to workers and even to the lowly apprentice workers who toiled in the deepest burrows and worked endlessly to keep the omnipresent ooze from flooding the undertunnels.

Rumors abounded. Workers whispered of a flaming rain that had fallen from the sky and destroyed hundreds of brood platforms. Or they told of tons of carefully hoarded foodstuffs invaded and ruined by spore rot. Or that the sun had appeared for three consecutive days, or that several of the Royal Court had been discovered feeding on the corpse of a mere worker and had been summarily dismissed.

The truth was far worse than the rumors. Those who knew hid in fear and went about their daily business always looking over their shoulders (those who could look over their shoulders, for some had no necks . . . and some no shoulders).

Hunter packs took every opportunity to get away from the capital city, on the pretext of adding still further to the enormous stocks of supplies. Official auditors bent low over their tallies. All were affected by the panic, a panic that reached beyond sense, beyond normal fears of mortality, to affect even quivering grubs within their incubation cocoons.

The Empress Skrritch was on a rampage. Blood and bits of loose flesh trailed in her wake as she stormed through the rooms and chambers of the labyrinthine central palace.

Safe from her wrath, endless legions of mandibled, facet-eyed troops drilled mechanically on the mossy plains outside the city. As if fearful of reaching the ground, the rays of the sun penetrated the dun-colored sky only feebly.

Guards and servants, scurrying messengers and bureaucrats alike felt the Empress' temper. Eventually the rage spent itself and she settled herself down in one of the lesser audience chambers.

Her thoughts were on her own fear. Idly she nibbled the headless corpse of a still twitching blue beetle chamberlain who'd been too slow to get out of her way. Chitin crunched beneath immensely powerful jaws.

It was some time before Kesylict the Minister dared to stick fluttery antennae around the arched doorway into the chamber. Sensing only simmering anger and the absence of blind fury he poked first his head and then the rest of his antlike body into the room.

A glance revealed a ruby the size of a man's head and redder than his blood. In the top facet Kesylict saw the reflection of the Empress. She was squatting on four legs. The body of the unfortunate chamberlain dangled loosely from one hand while the beautifully symmetrical porcelain-inlaid face of the Empress stared out without seeming to see him.

Though not as lavishly decorated as the main audience chamber or the sinister den of death designated as the royal bedroom, this chamber was still lush with gems and precious metals. The Greendowns were rich in such natural wealth, as though the earth had compensated the land for its noisome, malodorous surface and eternal cloud cover.

They were much appreciated by the hard-shelled denizens of those lands. In the absence of the sun, their sparkle and color provided much beauty. All the varieties of corundum were mined in great quantities: beryl, sapphire, ruby. Rarer diamond framed the windows in the chamber, and thousands of lesser gems, from topaz to chrysoberyl, studded furniture and sculpture and the ceiling itself.

But Kesylict had not kept his head by mooning like a bemused grub at commonplace baubles. He waited and was ready when the triangular emerald green skull jerked around and huge multifaceted eyes dotted with false black pupils glared down at him.

Kesylict debated whether it might not be prudent to retire and wait a while longer before attending his Empress. However, cowardice could cause him to go the way of the chamberlain. That former servitor was now only an empty husk that had been neatly scraped clean by the voracious Empress.

"Why do you cower in the doorway, Kesylict? Yes, I recognize you." Her voice was thick and raspy, like sandpapered oil. Useless wings twitched beneath a long flowing cape of pure silk inlaid with ten thousand amethysts and morions shaped by the empire's finest gem-cutters and polishers, and attached to the cape by a dozen royal seamstresses.

"Pardon, Your Majesty," said the hopeful Kesylict, "but I do not cower. I only hesitate because while I have hoped to talk with you for the past several hours, your mood recently has not been conducive to conversation." He gestured at the corpse-shell of the chamberlain. "Mutual conversation is difficult when one of the participants is forced to function minus his head."

That glowering, fixed skeleton shape could not twist her mouth parts into a smile, and such an expression would have been foreign to her anyway. Nonetheless, Kesylict felt some of the tension depart the room.

"A sense of humor when one's own possible demise is at stake is a finer recommendation of courage than the most dry and somber brilliance, my Kesylict." She tossed the empty shell of the chamberlain into a far corner, where it shattered like an old dish. A couple of legs fell away and rolled up against a far door. The corner was rounded, as were all in the room. The inhabitants of the Greendowns disliked sharp angles.

She turned away from the window. "Anyway, I am full, and tired. But there is more than that." Both knife-edged arms crossed in front of the green thorax, and the decorated head rested on the crux they formed, producing a frozen image of an insectoid odalisque.

"I am worried."

"Worried, Your Majesty?" Kesylict scuttled into the chamber, though taking care to try and remain unobtrusively out of her reach. One could not escape the lightning-swift grasp of the mantis unless one remained beyond its range. So Kesylict approached no closer than protocol demanded. None could tell when the mercurial desires of the Empress might change from a request for advice to a craving for dessert.

"What could possibly be enough to worry Your Majesty? The preparations?" He waved toward the far window. Outside and below were the busy streets of Cugluch, capital of the Empire of the Chosen, their most powerful city. Teeming thousands of dedicated citizens dutifully slaved for the glory of their Empress and their society. Their own lives were filled with the shared glory of their race, and each lowly worker was ready to share in the coming conquests. Preparations were proceeding with the usual efficiency.

"We ready ourselves better than ever before in the history of the Empire, and this time we cannot fail, Majesty."

"There has been no trouble with the stores?"

"None, Majesty." Kesylict sounded genuinely concerned. Though fearful for his personal safety, he was nevertheless a loyal and devoted servant of his Empress, and she did indeed seem worried.

"The training and mobilization also proceeds smoothly. Every day more grubs shed their larval skin and develop arms and the desire to bear weapons. Never has our army been as powerful, never has the desire of its troops been greater. Not one but three great armies stand ready and anxious for the ultimate assault on the lands to the west. Victory is within our grasp. Or so generals Mordeesha and Evaloc have been saying for over a year now. The whole Empire pulses with desire and readiness for battle.

"Yet by wisdom we wait, grow stronger still, so that we can now overwhelm the hated soft ones with but a third of our strength."

She sighed, a low hiss. "Still, we have many thousands of years of failure behind us to show the folly of brave words. I will not give the order to move unless I am certain of success, Kesylict." Her head twitched to one side and she used an arm to clean a bulging eye.

"No trouble then with the Manifestation?"

"Why, no, Majesty." Kesylict was appalled at the thought. For all his talk of strength and desire, he knew that the Empress and general staff were pinning their ultimate hopes on the Manifestation.

"What could be wrong with it?"

She shook a cautionary claw at him. "Where magic is involved, anything is possible. This development is so different it frightens even Eejakrat, who is responsible for it. The greatest care must be exercised to insure its safety and surroundings."

"So it has been, Majesty. Any unauthorized who have come within a hundred zequets of it have been killed, their bodies buried without even the meat being consumed. Greater security has never been exercised in the whole history of the Empire." He peered hard at her.

"Even still, my Majesty worries?"

"Even still." She made as if to rise from her squat. Kesylict took a nervous step backward. She gestured casually, slowly, with an armored arm.

"Be at ease, my valued servant. I am sated physically. It is my mind that hungers for surcease, and your counsel that I require. Not your meat."

"Gladly will I offer my poor advice to Your Majesty."

"This is not for you alone, Kesylict. Summon High General Mordeesha and the sorcerer Eejakrat. I have need of their thoughts as well."

"It will be done, Your Majesty." The Minister turned, his cushioned shoes scraping on the extruded stone floor. He was grateful for the respite but at the same time concerned for the health of his Empress.

Everything was going so well. What could possibly have happened to upset her to the point where she was worried about the outcome of the Great Enterprise?

Later, squatting with the others, Kesylict felt by far the most vulnerable, to both physical abuse and criticism.

To his left rested the heavily armored and aged beetle shape of High General Mordeesha. Battle armor drooped from his soft underbody. Insignia of rank and the less symmetrical wounds of war were cut into his thick dorsal wing covers. Sharp curving horns made of metal protruded from the helmet that fit over his own horny skull. Sweeping metal flanges shielded his eyes.

From his neck hung tiny skulls and teeth taken from the corpses of those the General had personally vanquished. They clanked hollowly against his metal thorax plate as he shifted his position.

Nearby was the Grand Sorcerer Eejakrat, a thin, delicate insect-specter. Pure white enamel decorated his wing cases and chitin. Strings of long white and silver beads dangled fringelike from both sides of his maxilla. An artificial white and silver crest ran from his forehead down between the dark compound eyes to disappear in the middle of his back. It included his insignia of office, of wisdom and knowledge, and marked him as the manipulator of magic most exalted.

Alongside the General, whose great physical skills could crush him easily, and Eejakrat, whose arcane abilities could turn him back into a grub, the Minister felt very inadequate indeed. Yet he squatted in the audience chamber amid the glittering gems and thousand shafts of light they threw back from the dozens of candles and the crystal candelabra overhead, as an equal with the others. For Kesylict possessed an extraordinary reservoir of common sense, an ability most Plated Folk lacked. It was for this that the Empress valued him so much, as a counterweight to the blind drive of the General and the intricate machinations of the Sorcerer.

"We've heard about your distress, Majesty," said the General tactfully. "Is it so important that you must summon us to council now? The critical time nears. Drill and redrill are required more than ever."

"I wish, though," responded Eejakrat in a voice that was almost a whisper between his mandibles, "I could persuade you to wait at least another year, General. I am not yet confident enough master over the Manifestation."

"Wait and wait," grumbled the General, skulls tinkling against his thorax. "We've waited more than a year already. Always building, always preparing, always strengthening our reserves. But there comes a time, good brother, much as I respect your learning, when even a soldier as unthinkingly devoted as those of the Empire grows overdrilled and loses that keen edge for slaughter his officer has worked so long and hard to instill in him. The army cannot retain itself at fever-ready forever.

"Probably we will overwhelm the soft ones by sheer weight of numbers this time, and will have no need of your obscure learning. You can then relax in your old age and toy with this wonder you have conjured up. The final victory shall be ours no matter what."

The General's voice trembled at the thought of the Great Conquest awaiting him, a conquest that would alter forever the history of the world.

"Even so," said the Sorcerer softly, "you are glad to have both my old age and my wonder in reserve, since in twenty thousand years we have shown ourselves unable to defeat the soft ones, despite all our preparations and boastings."

As always, the General was ready to reply. Skrritch waved

a knife-studded green arm. The movement was slow to her, awesomely fast to her attendants. They quieted, waited respectfully for what she might say.

"I have not called you here to discuss timing or tactics, but to listen to a memory of a dream." She gazed at Mordeesha. "In dreams, General, it is Eejakrat who is master. But I may want your opinion nonetheless." Obediently the General bowed low.

"I am no jealous fool, Majesty. Now, of all times, we must put aside petty rivalries to work for the greater glory of Cugluch. I will give my opinion if it is asked for, and I will defer to my colleague's ancient wisdom." He nodded to Eejakrat.

"A wise one knows his own limitations," observed a satisfied Eejakrat. "Describe the dream, Majesty."

"I was resting in the bedchamber," she began slowly, "half asleep from the orgy of mating and conversing with my most recent mate preparatory to his ritual dispatching, when I felt a great unease. It was as if many hidden eyes were spying upon me. They were alien eyes, and they burned. Hot and horribly moist they felt. I believed they were seeing into my very insides.

"I gave a violent start, or so my attending mate later said, and struck violently, instinctively, at the empty air. The cushions and pillows of my boudoir are flayed like the underbellies of a dozen slaves because I struggled so fiercely against nothingness.

"For an instant I seemed to see my tormentors. They had shape and yet no shape, form without substance. I screamed aloud and they vanished. Awake, I flew into a frustrated rage from which I have only just recovered." She looked anxiously at Eejakrat.

"Sorcerer, what does this portend?"

Eejakrat located a clean place amid the royal droppings and rested on his hind legs. The tip of his abdomen barely touched the floor. Minims, foot-long subservitors, busied themselves cleaning his chitin.

"Your Majesty worries overmuch on nothing." He shrugged and waved a thin hand. "It may only have been a bad hallucination. You have so much on your mind these days that such upsets are surprising only in that you have not experienced many before this. In the afterdaze of postcoital subsidence such imaginings are only to be expected."

Skrritch nodded and began to clean her other eye, shooing away the distraught minims. "Always the soft ones have managed to defeat us in battle." General Mordeesha shifted uncomfortably.

"They are fast and strong. Most of all, they are clever. We lose not because our troops lack strength or courage but because we lack imagination in war. Perhaps my imagining is, after all, a good sign. Do not look so uncomfortable, General. You are about to receive the word you have waited for for so long.

"I believe the time has come to move." Mordeesha looked excited. "Yes, General. You may inform the rest of the staff to begin final preparations."

"Majesty," put in Eejakrat, "I would very much like another six months to study the ramifications of the Manifestation. I do not understand it well enough yet."

"You will have some time yet, my good advisor," she told him, "because it will take a while to get so vast an enterprise in motion. But General Mordeesha's words concerning the morale and readiness of the troops must be acknowledged. Without that, all your magic will do us no good."

"I will give you all the time I can, wizard," said Mordeesha. "I wish your support." His eyes glittered in the candlelight as he rose to a walking position. He bowed once more.

"By your leave, Majesty, I will retire now and initiate preparations. There is a great deal to do."

"Stay a moment, General." She turned her attention to the sorcerer. "Eejakrat, I like not rushing the wise ones among us who serve with you in this great undertaking. We have been defeated in the past because we acted without patience or stealth. But I feel the time is right, and Mordeesha concurs. I want you to understand I am not favoring his advice over yours." She looked at Kesylict.

"I am neither general nor wizard, Majesty," the Minister told her, "but my instincts say, 'act now.' It is the mood of the workers as well."

Eejakrat sighed. "Let it be so, then. As to the dream-hallucination, Majesty . . . there are many masters of magic among the soft ones. We can despise them for their bodies but not for their minds. Perhaps I am paranoid with our plans so near fruition, but it is not inconceivable that the shapes you think were watching you were knowledgeable ones among the soft folk. Though," he admitted, "I know of no wizardly power strong enough to reach all the way from the warmlands to Cugluch and then penetrate the Veils of Confusion and Conflict I have drawn about the Manifestation. Nevertheless, I shall try to learn more about what occurred.

"If that happened to be true, however, it means that the sooner we act the surer we shall be of surprise and victory." He turned to the General. "See, Mordeesha, how my thoughts give support to your desires against my own hopes. Perhaps it is for the best. Perhaps I grow overcautious in my old age.

"If you are ready, if the armies are ready, then I will force myself to be ready also. To the final glory, then?"

"To the final glory," they all recited in unison.

Skrritch turned, pulled a cord. Three servitors appeared. Each carried a freshly detached, dripping limb from some unfortunate, unseen source. These were distributed. The four in council sucked out the contents of the arms by way of mutual congratulations.

They then took their leave, the General to his staff meeting, Eejakrat to his quarters to ponder a possible impossible mental intrusion into Cugluch, and Kesylict to arrange the mundane matters of mealtimes and official appointments for the following day.

The Minister had good reason to ponder the Empress' words concerning the notorious cleverness of the soft ones. By such similar adroitness had he retained his head upon his neck, even to agreeing with the others that the time to move had arrived. Privately he thought Eejakrat should be given all the time he wished. Kesylict had read the forbidden records, knew the litany of failure of past battles with the soft ones. So while he was as ignorant of the complexities of the Manifestation as any of the Royal Council, he knew that in Eejakrat's manipulation of it lay the Plated Folk's hopes for final victory over their ancient enemies, and not in General Mordeesha's boasts of superior military strength.

Alone, Skrritch pulled a second call cord. A servitor appeared with a tall, narrow-spouted drinking vessel. The Empress washed down the remnants of the recent toast, then turned and stared once more out the window.

Thickening mist obscured even the ramparts of the Keep. The city of Cugluch and its milling thousands were blotted out as though they did not exist. Day turned toward night as the mist and fog grew darker, indicating the down passage of the sun.

Mordeesha and his fellow generals had been chafing at the bit for several laying periods. She had held off as long as possible in order to give Eejakrat still more time to study his Manifestation. But knowing the wizard, such study could go on forever.

The elastic of patience had been broken now. Soon the word would spread throughout the Greendowns that the war had begun.

For an instant she thought again of the disturbing dream. Perhaps it had been no more than a daymare. Even empresses were subject to strain. Eejakrat did not seem overly concerned about it, so there was no reason for it to continue to trouble her thoughts.

There were promotions and demotions to be bestowed, executions to order, punishments to decide, and rewards to be handed out. Tomorrow's court schedule, so ably organized by the prosaic Kesylict, was quite full.

Such everyday activities seemed superfluous, now that the first steps toward final victory had been initiated. She savored the thought. Of all the emperors and empresses of the far-flung Empire she would be the first to stride possessively through the gentle lands of the soft ones, the first to bring back plunder and thousands of slaves from the other side of the world.

And after that, what might she not accomplish? Even Eejakrat had voiced thoughts about the possibilities the Manifestation might create. Such possibilities extended beyond the bounds of a single world.

She turned on her side and leaned back against a hundred glowing red rubies and crimson cushions. Her ambition was as boundless as the universe, as far-reaching as Eejakrat's magic. She could hardly wait for the war to begin. Glory would accrue to her and to Cugluch. With the wizard's assistance why should she not become Empress of the Universe, supreme ruler of as yet unknown beyonds and their inhabitants?

Yes, she would have the exquisite pleasure of presiding over destruction and conquest instead of records and stupid, fawning, peaceful citizens. Cugluch was on the march, as it should be. Only this time it would swell and grow instead of sputtering to an ignominious halt!

The hallucination faded until it was only an amusing and insignificant memory. . . .

XV

Jon-Tom was split down the middle. Half of him was cool and damp from the early morning mist. The other side was warm and dry, almost hot with the weight leaning against it.

He opened his eyes with that first lethargic movement of awakening and saw a white-and-black-clad form snuggled close against his own. Flor's long black hair lay draped over his shoulder. Her head was nestled in the crook of his left arm.

Instead of moving and waking her, he used the time to study that perfect, silent face. She looked so different, so childlike in sleep. Further to his left slumbered the silent shape of the wizard.

With his head and limbs retracted Clothahump was a boulderish form near a clump of bushes. Jon-Tom started to look back down at his sleeper when he became aware of movement just behind him. Startled, he reached automatically for his war staff.

"Rest easy, Jon-Tom." The voice was less reassuring than the words it spoke. Talea moved down beside him, staring morosely at the recumbent couple. "If I murder you, Jon-Tom, it won't ever be in your sleep." She stepped lithely over them both and trotted over to Clothahump.

She bent and rapped unceremoniously on the shell. "Wake up, wizard!"

A head soon appeared, followed by a pair of arms. One

hand held a pair of spectacles which were promptly secured before the turtle's eyes. Then the legs appeared. After resting a moment on all fours, the wizard pushed back into a squat, then stood.

"I am not accustomed," he began huffily, "to being awakened in so brusque a fashion, young lady. If I were of less understanding a mind . . ."

"Save it," she said, "for him." She pointed to the unsteady shape of Pog. The sleepy bat was fluttering awkwardly over to attend to his master's early morning needs. He'd been sleeping in the branches of the great oak overhead.

"What's da matter?" he asked tiredly. "What's all da uproar? Can't ya let a person sleep?"

"C'mon," Talea said curtly, "everybody up." She looked back at Jon-Tom, and he wondered at something he thought he saw in her gaze. "Well," she asked him, "are you two going to join this little session or aren't you? Or do you intend to spend the rest of your life practicing to be a pillow?"

"I might," he shot back, challenging her stare and not moving. She looked away. "What's the trouble, anyway? Why the sudden fanaticism for an early start? I've never noticed you passing up any chance for a little extra sleep."

"Ordinarily I'd still be asleep, Jon-Tom," she replied, "but what made me wake up wasn't too much sleep but the lack of something else. Isn't it obvious to any of you yet?" She spread both hands and turned a half circle. "Where's Mudge?"

Jon-Tom eased Flor off his shoulder. She blinked sleepily and then, becoming aware of her position, slid to one side. Her cat stretch made it difficult for him to concentrate on the problem at hand.

"Mudge is gone," he told her as he rose, trying to work the kinks out of shoulders and legs.

"So da fuzzy little bugger up and split." Pog used the tip of one wing to clean an ear, grimacing as he did so. "Don't surprise me none. He as much as said he was gonna do it first chance he got.''

''I thought better of him.'' Jon-Tom looked disappointedly at the surrounding woods.

Talea laughed. ''Then you're a bigger fool than you seem. Don't you realize, the only thing that kept him with us this far was wizardly threats.'' She jabbed a thumb toward Clothahump.

''I am most upset,'' said the wizard quietly. ''Despite his unfortunate predilection for illegal activities, I rather liked that otter.'' Jon-Tom watched the turtle's expression change. ''Well, I cannot bring him back, but I can fix him, where he is. I'll put a seekstealth on him.''

Inquiry revealed that a seekstealth was something of a magical delayed-action bomb. Possessed of its own ethereal composition, it would drift about the world invisibly until it finally tracked down its assigned individual. At that point the substance of the spell would take effect. Jon-Tom shook at how devastating such a Damoclean conjuration could be. The unfortunate subject could successfully elude the seekstealth for years, only to wake up one morning having long since forgotten the original incident to discover that he now had, for example, the head of a chicken. How could this happen to his friend Mudge? Wait one hour, he begged the wizard, who reluctantly agreed.

One hour later Clothahump commenced forming the complex spell. He was halfway through it when a figure appeared out of the forest. Jon-Tom and Flor turned from preparing breakfast to observe it.

Several small, bright blue lizard shapes dangled from its belt, their heads scraping the ground. In all other respects it was quite familiar.

Mudge detached the catch from his waist and tossed the limp forms near the cookfire. Then he frowned curiously at the half circle of gaping onlookers.

'' 'Ere now, wot's with all the fish-faces, wot?'' He bent over the lizards, pulled out his knife, and inserted it in one of the bodies. "Take me a moment, mates, t' gut these pretties and then we can set t' some proper fryin'. Takes a true gourmet chef, it does, t' prepare limnihop the right way."

Clothahump had ceased his mumbling and gesticulating. He looked quite angry.

"Nice mornin' for huntin'," said the otter conversationally. "Ground's moist enough t' leave tracks everwhere, so wakin' up early as I did, I thought I'd 'ave a go at supplementin' our larder." He finished the last lizard, began to skin them. Then he paused, whiskers twitching a touch uncertainly as he noticed everyone still staring at him.

"Crikey, wot's the bloomin' matter with you all?"

Jon-Tom walked over, patted the otter on the back. "We thought for a moment that you'd run out on us. I knew you wouldn't do that, Mudge."

"The 'ell I wouldn't," came the fervent reply. Mudge gestured toward Clothahump with the knife. "But I've no doubt 'Is Brainship 'ere would keep his wizardly word t' do somethin' rotten t' meself, merely because I might choose t' exercise me own freedom o' will. Might even do me the dirty o' puttin' a seekstealth on me."

"Oh, now I don't know that I would go that far," muttered Clothahump. Jon-Tom looked at him sharply.

"Now don't get me wrong, mate," the otter said to Jon-Tom. "I like you, and I like the two dear ladies, even if they are a bit standoffish, and even old Pog 'ere can be good company when 'e wants to." The bat looked down from his branch and snorted, then returned to preening himself.

"It's just that I'm not lookin' forward t' the prospect o' possible dismemberment. But then, I've said all this before, 'aven't I." He smiled beatifically. " 'Tis the threat that keeps me taggin' along. I know better than t' try and run off."

"It is not that we believed you had actually done that. Which is to say, we were not entirely certain that . . ."

"Stow it, guv'nor. I don't pay it no mind." He set the fillets on the fire, moved to a mossy log, and pulled off one boot. Furry toes wiggled as he turned the boot upside down and tapped the heel with a paw. Several small pebbles tumbled out.

"Some bloody deep muck I 'ad t' slop through t' run that set down. 'Twas worth it, I think. They're young enough t' be sweet and old enough t' be meaty. Truth t' tell, I was gettin' tired o' nuts and berries and jerky." He shoved his foot back into the boot.

"Come on, now. Surely none o' you seriously thought I'd taken the long hike? Let's get t' some serious business, right? Breakfast!" He ambled toward the fire. "I may be ignorant, foul-mouthed, lecherous, and disreputable," he reached for the proximate curves of Talea's derrière and she jumped out of the way, "but there be one thing I am that's good. I'm the best camp cook this side o' the Muddletup Moors." He winked at Jon-Tom.

"Comes from 'avin' t' eat on the run all your life."

There was no more talk of desertion. The lizards looked rather more ghastly than the average hunk of cooked meat. Flor bit into her section with obvious gusto, so Jon-Tom could hardly show queasiness. Meat was meat, after all, and he'd eaten plenty of reptile in the past weeks. It was just that they'd been such cute little blue things.

"Muy bueno," Flor told Mudge, licking her fingers. "Maybe one of these days I'll have a chance to make you my *quesadillas.*"

Mudge was repacking his gear. "Maybe one o' these days I'll 'ave a chance to sample some *quintera.*"

"No, no. '*Quesadilla.*' *Quintera* is my . . ." She gaped, and then to Jon-Tom's considerable surprise, she blushed. The flush was very becoming on her dark skin. He wanted to say something but somehow the idea of admonishing an otter about a ribald remark upset him. He simply could not visualize the furry joker as a rival. It was inhuman. . . .

They shouldered their packs and started across the glade. Jon-Tom chatted with Mudge and Clothahump while Flor engaged the gruff but willing Pog in conversation. She was curious about the functions of a famulus, and he readily supplied her with a long list of the mostly unpleasant activities he was regularly required to perform. He spoke softly, out of the wizard's hearing.

Water occasionally lapped at their boots. The night's rain had littered the glade with little pools. They avoided the largest without anyone noticing that several of the depressions were identical in outline: the shape of hooves had been melted into the rock.

Jon-Tom was not prepared for his first sight of the river. The Tailaroam was anything but the modest stream he'd expected.

It was broad and wild, with an occasional flash of racing white water showing where the current ran from east to west. He had no way of knowing its depth, but it seemed substantial enough to support a very large vessel indeed. It reminded him of pictures he'd seen of the Ohio in colonial times. Not that he expected to see anything as technologically advanced as a steamship or sternwheeler.

Possibly it was the contrast that made the river seem so big. This was the first time he'd seen anything larger than a rivulet or creek, and the Tailaroam was enormous in comparison. Willow and cypress clustered thickly along the banks. Here and there, scattered stands of birch thrust thin skeletal fingers toward a cloud-flecked sky.

They turned eastward and moved steadily upstream. The dense undergrowth that hugged the river made progress slow. Tangled clumps of moonberry bushes often forced them to change direction, and brambles stuck to their capes and tried to work their way to the skin beneath.

Eventually they found what Clothahump had been searching for: a flat peninsula of sand and gravel that jutted out into the water. Only a few bushes clung tenaciously to the poor soil. In high-water weather the little spit would be submerged. For now it formed a natural landing place and a good one, the wizard explained, from which to hail a passing ship.

Day slid into day, however, without any sign of river travel.

"Commerce is thin this time of year," Clothahump told them apologetically. "There are more ships in the spring when the river is higher and the upper rapids more navigable. If we do not espy transport soon, we may be reduced to constructing our own." He sounded irritated and perhaps a little peeved that Talea might have been right in suggesting they travel overland.

The next two days offered only hopeful signs. Several boats passed them, but all were traveling downstream toward the Glittergeist Sea and distant Snarken.

Jon-Tom used the time to practice his duar, working to master the difficult double-string arrangement. He was careful only to play soft music and not to sing any songs for fear of accidentally conjuring something distressing. Clouds of gneechees seemed to swarm about him at such times. He was learning to resist the constant temptation to spend all his time trying to catch one in his gaze.

Once something like a foot-long glowworm crawled out of the shallows to dance and writhe near his feet. It did nothing else, and shot back into the water the instant he stopped playing.

Flor was fascinated by the instrument. Despite Jon-Tom's initial worries she insisted on trying it herself. She succeeded only in strumming a few basic chords, and went back to listening to him play.

She was doing so one morning when a cry came from Talea.

"A ship!" She stood on the end of the sandy point and gestured to the west.

"How big?" Clothahump puffed his way over to stand next to her. Jon-Tom slipped the duar back across his chest, and he and Flor moved to stand behind them.

"Can't tell." Talea squinted, shielded her eyes. The cloud

cover now restricted the sunlight, but the glare from the surface of the river was still strong enough to water unwary eyes.

Soon the vessel hove into full view. It was stocky and pointed at both ends. Two square-rigged sails were mounted on separate masts set fore and aft. There was a central cabin abovedeck and a narrow high poop from which a figure was steering the ship by means of an enormous oar.

There were also groups of creatures moving from east to west along the sides of the ship. They shoved at long poles. Jon-Tom thought he could make out at least a couple of humans among the fur.

"Looks like a cross between a miniature galleon and a keelboat," he murmured thoughtfully. Wetting a finger, he tested the wind. It was blowing upstream. That would propel a sailboat against the current, and the ship could then down sail and take the current back downstream. Except on days such as today. The breeze was weak, and the keel poles had been brought into play to keep the vessel moving.

"Are they flying a merchant's pennant?" Clothahump fiddled with his spectacles. "One of these days I really *must* try and master that spell for myopia."

"Hard to tell," Talea said. "They're flying something."

"There seem to be an awful lot of people on deck." Jon-Tom frowned. "Not all of them are pushing on those poles. Some of them seem to be running around the edge of the ship. Could they be exercising?"

"Are you more than 'alf mad, mate? Anyone not workin' 'is arse off would be below decks restin' out o' the way."

"They're running nonetheless." Jon-Tom frowned, trying to make some sense out of the apparently purposeless activity taking place on the ship.

"Pog!"

The bat was instantly at Clothahump's side. "Yes, Master?" He hastily tossed away the lizard leg he'd been gnawing on.

"Find out who they are, how far upstream they are traveling, and if they will take us as passengers."

"Yes, Master." The bat soared out over the water, heading for the boat. Jon-Tom followed the weaving shape.

Pog appeared to circle above the vessel. It was now almost opposite their little beach, though on the far side of the river. It wasn't long before the famulus came speeding back.

"Well?" Clothahump demanded as the bat fluttered to a resting stance on the ground.

"Boss, I don't think they're much in the mood for talking business." He raised a wing and showed them the shaft of the arrow protruding from it. Plucking it free, he threw it into the water and studied the wound. "Shit! Needle and thread time again."

"Are you certain they were shooting at you?" asked Flor.

Pog made a face, which on a bat can be unbearably gruesome. "Yes, I'm sure dey were shooting at me!" he said sarcastically, mimicking her voice. "So sorry I couldn't bring more proof back wid me, but unfortunately I managed ta dodge da other dozen or so belly-splitters dey shot at me."

He was fumbling in his backpack. Out came a large needle and a spool of some organic material that Jon-Tom knew could not be catgut. As the bat sewed, he spoke.

"Dere seemed ta be some kind of riot or fight taking place on da deck. I just kinda circled overhead trying ta make some sense outta what was going on. Eventually I gave up and drifted over da poop deck. Tings were quieter dere and it's where I'd expected ta find da captain. I tink one of 'em was, because he was better dressed dan any of da odders, but I couldn't be sure, ya know?" He pushed the needle through the membrane without any sign that it pained him, stuck it around and in again, and pulled smoothly. The hole was beginning to close.

"So I shout down at dis joker about us needing some transportation upstream. First ting he does is call me a

black-winged, gargoyle-faced, insect-eating son-of-a-bitch."
He shrugged. "Da conversation went downhill from dere."

"I don't understand such hostility," murmured Clothahump,
watching as their hoped-for transport began to slip out of
sight eastward. No telling how long it might be before
another going that way might pass them.

"I just got da impression," continued Pog, "that da
captain and his crew were pretty fucking mad about someting
and was in no mood to talk polite to anyone including dere
own sweethearts, if dey got any, which I doubt. Why dey
were so mad I don't know, an' I wasn't about ta hang around
an make no pincushion of my little bod ta find out."

"We might find out anyway." Everyone looked toward
Mudge. The otter was staring out across the river.

"How do you mean?" asked Flor.

"I believe they just threw somebody overboard."

Distant yelling and cursing came from the fading silhouette
of the ship. Several splashes showed clearly now around the
ship's side. Even Jon-Tom saw them.

"Somebody's jumped in after the first," said Talea. "I
don't think anyone's been thrown, Mudge. There! The three
that just jumped are being pulled back aboard. The first is
swimming this way. Can you make out what it is?"

"No, not yet, luv," replied the otter, "but it's definitely
comin' toward us."

They waited curiously while the ship slowly receded from
sight, trailing a philologic wake of insult behind it.

Several long minutes later they watched as a thoroughly
drenched figure nearly as tall as Flor emerged dripping from
waist-deep water and slogged toward them. It was a biped
and clad in what when dry would be an immaculate silk
dressing jacket lined with lace at cuffs and neck. A lace shirt
protruded wetly from behind the open jacket, the latter a
green brocade inlaid with gold thread. The white lace was
now dim with river muck.

Matching breeches blended into silk knee-length stockings

which rose from enormous black shoes with gold buckles. The shoes, Jon-Tom estimated hastily, were comparable to a size twenty-two narrow for a human, which the damp arrival was not.

It stopped, surveyed them with a jaundiced eye, and began wringing water from its sleeves. A monocle remained attached to the jacket by means of a long gold chain. After adjusting it in his right eye, the rabbit said with considerable dignity: "Surely you would not set upon a traveler in distress. I am the victim of antisocial activities." He gestured tiredly upstream to where the boat had vanished.

"I cast myself on your mercies, being too exhausted to fight or flee any farther."

"Take it easy," said Talea. "You play square with us and we'll be square with you."

"An estimable offer of association, beautiful lady." Bending over, the rabbit shook his head and ran a clutching paw down each long white and pink ear. Water dripped from their ends.

A few isolated patches of brown and gray spotted the otherwise white fur. Nose and ears were partly pink. From a hole in the back of his breeches protruded a white tail. At the moment it resembled a soggy lump of used cotton.

Mudge had been assisting Pog in trimming and tying off the end of his stitchery. At first he'd paid the new arrival only cursory attention. Now he left the bat and moved to join his companions. As he did so he had a better view of the bedraggled but still unbowed refugee, and he let out an ear-splitting whistle.

Expecting the worst, the rabbit flinched back, thinking he was now about to be attacked despite Talea's announcement of assistance. But when he got his first look at the otter he let out a sharp whistle of his own. Mudge flung himself into the taller animal's arms and the two spent several minutes apparently trying to beat each other to death.

"Bugger me for a fag ferret!" Mudge was shouting gleefully. "Imagine seein' you 'ere!" He turned, panting, to find his friends staring dumbfoundedly at him. "'Ere now, you chaps don't know who this be, do you?" He whacked the rabbit on the back once more. "Introduce yourself, you vagrant winter coat!"

The rabbit removed his monocle carefully and cleaned it with a dry sleeve. "I am Caspar di Lorca di l'Omollia di los Enansas Giterxos. However," and he slipped the now sparkling eyepiece back in place, "you may all call me Caz."

He frowned as he examined his silk stockings and pants. "You must please excuse my dreadful appearance, but circumstances compelled that I exit hastily and by unexpected aquatic route from my most recent method of conveyance."

"Good riddance ta 'em," snorted Pog, giving the horizon the finger.

"Ah, the aerial disruption that facilitated my departure." The rabbit watched as Pog tested his repaired wing. "It was because of your arrival that I was able to take leave so unbloodily, my airborne friend. Though I had little time for extraneous observation I saw the disgusting manner in which you were treated. It was rather like my own situation."

Clothahump had little time for individual tales of woe, no matter how nicely embroidered. "Talea said that we would treat you fairly, stranger. So we shall. I must tell you immediately that I am a wizard and that," he pointed at Jon-Tom, "is an otherworldly wizard. With two wizards confronting you, you dare not lie. Now then, be good enough to tell us exactly why you jumped off that boat and why several members of its crew chased you into the water themselves?"

"Surely the sad details of my unfortunate situation would only bore you, wizened sir."

"Try me." Clothahump wagged a warning finger at the rabbit. "And remember what I said about telling the truth."

Caz looked around. He was cut off from the rest of the shore. Two humans of enormous size towered expectantly over him. If the turtle was no wizard, he was clearly convinced he was one.

"Best do as 'Is Smartship says, mate," Mudge told him. " 'E's a true wizard as 'e says. Besides," the otter hunkered down on his haunches against a smooth section of sand, "I'm curious meself."

"There's not much to relate." Caz moved over to their smoking camp fire and continued to dry himself. "It was in the nature of a childish dispute over a game of chance."

"That sounds about right." Talea grinned tightly. "They did throw you overboard, then?"

The rabbit smiled slightly, turned, and shoved his tail end toward the fire. "Sadly, they would not have been content with that. I fear they had somewhat more lethal designs on my person. I was forced to fend them off until your friend with the wings momentarily distracted them, thus enabling me to enter the river intact. Though I first tried my best to reason with them."

"Yeah," said Pog from nearby, "I saw how ya was reasoning wid dem." He flapped experimentally, rose a few feet into the air. "Dey reasoned ya all over da ship!"

"Ignorant peddlars of trash and quasi-pirates," said Caz huffily. He studied his sodden lacework in evident distress. "I fear they have caused me to ruin my attire."

"What did they catch you cheating at," asked Flor casually, "cards?"

"I beg your pardon, vision of heaven, but that is an accusation so vile I cannot believe it fell from the lips of one so magnificent as to constitute a monument to every standard of beauty in the universe."

"It fell," she told him.

"I never cheat at cards. I have no need to, being something of an expert at their manipulation."

"Which means they caught you cheating at dice," Talea said assuredly.

"I fear so. My expertise with the bones does not match my skill at cards."

Talea laughed. "Meaning it's a damnsight harder to hide a dice up your sleeve than a card. No wonder your shirt boasts so much lace."

The rabbit looked hurt, ran fingers through the fur on his forehead and then up one ear. "I had hoped to find refuge. Instead I am subject to constant ridicule."

"Truth, you mean."

Caz readied another reply, but Flor interrupted him. "Never you mind. We're all busy showing each other how tough we can be. We'll just have to make sure not to gamble with you."

"Where such loveliness is present, I never gamble," he informed her. Flor looked nonplussed.

"Well, you're well out o' it, mate," observed Mudge. "From the look o' you, squelchy as a fish or not, you've done right well since the last we met."

"I recall that encounter clearly." Now the rabbit was cleaning his buckled shoes. "If I remember correctly, that was also an occasion that demanded a hasty departure."

High otter-laugh whistled over the water. "I'll never forget it, guv. The look on that poor banker clerk's face when 'e found out 'ow 'e'd been duked!" Their voices blended as they reminisced.

Talea listened for a few minutes, then walked to the water's edge. Flor was sitting there, watching the two furry friends converse.

"Otherworlder," Talea began, "that Caz had a certain look in his eye when he was talking to you. I know his type. Fast talk, fast action, fast departure. You watch yourself."

Flor looked up, then stood. She shaded the comparatively diminutive Talea.

"Thanks for the advice, but I'm a big girl now. I can take care of myself. *Comprende*?"

"Size and wise don't necessarily go together," the redhead said. "I was just giving you fair warning."

"Thanks for your concern."

"Just remember one thing about him." Talea nodded toward the chattering Caz. "He'll probably screw anything that walks and likely a few things that don't. Old Mudge is a talker, but this one's a doer. You can tell."

"I'm sure I can rely on your experienced judgment," replied Flor evenly. She moved away before Talea could ask exactly what the last comment meant.

"That is my recent history," the rabbit was saying. He examined the otter's companions. "What then are you bound to, old friend? This does not appear to me to be a typical robber band, though if such is their wont I daresay they would be efficient at it. Those are two of the biggest humans I've ever seen. And the turtle called the man an 'otherworld-ly' wizard."

"I don't wonder at your wonderin', mate," said Mudge. " 'Tis all part o' the strangest tale ever a 'alf-senile wizard wove. I'd give me left incisor if I'd never o' become involved with this bunch." His voice had dropped to a whisper.

"Now don't you go botherin' yourself about it. You can't 'elp me. You get on your way afore 'is 'ard-shelled and 'ard-'eaded wizardship there conscripts you also. 'E's a no-nonsense sorcerer 'e is, and 'e's dragged us all off on some bloody crusade to save the world. Don't think o' doubtin' 'is magic, for 'e's the real article, 'e is, not some carnival fakir. The tall 'uman man with the slightly stupid expression, 'im I still ain't figured out. 'E seems as naïve sometimes as a squallin' cub, but I've seen with me own eyes the magic 'e can work. 'E's a spellsinger."

"What about the tall human woman. Is she a sorceress?"

"Not that she's shown so far," said Mudge thoughtfully. "I don't think she is. Sure is built, though."

"Ah, my friend, you have no appreciation for the arts of higher learning. Even in our brief exchange I could tell that she is of a noble order of initiates on whom high intellectual honors are bestowed.''

"Like I said," reiterated the otter, "she sure is built."

Caz shook his head dolefully. "Will you never lift your thoughts from the gutter, friend Mudge?"

"I like it in the gutter," was the response. " 'Tis warm and friendly down there, and you meet up with all manner o' interestin' folk. What's 'appened t' me since I made the mistake o' temporarily comin' out o' the gutter is that I was stuck as wet-nurse t' the lad, and now I've got meself sort o' swept along a course I can't change or swim out of. As I've said afore, mate, the company is nice but the situation sucks. Shssh, be quiet, an' watch your words. 'Ere 'e comes now."

Clothahump had waddled over to them. Now he looked sorrowingly down at Mudge. "My dear otter," he said, peering over his spectacles, "do you never stop to consider that one who is capable of calling up elemental forces from halfway across the universe is also quite able to hear what is being said only a few yards behind him?"

Mudge looked startled. "You 'eard everythin', then?"

"Most everything. Oh, don't look like a frightened infant. I'm not going to punish you for expressing in private an opinion you've made no secret of in public." The otter relaxed slightly.

"I didn't imagine you might 'ave a 'earın' spell set on yourself, Your Niceness."

"I didn't," explained the wizard. "I simply have very good hearing. A compensation perhaps for my weak eyesight." He regarded the watchful Caz. "You, sir, you have heard what our mutual friend thinks. Allow me to explain further, and then see if you think our 'crusade' is so insane."

He proceeded to give the rabbit a rundown on both their purpose and progress.

When he'd finished, Caz looked genuinely concerned. "But of course if what you say is imminent, then I must join your company."

"*Wot*?" Mudge looked stunned, and his whiskers twitched uncontrollably.

"That's damn decent of you," said Jon-Tom. "We can use all the help we can get."

"It simply seems to me," said the rabbit slowly, "that if the sorcerer here is correct, and I have no reason to doubt him, then the world as we know it will be destroyed unless we do our best to help prevent the coming catastrophe. That strikes me as quite an excellent cause to commit oneself to. Yes, I shall be honored to join your little expedition and give what assistance I may."

"You're daft!" Mudge shook his head in despair. "Downright balmy. The water's seeped into your brain."

"Idiot," was all Pog said, confirming Mudge's assessment of Caz's action. But there were congratulations and thanks from Clothahump and the two otherworldly humans.

Even Talea ventured a grudging kind of admiration. "Not many people around who'll do the honorable thing these days."

"That's true of at least one other world, too," added Flor tentatively.

"It is sad, but honor is a dying attribute." Caz put a paw over his heart. "I can but do my slight best to help restore it."

"We're certainly glad to have you with us." Clothahump was clearly overwhelmed by this first voluntary offer of help. "Do you have a sword or something?"

"Alas," said the rabbit, spreading his paws, "I have nothing but what you see. If I can procure a weapon I will naturally carry it, though I have found that my most efficient methods of disarming an opponent involve the employment of facile words and not sharp points."

"We need sword arms, not big mouths," grumbled Talea.

"There are times, head and heart of fire, when a large mouth can smother the best attack an antagonist can mount. Do not be so quick to disparage that which you do not possess."

"Now look here, are you calling me dumb, you fuzz-faced son of . . . !"

Clothahump stepped between them. "I will not tolerate fighting among allies. Save your fury for the Plated Folk, who will absorb all you can muster." He suddenly looked very tired.

"Please, no more insult-mongering. Not direct," and he glared at Talea, "or veiled," and he glanced over his shell at Caz.

"I shall endeavor to control an acid tongue," said the rabbit dutifully.

"I'll keep my mouth shut if he does the same," Talea muttered.

"Good. Now I suggest we all relax and enjoy the midday meal. Have you eaten recently, sir?"

The rabbit shook his head. "I fear I had to depart before lunch. This has not been my day for timing."

"Then we will eat, and wait. . . ."

XVI

But no other vessel appeared while they ate. Nor all the rest of that day or the morning of the next.

"In truth, we passed much commerce moving downstream toward the Glittergeist," Caz informed them, "but practically none save ourselves moving in the other direction. The winds are capricious this time of year. Not many shipowners are willing to pay the expense of poling a cargo all the way up the Tailaroam. Good polers are too expensive. They make profit most uncertain.

"We shall be fortunate to see another ship moving upstream, and even if we should, there's no guarantee they'd have room aboard for so many passengers. My vessel was quite crowded and I was the only noncrewmember aboard." He spat delicately at the sand. "A distinction I should have avoided."

Clothahump sighed. He struggled to his feet and trundled to the water's edge. After a long stare at the surface, he nodded and told them, "This part of the Tailaroam is wide and deep. It should be full of docile but fast-swimming salamanders. They will be safer and cheaper than any ship." He cleared his throat. "I will call several from the deeps to carry us."

He raised short arms over the gently lapping water, opened his mouth, and looked very confused. "At least, I believe I will. That spell . . ." He began searching the drawers in his plastron. "Salamanders . . . salamanders . . . Pog!"

The bat appeared, hovered in front of him. "Don't ask me, boss. I don't know where ya put it, either. I don't tink I ever remember hearin' about it. When was da last time ya had ta use it? Maybe ya can goose me memory if not your own."

The wizard looked thoughtful. "Let me see . . . oh yes, it was about a hundred years ago, I think."

Pog shook his head. "Sorry, Master. I wasn't around."

"Damm it," Clothahump muttered in frustration, still sorting through his shell, "it has to be in here someplace."

Jon-Tom turned his attention to the water. Everyone's attention was on the wizard. He swung the duar around from his back, experimented with the strings. Notes floated like Christmas ornaments over the surface.

"Allow me, sir," he said importantly, watching out of the corner of an eye to see if Flor was paying attention.

"What, again?"

He waded ankle-deep out into the water. It swirled expectantly about his boots. "Why not? Didn't I do well the last time we needed transportation?" Yes, Flor was definitely watching him now.

"You did well indeed, boy, but by accident."

"Not entirely accident. We needed transportation, I called for it, we got it. The outlines were a little different, that's all. I should have more control over it this time."

"Well . . . if you think you're ready." Clothahump sounded uncertain.

"Ready as I can be."

"Then you know a proper salamander song?"

"Uh . . . not exactly. Maybe if you'd describe one."

"We should need six of them," the turtle began. "Pog has his own transportation. Salamanders are about twelve feet long, including tail. They have shiny gray bodies tending to white on their bellies, and their backs and sides are covered with red and yellow splotches. They have small but sharp teeth, long claws on webbed feet, and are dangerous only when threatened. If you can induce them up, I can put a

251

control spell on them that will allow us to manage them all the way to Polastrindu." He added under his breath, "Know that stupid thing's around here somewhere."

"Twelve feet long, gray to white with red and yellow spots, claws and teeth but dangerous only when threatened," Jon-Tom muttered. He was stalling for time, aware of everyone's eyes on him. "Let's see . . . something by Simon and Garfunkle maybe? No, that's not right. Zepplin, Queen, Boston . . . damn. There was a song by the Moody Blues . . . no, that's not right."

Flor leaned close to Talea. "What's he doing?"

"Preparing the proper spellsong, I suppose."

"He sounds confused to me."

"Wizards often sound confused. It's necessary to the making of magic."

Flor looked doubtful. "If you say so."

Eventually Jon-Tom reached the conclusion that he'd have to play something or admit defeat. That he would not do, not with Flor watching him. He fiddled with the mass and tremble controls, ran fingers over both sets of strings, strumming the larger and plucking at the smaller. No doubt he'd have been better off asking Clothahump for help, but the fear of self-failure pushed him to try.

Besides, what could go wrong? If he conjured up fish instead of salamanders they might not be on their way any sooner, but at least they would eat well while waiting.

Let's see . . . why should he not modify a song to fit the need of the moment? Therefore, ergo, and so forth. . . . "Yellow salamander" didn't scan the same as "yellow submarine," but it was close enough. "We all live on a yellow sal'mandee, yellow sal'mandee, yellow sal'mandee. . . ."

At the beginning of the chorus there was a disturbance in the water. It broadened into a wide whirlpool.

"They're down there, then," murmured Clothahump excitedly, peering at the surface. He tried to divide his attention between the river and the singer. "Maybe a little longer on the verbs, my boy. And a little more emphasis on the subjects of seeking. Sharply on the key words, now.''

''I don't know what the key words are,'' Jon-Tom protested between verses. ''But I'll try.''

What happened was that he sang louder, though his voice was not the kind suited to shouting. He was best at gentle ballads. Yet as he continued the song became easier. It was almost as if his brain knew which of the words catalyzed the strange elements of quasi-science Clothahump called magic. Or was the wizard right, and science really quasi-magic?

This was no time, he told himself furiously as he tried to concentrate on the song, for philosophizing. A couple of jetboats might be even more useful. . . .

Careful, remember the riding snake! Ah, but that was a fluke, the natural result of an uncertain first-time try at a new discipline. Sheer accident. At the time he'd had no idea of what he'd been doing or how he'd been doing it.

Salamanders Clothahump wanted and salamanders he'd get.

Now the water in the vicinity of the whirlpool was beginning to bubble furiously.

''There they are!'' yelled Talea.

''Blimey but the lad's gone an' done it.'' Mudge looked pridefully at his wailing ward.

For his part Jon-Tom continued the song, sending notes and words skipping like pebbles out across the disturbed river. Water frothed white at the center of the whirlpool, now bubbling to a respectable height. Occasionally it geysered twenty feet high, as if something rather more massive than a lowly salamander was stirring on the river bottom.

Talea and Caz were the first to frown and begin backing away from the shore. ''Jon-Tom,'' she called to him, ''are you sure you know what you're doing?''

Oblivious now to outside comments, he continued to sing. Clothahump had told him that a good wizard or spellsinger had to always concentrate. Jon-Tom was concentrating very hard.

"My boy," said Clothahump slowly, rubbing his lower jaw with one hand, "some of the words you're using . . . I know context is important, but I am not sure . . ."

Bubbles and froth rose three times the height of a man. There was a watery rumble and it started moving toward shore. If there were any amphibians out there, it was apparent they now likely numbered more than half a dozen.

The violence finally penetrated Jon-Tom's concentration. It occurred to him that perhaps he might be better off easing back and trying a new song. But Flor was watching, and it was the only watery song he knew. So he continued on despite Clothahump's voiced uncertainty.

At least something was out there.

There was thunder under the water now. Suddenly, a head broke the froth, a head black as night with eyes of crimson. There was a long narrow snout, slightly knobbed at the tip and crowded with razor ivories. Bat-wing ears fluttered at the sides and back of the skull. The head hooked from a thickly muscled, scaly neck and ran into a massive black chest shot through with lines of iridescent purple and azure. Red gills ran half the length of the neck.

A forefoot rose up out of the water. It was bigger than Jon-Tom, whose fingers had frozen on the strings of the duar as completely as the remaining words of the stanza had petrified in his mouth.

The sun continued to shine. Only a few dark clouds pockmarked the sky, but around them the day seemed to grow darker. The thick, leathery foot, dripping moss and water plants from black claws the length of a man's arm, moved forward to land in a spray of water. Webbing showed between the digits.

The elegant nightmare opened its mouth. A thin stream of organic napalm emerged in a spray that turned the water several yards short of the sandy peninsula into instant cloud.

"Ho!" said a distinct, rumbling voice that made Pog sound positively sweet by comparison, "who dares to disturb the hibernation of Falameezar-aziz-Sulmonmee? Who winkles me forth from my home inside the river? Who seeks," and the great toothy jaws curved lower on the muscular neck-crane, "to join great Falameezar for lunch?"

Mudge had scuttled backward and was nearing the edge of the forest. The dragon tilted its head, sighted, and closed one eye. His mouth tightened and he spat. A tiny fireball landed several feet ahead of Mudge, incinerating some bushes and a medium-sized birch. Mudge halted instantly.

"You have summoned me . . . but I have not dismissed you." The head was now almost drooping directly over Jon-Tom, who was developing a crick in his neck from looking up at it.

"Know that I am Falameezar-aziz-Sulmonmee, Three Hundred and Forty-Sixth of the line of Sulmonmeecar, Dragons of all the River, who guard the fast depths of all the rivers of all the worlds! Who, practitioner of rashness, might you be?"

Jon-Tom tried to smile. "Just a stranger here, just passing through, just minding my own business. Look now, uh, Falameezar, I'm sorry I disturbed you. Sometimes I'm not too prudent in certain things. Like, my elocution never seems able to keep up with my enthusiasm. I was really trying to summon some salamanders and—"

"There are no salamanders here," thundered the voice from behind the teeth. The dragon made a reptilian smile. A black gullet showed beyond the teeth. "I have already eaten all who swam hereabouts. The others have fled to safer waters, where I must soon follow." The smile did not fade. "You see, I am often hungry, and must take sustenance where I can find it. To each according to his needs, isn't that right?"

Clothahump raised his hands.

"Ancestor of the lizard neat,
  Troubler of our tired feet,

255

On your way I bid you go,
Lest we your internal temp'rature low."

The dragon glanced sharply at the turtle. "Cease your mumblings, old fool, or I'll boil you in your shell. I can do that before you finish that incantation."

Clothahump hesitated, then fell silent. But Jon-Tom could see his mind working furiously. If someone could give him a little more time . . .

Without thinking, he took several steps forward until the water was lapping at the tops of his boots. "We mean you no harm," there was a faint dragon-chuckle and puffs of smoke drifted from scaly nostrils, "and I'm sorry if we disturbed you. We're on a mission of great importance to—"

"The missions and goings and comings of the warmlanders are of no interest to me." The dragon sounded disgusted. "You are all economically and socially repressive." His head dipped again and he moved closer, a black mountain emerging from the river. Now Falameezar was close enough to smash the duar player with one foot.

Somewhere behind him he could hear Flor whispering loudly, "A *real dragon*! How wonderful!" Next to her, Talea was muttering sentiments of a different kind.

"You live or become food," said the dragon, "at my whim. That is the way of dragons who chance upon travelers. As is our way, I will offer you the chance to win your freedom. You must answer a riddle."

Jon-Tom sloshed water with one foot. "I'm not much at riddles."

"You have no choice. In any case, you need not worry yourself much." Saliva was trickling from his lower jaw. "Know that not one who has come my way has been able to answer my riddle."

" 'Ere now, mate," Mudge called to him encouragingly, "don't let 'im intimidate you. 'E's just tryin' t' frighten you out o' careful consideration o' your reply."

"He's succeeding," Jon-Tom snapped back at the foolhardy otter. He looked back up at the mouth waiting to take him in one bite. "Isn't there some other way we can settle this? It's not polite to eat visitors."

"I did not invite you," growled the dragon. "Do you prefer to end it now by passing over your right to try and answer?"

"No, no!" He glanced sideways at Clothahump. The wizard was clearly mumbling some sort of spell soft enough so the dragon could not overhear, but either the spell was ineffective or else's the wizard's capricious memory had chosen this inopportune moment to turn to mush.

"Go ahead and ask," he said, still stalling. Sweat was making his indigo shirt stick to his back.

The dragon smelled of mud and water and pungent aquatic things. The thick smell gave Jon-Tom something to concentrate on besides his fear.

"Then riddle me this," rumbled the dragon. He lolled in the shallow water, keeping a sharp, fiery eye on the rest of the frightened group.

"What is the fundamental attribute of human nature . . . and of all similar natures?" He puffed smoke, hugely enjoying Jon-Tom's obvious confusion.

"Love!" shouted Talea. Jon-Tom was shocked at the redhead's uncharacteristic response to the question.

"Ambition," suggested Flor.

"Greed." No need to see who'd said that. It could only have come from Mudge.

"A desire to better one's self without harming one's fellows." That was Caz's graceful offering. At least, it was graceful until he added, "Any more than necessary."

"Fear," said the stuttering Pog, trying to find a tree to hide behind without drawing the dragon's attention.

"The wish to gain knowledge and become wise," said Clothahump, momentarily distracted from his spell weaving.

"No, no, no, no, and no!" snorted the dragon contemptuously, searing the air with a gout of flame. "You are ignorant as all. All that fools have to recommend themselves is their taste.''

Jon-Tom was thinking hectically about something the dragon had said before. Yes . . . his comment about the warmlanders being "economically and socially repressive." Now the riddle sounded almost familiar. He was sure he recognized it, but where, and was there more to it that might be the answer? His brain fumbled and hunted desperately for the distant memory.

Falameezar hissed, and water boiled around Jon-Tom's boots. He could feel the heat even through the thick leather. He wondered if he would turn red, like a lobster . . . or black, like burnt toast.

Perhaps the dragon could read minds as well as he could pose riddles. "I will now give you another choice. I can have you steamed or broiled. Those who would prefer to be steamed may step into the river. Those who prefer broiling remain where you are. It is of no matter to me. Or I can eat you raw. Most meals find precooking preferable, however."

Come *on*, meal, he chided himself. This is just another test, but it may be the last one if you don't . . .

"Wait. Wait a minute! I know the answer!"

The dragon cocked a bored eye at him. "Hurry up. I'm hungry."

Jon-Tom took a deep breath. "The fundamental attribute of human nature is . . . productive labor." For good measure he added casually, "Any fool knows that."

The dragon's head reared back, dominating the sky. Bat-wing ears fluttered in confusion, and for a moment he was so startled he choked on his own smoke.

Still menacingly, but uncertain now, he brought his massive jaws so near that Jon-Tom could have reached out and caressed the shiny black scales. The air was full of dampness and brimstone.

"And what," he rumbled, "determines the structure of any society?"

Jon-Tom was beginning to relax a little. Unbelievable as it seemed, he felt safe now. "Its economic means of production."

"And societies evolve . . . ?"

"Through a series of crises caused by internal contradictions," Jon-Tom finished for him.

The dragon's eyes flashed and his jaws gaped. Though confident he'd found the answer, Jon-Tom couldn't help but back away from those gnashing teeth. A pair of gigantic forefeet rose dripping from the water. Tiny crustaceans scrambled frantically for cover.

The feet lunged toward Jon-Tom. He felt himself being lifted into the air. From somewhere behind him Flor was yelling frantically and Mudge was muttering a dirge.

An enormous forked tongue as startlingly red as the slitted eyes emerged from the mouth and flicked wetly at Jon-Tom's face.

"*Comrade!*" the dragon declaimed. Then Jon-Tom was gently deposited back on dry land.

The dragon was thrashing at the water in ecstasy. "I *knew* it! I knew that *all* the creatures of this world could not exist ignorant of the true way." He was so happy he blew fire simply from pure joy, though now he carefully directed it away from his stunned audience.

The otter ran out onto the sand, sidled close to the tall human. "Crikey, mate, be this more o' your unexpected wizardry?"

"No, Mudge." He wiped dragon spit from his cheeks and neck. It was hot to the touch. "Just a correct guess. It was sparked by something he'd said to us earlier. Then it came back to me. What I don't understand is how this bonafide dragon was transformed into a dedicated Marxist."

"Maziwhich? Wot's that? Some otherworldly magickin', maybe?"

"Some people think so. Others would regard it more as pure superstition. But for God's sake, don't say anything like that to him or we'll all find ourselves in the soup, literally."

"Pardon my curiosity," he called to the dragon, "but how did you happen to stumble on the," he hesitated, " 'true way'?"

"It happens on occasion that dragons stumble into interdimensional warps," Falameezar told him as he calmed himself down. "We seem prone to such manifestations. I was suspended in one for days. That is when it was revealed to me. I have tried to make others see but," he shrugged massive black shoulders, "what can but one do in a world aswarm with voracious, ravenous capitalists?"

"What indeed?" murmured Jon-Tom.

"Even if one is a dragon. Oh, I try now and then, here on the river. But the poor abused boatmen simply have no comprehension of the labor theory of value, and it is quite impossible to engage even the lowliest worker in an honest socialist dialectic."

"I know the problem," said Jon-Tom sympathetically.

"You do?"

"Yes. As a matter of fact, we're all embarked on a journey right now, we seven comrades, because this land which you say is filled with capitalists is about to be invaded and overrun by an entire nation of totalitarian capitalists, who wish to enslave completely the, uh, local workers to a degree the primitive bosses hereabouts can't begin to match."

"A terrible prospect!" The dragon's gaze turned to the others. "I apologize. I had no idea I was confronting fellow crusaders of the proletariat."

"Dead right," said Mudge. "You ought t' be ashamed o' yourself, mate." He began cautiously moving back toward the sand. Clothahump looked at once intrigued and puzzled, but for the moment the wizard was quite content to let Jon-Tom do the talking.

"Now then, comrade." The massive black shape folded its forelegs and squinched down in the sandy shallows. "What can I do to help?"

"Well, as you would say, from each according to his ability to each according to his need."

"Just so." The dragon spoke in a tone usually employed for the raising of saints.

"We need to warn the people against the invasion of the bosses. To do so we must warn the local inhabitants of the most powerful center of government. If we could get upstream as quickly as possible—"

"Say no more!" He rose majestically on hind legs. A great surge of water nearly washed away their packs. As the dragon turned, his thick black and purple tail, lined with rigid bumps and spinal plates, stretched delicately onto the sand.

"Allow me the honor. I will take you wherever you wish, and far more quickly than any capitalist pig of a boat master could manage. On one condition." The tail slipped partway back into the river.

Jon-Tom had been about to start up the tail and now hesitated warily. "What's that?"

"That during the course of our journey we can engage in a decent philosophical discussion of the true nature of such matters as labor value, the proper use of capital, and alienation of the worker from his output. This is for my own use. I need all the ammunition I can muster for conversing with my fellows. Most dragons are ignorant of the class struggle." He sounded apologetic. "We tend to be solipsists by nature."

"I can understand that," said Jon-Tom. "I'll be happy to supply whatever arguments and information I can."

The tail slid back onto the sand. Jon-Tom began the climb up the natural ladder and glanced back at his companions.

"What are you all waiting for? It's safe. Falameezar's a fellow worker, a comrade."

The dragon positively beamed.

When they had all mounted and found seats and had secured their baggage, the dragon moved slowly out into the water. In a few minutes they had reached the center of the river. Falameezar turned upstream and began to swim steadily and without apparent effort against the considerable current.

"Tell me now," he said by way of opening conversation, "there is a thing I do not understand."

"There are things none of us understand," said Jon-Tom. "Just now I'm not too sure I understand myself."

"You are introspective as well as socially conscious. That's nice." The dragon cleared his throat, and smoke drifted back over the riders.

"According to Marx, the capitalists should long since have been swept away and the world should now exist in a stateless, classless society. Yet nothing could be further from the truth."

"For one thing," Jon-Tom began, trying not to sound too much like a tutor, "this world hasn't yet fully emerged from the feudal stage. But more importantly . . . surely you've heard of Rosa Luxemburg's *Accumulation of Capital*?"

"No." A crimson eye blinked curiously back at him. "Please tell me about it."

Jon-Tom proceeded to do so, with caution and at length.

They had no problems. Falameezar could catch more fish in one snap than the entire party could in a day's trying, and the dragon was quite willing to share his catch. Also to cook it.

The assured, easy supply of fresh food led Mudge and Caz to grow exceedingly lazy. Jon-Tom's biggest worry was not occupying Falameezar but that either of the two dragon-borne lotus-eaters might let something slip in casual conversation which would tell the dragon that they were no more Marxists than they were celibate.

At least they were not merchants or traders. Mudge, Caz, and Talea qualified as free agents, though Jon-Tom couldn't stretch the definition of their erstwhile professions far enough to consider them craftsmen. Clothahump could be considered a philosopher, and Pog was his apprentice. With a little coaching from Jon-Tom, the turtle was able to acquire a semantic handle on such concepts as dialectical materialism and thus assist with some of the conversational load.

This was necessary because while Jon-Tom had studied Marxism thoroughly it had been over three years ago. Details returned reluctantly. Each was challenged by the curious Falameezar, who had evidently committed to memory every word of both *The Communist Manifesto* and *Das Kapital*.

There was no talk of Lenin or Mao, however, for which Jon-Tom was thankful. Any time the subject of revolution arose the dragon was apt to wonder if maybe they oughtn't to attack this or that town or cluster of traders. But without much of a practical base on which to operate he grew confused, and Jon-Tom was able to steer their debate to less violent aspects of social change.

Fortunately, there were few traders plying the river to stimulate the dragon's ire, and the moment they spotted the black silhouette of Falameezar they hastily abandoned both their boats and the water. The dragon protested that he would like to talk with the crews as much as he would like to cremate the captains, but sadly admitted he did not seem to have the ability to get close to people.

"They don't understand," he was saying softly one morning. "I merely wish to be accepted as an equal member of the proletariat. They will not even stop to listen. Of course, most of them do not have the necessary grasp and overview of their society's socioeconomic problems. They rant and rave and are generally so abusive that they give me heartburn."

"I remember what you said about your fellow dragons' independent natures. Can't you organize them at all?"

Falameezar let out a disgusted snort, sending orange fire across the water's surface. "They will not even stop to listen. They do not understand that to be truly happy and successful it is necessary for all to work together, each helping his comrade as we march onward toward the glorious, classless, socialist future."

"I didn't know dragons had classes."

"It embarrasses me to admit it, but there are those among us who hold themselves better than their fellows." He shook his great head dolefully. "It is a sad, confused world we live in, comrade. Sad and exploitative."

"Too true," agreed Jon-Tom readily.

The dragon brightened. "But that makes the challenge all the greater, does it not?"

"Absolutely, and this challenge we go to confront now is the most dangerous one ever to face the world."

"I suppose." Falameezar looked thoughtful. "But one thing puzzles me. Surely among all these invaders-to-come there must be *some* workers? They cannot all be bosses."

Oh, lord, now how, Jon-Tom? "That's the case, I suppose," he replied as quickly as he could, "but they're all irrevocably imbued with the desire to be bigger bosses than those they now serve." Falameezar still seemed unsure.

Inspiration served. "And they also believe implicitly that if they can conquer the rest of the world, the warmlands and the rest, then they will become capitalist bosses over the workers here, and their old bosses will remain master over them. So they will give rise, if successful, to the most implacable class of capitalists the world has ever known, a class of bosses' bosses."

Falameezar's voice echoed like an avalanche across the water. "This must be stopped!"

"I agree." Jon-Tom's attention for the past hour had been more and more on the shoreline. Hills had risen in place of low beaches. On the left bank they merged into sheer rock walls almost a hundred feet high, far too high for even the powerful Falameezar to negotiate. The dragon was swerving gradually toward his right.

"Rapids ahead," he explained. "I have never traveled beyond this point. I dislike walking and would much rather swim, as befits a river dragon. But for the cause," he said bravely, "I will of course dare anything, so I will walk the rapids."

"Of course," Jon-Tom murmured.

It was growing dark. "We can camp the first place you can easily climb ashore, comrade Falameezar." He looked back in distaste. Mudge and Caz were playing at dice on a flat section of the dragon's back. "For a change maybe our 'hunters' can find us something to eat besides fish. After all," he murmured with a wicked grin, "everyone must contribute to the welfare of the whole."

"How very true," said the dragon, adding politely, "not that I mind catching you fish."

"It's not that." Jon-Tom was enjoying the thought of the two somnolent gamblers slogging through the muck to find enough meat to feed the voracious dragon. "It's time some of us did some real work for you. You've sure as hell done enough for us."

"Well put, comrade," said the dragon. "We must bow to social decorum. I would enjoy a change from fish."

The hilly shore bordered a land of smaller trees, narrower of bole and widely scattered amid thick brush. Despite his insistence that he preferred water to land, the dragon had no trouble smashing hs way through the foliage bulwarking the water's edge.

A small clearing close to the river was soon located. They settled into camp to the accompaniment of rising moonlight. Ahead was the steady but soothing roar of the rapids Falameezar would have to negotiate the next day.

Jon-Tom dumped a load of wood by the fire, brushed bark and dirt from his hands, and asked Caz, "What do ships traveling past this point do about the rapids?"

"Most are constructed and designed so as to make their way safely through them when traveling down to the Glittergeist," the rabbit explained. "When traveling upstream it is necessary to portage around. There are places where it can be done. Logs have been laid across ancient, well-known paths. The ships are then dragged across this crude cellulose lubrication until quieter water is reached." He nodded curiously toward the dragon. Falameezar lay contentedly on the far side of the clearing, his tail curled across his jaws.

"How did you ever manage to talk the monster into conveying us atop his belly instead of inside it? I understood nothing of his riddle or your reply, nor of the lengthy talk you have engaged in subsequently."

"Never mind," said Jon-Tom, stirring the fire with a twig. "I'll take care of the dialectic. You just try to say as little as possible to him."

"No fear of that, my friend. He is not my idea of a scintillating conversationalist. Nor do I have any desire to become someone's supper through misapplication of a word or two." He patted Jon-Tom on the back and grinned.

Despite the rabbit's somewhat aloof bearing, Jon-Tom couldn't help liking him. Caz was inherently likable and had already proven himself a willing and good-natured companion. Hadn't he volunteered to come on what was likely to be a dangerous journey? To be quite fair, he was the only true volunteer among them.

Or was there some other motive behind the rabbit's participation that so far he'd kept well hidden? The thought gave Jon-Tom an unexpected start. He eyed the retreating ears. Maybe Caz had reasons of his own for wanting to travel upstream, reasons that had nothing to do with their mission. He might desert them at the first convenient opportunity.

Now you're thinking like Clothahump, he told himself angrily. There's enough for you to worry about without trying to analyze your companion's thoughts.

Speaking of companions, where the devil had Mudge got himself to? Caz had returned a few moments ago with a fat, newtlike creature. It drew deprecatory comments from Talea, the designated chef for the evening, so they'd given it to the delighted Falameezar.

But Mudge had been gone a long time now without returning. Jon-Tom didn't think the mercurial otter would try to split on them in so isolated a place when he'd already passed up excellent opportunities to do so in far more familiar surroundings.

He walked around the fire, which was now crackling insistently for fuel, and voiced his concern to Clothahump. As usual, the wizard sat by himself. His face shone in the firelight. He was mumbling softly to himself, and Jon-Tom wondered at what lay behind his quiet talk. There was real magic in the sorcerer's words, a source of never ending amazement to Jon-Tom.

The wizard's expression was strained, as befitted one on whose shoulders (or shell) rested the possible resolution of a coming Armaggedon.

Clothahump saw him without having to look up. "Good eve to you, my boy. Something troubles you." Jon-Tom had long since overcome any surprise at the wizard's sensitivity.

"It's Mudge, sir."

"That miscreant again?" The aged face looked up at him. "What has he done now?"

"It's not what he's done so much as what he hasn't done, sir, which is come back. I'm worried, sir. Caz returned a while ago, but he didn't go very far into the forest and he hasn't seen Mudge."

"Still hunting, perhaps." Most of the wizard's mind seemed to be on matters far off and away.

"I don't think so, sir. He should have returned by now. And I don't think he's run off."

"No, not here, my boy."

"Could he have tried to catch something that caught him instead? It would be like Mudge to try and show off with a big catch."

"Not that simpleton coward, boy. But as to something else making a meal of him, that is always a risk when a lone hunter goes foraging in a strange forest. Remember, though, that while our otter companion is somewhat slow upstairs, there is nothing sluggish about his feet. He is lightning fast. It is conceivable that something might overpower him, but it would first have to surprise him or run him down. Neither is likely.''

"He could have hurt himself," persisted a worried Jon-Tom. "Even the most skillful hunter can't outrun a broken leg."

Clothahump turned away from him. A touch of impatience crept into his voice. "Don't belabor it, boy. I have more important things to think upon."

"Maybe I'd better have a look for him." Jon-Tom glanced speculatively at the silent ring of thin trees that looked down on the little clearing.

"Maybe you had." The boy means well, Clothahump thought, but he tends not to think things through and to give in to his emotions. Best to keep a close watch on him lest he surrender to his fancies. Keep him occupied.

"Yes, that would be a prudent thing to do. You go and find him. We've enough food for the night." His gaze remained fixed on something beyond the view of mere mortals.

"I'll be back with him soon." The lanky youth turned and jogged off into the woods.

Clothahump was fast sinking into his desired trance. As his mind reeled, something pricked insistently at it. It had to do with this particular section of Tailaroam-bordered land. It was full night now, and that also was somehow significant.

Was there something he should have told the boy? Had he sent him off unprepared for something he should expect to encounter hereabouts? Ah, you self-centered old fool, he chided himself, and you having just accused *him* of not thinking things through.

But he was far too deeply entranced now to slip easily back into reality. The nagging worries fell behind his probing, seeking mind.

He's a brave youngster, was his fading, weak appraisal. He'll be able to take care of himself. . . .

Untold leagues away, underneath the infectious mists of the Greendowns in the castle of Cugluch, the iridescent Empress reclined on her ruby pillows. She replayed her sorcerer's words mentally, lingering over each syllable with the pleasure that destruction's anticipation sent through her.

"Madam," he had bowed cautiously over this latest pronouncement, "each day the Manifestation reveals powers for which even I know no precedent. Now I believe that we may be able to conquer more thoroughly than we have ever dreamed."

"How is this, Sorcerer?—and you had better be prepared to stand by any promises you make me." Skrritch eyed his knobby legs appraisingly.

"I will give you a riddle instead of a promise," Eejakrat said with untoward daring. Skrritch nodded.

"When will we have completed the annihilation of the warmlands?" he asked her.

"When every warmlander bows to me," she answered without hesitation.

The wizard did not respond.

"When every warmlander has been emptied to a dead husk?"

Still he did not reply.

"Speak, Sorcerer," Skrritch directed testily.

"The warmlands will be ours, my lady, when every warmblooded slave has been returned to the soil and in his place stands a Plated subject. When the farmlands, shops, and cities of the west are repopulated with Plated Folk your empire will know no limit!"

Skrritch looked at him as if he'd gone mad and began to preen her claw tips. Eejakrat took a prudent step backward, but his words held the Empress in mid-motion.

"Madam, I assure you, the Manifestation has the power to incinerate entire races of warmlanders. Its death-power is so pervasive that we shall not only crush them, we will obliterate their memory from the earth. Your minions will march into their cities to find the complete welcome of silence."

Now Skrritch smiled her weird, omniverous smile. The

wizard and his queen locked eyes, and though neither really understood the extent of the destruction at their disposal, the air reverberated with their insidious obsession to find out. . . .

It was very dark in the forest. The moon made anemic ghosts of the trees and turned misshapen boulders to granite gargoyles. Bushes hid legions of tiny clicking things that watched with interest and talked to one another as the tall biped went striding past their homes.

Jon-Tom was in fair spirits. The nightly rain had not yet begun. Only the usual thick mist moistened his face.

He carried a torch made from the oil rushes that lined the river's edge. Despite the persistent mist the highly combustible reeds readily caught fire when he applied the tip of the well-spelled sparker Caz had lent to him. The torch lit readily and burned with a satisfying slowness.

For a moment he had thoughts of swinging round his duar and trying to conjure up a flashlight or two. Caution decided him against the attempt. The torch would serve well enough, and his accuracy where conjuration was involved thus far left something to be desired.

The ground was damp from the mist-caress of late evening, and Mudge's tracks stood out clearly. Occasionally the boot marks would cross each other several times in one place, indicating where the otter had rested behind a large boulder or fallen log.

Once the gap between the prints abruptly lengthened and became intermixed with tiny polelike marks, evidence that Mudge had given chase to something. The pole prints soon vanished and the otter marks shortened in stride. Whether the otter had made a successful kill or not Jon-Tom couldn't tell.

Oblivious to the fact that he was moving steadily deeper into the woods, he continued to follow the tracks. Unexpectedly the brush gave way to an open space of hard-packed earth that had been raised several inches above the level of the surrounding surface. The footprints led up to the platform and disappeared. It took Jon-Tom long minutes before he could locate traces of them, mostly scuffs from the otter's boot heels. They indicated he'd turned off to his right along the artificial construct.

"Come on back, Mudge!" There was no reply, and the forest swallowed any echo. "Caz brought in something already, and everyone's getting worried, and my feet are starting to hurt!" He started jogging down the platform.

"Come on out, damn you! Where the hell have—?"

The "you" was never uttered. It was replaced by a yelp of surprise as his feet went out from under him. . . .

XVII

He found himself sliding down a gentle incline. It was slight enough and rough enough so that he was able to bring himself to a halt after having tumbled only a few yards. The torch bumped to a stop nearby. It had nearly gone out. Flames still flickered feebly at one corner, however. Leaning over, he picked it up and blew on it until it was once more aflame. Try as he would, though, he couldn't induce it to provide more than half the illumination it had supplied before.

The reduced light was barely sufficient to show that he'd stumbled into an obviously artificial tunnel. The floor was flat and cobbled with some dully reflective stone. Straight walls rose five feet before curving to a slightly higher ceiling.

Having established that the roof was not about to fall in on him, he took stock of himself. There were only bruises. The duar was scratched but unbroken. Ahead lay a blackness far more thorough and intimidating than friendly night. He wished he hadn't left his staff back in camp. There was nothing but the knife strapped to his belt.

He stood, and promptly measured the height of the ceiling. Carefully turning around, he walked awkwardly back toward the circle of moonlight he'd fallen through. Nothing materialized from the depths of the tunnel to restrain him, though his neck hairs bristled. It is always easier to turn one's back on a known enemy than on an unknown one.

He crawled up the slight incline and was soon staring out at the familiar forest. The lip of the gap was lined with neatly worked stone engraved with intricate designs and scrollwork. Many twisted in upon themselves and were set with the same dimly reflective rock used to pave the tunnel.

He started to leave . . . and hesitated. Mudge's last boot prints had been moving in this direction. A close search of the rim of the hole showed no such prints, but the earth there was packed hard as concrete. A steel rod would not have made much of an impression upon it, much less the boot of an ambling otter.

The paving of the slope and tunnel was of still tougher material, but when he waved the torch across it the light fell on something even more revealing than a boot print. It was an arrow of the kind Mudge carried in his hunting quiver.

Crawling back inside, he started down the tunnel. Soon he came across another of the orphaned shafts. The first had probably fallen from the otter's quiver, but this one was cleanly broken. He picked it up, brought the torch close. There was no blood on the tip. It might have been fired at something and missed, to shatter on the wall or floor.

It was possible, even likely, that Mudge was pursuing some kind of burrow-dwelling prey that had made its home in the tunnel. In that case Jon-Tom's worries might prove groundless. The otter might be just ahead, busily gutting a large carcass so that he'd have to carry only the meat back to camp.

The thought of traveling down into the earth and leaving the friendly exit still further behind appalled him, but he could hardly go back and say truthfully he'd been able to track Mudge but had been too afraid to follow the otter the last few yards.

There was also the possibility that his first assumption might prove correct, that the creature Mudge had been pursuing had turned on him and injured him. In that case the otter might lie just a little ways down the tunnel, alive but helpless and bleeding.

In his own somewhat ambivalent fashion Mudge *had* looked

out for him. Jon-Tom owed him at least some help, with either bulky prey or any injuries he might have suffered.

With considerable trepidation he started moving down the tunnel. The slope continued to descend to the same slight degree. From time to time torchlight revealed inscriptions on the walls. There also were isolated stone tablets neatly set into recesses. Directions perhaps . . . or warnings? He wondered what he would do if he reached a place where the tunnel split into two or more branches. He was too intent on the blackness to study the revealing frescoes overhead.

He had no desire to become lost in an underground maze, far from surface and friends. No one knew where he was, and when the night rain began it would obliterate both Mudge's tracks and his own.

Holding the torch ahead and to one side, he continued downward.

Mmmmmm-m-m-m-m-m . . .

He stopped instantly. The eerie moaning came clearly to him, distorted by the acoustics of the tunnel. He knelt, breathing hard, and listened.

Mmmm-lllll-l-l-l-l . . .

The moan sounded again, slightly louder. What unimaginable monster might even now be treading a path toward him? His torch still showed only blackness ahead. Had the creature already devoured the poor otter?

He drew the knife, wishing again for the staff and its foot-long spear point. It would have been a particularly effective weapon in the narrow tunnel.

There was no point in needlessly sacrificing himself, he thought. He'd about decided to retreat when the moan unexpectedly dissolved into a flurry of curses that were as familiar as they were distinct.

"Mmmm-l-l-l-let me go or I'll slice you into stew meat! I'll fillet you neat and make wheels out o' your 'eads! I'll pop wot little eyeballs you've got out o' their sockets, you bloody blind-faced buggerin' ghouls!"

A loud *thump* sounded, was followed by a bellow of pain and renewed cursing from an unfamiliar source. The source of the first audible imprecations was no longer in doubt, and if Mudge was cursing so exuberantly it was most likely for the benefit of an assailant capable of reason and understanding and not blind animal hatred.

Jon-Tom hurried down the corridor, running as fast as possible with his hunched-over gait. There were still no lights showing ahead of him, so he had burst around a bend and was on top of the busy party before he realized it.

Letting out an involuntary yell at the sight, he threw up his arms and fell back against a wall, waving knife and torch to keep his balance. The effect produced among Mudge's attackers was unexpected, but highly satisfactory.

"Lo, a monster! . . . Daemon from the outer world! . . . Save yourselves! . . . Every mole for hisself . . . !"

Amid much screaming and shrieking he heard the sounds of tiny shoes slapping stone racing not toward but away from him. This was mixed with the noise of objects (weapons, perhaps) being thrown away in great haste by their panicky owners.

It occurred to him that the sight of a gigantic human clad entirely in black and indigo, flashing a reflective green lizard-skin cape and brandishing a flaming torch and knife, might be something which could truly upset a tunnel dweller.

When the echoes of their flight had finally faded away, he regained control of his own insides and lowered the torch toward the remaining shape on the floor.

"'Ad enough, then, you bloomin' arse'oles?" The voice was as blustery as before, if softer from lack of wind. "Be that you, mate?" A pause while otter eyes reflected the torchlight. "So 'tis, so 'tis! Untie me then mate, or give me the knife so's I can cut—"

"If you make a move, outworlder," said a new voice, "I will slit what I presume to be your friend's throat. I can get to it before you can reach me."

Jon-Tom raised the torch higher. Two figures lay on the floor of the tunnel. One was Mudge. His feet were bound at the ankles and knees and his arms done up similarly at wrists and elbows. A carrying pole had been slipped neatly between the bindings.

Leaning over the otter was a furry creature about four feet tall. His attire was surprisingly bright. He wore a yellow vest studded with blue cabochons and held together across the chest with blue laces. Additional lacings held the vest bottom securely to what looked like lederhosen.

A ringlet much like a thin tiara sat askew on the brown head. It was fastened under the chin by yellow straps. Broad sandals were laced across its feet. The sandals were pointed at toe and heel, possibly a matter of design, perhaps to aid in digging, giving freedom to the long thick claws on each hind foot.

One hand was fitted with a yellow metallic glove. This covered the creature's face as he squinted sideways through barely spread fingers, though he was trying hard to look directly at Jon-Tom and his torch.

The other hand held the sickle-shaped weapon that was resting on the otter's throat. Mudge's own weapons lay scattered on the floor nearby, even to his secret heel-boot knife. His arrows, sword, and bow shared space with the spears and wicked-looking halberds abandoned by those who had fled at Jon-Tom's appearance.

"I say to you again," repeated the determined gopher, his grip tightening on the sickle-knife, "if you move I'll open this thief's neck and let out his life among the stones."

"Thief?" Jon-Tom frowned as he looked back down at the tightly trussed otter.

"Ah, you fart-faced worm eater, that's the biggest lie since Esaticus the eagle claimed to 'ave done it flyin' underwater!"

Jon-Tom settled back against the cool wall and deliberately lowered his knife, though he didn't go so far as to replace it in its sheath. The gopher watched him uncertainly.

"What has been going on here, Mudge?" he asked the otter quietly.

"I'm tellin' you, mate! I was out huntin' for our supper when I tripped while chasin' a fine fat broyht. I fell down into this pit o' 'orrors, where I was promptly set upon by this 'orde o' rabid cannibals. They're blood-drinkers, lad. You'd best take care o' this one with your magical powers afore—"

"That's enough, Mudge." He looked up at the gopher. "You can put up your sickle, or knife, or whatever you call it, sir. That position can't be too comfortable." He set the torch down on the floor. "I'm sorry if my light hurts your eyes."

The gopher was still wary. "Are you not this one's friend?"

"I'm his associate in travel. I'm also a believer in the truth. I promise not to attack you while we talk, or make a hostile move of any kind."

"Lad, you don't know wot you're sayin'! The minute you put up your knife 'e's likely to—"

"Mudge . . . shut up. And be glad I'm here instead of Clothahump. He'd probably just leave you." The otter went quiet, muttering under his breath.

"You have my word," Jon-Tom informed the gopher, "as a traveler in your country and as a," he thought rapidly, "as a wizard who means you no harm. I swear not to harm you on my, uh, sacred oath as a spellsinger."

The gopher noted the duar. "Wizard it may be, though it was more of a daemonic effect you had upon my men." Reluctantly the scythe blade moved away from Mudge's throat.

"I'm Jon-Tom."

"And I am called Abelmar." The gopher moved his hand away from his eyes and squinted painfully at the man. "It was your light as well as your appearance which startled my troop. Most of them are moles and the light is far more hurtful to them than to me, for my kind occasionally make daytime forays when the city so requires it. Some daytime activity is necessary for the maintenance of normal commerce, much as we of Pfeiffunmunter prefer to keep to ourselves.'' He looked meaningfully down at Mudge.

"Except when we are intruded upon by cutthroats and thieves."

" 'Tis all a bloody lie!'' Mudge protested. "When I get out o' these blinkin' ropes I'll do some intrudin' you'll never forget. Come on now, mate,'' he said to Jon-Tom, "untie me.''

Jon-Tom ignored the twisting, writhing otter. "I meant no intrusion, Abelmar. My friend says that you attacked him. You've called him a thief.''

"I am in charge of the east-end morning patrol,'' explained the gopher. He looked worriedly back down the tunnel. "Citizens will soon be appearing on nightly business, awakening from the day's sleep. It would be embarrassing for them to see me this way. Yet I must carry out my duty.'' He stiffened.

"Your associate is guilty of attempted theft, a sadly common crime we must continually face when we deal with outlanders. Yet it is not the theft that troubles us so much as the vandalism.''

"Vandalism?'' Jon-Tom looked accusingly at Mudge.

"Yes. It is not serious, but if left unchecked could become a serious threat to our neatly built community. Do you have any idea, Jon-Tom, how taxes go up when the public thoroughfares are torn to pieces by strangers?''

" 'E's lying through those oversized teeth o' 'is again, mate,'' Mudge protested, though with less conviction this time. "Why would I want t' go around rippin' up 'is blinkin' street?''

Abelmar sighed. "I suppose it is our own fault, but we are aesthetes by nature. We enjoy a bit of brightness in our city, for all that it gives us problems with ignorant travelers such as this,'' and he kicked Mudge in the back. "But I see you still do not understand.'' He'd grown accustomed enough to Jon-Tom's torch to look without blinking now.

''Look,'' and he bent toward Mudge.

''Careful!'' Jon-Tom took a step forward and raised his knife.

''Easy move, Jon-Tom stranger,'' said the gopher. ''If you are suspicious of my movements, then look instead at your own feet. Or can it be in truth you have not looked closely at our fine streets?''

Jon-Tom knelt cautiously, still keeping an eye on the gopher. Moving the torch, he stared intently at the closely laid bricks. They gleamed as dully as those he'd encountered near the tunnel entrance, only with the torch resting directly on them the glow intensified. They threw back a half-familiar, reddish-yellow light.

''Gold?'' he asked uncertainly.

''Common enough below Pffeifunmunter,'' said the gopher with a trace of bitterness, ''but not to those who come along and try ripping it out of our beautiful pathways and boulevards. It makes for pretty paving, don't you think?''

''Surely now that you understand you can excuse me the temptation, mate,'' said Mudge defensively. ''You wouldn't think these grave diggers would be so greedy they'd resent a poor visitor a few cobblestones.''

''Excuse me.'' Jon-Tom rose and almost cracked his head again on the low ceiling. ''I apologize to you for any damage, Abelmar.''

''It's not too bad. You have to understand,'' the gopher told him, ''that if we let this sort of thing persist and word of it spread 'round the outworld, before too long we'd have mobs of sunlifers down here destroying all our public thoroughfares, our roads, and our very homes. It would be the end of civilization as we know it.''

He paused. Noise was growing behind him, moving up from the depths of the tunnel. ''Travelers out for an evening walk,'' the gopher surmised, ''or else my men, the cowardly bastards, coming back to see if anything's left of me.'' He sighed. ''I have my duty, but I can face reality as well. We have something of a standoff here, friend spellsinger. I must confess I am now more interested in punishing my men than in your pitiful petty thief of a friend.

''If you will get him out of here and promise not to let him return, and will do so without disturbing any municipal construction, I won't report this incident to the Magistrates, or cut your friend's throat. Well though he deserves it!''

''I'd appreciate that, and I agree,'' said Jon-Tom.

''So do I, guv'nor.'' Mudge smiled toothily up at the gopher.

Abelmar hesitated, then used the curved blade on the otter's ropes before slipping it through a catch in his lederhosen straps. Mudge scrambled across the floor until he was standing next to Jon-Tom. He stretched luxuriously, working the kinks out of his muscles and joints.

''Now mate, quick now, while there still be time!'' He bent and hefted one of the loose golden bricks. ''Cover me with the knife while I slip a few o' those into me quiver an' pants.'' He hurried to recover his own weapons. ''You're bigger than 'im, and you've got the light.''

When the otter had finished gathering up his possessions, Jon-Tom said tiredly, ''All right, Mudge. Put down the gold and let's go.''

The otter stared at him, both arms now full of gleaming pavingstones. ''You gone daft, mate? I'm 'oldin' a bloody fortune right now. We've got us a chance t'—''

''*Put it down, Mudge!*'' The knife moved threateningly, not at the gopher now. ''Or I swear I'll leave you the way I found you.''

''Cor,'' muttered the otter. Reluctantly he opened his arms. There was a heavy clattering as the gold bricks dented the pavement. Abelmar was nodding and looking satisfied. The cries of the approaching patrol were intelligible now. He peered down the tunnel and thought he could see dim, snouty shapes approaching. They wore gold earrings, clothing similar to Abelmar's, and very dark sunglasses. Their newly acquired weapons shone in the faint torchlight. Jon-Tom idly noted that the gopher's sickle-knife was made of gold.

"You're a man of your word," said the gopher, "which is rare among sunlifers. Go in peace." He glared at Mudge. "If I ever run across your flea-flecked body again, sir, I'll see you skinned and thrown to the carrion herds."

Mudge made quick use of the middle digit of his right hand. "Up yours, shit face!" He turned to Jon-Tom. "Right, then. It's done. You've kept your part o' the bloody bargain, but you've no guarantee 'is men will keep theirs."

"Let's get going, then." They started back up the tunnel.

"No need to worry," Abelmar shouted to them, "my men will be busily engaged." He turned to face down the tunnel.

"So, you cowards have come back, have you?"

Angry mutterings sounded from the ranks of armed moles. A few gophers were scattered among them.

"They're getting away, sir!" shouted one of the moles, pointing up the tunnel.

"When I'm finished with you lot you'll wish you'd gone with them!" roared Abelmar, letting loose a string of curses that reverberated around the tunnel. Their echoes followed Jon-Tom and Mudge out.

"Keep going, Mudge." Jon-Tom gave the otter a gentle but insistent shove.

"'Ere now, mate, let's not panic, shall we? That officer's stopped t' give 'is troop a thorough bastin'. There's still plenty o' pavin' 'ereabouts." He stomped on the bricks with one boot. "It wouldn't 'urt no one if we took a few minims 'ere and did a nice little bit 'o work. There be no way that buck-toothed flat-faced cop would know we were the ones responsible. Perhaps if I just—"

"Perhaps if I just stick this torch up your ass," Jon-Tom told him firmly.

"All right, all right. It were only a thought, lad."

The moon was bright when they emerged again into the forest. There were no indications of pursuit, though he had a feeling of movement from behind them. It was a distant rumbling, the sounds carried through the earth that indicated the burrow city of Pfeiffunmunter was coming awake for another busy night.

"Just be thankful I got there when I did," he told the otter. "He might've cut your throat without waiting to present you to the Magistrates."

"Poppycock," snorted Mudge. "I could've made me way loose eventual-like." He straightened his vest and tugged his cap tight on his head. "All that beautiful gold!" He shook his head regretfully. "More gold than even wizards can make! An' those bloody dirt-eaters defile it by usin' it just t' walk upon."

"That's better than the other way around."

"Huh?" Mudge eyed him perplexedly. "Are you wizard riddlin' me, mate?"

"Not at all." They turned off into the woods.

The otter looked bemused. "You be either the sharpest spellsinger that ever came up the river, mate, or else the biggest fat'ead."

Jon-Tom smiled faintly. "Hardly much thanks for the one who saved your life." He pushed at the clinging brush.

"Better to die tryin' for wealth than to live in poverty," the otter grumbled.

"Okay. Go on back to the entrance, then. I won't try to stop you. See if you can help yourself to some pavement. I'm sure Abelmar and his troops will be happy to welcome you. Or do you think him fool enough to trust us to the point of leaving the gateway unguarded?"

"On the other 'and," Mudge said, without breaking stride, "'tis a wise chap who bides 'is time and rates 'is chances. I told you once I ain't no gambler, not like old Caz. But if you'd come back an' give me a 'and, lad. . . ."

"No way." He shook his head. "I gave my word."

The otter looked crushed, shoved aside a branch, and cursed his foul luck as he stumbled over a projecting root.

"If you expect to make anythin' o' yourself 'ere, mate, you're goin' to 'ave to discard these otherworldly ethical notions."

"That sounds funny coming from you, Mudge. If you'll think a moment, you'll remember that you're embarked on an ethical sort of journey."

"Under duress," Mudge insisted.

Jon-Tom looked back and smiled at him. "You know, I think you use that as an excuse to keep from having to admit your real feelings." The otter grumbled softly.

"We'il tell them you had an unsuccessful hunt, which is hardly a lie. That'll do you better than telling them what a greedy, self-centered little prick you really are."

"Now that 'urts me to me 'eart, lad," Mudge said in mock pain.

"It would have hurt you a lot more if you'd returned with your arms full of gold and Falameezar saw you. Or hadn't you stopped to consider that? Considering the strength of his feelings where personal accumulation of wealth is concerned, I don't think even I could have argued him out of making otter chips out of you."

Mudge appeared genuinely startled. "You know wot, mate? I truly 'adn't given the great beastie a thought. 'E is a mite quick-tempered, even for a dragon."

"Not quick-tempered at all," Jon-Tom argued. "He simply believes in his own ethical notions. . . ."

The beginnings of real distress were stirring through the camp when they finally walked into the glow of the camp fire. Falameezar was vowing he'd burn down the entire forest to find Jon-Tom, while Pog had volunteered to lead a night search party.

It was difficult for Jon-Tom to restrain himself from telling them the truth as he watched Talea and Flor fawn over the otter.

"Are you all right?" asked Flor, running concerned fingers through the fur of his forehead.

"What happened out there?" Talea was exhibiting more concern than she had for anyone since the journey'd begun.

" 'Twas a chameleon," said Mudge bravely, sitting down on a rock near the fire with the look of one who'd run far and hard. "You know 'ow dangerous they can be, Talea. Blendin' their colors in with the landscape and waitin' with those great sticky tongues o' theirs for some unwary travelersby."

"Chameleons?" Flor looked confusedly over at Jon-Tom. He muttered something about much of the reptilian life growing to the size of buffaloes and why should chameleons be any exception.

"I just 'ad crept up on 'im and was drawin' back me bow," said Mudge tensely, warming to his story, "when the brute saw me against a light-barked tree. Turned on me right there, 'e did, with all three horns a flashin' in the moonlight an 'im so close I could smell 'is fetid breath."

"What happened then?" wondered Flor, leaning close. The exhausted otter rested the back of his head against the cushion of her bosom and tried with difficulty to concentrate on his spellbinding invention, while Talea soothingly stroked one limp arm.

"I 'eard that slick raspy noise they make when they open their jaws just afore the strike, so I dove right back between two trees. That tongue came after me so fast you'd o' swore it 'ad wings o' its own. Came right between the trees after me an' went over me 'ead so near it took off the top o' me cap.

"I started runnin' backward, just to keep 'im in sight. The damn persistent cham followed 'is tongue right through those trees. I tell you, 'is nose 'orn 'twere no farther from me 'eart than you are from me now." He patted the cushion against which he rested.

"Then how did you get away?" asked the rapt Flor, her black hair mixing in his short fur.

"Well, 'e charged so fast and reckless, so 'ungry was 'e

for me flesh, that 'e gets 'imself pinned between the trunks, 'is top right 'orn pierced 'alfway through one. For all I know 'e's still there a-tuggin' and a-pullin', tryin' to free 'imself.'' Whiskers twitching, the otter wiped a hand across his forehead.

'' 'Twere a near thing, luv.''

A disgusted Jon-Tom was angrily tossing twigs into the fire. A warm paw came down on his shoulder. He looked up to see Caz, the orange firelight sparkling on his monocle, grinning down at him around a pair of blunt white incisors.

"Something less than the truth to our friend's tale, Jon-Tom?" Another twig bounced into the flames. "I know, I've heard him spin stories before. What he lacks in literacy he compensates for with a most fecund imagination. By the time he finishes he will half believe it actually happened."

"I don't mind him spinning a yarn," Jon-Tom said, "it's the way those two are lapping it up."

"Don't let it dig at you, my friend," said the aristocratic lepus. "As I said, it is his enthusiasm that carries his storytelling. Before very long cleverness instinctively gives way to a natural lack of subtlety coupled with an inability to let well enough alone."

In confirmation, a startled yelp came from the other side of the fire, followed by the sound of a hand striking furry flesh. An argument filled the misty night air. Jon-Tom saw both Flor and Talea stalking angrily away from the recumbent and protesting otter.

"You see?" Caz sounded disapproving. "Mudge is a good fellow, but at heart he is crude. No style."

"What about you?" Jon-Tom looked curiously up at his companion. "What's your style? What do you expect to get out of this journey?"

"My style . . . is to be myself, friend." It was spoken with dignity. "To be true to myself, my friends, and forgiving to my enemies."

"Including those who chased you off the boat?"

"Tut! They were justified in their feelings, if not the

extremity of their reaction." He winked with his unglassed eye. "I was doubtless guilty of some indelicate prestidigitation of the dice. My mistake was that I was found out.

"If they had actually caught and killed me, of course, I would have been somewhat more upset."

Jon-Tom couldn't help breaking into a grin.

"As to what I expect to 'get out of this journey,' I have already stated that I feel assisting this worthy cause is reason and therefore satisfaction enough. You have been too long in the company of likable but amoral types such as Mudge and Talea. I believe implicitly everything our currently comatose wizard leader says.

"I have been studying him closely these past few days. Any idiot can see plainly that all the woes of the world weigh squarely upon his head. I am no hero, Jon-Tom, but neither am I such a fool that I cannot see that the destruction of the world as it currently exists would mean the end of my pleasant manner of living. I'm quite fond of it.

"So you see, it is in my own best interest to go along with and to help you, as it would be for any warmlander satisfied with his existence. I will help Clothahump in any way I can. I am not much for soldiering, but I have some skill in the use of words. Even he realizes, I think, that he has a tendency to be impatient with fools. On the other hand I am quite used to dealing with them."

"This group could sure use a diplomat," agreed Jon-Tom. "I've tried my best at mediating but . . . I guess I just don't have the experience for it."

"Do not belittle that which you have no control over, which is your youth, my friend. You strike me as wise for your years. That's more than anyone could ask, from what I've learned of your unwilling presence here. It strikes me you want not for ability but for goals.

"Though I have more experience than you, I am always willing to listen to others. And I could never do what you've done with the dragon. There is experience and there is experience. You handle him who breathes fire and I will take care of those who breathe insults and threats. We will complement each other. Agreed?''

''Fair enough.'' Man and rabbit shook hands warmly. The sensation no longer surprised Jon-Tom. It was like shaking hands with someone wearing mittens.

Camp was growing quiet and the nightly rain had hesitantly begun a late fall.

''You see?'' Caz pointed to the motionless figure of Clothahump, still seated on his log. He seemed not to have moved since Jon-Tom left the camp to search for Mudge. Now he sat glaze-eyed and indifferent to the falling rain.

''Our friend broods on larger matters. Yet often is the greater lost for lack of attention to the lesser.''

''Meaning what?''

''Meaning that we have posted no sentries. This is strange country to all of us.''

''In this case I don't think we have to worry. You're forgetting something.'' He pointed.

'' 'Pon my soul,'' laughed the rabbit, ''so I have.'' He sounded embarrassed. ''It is not easy to forget a dragon. How quiet he is, though.''

''Dreaming sweet dreams of a classless society, no doubt.''

Caz removed his monocle, absently polished it with the hem of his beautiful shirt. ''Then it seems we can sleep soundly ourselves. The dragon's presence is worth more than any hundred sentries. I will enjoy the security of sleeping near to so powerful an ally.''

''Just be careful he doesn't turn in his sleep.'' Caz waved smilingly back to him, and Jon-Tom watched the bobbing white tail recede toward the black bulk shielding their camp.

A gentle voice reached back to him. ''Dragons don't toss and turn in their sleep, my friend. They're not built that way. But I surely hope he does not snore. I wouldn't enjoy waking up with my pants on fire.''

Jon-Tom laughed with him. Pog was asleep, dangling like

a dark decoration from the branch of an overhanging oak. Talea and Flor were chatting quietly beneath bedrolls on the other side of the fire. He thought of joining them, shrugged, and spread out his own blanket. He was dead tired, and it would soon be morning.

Right then his body needed comforting more than his ego. . . .

XVIII

Two days of climbing the rapids followed, during which the only danger they had to cope with was the burning in Jon-Tom's ears as he was compelled to endure Mudge's reciting and embroidering of the story of his escape from the monstrous chameleon. When the horned color-changer grew to twice the size of Falameezar, even Flor threatened to beat the glib otter.

On the fourth day they encountered signs of habitation. Plowed fields, homes with neatly thatched or slate-tiled roofs, smoking chimneys, and small docks with boats tied to them began to slip past.

Falameezar would glide deeper in the water, keeping only his eyes, ears, and passengers above the surface as he breathed through his gills. Anyone on shore watching would think the several travelers were floating atop a peculiarly low boat.

On the tenth day Clothahump noted a group of low hills off to their left. Rapids lay directly ahead, though they were not nearly as swift as those that cut through the Duggakurra hills close by buried Pfeiffunmunter.

"You may put us ashore here, friend dragon. We are quite close to the city."

"But why?" Falameezar sounded disappointed. "The river is still deep and the current not too strong." He puffed smoke ahead. "I can pass on easily."

"Yes, but your presence with us might panic the inhabitants."

"I know." The downcast dragon let out a sigh. "I shall put you in to land, then. What shall I do next?"

Jon-Tom threw Clothahump a look, and the wizard subsided in the youth's favor. "I'll talk to the commissars of the Polastrindu commune. Perhaps they might accept you as a member."

"Do you think so? I had no idea so enlightened a community existed." Fiery eyes stared back down at Jon-Tom hopefully. "That would be wonderful. I'm certainly willing to do my share of the work."

"You've already done more than that this trip, comrade Falameezar. Clothahump is right, though, in suggesting you wait here in the river. Even the most educated comrades can sometimes react thoughtlessly when confronted by the unfamiliar." He leaned forward, and the dragon bent his neck back and down as Jon-Tom whispered to him, "There are counterrevolutionaries everywhere!"

"I know. Be on your guard, comrade Jon-Tom."

"I will."

The dragon eased into shore. They marched down his back and tail, passing supply packs from hand to hand. A well-used track halfway between a wide trail and a small road led over the hills. Jon-Tom looked back for a moment. The others had already started up the road. Flor was alive with excitement at the prospect of entering the strange city. Her enthusiasm made her glow like the lining of clouds after a storm.

He waved to the dragon. "Be well, comrade. Up the revolution."

"Up the revolution!" the dragon rumbled back, saluting him with a blast of fire and smoke. Then the ferocious head dipped beneath the surface. A flurry of bubbles and some fading, concentric ripples marked with a watery flower the place where the dragon sank. Then they too were gone.

Jon-Tom waded, his long legs and walking staff soon bringing him up alongside his companions, despite the burden of guilt he carried. Falameezar was far too nice a dragon to have been so roundly deceived. Perhaps they'd left him happier than he'd been before, though.

"What do you think he'll do?" Caz moved next to Jon-Tom. "Will he stay and wait for you to return?"

"How should I know? I'm no expert on the motivations of dragons. His political beliefs seem unshakable, but he tends more to philosophizing than action, I think. He might simply grow bored and swim back downstream to his familiar feeding grounds." He looked sharply at the rabbit. "Why? Do you expect trouble in Polastrindu?"

"One never knows. The larger the city, the more arrogant the citizens, and we're not exactly the bearers of good news. We shall see."

An hour's hike had brought them to the crest of the last hill. Finally the destination of so many days' traveling lay exposed to their sight.

It was wonderful, yes, but it was a flawed wonderment. They started down the hill. Why should a city here be so very different from any other? he thought sardonically.

There was a massive stone wall surrounding the city. It was intricately decorated with huge bas-reliefs and buttressed at ground level. Several gates showed in the wall, but the traffic employing them was sparse.

It was not a market day, Caz explained. Farmers were not bringing produce into the city, nor distant craftsmen and traders their wagon-borne wares.

There was somewhat more activity to the south of the city. The great wall ran almost to the river there. At least a dozen vessels were tied to the rotting docks. Some were similar to the sail-and-oar-powered keel-type boat that Caz had fled from that day on the river. Jon-Tom wondered if that very same ship might be among those bobbing gently at anchor below them. Barges and fishing vessels comprised the rest of the motley but serviceable flotilla.

"The main gate is on the opposite side of the city, to the northwest and facing the Swordsward."

"What's that?" Flor wondered aloud. "Have you been there? It seems like you've been everywhere."

Caz cleared his throat. "No, I have not. I've been no farther than anyone else, I should say. It is a vast, some say endless, ocean of vegetation inhabited by vile aborigines and dangerous creatures.

"We have no need to march around the whole city. The harbor gate should be a quite satisfactory ingress."

They continued down the winding path, which had now expanded to road size. Curious fellow travelers let their gaze linger long on the unusual group.

Lizard-drawn wagons and carts trundled past them. Sometimes riders on individual mounts would run or hop past. There was even a wealthy family on a small riding snake.

Clothahump was enjoying himself. He moved with much less effort downhill than up. His glance turned upward. "Pog! Anything to report, you useless miscreant?"

The bat yelled down to them as he dipped lower in the sky. "Da usual aerial patrol. A couple o' armed jays overflew us a few minutes ago. I don't tink dey saw us wid da dragon, though. Dey've long since turned 'round and flown back to report. Dey didn't act excited."

Clothahump appeared satisfied. "Good. I have no time for intermediaries. Polastrindu is too big for them to bother with every odd group of visitors, even if we are a bit odder than most."

"We may not seem so from the air, sir," Jon-Tom pointed out.

"Quite so, my boy."

They strolled into the docks without anyone challenging them. They watched as busy stevedores, mostly broad-shouldered wolves, margays, and lynxes, laboriously loaded and unloaded stacks of crates and bales. Exotic goods and crafts were stacked neatly on shore or loaded carefully onto dray wagons for transport into the city.

Along the docks the aroma was pungent but something less

than exotic. Even the river was darker here than out in midstream. The gray coloration derived not from some locally dark soil, as Jon-Tom first thought, but from the effluent pouring out of pipes and gutters. The raw sewage abraded much of the initial glamor he'd come to associate with Polastrindu.

Flor's expression twisted in disgust. "Surely it's not this bad in the city."

"I sure hope not." Talea sniffed once, tried to close down her sense of smell.

"It is said that the larger the town, the dirtier the habits of its citizens." Caz trod lightly on the filthy paving lest it sully the supple leather of his enormous shoes. "This derives from the concentration of the inhabitants on the making of money. Fastidiousness follows financial independence, not hard work."

One narrow stone arch bridged an open trench. As they crossed, the stench nearly knocked Flor unconscious. Jon-Tom and Caz had to help her across. Once past she was able to stand by herself and inhale deep drafts of only partly tainted air.

"*Mierda,* what a smell!"

"It should be less overwhelming once we are inside the city gate." Clothahump did not sound particularly apologetic. "There we will be away from the main sewer outfalls."

A rattling warning fell on them as Pog dipped close. "Master, soldiers come from da gate. Maybe dat overfly patrol wasn't so indifferent as it seemed. Maybe we in for some trouble."

Clothahump waved him away as one might a large house-fly. "Very good, Pog, but you worry overmuch. I will deal with them."

It was a well armed if motley-looking knot of soldiers that soon came into view, marching toward them. Between twenty and thirty, Jon-Tom guessed. He slipped his club-staff from its lacings and leaned on it expectantly. Other hands drifted in the vicinity of sheathed swords. Mudge made a show of inspecting his bow.

The troop was led by a heavily armored beaver, a thickset individual with a no-nonsense gleam in his eyes. Catching sight of the column, sailors and stevedores scattered for cover. While at first they had ignored the newcomers, they now shied from them as if they carried plague.

Boots, sandals, and naked feet generated a small rumble of retreat as other onlookers scurried for safety. Ten soldiers detached themselves with forced casualness from the main body. They quick-marched to the left to get behind the newcomers and cut off any possible retreat.

"That doesn't look promising." Jon-Tom's grip tightened on the staff as he watched the maneuver.

"Easy, my friend." The imperturbable Caz stepped forward. "I will handle this."

"They would not dare to attack us," said an outraged Clothahump. "I am an emissary to the Council of Wizards and as such my person is inviolable and sacred."

"Don't tell me, good sir," said Caz, gesturing at the nearing troops. "Tell them."

Now the walls had become menacing instead of beautiful. Their stone towers cast threatening shadows over the travelers. From ships and other places of concealment the mutterings of watchful sailors and merchants could be heard.

Finally the main body of soldiers drew up in a crescent facing them. Their leader stepped forward, pushed his helmet back on his furry forehead with a muscular paw, and studied them curiously. In addition to his chain mail, helmet, and thicker steel plates protecting particularly vulnerable places there was an unusual moon-shaped iron plate strapped to the thick, broad tail. It was studded with sharp spikes and would make a devastating weapon if it came to close-quarter fighting.

"Well," he said, speaking with a distinct lisp, "what have we here? Two gianth, a tough-looking little female"—Talea spat at the ground—''a dithreputable otter type, a fop, and an elderly gentleman of the amphibian perthuathion.''

''Good sir.'' Caz bowed slightly. ''We are travelers from downriver on a mission that is of great importance to Polastrindu and the world.''

''Thath motht interethting. Whom do you reprethent?''

''By and large we represent ourselves for now, primarily in the person of the great wizard Clothahump,'' and he gestured toward the impatient turtle. ''He carries information vital to our survival that he must present to the city council.''

The beaver was casually twirling an ugly skull-splitter of a mace, indifferent to where the spike-studded ball might land.

''Thath all very nice, but it remainth that you're not citithenth of thith city or county. At leatht, I athum you are not. Unleth of courth you can produth your identity chith.''

''Identity chits?''

''Everyone who liveth in the county or thity of Polathrindu hath an identity chith.''

''Well, since we don't come from the county or city of Polastrindu, as you've just been informed, obviously we don't have any such thing,'' Jon-Tom said in exasperation.

''That doth not nethetherily follow,'' said the beaver. ''We get many vithitoth. They all have properly thtamped identity chith. To be freely admitted to the thity all you have to do ith apply for and rethieve your proper chith.'' He smiled around enormous teeth. ''I will be happy to provide you with thom.''

Jon-Tom relaxed a little. ''Good. We'll need theven.''

''You very funny, big man. Thinth you have thuch a good thenth of humor, for your party it will cotht only''—the beaver performed some silent cogitation—''theven hundred silver pietheth.''

''Seven hundred . . . !'' Clothahump sputtered all over the pavement. ''That's extortion! Outright robbery! I am insulted. I, the great and wise and knowing Clothahump, have not been so outraged in a hundred years!''

''I believe that our leader,'' said Caz quietly, ''is somewhat disinclined to pay. Now if you will just convey word of our arrival to your superiors, I am sure that when they know why we have come—''

"They won't hear why you have come," broke in the beaver, "until you pay up. And if you don't pay up, they won't hear why you were overcome." He grinned again. His huge teeth were badly stained by some dark brown liquid. "Actually, ith eighty silver pietheth per party for identity cardth, but my men and I have to make a living of thom kind, don't we? A tholdierth pay ith pretty poor.''

There were angry murmurs of agreement from the troops standing behind him.

"We will depart peacefully then," said Caz.

"I don't think tho," said the beaver. The ten soldiers who had detached themselves earlier now moved in tightly behind the travelers, blocking their path. "I don't want you going around to the other gateth.''

Flor whispered to Mudge, "Are all your cities so hospitable?"

Mudge shrugged. "Where there's wealth, luv, there's corruption. There's a lot of wealth in Polastrindu, wot?'' He eyed the soldiers nervously.

Some of them were already fingering swords and clubs in anticipation of a little corrective head-bashing. They looked healthy and well fed, if not especially hygienic.

" 'Ere now, your wizardship, why don't we just pay up? These blokes look as though they'd rather 'ave themselves a good massacre than anythin' else. If we wait much longer we won't 'ave ourselves much o' a choice.''

"I will not pay." Clothahump obstinately adjusted his spectacles. "Besides, I can't remember that asinine silver spell.''

"You won't pay, eh?" The beaver waddled over until he was glaring eye to eye with the turtle. "Tho you're a great withard, eh? Leth thee how much of a withard you really are," and he flipped the mace around, snapped his wrist, and struck Clothahump square on the beak.

The sorcerer let out a startled cry and sat down hard. "Why you impudent young whelp!" He fumbled for his glasses, which had been knocked loose but not broken. "I shall show you who is a wizard. I will disembowel you, I'll...!"

"Port armth!" the beaver barked. Instantly a cluster of spears and clubs was pointed at the travelers. The officer said sourly, "I've had jutht about enough of thith foolithneth. I don't know who you are, where you come from, or what kind of game you're trying to play with me, but we don't take kindly to vagranth here. Ith dragged off to the thellth you're to be, and methily, too, unleth you come up with thom cash."

There was stone wall to his right and sharp steel ahead and behind, but nothing blocked Jon-Tom's path as he'd worked his way to the water's edge. He cupped his hands and yelled desperately, "Falameezarrrr!"

"What, thereth more of you then?" The beaver's whiskers twitched as he turned to face the stagnant water. "Where ith thith one? Hiding on a boat? Ith going to cotht you another hundredth silver piethes. I'm growing tired of thith. You'll pay me right now or elth..." and he twirled the mace menacingly.

A great tired creaking drowned out the last words of the threat as two ships were bodily shouldered aside. Dock planking gave under irresistible pressure from below. A huge black head emerged from beneath, trailing water and shattered boards. Great claws dug into broken stone, and coal-eyes glared down at the group.

The beaver stared open-mouthed up at the wet, shiny teeth clashing just above him. "D-d-d-d—!" He never did get the whole word out, but managed to outwaddle half his subordinates in the race for the main gate.

Sailors hastily abandoned their ships in the mad rush for the gate. Vendors and merchants abandoned their stocks and wharfside businesses in favor of drier territory. There was panic on the city wall as rudely awakened troops ran into one another in their rush to take up defensive positions.

The now solitary band of travelers put up their own weapons.

"A timely appearance, comrade," said Jon-Tom. "I'd hoped you might still be nearby, but I had no idea it would be quite this near."

Falameezar gazed at the terrified faces peeking over the top of the wall. "What is wrong with them?" He was more curious than angry. "I heard your call and came as promised, but I thought they surely would treat you as fellow comrades-in-arms in the great struggle to come."

"Yes, but you recall what I told you about the presence of counterrevolutionaries?" Jon-Tom said darkly.

"Oho, so that's it!" Falameezar let out a furious hiss and a trio of small shops burst into flame.

"Careful. We just want to get inside, not burn the city down."

A massive tail lashed at the water and instantly put out the small fires, though he did the innocent shops no more good than had the flames.

"Keep your anger in check, Falameezar," Jon-Tom advised. "I'm sure we'll have this all straightened out as soon as we can get to talk with the city's commissars."

"I should certainly think so!" said the dragon huffily. "The idea of letting counterrevolutionaries interdict innocent travelers."

"It's hard to tell the true revolutionaries from their secretive enemies."

"I suppose that's so," the dragon admitted.

"There might be even worse yet to come," Jon-Tom informed him as they all sashayed across the stones toward the now tightly barred wooden gate.

"Like what, comrade?"

Jon-Tom whispered, "Revisionists."

Falameezar shook his head and muttered tiredly, "Is there no decency left in the world?"

"Just keep your temper under control," Jon-Tom told him. "We don't want to accidentally incinerate any honest proletarians."

"I will be careful," the dragon assured him, "but inside I am trembling with outrage. Yet even a filthy revisionist can be reeducated."

"Yes, it's clear that the formation of instructional cadres should be a priority here," Jon-Tom agreed.

The city of Polastrindu had suddenly taken on the aspect of a ghost town. At the dragon's continued approach all interested faces had vanished from the wall. Only an occasional spear showed itself, and that was the only sign of movement.

Jon-Tom could feel the eyes of hidden sailors and stevedores on his back, but there was nothing to worry about from that quarter. In fact, so long as Falameezar remained with them there was little to fear from anywhere.

He glanced at Caz. The rabbit smiled and nodded back at him. Being the one in control of the dragon, it behooved Jon-Tom to do the talking. So he marched up to the gate and rapped arrogantly on the wood.

"Captain of the Gate, show yourself!" When there was neither a reply nor hint of movement from within, he added, "Show yourself or we'll burn down your gate and make you Captain of Ashes!"

There were sounds of argument from within. Then a slight groaning of wood as the massive portal opened just wide enough to permit the egress of a familiar figure. The gate shut quickly closed behind him.

"That's better." Jon-Tom eyed the beaver, who looked considerably less belligerent now. "We were discussing something about 'identity chits'?"

"They're being prepared right now," the officer told him, his gaze continually darting up at the glowering crimson-eyed face of the dragon.

"That's nice. There was also the matter of a large number of silver pieces?"

"No, no, no. Don't be ridiculouth. And abthurd mithunderthanding!"

A moment later a grateful expression came over his face as the gate opened again. He disappeared inside and came back with a handful of tiny metal rectangles. Each was stamped with tiny symbols and a few words.

"Here we are." He passed them out quickly. "You are to have your own nameth engraved here." He indicated a wide blank place on each chit. "At your leithure, of courth," he added obsequiously.

"But there are only seven chits here." The beaver looked confused. "Remember, by your own recognition there are now eight in our party."

"I don't underthand," said the nervous officer. He nodded slightly in Falameezar's direction. "Thurely *that* ith not coming into the thity?"

"A bourgeois statement if ever I heard one!" The dragon leaned close enough for the smell of brimstone and sulfur to overpower the odor of spilling sewage. That he could swallow the officer in one snap was a fact not lost on that worthy.

"No, no . . . a mithunderthanding, thath all. I . . . I'm truly thorry, thir dragon. I didn't realize you were a part of thith party . . . not jutht . . . if you'll excuth me, pleath!" He backpedaled through the opening faster than Jon-Tom would have believed those bandy legs could carry him.

Several minutes went by this time before he reappeared. "The latht chit," he said, panting as he proferred the freshly stamped metal plate.

"I'll take charge of it." Jon-Tom slipped it into a shirt pocket. "And now if you'd be so kind as to open the gate?"

"Open up in there!" yelled the officer. The newcomers strolled through. Falameezar had to duck his head and barely succeeded in squeezing through the opening.

They found themselves in a deserted courtyard. Hundreds

of anxious eyes observed them from behind dozens of barely opened windows.

Huge stone structures marched off in all directions. As in Lynchbany, they gave the impression of dozens of smaller buildings that had grown together, only here the scale was larger. The city had the appearance of a gray sand castle. Some of the structures were six and seven stories tall. Ragged apartment buildings displayed odd windows and individual balconies.

The streets they could see were much wider than in provincial Lynchbany, though overhanging porches and window boxes made them appear narrower. The street that opened into their courtyard led to the harbor gate. It was only natural that it be wider than most. Undoubtedly the city possessed its share of alleys and closes.

Evidence of considerable traffic abounded, from the worn domes of the cobblestones that projected like the bald skulls of buried midgets to the huge piles of discarded trash. Several dozen stalls ringed the courtyard square.

Jon-Tom suspected that until a little while ago these had been crowded with busy vendors hawking wares to sailors and shoppers alike. A few salespeople still cowered within, too weak or too greedy to flee. Some of the fgithtened faces were furry, a few humanly smooth.

"Look at 'em, ashrinkin' behind their bellies." Mudge made insulting faces at the half-hidden onlookers, feeling quite invulnerable with the bulk of Falameezar immediately behind him. "Welcome to wonderful Polastrindu. Pagh! The streets stink, the people stink. Sooner we've done with this business and can get back to the clean forest, the better this 'ere otter'll like it." He cupped his hands and shouted disdainfully.

"You 'ear me, you quiverin' cowardly buggers! Yer 'ole city sucks! Want to argue about it?"

No one did. Mudge looked satisfied, turned to face Jon-Tom. "What now, mate?"

"We must meet with the local sorcerers and the city council," said Clothahump firmly, "during which meeting you will do me the pleasure of restraining your adolescent outpourings."

"Ah, they deserve it, guv."

"Council?" That ominous rumble came from a quizzical Falameezar.

"Council of commissars," explained Jon-Tom hastily. "It's all a matter of semantics."

"Yes, of course." The dragon sounded abashed.

Looking around, Jon-Tom spotted the beaver hovering uncertainly in a nearby doorway. "You there, come here." The officer hesitated as long as possible.

"Yes, you!"

Reluctantly he emerged. Halfway across the square, perhaps conscious of all the eyes watching him from numerous windows, he seemed to regain some of his former pride and dignity. If he was going to his death, seemed to be his thinking, then he might as well make a good showing of it. Jon-Tom had to admire his courage, belated though it might be.

"Very well," the beaver told him calmly. "You've bullied your way into my city."

"Which was necessary only because you tried to bully us outside," Jon-Tom reminded him. "Let's say we're even now. No hard feelings."

The beaver shot a whiskery glance at the quiescent form of Falameezar before staring searchingly back at Jon-Tom.

"You mean that, thir? You are not going to take your revenge on me?"

"No. After all," Jon-Tom added, hoping to gain a local ally, "you were only doing your duty as you, uh, saw it."

"Yeth. Yeth, thath right." The officer was still reluctant to believe he wasn't being set up and that Jon-Tom's offer of friendship was genuine.

"We have no grudge against you, nor against any citizen of Polastrindu. We're here to help you."

"And every sentient inhabitant of our warmland world," Clothahump added self-importantly.

The officer grunted. Clearly the beaver prefered talking with Jon-Tom, though staring up at the towering human hurt his short neck.

"What then can I do to be of thervith to you, my friend?"

"You could arrange for us to meet with the city council and military administrators and the representatives of the wizards of this region," Jon-Tom informed him.

The beaver's eyes widened. Massive incisors clicked against lower teeth. "Thath quite a requetht, friend! Do you have any idea what you're athking?"

"I'm sorry if it's going to be difficult for you, but we can't settle for anything less. We would not have traveled all this way unless it was on a matter of critical importance."

"I can believe that. But you got to underthand I'm jutht a thuboffither. I'm not in a pothition to—"

Shouts came from behind him. Several of his soldiers were emerging from the door behind which they'd taken refuge and pointing up the main street.

An elaborate sedan chair was approaching. It was borne aloft by six puffing mice. They hesitated at their first view of Falameezar, but shouts from inside the chair and the crack of the shrewish driver's whip forced them onward. The shrew was elegantly dressed in lace and silk, complete to lace cap.

The chair halted a modest distance away. The three-foot-tall driver descended rapidly and opened the door, bowing low. The abused bearers slumped in their harnesses and fought to catch their breath. They'd apparently run most of the way.

The individual who emerged from the vehicle was clad in armor more decorative than functional. It was heavily gilded, befitting its owner's high station and haughty demeanor. He appraised the situation in the square and ambled over.

Open paw slapping across his chest, the beaver saluted sharply as the newcomer neared. A faint wave from the other was all the acknowledgment he gave the officer.

"I am Major Ortrum, Commandant of the City Guard," the raccoon said unctuously. He managed the considerable feat of ignoring Falameezar as he talked to the rest of the arrivals.

The dragon caught Jon-Tom's attention. The youth edged back alongside the black bulk while the raccoon recited some sort of official greeting in a bored voice.

"Those poor fellows there," said the dragon angrily, nodding toward the exhausted bearers of the sedan chair, "appear to me the epitome of the exploited worker. And I don't care for the looks of this one now talking."

Jon-Tom thought very fast. "I expect they take turns. That's only fair."

"I suppose," said the dragon doubtfully. "But those workers," and he indicated the panting mice, "are all of the same kind, while the speaker is manifestly different."

"Yeah . . . but what about the driver? He's different, too."

"Yes, but . . . oh, never mind. It is my suspicious nature."

Too suspicious by half, Jon-Tom thought, breathing a mental sigh of relief at having once again buffaloed the dragon. He hoped to God the Major didn't take his leave by kicking one or two of the bearers erect.

"I gather," the raccoon was saying, inhaling a choice bit of snuff, "that you are here on some silly sort of important mission?"

"That's true." Clothahump eyed the Major distastefully.

"Ah, you must be the wizard who was mentioned to me." Ortrum performed a smooth, aristocratic bow. "I defer to one who has mastered the arcane arts, and to whom all must look up to." There was a short, sharp guffaw from the bat fluttering overhead, but Clothahump's opinion of the Major underwent a radical change.

"At last, someone who recognizes the worth of knowledge! Maybe now we will get somewhere."

"That will depend," said the Major. "I am told you seek an audience of the council, the military, and the sorceral representatives as well?"

"That's right," said Mudge, "an' if they know wot's good for them they'll give us a hard listen, they will."

"Or . . . ?"

"Or . . ." Mudge looked helplessly at Clothahump.

"A crisis that threatens the entire civilized world looms closer every day," said the wizard. "To counter it will require all the resources of the warmlands."

"Understand that I do not dispute your word, knowledge-able sir," the Major said, closing his silver snuffbox, "but I am ill prepared to consider such matters. Therefore I suppose you must have your audience. You must realize how difficult it will be to gather all the notables you require in a brief period of time."

"Nevertheless, it must be done."

"And at the audience you will of course substantiate all your claims."

"Of course," said the turtle irritably.

Jon-Tom took note of the implied threat. There was more to Major Ortrum than met the eye, or the nose. It took considerable bravery to stand there showing apparent disregard for the massive presence of Falameezar. Even Jon-Tom himself, at first sight, made many of the locals pause.

Then it occurred to him that bravery might have nothing to do with it. He wondered at the contents of the snuffbox. Major Ortrum might be stoned out of his socks.

"It will take a little time."

"As soon as possible, then," said Clothahump with a harrumph of impatience.

"Naturally, you will give me the particulars of this supposed threat, so that the sorcerers at least will know, excuse my boldness sir, that they are not being dragged from their burrows and dens to confront only the ravings of a senile fraud.'' He put up a mollifying hand. ''Tut, tut, sir. Think a moment. Surely you yourself would want some assurance if the positions were reversed?''

''That seems reasonable enough. The wizards of the greater territories are a supercilious bunch. They must be made to understand the danger. I will give you such information as will be sufficient to induce them to attend the audience.'' He hunted through his plastron.

''Here, then.'' He removed a handful of tiny scrolls. ''These are curse-sealed.''

''Yes, I see the mark,'' said the raccoon as he carefully accepted them.

''Not that it would matter if you saw their contents,'' Clothahump told him. ''All the world will know soon enough. But there are certain snobbish types who would resent the intrusion of mere laymen into sorceral affairs.''

''Rest assured they will not be tampered with,'' said the Major with a fatuous smile. He placed the scrolls in his side purse.

''Now to less awesome matters. It is growing late. Surely you must be tired from the day's work''—he eyed the unfortunate beaver sharply—''and from your extensive journeying. Also, it would help settle the populace if you would retire.''

Caz brushed daintily at his lace cuffs and silk stockings. ''I for one could certainly use a bath. Not to mention something more elaborate than camp cuisine. Ah, for an epinard and haricot salad with spiced legume dressing!''

''A gourmet.'' Major Ortrum looked with new interest at the rabbit. ''You will pardon my saying so, sir, but I do not understand you falling in with this kind of company.''

''I find my present company quite satisfactory, thank you.'' Caz smiled thinly.

Ortrum shrugged. ''Life often places us in the most unexpected situations.'' It was clear he fancied himself something of a philosopher. "We will find you your bath, sir, and lodgings for you all."

The beaver leaned close, still stiffly at attention, and jerked his head toward the dragon. "Lodgings, thir? Even for that?"

"Yes, what about Falameezar?" Jon-Tom asked. "Comrades are not to be separated." The dragon beamed.

"No trouble whatsoever," the raccoon assured him. He pointed behind them. "That third large structure there, behind you and to your left, is a military barracks and storehouse. At present it is occupied only by a small maintenance crew, who will be moved. Should your substantial reptilian friend desire to return to his natural aquatic habitat, whether permanently or merely for a washup, he will find the river close at hand. And there is ample room inside for all of you, so you will be able to stay together.

"If you will please follow me?" He returned to his chair. Curses and urgings came from the driver. Though high-pitched and squeaky, they were notable for their exceptional vileness.

Divide and promote a selected few, Jon-Tom thought angrily. That's how to keep the oppressed in line. The treatment of the smaller rodents was a source of continuing unease to him.

They followed the chair to the entrance of a huge wooden building. A pair of towering sliding doors were more than large enough to admit Falameezar.

"This building is often used to house large engines," Ortrum explained. "Hence the need for the oversized portal.

"I will leave you here now. I must return to make my report and set in motion the requests you have made. If you need anything, do not hesitate to ask any of the staff inside for assistance. I welcome you as guests of the city."

He turned, and the chair shuffled off under the straining muscles of the mice. . . .

XIX

Their quarters were Spartan but satisfactory. Falameezar declared himself content with the straw carried in from the stables, the consistency being drier but otherwise akin to the familiar mud of his favorite riverbottom.

"There are some ramifications of communal government I would like to discuss with you, comrade," he said to Jon-Tom as the youth was walking toward his own quarters.

"Later, Falameezar." He yawned, nearly exhausted by the hectic day. It had turned dark outside. The windows of Polastrindu had come alive like a swarm of fireflies.

Also, he was plain tired of keeping the dragon's insatiable curiosity sated. His limited store of knowledge about the workings of Marxism was beginning to get a little threadbare, and he was growing increasingly worried about making a dangerous philosophical mistake. Falameezar's friendship was predicated on a supposedly mutual affinity for a particular socioeconomic system. A devastating temper lay just beneath those iridescent scales.

A hand clutched his arm and he jumped. It was only Mudge.

"Take 'er a mite easier, mate. Yer more knotted up than a virgin's girdle. We've made it 'ere, an' that were the important thing, wot? Tonight we'll go out an' find ourselves a couple of less argumentative ladies than the pair we're travelin' with and 'ave ourselves a time of it, right?"

Jon-Tom firmly disengaged his arm. "Oh no. I remember the last tavern you took me into. You nearly got my belly opened. Not to mention abandoning me in Thieves' Hall."

"Now that were Talea's doin', not mine."

"What was my doing?" The redhead had appeared in the doorway ahead.

"Why nothin', luv," said Mudge innocently.

She eyed him a moment longer, then decided to ignore him. "Anybody noticed that there are dormitories at each end of this masoleum? They're full of soldiers. We've been given the officer's quarters, but I don't like being surrounded by the others."

"Afraid of being murdered in your sleep?" Flor had joined the discussion.

Talea glared at her. "It's been known to happen, usually to those who think their beds safe. Besides, that Major Maskface said there was normally only a 'maintenance crew' living here. Then where'd all the bully-boys come from, and why?"

"How many are there?" inquired Caz.

"At least fifty at each end. Possums, weasels, humans; a nice mix. They looked awfully alert for a bunch of broom-pushers. Well armed, too."

"It's only natural for the city to be nervous at our presence," Jon-Tom argued. "A few guards are understandable."

"A few yes, a hundred I'm not so sure."

"Are you saying we're prisoners?" said Flor.

"I'm saying I don't sleep well knowing that over a hundred 'nervous' and well-armed soldiers are sleeping on either side of me."

"Wouldn't be the first time," Mudge murmured.

She looked at him sharply. "What? What did you say, you fuzz-faced little prick?"

"That it wouldn't be the first time we've been surrounded, luv."

"Oh."

"There's one way to find out." Caz moved to the small

door set in one of the huge sliding panels hung from the west wall. He opened it and conversed with someone unseen. Presently the beaver officer they'd first encountered outside the city appeared. He looked unhappy, tried to avoid their stares.

"I underthand you would like an evening meal."

"That's right," said Caz.

"They will be brought in immediately. The betht the city can offer." He started to leave. Caz restrained him.

"Just a moment. That's a very kind offer, but some of us would prefer to find our own dinery." He picked absently at his tail, whiskers twitching. "That's all right, isn't it?" He took a step toward the open door.

The officer reluctantly moved to block his path. "I'm truly thorry, thir." He sounded as if he meant it. "But Major Ortrum gave thrict inthructions on how you were to be quartered and fed. Your thafety ith of much conthern to the authoritieth. They are worried that thertain radical foolth among the population might try to attack you."

"Their concern for our health is most kind," replied, Caz, "but they needn't worry. We can take care of ourselves."

"I know that, thir," admitted the officer, "but my thuperiorth think otherwithe. Ith for your own protecthion." He backed out, closing the door tightly behind him.

"That's it, then," snapped an angry Talea. "We're under house arrest. I knew they were up to something."

Flor was playing with her knife, cleaning her long nails and looking quite ravishing as she leaned against a wall, legs crossed and her black cape framing her figure.

"That's easily fixed. *Un poco sangre* and we'll go where we please, *¿no es verdad?* Or we could wake up Jonny-Tom's fire-breathing *compadre* and make charcoal of that door." She gestured at the huge sliding panels with the knife.

"These aren't the enemy, Flor. Now is a time for diplomacy," he told her. "In any case, I can't risk leaving Falameezar."

Black eyes flashed at him and she stood away from the

wall, jabbed the knife into the wood. "Maybe so, but I'm like Talea in this. I don't like being told where I can and can't go even if it supposedly is for my own 'protection'! I had twenty years of older brothers and sisters telling me that. I'll be damned if I'm going to let some oversized stuffy coon dictate the same thing to me now."

"Tch, tch . . . children, children."

They all turned. The squat figure of Clothahump was watching them, clucking his tongue in disapproval.

"You will all be valuable on the battlefield in the war to come, but that war is not yet, nor here. The fleshpots of the city do not interest me in the least, so," and he smiled up at Jon-Tom, "I will remain here to satisfy our large companion's desire for conversation."

"Are you sure . . . ?" Jon-Tom began.

"I have listened closely to much of your chatter, and you have instructed me well. The underlying principles to which this dragon adheres so fanatically are simple enough to manipulate. I can handle him. Besides, it is the nature of wizards and dragons to get along with one another. There are other things we can talk about.

"But you should all go, if you so desire. You have done all I have asked of you so far and deserve some relaxation. So I will occupy the attention of the dragon when required, and will aid you in slipping away."

"I don't know." Jon-Tom studied the snoring figure of the dragon. "He has a pretty probing, one-track mind."

"I will endeavor to steer our talk away from economics. That seems to be his main interest. After you have departed I shall bar the door from the outside . . . a simple bit of levitation. With the bars in place and the sounds of conversation inside, the other guards will assume all are still here.

"That shouldn't be too 'ard to do, wot?"

Mudge jumped. The wizard had mimicked his voice perfectly.

A dark form descended from the rafters. "What about me, Master?" Pog looked imploringly at him.

"Go with them if you will. I will have no need of you here tonight. But stay away from the brothels. That's what got you into this in the first place, remember. You will end up indenturing yourself to a second master."

"Not ta worry, boss. And thanks!" He bowed in the air, dipping like a diving plane.

"I don't believe you, but I will not hold you back and let the others go. Moral dessication," he muttered disgustedly. Pog simply winked at Jon-Tom.

"You said you'd help us get out. What are you going to do," Flor wondered, "dissolve the wall?"

Clothahump frowned at her as much as his hard face would allow. "You underestimate the resources available to a sophisticated worker of miracles such as myself. If I were to do as you suggest, it would be immediately evident to those watching us what had taken place. Your temporary departure must go unnoticed.

"When it is but a little darker I will allow you to pass safely and unseen into the city."

So it was that several hours later the little group of sightseers stood clustered in a narrow side street. Oil lamps flickered in the night mist. Light struggled to escape from behind closed shutters. Around them drifted the faint sounds of a city too big and bustling to go to sleep at night.

Behind them, across the deserted square, bulked the shadowy, barnlike barracks in which they'd been confined only moments earlier.

Jon-Tom had expected Clothahump to do something extraordinary, such as materializing them inside another building.

Instead, the wizard had moved to another small side door. His gift for mimickry, magical or otherwise, had been used to throw the studied voice of one snoozing guard. Through the use of ventriloquism he had cast rude aspersions on the ancestry of the other guard. Violently waking up his supposedly insulting companion, this victim and his associate soon fell to more physical discussion.

At that point it was a simple matter for Caz and Talea to slip up behind them and via the judicious application of some loose cobblestones, settle the argument for the duration of the evening.

It was not quite the miraculous manipulation of magic Jon-Tom had expected from Clothahump, but he had to admit it was efficient.

No one troubled them or challenged them as they walked down the deserted thoroughfare. Citizens were voluntarily or else by directive giving the barracks area a wide berth.

Soon they began encountering evening pedestrian traffic, however, and despite the size of Jon-Tom and Flor, they attracted little attention. Talea and Mudge had never been inside a city the size of Polastrindu. They were trying hard to act blasé, but their actual feeling was awe.

Jon-Tom and Flor were equally ignorant of the city's customs, though not of its size, and so was Pog. So it was left unspoken that Caz would lead them. After a while Jon-Tom felt almost comfortable walking the rain-soaked streets, his cape up over his head. With its overhanging balconies and flickering oil lamps it was not unlike Lynchbany. The principal difference was the increased volume of bickering and fighting, of the sounds of loving and playing and cursing and crying cubs that issued from behind doors and windows.

As in Lynchbany the uppermost garret levels were inhabited by the various arboreal citizens. Bats like Pog, or kilt-clad birds. Night-fliers filled the sky and danced or fought in silhouette against the cloud-shrouded moon.

A group of drunken raccoons and coatis ambled past them. Their capes and vests were liquor-stained. One inebriated bobcat tottered in their midst. She was magnificently dressed in a long flowing skirt and broad-rimmed hat. With short tail switching and cat-eyes piercing the night she looked as if she might just have emerged from a stage version of *Puss n' Boots*, though the way her companion coati was pawing her was anything but fairytalish.

They encountered a group of voles and opossums on their way to work. Having just arisen from a long day's sleep, the workers were anxious to reach their jobs. The revelers would not let them pass. There was shoving and pushing, much of it good-natured, as the workers made their way at last up the street.

"Down this way," Caz directed them. They turned down a narrow, winding road. The lighting was more garish, the noise from busy establishments more raucous. Heavily made-up faces boasting extreme coloration of fur and skin only partly due to cosmetics beckoned to them from various windows. By no means were all of them of a female cast. Flor in particular studied them with as much interest as ever she'd devoted to a class in the sociology of nineteenth-century theater.

Occasionally these faces would regard them with more than usual intent. These stares were reserved primarily for the giants Flor and Jon-Tom. Some of the comments that accompanied these looks were as appreciative as they were ribald.

"My feet are beginning to hurt," Jon-Tom told Caz. "How much farther? You know where you're taking us?"

"In a nonspecific way, yes, my friend. We are searching for an establishment that combines the best of all possible worlds. Not every tavern offers sport. Not every gaming house supplies refreshment. And of the few that offer all, not many are reputable enough to set foot in."

Still another corner they turned. To his surprise Jon-Tom noted that Talea had sidled close to him.

"It's nice to be out," he said conversationally. "Not that I was so uncomfortable back there in the barracks, but it's the principle of the thing. If they think they can get away with restricting our movements, then they'll be more inclined to do so, and less respectful of Clothahump's information."

"That's so," she said huskily. "But that's not what concerns me now."

"No?" He put his arm around her experimentally. She

didn't resist. He thought back to that morning in the forest when he'd awakened to find her curled up against his shoulder. That warmth communicated itself now through her shirt and cape. It traveled through his fingers right up his arm and down toward nether regions.

"What does concern you, then?" he asked affectionately.

"That for the past several minutes we've been followed." Startled, Jon-Tom started to look back over his shoulder when a hand jabbed painfully into his ribs.

"Don't look at them, you idiot!" He forced his eyes resolutely ahead. "There are six or seven of them, I think."

"Maybe it's just another group of party-goers," he said hopefully.

"I don't think so. They've neither fallen behind us, turned off on a different street, nor come any nearer. They've kept too consistent a gap between us to mean well."

"Then what should we do?" he asked her.

"Probably turn into the next tavern. If they mean us any harm, they'll be more reluctant to try anything in front of a room full of witnesses."

"We can't be sure of that. Why not send Pog back to check 'em out," he suggested brightly, "before we jump to any conclusions? At the least he can tell us exactly how many of them there are and how heavily armed they are."

She looked up at him approvingly. "That's more like it. The more suspicious you become, Jon-Tom, the longer you'll live. Pog! *Pog*?" The others looked back at her curiously.

"Pog! Good-for-nothing parasitic airborne piece of shit, where the hell—?"

"Stow it, sister!" The bat was abruptly fluttering in front of them. "I've got some bad news for ya."

"We already know," Talea informed him.

He looked puzzled, remained hovering a couple of feet in front of them as they walked. "You *do*? But how could you? I flew on ahead because I was getting bored, and surely ya can't see . . . ?"

"Wait . . . wait a second," muttered Jon-Tom. "*Ahead*? But," and he jerked a thumb back over his left shoulder, "we were talking about the group that's be—"

"That's far enough!" declaimed a strange voice.

"Whup . . . see yas." Pog suddenly rocketed straight up into the darkness formed by garrets and overhanging beams.

Jon-Tom hastily searched the street. The nearest open doorway from which music and laughter emerged was at least half a block ahead of them on the left. At the moment there was nothing flanking them save a couple of dark portals. One led into a close that pierced a labyrinth of stairways. The other was heavily barred with iron-studded shutters.

There was no one else in sight. Not a single stray celebrant, or better still, any of the city's night patrol.

In front of them waited perhaps a dozen heavily armed humans. Most boasted long scraggly hair and longer faces. They hefted clubs, maces, quarterstaffs, and bolas. It was an impressive assortment of armament. Not until much later did he have time to reflect on the fact that there was not a single serious killing weapon, not one knife or spear or sword, among them.

The humans had spread themselves into a semicircle across the street, blocking it completely. Jon-Tom considered the narrow close a last time. It had more the look of a trap than a means of escape.

Two-thirds of the humans were male, the rest female. None wore decent clothes or pleasant looks. All were roughly Talea's height. Even Caz was taller than most of them. Their attention was on Jon-Tom and Flor, whom they regarded with unconcealed interest.

"We'd appreciate it if you'd come along with us." This request was made by a stocky blond fellow in the middle of the group. His beard seemed to continue right down into his naked chest, as did the drooping mustache. In fact, he displayed so much hair that Jon-Tom wondered in the darkness if he really was human and not one of the other furry local citizens.

That led him to consider the unusual homogeneity of the group. Up till now, every gathering of locals he'd encountered, whether diners or merchants, sailors or pedestrians, had been racially mixed.

He looked backward. The lot who'd been trailing them had spread out to block any retreat back up the street and yes, they were also wholly human, and similarly armed.

"That's nice of you," Caz said, replying to the invitation, "but we have other plans of our own." He spoke for all his companions. Jon-Tom casually swung his staff around from his back, slipped the duar out of the way. Talea's hand dropped to her sword. There was some uneasy shuffling among the humans confronting them.

"I'm sorry. We insist."

"I wish you would encyst," said Flor cheerfully, "preferably with something cancerous."

The insult was lost on the man, who simply blinked at her. Both clusters began to crowd the travelers, edging in from front and back.

There was a light metallic sound as Talea's sword appeared in her hand. "First one of you rodents lays a hand on me is cold meat."

In the dim light from the oil lamps Jon-Tom thought she looked lovelier than ever. But then, so did Flores Quintera.

She'd assumed an amazonian stance with her own short sword and mace held expectantly in front of her, the light gleaming off the saw teeth lining the steel.

"*Ovejas y putas*, come and take us ... if you can."

"Ladies, please!" protested Caz, aghast at the manner in which his attempted diplomacy was being undermined from behind. "It would be better for all of us if ... excuse me, sir." He'd been glancing back at Talea and Flor but had not lost sight of their opponents. One of them had jumped forward and attempted to brain the rabbit with a small club, whereupon Caz had hopped out of the way, offered his apologies, and stuck out a size twenty-two foot. His assailant had gone tumbling over it.

"Dreadfully sorry," murmured Caz. His apology did nothing to stem the rush which followed as the two groups of encircling humans attacked.

The narrowness of the street simplified defensive tactics. The set-upon arranged themselves back to back in a tight circle and hacked away at their antagonists, who threw themselves with shocking recklessness against swords and knives. The light and sweat and screaming swam together around Jon-Tom. The duar was a heavy weight bouncing under his arm as the blunt end of his staff-club sought out an unprotected face or groin.

It occurred to him that a little magic might have frightened off their assailants. He cursed himself for not thinking of it earlier. It was too late now for singing. He couldn't stop defending himself long enough to swing the duar around.

Three frustrated attackers were trying to get beneath his enormous reach. He held them off with the club. One slipped underneath the staff and raised a mace. Jon-Tom thumbed a stud on the staff and flipped it around in an arc as he'd been shown. The spring-loaded spearpoint sliced across the mace-wielder's thighs. He collapsed, moaning and holding his legs.

Something dark covered Jon-Tom's eyes as he was hit from below and behind. Flailing wildly with the staff, he went over backward. The staff intercepted something yielding, which yelped once.

A heaviness pressed down on his senses as well as his eyes. Then everything turned to mush, including the noise of fighting. His thoughts swam sluggishly as though he were trying to think through Jell-O. Dimly he could still make out shrieks and screams from the continuing battle, but they sounded faint and far away.

He recognized the high-pitched challenge of Talea alternating with Mudge's taunts and curses. Flor was yowling war cries in an interesting mixture of English and Spanish. The last sight he'd glimpsed before the black cloth or bag or whatever it was had been slipped over his head showed a starlit sky mottled with clearing rain clouds and a sickle moon beaming bluely down between peaked roofs that overhung the street like cupped hands. He hoped they were formed in prayer for him.

Then even that wish faded, along with the remnant of his consciousness. . . .

XX

At first he thought a fly had somehow tumbled into his brain. It was beating against the sides, trying to get out. When the fly-feeling gave way to a certainty that the buzzing came from elsewhere, he opened his eyes and hunted for its source.

An oil lamp burned on a simply hewn wood table. A gruff announcement came from someone unseen.

"He's awake!"

This was followed by the pad-padding of many feet. Jon-Tom struggled to a sitting position. Gravity, or something, tried to pull off the back of his head. He winced at the pain. It slowly dribbled away, down his neck and into oblivion.

He discovered he was sitting on the edge of a cot. In the dim lamplight he could now make out the familiar shapes of his staff and duar leaning against the far wall of the room.

Flanking his possessions were two of the humans who'd attacked him. One wore a bandage across his forehead and over one ear. The other exhibited a deep purple bruise and knot over his right eye. His mouth also showed signs of having been cut.

Normally an exceptionally pacific person, Jon-Tom experienced an uncharacteristic surge of pleasure at this evidence of the damage he and his companions had done. He'd made up his mind to make a rush for the club-staff when a door opened on his left and half a dozen people marched in.

Leaning forward, he was disappointed to discover he could

see nothing past the door except a dimly lit corridor, though he could hear distant conversation.

The new arrivals stationed themselves around the room. Three of them took up positions in front of the door while another closed it behind them. Two additional lamps were lit. Everyone in the room looked very determined. Another trio sat down at the table. Someone brought a few roughly forged goblets and a couple of plates piled high with steaming meat and a close relative of boiled potatoes.

There were no windows in the room. The only light came from the three oil lamps and the crack beneath the door. Captors and captive examined each other with interest for long minutes.

Then one of the three seated at the table spoke to him, and Jon-Tom recognized the blond spokesman who had confronted him in the street.

"You hungry?" Jon-Tom shook his head. "Thirsty?" Again the negative motion, accompanied by a smile and an obscene gesture. Jon-Tom was not thinking like a would-be lawyer now. He was still light-headed and maybe just a little crazy.

His actions and silence did not seem to upset his interrogator, who shrugged and said, "Suit yourself. I am." He picked up a potato-thing and spread some sort of transparent glaze over it, using a spoon set in a small jar. Taking a bite out of it, he chewed noisily. Glaze slid down his chin and onto his chest.

When he'd finished half the tuber he looked again at Jon-Tom. Then he asked bluntly, "Head hurt?"

"You know goddam well it does," Jon-Tom told him, feeling of the lump that was maturing on the back of his skull.

"We're sorry about that." And to Jon-Tom's surprise the man sounded honestly contrite. "But you wouldn't come with us voluntarily, and we didn't have much time to talk. Patrol could've come along."

"If you've been facing twelve armed people in an unfamiliar street, would you have gone along?"

The blond smiled wryly. "I suppose not. We're not much
on tact, I guess. But it was imperative you come with us, and
we had to get you away from the animals."

That made Jon-Tom take another anxious look around the
room. No question about it, he was the sole captive present.

"Where are the others? Where are my friends?"

"Where we left them. Scattered around the alleys of the
Loose Quarter. Oh, they didn't seem badly hurt," he added
when Jon-Tom looked ready to rise from the cot. "Far less so
than our own people. We simply led the fight away from you
once we had you drugged and under control."

"Why me?" He leaned back against the rock wall. "What's
so interesting about me?"

The stocky speaker peered hard at him. "It is said that you
are a wizard, a spellsinger, from another world." He seemed
at once skeptical and yet anxious to have that skepticism
disputed.

"Yes . . . yes, that's right." Jon-Tom stretched out his arms
and waved his fingers. "And if you don't let me out of here in
ten seconds I'm going to turn you all into mushrooms!"

The leader shook his head, looking down at the floor and
then up again to smile at Jon-Tom. He clasped both hands
together on his lap.

"Any spellsinger requires his instrument to make magic."
He nodded in the direction of the closely guarded duar. "You
threaten emptily. I had heard that you controlled a river
dragon. That plus your admission just now is proof enough
for me."

"How do you know that I'm controlling the dragon?
Maybe I'm just trying to frighten you into releasing me.
Clothahump the turtle is still back at our barracks, and he's a
powerful wizard, much more powerful than I am. Maybe he's
controlling the dragon and even now setting up a spell to
dissolve all of you like so much tea."

"We know of the hard-shelled bumbler who accompanied you. We know also that he and the great dragon are even now arguing absurdities back in the harbor barracks. We know this not through magic but through our well-organized and loyal network of observers and spies." Again the smile. "Sometimes that is worth more than magic."

Network, Jon-Tom thought? What's this talk of spies and networks? Something else, something about the attitude of the people in the room, their attacking with nonlethal weapons, all bespoke something deeper than your everyday garden-variety robbers.

"Who do you spy for? Aren't you all citizens of the city or county of Polastrindu?"

"By birth," admitted the man, and there were murmurs of agreement from the others in the room, "but not by inclination, or belief."

"You're losing me."

"We don't want to do that," said the man, unclasping his hands. "We want you to join us."

"Join you? In what? I haven't got time to join anything else. I'm already into something vitally important to your whole world." He started to recite Clothahump's warning about the coming cataclysm.

"The Plated Folk are readying their greatest invasion of these lands in their history, and they have—"

"We know all that," said one of the other guards impatiently.

Jon-Tom gaped at the woman who'd spoken. She was one of the trio blocking the doorway. "You know?" Nods of assent came from several of the others.

"But I thought . . . Clothahump said he was the only one perceptive enough to . . . but *how* do you know?"

"Patience," the blond urged him. "All will be explained.

"You asked if we were not citizens of the city, and what we wanted you to join us for. We are citizens of this city, yes, and we are something more, we believe. As for what we want

323

you to join, I have already told you. We want you to join us."

"What the hell do you mean by 'us'? Some kind of political organization?"

The man shook his head. "Not really. Us. *Us* . . . we humans." He spoke patiently, as though explaining to a child.

"I still don't follow you."

The man looked in exasperation at his companions, then once more back at Jon-Tom. "Listen to me carefully, spellsinger. For tens of thousands of years mankind has been compelled to exist as a lowly equal with the animals. With the hordes of stinking, smelly, hairy beasts who are obviously our inferiors." This was said with casual disregard for his own unkempt mat of fur. "With those who are destined to be damned together with the rats and mice they so readily discriminate against themselves."

Jon-Tom didn't reply. The man almost pleaded with him. "Surely you have felt the inequality, the unnaturalness of this situation?" He paced in front of Jon-Tom's cot, occasionally shaking clenched fists at him.

"We are more than animals, are we not? Clearly nature has intended us to be superior, yet some unnatural force or circumstance has held us back from achieving our birthright. The time to change that is near. Soon mankind shall inherit this world, as nature intended him to!"

"You're talking, then," said Jon-Tom slowly, "about a race war?"

"No!" The stocky leader turned angrily on him. "This is to be a war for the race, for the human race, to place it in its rightful position as leader of civilization." He leaned near, stared searchingly into Jon-Tom's face. "Tell me then, spellsinger: do the humans of your otherworld exist equally with the animals?"

My God, Jon-Tom thought in panic. What do I say? How perceptive are they? Can they detect, through magic or otherwise, if I lie? And if so, and they learn the truth, will they use that to gather support among the humans here for their own hateful plans?

But are they after all so hateful? Do you hate what this man is saying, Jon-Tom, or do you hate the thought that you might agree with him?

"Well?" the man prompted.

No reply was worse than anything he might say, he decided. "The humans I've met are no more than the equal of the other animals here in size and intelligence. Some have shown themselves to be a damnsight less so. What makes you think you're so superior?"

"Belief, and inner knowledge," came the instant reply. "This cannot be the way nature meant things to be. Something is wrong here. And you have not yet answered my question about the relationship between humans and animals in your world."

"We're all animals together. Intelligence is the determining factor, and the other *persons* I've met here have been pretty much equal in intelligence."

"Ah . . . the other animals you've met *here*. What about your own world's 'animals'?"

Jon-Tom's voice rose in frustration. "God damn you, shape and size has nothing to do with it!"

"It confirms what the dream raiders told us," murmured someone in the back of the room. There were other unintelligible whispers, smug and self-satisfied. Jon-Tom found them unsettling.

"Anyway, I won't join you." He folded his arms. "I doubt that many will. I know plenty of humans already who can tell the difference between civilized and uncivilized, between intelligent and ignorant, without having to think about it, and it hasn't a fucking thing to do with body odor. So you can take your 'belief' and 'inner knowledge' and stuff it! Those are the kinds of groundless, half-assed reasons dictators have used throughout history for discriminating against others, and I don't want anything to do with it.

"Besides, humans are just another mammalian minority here. Even if they all went nuts and joined you, you're far too outnumbered to even think the kind of genocide you're contemplating has a chance of success."

"You're right on all counts," agreed the leader, "except one."

"I don't think I overlooked anything."

"Perhaps it would be better if *I* explained." The voice had a hoarseness to it that suggested a severe cold or laryngitis. The man who'd spoken stepped out into the light. He was as thickset as the leader and even more hirsute. Long black hair flowed below his shoulders, and his beard almost obscured his face. Brown and blue leathers were draped tentlike on his body.

Jon-Tom was by now almost too furious to think straight. "Who the hell are you, jack?" He was thinking of Mudge and Clothahump, of the aristocratic but friendly Caz, and the acerbic Pog. The idea that this motley mob of near barbarians considered themselves good enough to lord it over his new-won furry friends was almost more than he could stomach.

"My identity is perhaps better shown than stated," said the black-haired shape as he reached up and carefully removed his head.

The skull thus revealed was smaller than a human head, but occupied almost as much volume because of the bulging, bright green compound eyes. The chitin was bright blue spotted with yellow patches. A slash of maroon decorated the mandibles. Antennae drooped toward Jon-Tom. They were constantly in motion, alternating like a swimmer's arms.

It spoke again, the same harsh, rasping tone. The mouth did not move. Jon-Tom realized the insect was generating a crude approximation of normal speech by controlling the flow of air through its breathing spicules.

"I am Hanniwuz," said the apparition huskily. "This suit I wear is necessary lest the locals kill me on sight. They bear an unreasoning hatred for my people and have persecuted us for thousands of years.''

Jon-Tom had recovered from the initial shock of the revelation. ''The way I hear it, it's your people who have been doing the hating, trying to invade and enslave the locals for millenia.''

''I will not deny that we seek control, but we do not seek conquest. It is for our protection. We require security of some kind. The warmlanders grow constantly stronger. One day their hatred will overwhelm their lethargy and they will arise en masse to massacre the Plated Folk. Do we not have the right to self-defense?''

Oh boy, Jon-Tom thought: history and legalisms. He felt suddenly at home. ''Don't try and bullshit me. Whenever one nation claims it requires 'secure borders' with another, that border is usually the far border of the neighboring country and not the common one. That 'border' country gets swallowed up, and the secure borders have to be moved outward again, and then again. It's a never ending process. Security may never be satisfied that way, but greed usually is.''

The insect's head swiveled to look up at the blond man. ''Spellsinger or not, I think this one more dangerous than useful. I do not think he will be of use to us.'' Jon-Tom went cold and still.

''No, he's not as positive as he sounds.'' The leader turned imploringly, smilingly back to the lanky youth. ''Please tell Hanniwuz you'll join us.''

''I don't see the connection between you two.''

''The Plated Folk recognize that among the warmlanders only we humans think like they do. Only we have the ability to make war with detachment and then to govern properly. That's our natural right, and the Plated Folk are willing to recognize that. If we help them, they will allow us to rule in their stead. That will give them the security they seek.''

''You really believe that? Then you people are either dumb

or morally bankrupt. You have no 'natural right' to rule anything. Genetics has worked out differently here.''

One of the other guards said worriedly, "Careful, he speaks magic words.'' Candlelight glinted on swords and spears, a sparkling forest of death suddenly aimed threateningly at Jon-Tom.

"Watch your mouth, stranger! . . . Don't try magicking us!''

"See the effect he has?'' The leader turned to Hanniwuz. "Consider how important an ally he could be to the cause.''

" 'Could be' are the key words, my friend.'' The insect envoy lifted a hand, turned his head sideways, and preened his ommatidia. "He remains violently opposed.''

The stocky chieftain walked up to Jon-Tom, who tensed, but the man only put his hands on the youth's shoulders.

"Listen to me, spellsinger. You have the size and bearing of a warrior along with your gift for magicking. You could be a leader among us, one of those who lord it over these lands. The climate here suits not the Plated Folk. They have need of our services now and they will have need of them when the war is done.''

"So they say.'' Jon-Tom eyed the impassive insect. "It's astonishing how fast a conquerer can get acclimated.''

"Control your first reactions, spellsinger. Think rationally and without bitterness on what I say. With your stature and abilities you could rule whole counties, entire reaches of the Lands. A dozen or more cities like Polastrindu could be under your absolute control. Anything you wanted could be yours for the asking: riches, fine goods, slaves of any species or sex.

"You are a young man still. What future does your mentor Clothahump offer you in comparison? A chance to go to an unpleasant death? Is it so very wrong that humans rule over the animals? So you do not agree with the moral justification of our cause. Can you not rationalize what it would bring to you personally?

"Think hard, spellsinger, for the Plated Folk are destined

to conquer this time, no matter who or what opposes them. It is easy to support a martyr's death for others . . . but what about for yourself? Is that what you have hoped for all your life, to die young and bravely?'' His hand slashed at the air. "That is stupid."

"I don't think your victory is assured just yet," Jon-Tom said quietly, "despite your"—he caught himself just in time, having been on the verge of saying "despite your secret magic," and instead finished—"despite all the quislings you can recruit, and I don't think there'll be all that many."

"Then there are no circumstances under which you would consider joining us? Think hard! The world can be yours."

"Shit, I wouldn't know what to do with it. I don't . . ." He stopped.

Seriously now, what did he owe to this world into which he'd been rudely, unwillingly, and perhaps permanently yanked? If he ever succeeded in returning to his own place and time, what would he become? A corpulent attorney, fat and empty of real life? Or a sour, doped-up musician playing cheap bars and sweet-sixteen parties?

Here he could be one step above a mayor and one step below a god. Weren't all of them, for all their veneer of civilization and intelligence, nothing more than oversized animals? Mudge, Caz, Pog, all of them? He considered the way Flor had occasionally looked at Caz. Was it right that he should consider himself, even momentarily, in competition for the love of his life with an oversized hare? Was that less repugnant than cooperation with these people?

Why shouldn't he join them, then? Why should he not look out for himself for a change?

"That's very good, man," whispered Hanniwuz. "You think. Death, or ascension to a throne we will create for you. It seems an easy choice to make, does it not? The day we attack there will be uprisings of humans throughout the warmlands. They will flock to our cause. Together we shall force these bloated, soft, smelly creatures back into the dirt where they belong . . . aahhh-chrriick!''

''I'm not sure—'' Jon-Tom began.

Yells and shouts from the other side of the door and all eyes turned in that direction. Then the opening was full of flying bodies, blood, and steel. Talea darted in and out of the crowd, her sword taking bites out of larger and more muscular bodies. Caz wielded a rapier with delicacy but far more ferocity than Jon-Tom had suspected him of possessing, a furry white demon in the candlelight. Mudge charged into the thick of fray, his energy and activity compensating for his usual lack of good judgment.

Dim light was reflected from fast-moving metal. There were screams and curses and the sound of flesh hitting stone. Blood hit Jon-Tom in the face, temporarily blinding him. Flores Quintera towered above the mob, her black mane flailing the air as she cut with mace and her small saw edge at anyone who tried to get near her.

Above them all, clinging precariously to a chink in the roof and occasionally tossing a knife down into the milling cluster below, was Pog.

That explained how the others had tracked him. When the fight in the street had broken away from Jon-Tom, Pog had thoughtfully left the battle to shadow Jon-Tom and his captors. Then he'd returned to lead the others to the rescue.

A large, spiked mace rose in front of Jon-Tom's gaze. The man hefting it was bleeding badly from the neck and sanity had left his face.

''Die then, otherworld thing!''

Jon-Tom closed his eyes and readied himself for oblivion. There was the shock of concussion, but it was in his right shoulder instead of his forehead. Opening his eyes he found the mace-wielder sprawled across his legs. As he watched, the dying man slid to the floor.

Talea stood above the corpse, a knife in each hand, her clothes splattered with the darker stains of blood. She looked back into the room. Another door had opened in the far corner. His few surviving captors were retreating via the new exit. Of Hanniwuz there was no sign.

The redhead was breathing heavily, her chest heaving beneath the shirt. She had a wild look in her eyes. It became one of concern as she focused on the slumped shape of Jon-Tom. He blinked at her as he held his throbbing shoulder.

"I'm all right. But just barely. Thanks." He looked past her. "Pog? You responsible for this?"

"Dat a fact. Sometimes da coward's course is da best. When I saw da fight all revolving around you, I knew it was you dey were after. So I held myself in reserve in case I had ta follow or bring help."

"I'll bet you 'eld yourself in 'reserve,' you sanctimonious 'ypocrite!" bellowed Mudge from across the room. The last of Jon-Tom's captors had fled or been dispatched, and the otter was walking toward the table, wiping at a cut across his chest.

"Near ruined me best vest, bugger it! Cost me thirty coppers in Lynchbany." He smiled then at Jon-Tom and let out a pleased whistle-whoop. "But it don't matter much, mate, because you're awright."

"Your vest's in better shape than my shoulder." Jon-Tom sat up with Talea's help. She felt of it ungently, and he yelped.

"Don't be such a cub. It's not broken, but I wager you'll have the devil of a bruise for a few weeks." She cleaned one knife on a pants leg and used it to point at an overhead set of iron bars. Jon-Tom walked beneath them. They'd been invisible from his seat on the cot.

"Crawl space up there. We heard you talking with this bunch before we interrupted the party." She looked back at him interestedly. "What were you talking about?"

"Nothing much." He looked away. "They wanted me to join them."

"Huh! Join them in what?"

"Sort of an outlaw band," he muttered uncomfortably.

"And what were you going to do?"

He looked angrily at her. "I didn't give it a thought, of course!" He hoped he appeared suitably outraged. "What do you take me for?"

She regarded him silently for a moment before saying, "A confused, stubborn, naïve, brilliant, and I hope sensible guy."

With that she left him, joined Flor in inspecting the escape door to see if any wounded remained.

Caz was at his back, undoing his bonds. "Rather awkward situation, my friend."

"'Ere now, it were bloody well more than 'awkward,' flagears!" Mudge had adopted a familiar swagger, now that the fight was won. "When I shot into the room and saw that mace comin' down I was afraid we were goin' t' be a second too late. Good thing sweet flame-top's as fast with 'er 'ands as she is with 'er 'ips," and he glanced around quickly to make certain Talea hadn't overheard him.

"I'm okay, Mudge." The ropes came loose. Circulation stabbed back into his wrists. Rubbing them, he stood, towering once more over his rescuers.

Mudge, Caz, Pog. Not only were they not "animals," he decided, they were a hell of a lot more "human" than the so-called humans who'd kept him prisoner. The thought of betraying their trust on behalf of the Plated Folk now made him almost physically ill. As for dreams of power and mastery, they vanished from his thoughts. Not because they were unattainable, not because they were morally repugnant, but because Jon-Tom had always been utterly unable to do less than the Right Thing.

I'd make a lousy lawyer, he thought. And if I can't help thinking about power and mastery, well hell, I'm only human.

Maybe if I work real hard, he told himself, I can manage to overcome that.

"There was an insect envoy with them," he said. "One of

the Plated Folk. They're trying to find allies among the locals. We have to inform the authorities.''

''We'll do that for a fact, mate,'' said a startled Mudge. ''Cor, t' think o' one o' them great ugly bugs a-sneakin' about in this part o' the world!''

''How could he get in here?'' Caz wondered.

''He looked as human as any of the others,'' Jon-Tom told them. ''Clothahump should know.''

Talea and Flor crawled back out of the secret doorway. ''No sign of the one Jon-Tom says he saw here, nor the scum that got away.''

They moved cautiously to the main door. Jon-Tom gathered up his belongings. It felt good to have the smooth bulk of the duar under his arm and the staff in his hands. While his companions formed a protective cordon around him, Mudge checked the stairway. It was empty now.

Then they were racing up the hallway toward the street, Jon-Tom and Flor taking the steps two at a time. Mudge and Talea burst outward into the mist, one looking right, the other left.

''All clear,'' Talea called back. The others soon stood on the cobblestones.

They started back up the street. Eyes searched windows for drawn bows as they walked rapidly between dark buildings. Pog overflew alleys in search of ambush. But there was no sign of any attempt to block their progress.

Jon-Tom stumbled once as his shoulder flared with pain. Talea was alongside. She remained there despite his insistence that he was all right.

''This outlaw band,'' she inquired, still warily inspecting the street ahead, ''you sure you didn't consider joining up with them? They might do real well if they have Plated Folk support.''

''Why would I do an asinine thing like that?'' he snapped. ''I've no love for the insects.''

"They've done nothing to you or yours. Why should you not be as willing to join with them as with us?"

How much did she overhear through that grating? he wondered. Then it occurred to him that she was nervous, not angry. The unaccustomed expression of vulnerability made him feel suddenly and oddly warm inside.

"I didn't like those people," he told her calmly. "I didn't like that envoy Hanniwuz. And I do like you. And Caz, and Mudge, and the others."

"As simple as that?"

"As simple as that, Talea."

She seemed about to say something more, lengthened her stride instead. "Let's hurry it up." She moved out in front of them and the others, even the long-limbed spellsinger, had to hurry to keep pace.

A disturbed Pog suddenly dipped low overhead. "Jon-Tom, Jon-Tom! There's something wrong up ahead!"

"What? What's wrong, Pog?"

"Big commotion, boss. Many people running like da Naganuph's after dem. I can't see a cause yet."

They turned a corner and were nearly trampled. Dozens of citizens poured down the wide street, bumping into the new arrivals and each other. Anxious raccoons cuddled masked infants in their arms, squirrel tails bobbed hysterically, and nightgown-clad anteaters stumbled into panicky simians. All were screeching and yelling and bawling in fear, and all were obviously running away from something utterly terrifying.

"What's wrong, what's the matter?" Talea demanded of one of the fleeing inhabitants.

The elderly bobcat beat feebly at her with her cane. "Let me go, woman. He's gone mad, he has. He'll kill us all! Let me go!"

"Who's gone mad? What . . . ?"

In her other hand the feline carried a heavy purse, weighed down perhaps with the family gold horde. She struck at Talea's wrist with it and tore free of her grasp.

Humans in night clothes and sleeping caps were among the mob. With their smooth strides they were outdistancing some of their shorter-legged neighbors, but they were equally panicked. Only the occasional roos and wallabies bounded past them.

"Falameezar. It's got to be," Jon-Tom said fearfully. "Something's gone wrong at the barracks."

"Maybe it would be better," Mudge said, slowing slightly, "if some of us waited 'ere. Pog and I could stay in reserve in case of . . ."

"Not me," said the bat forcefully. "My master may be in trouble. I've got ta help him if he is."

"Loyalty from you, Pog?" Jon-Tom couldn't help saying aloud.

"Loyalty my airborne arse!" the bat snorted derisively. "Dat hard-shelled senile old turd and I have a contract, and he's not gonna get out of it by getting himself stepped on by some berserk overheated lizard!" He soared on ahead above the foot traffic, darting and weaving his way around the panicked birds and bats that flew toward him.

For a while it seemed as if they'd never make it back to the courtyard. Eventually the crowds of refugees started to thin, however. Soon they'd vanished altogether.

Ahead the evening sky was glowing brightly, and it wasn't from a rising moon. They turned a last corner and found themselves in the open square on the opposite side from the barracks. That massive structure was a mass of flame. Orange fire licked at the sky from several smaller buildings nearby, but the blaze had not yet spread to the large, closely packed residential structures lining the courtyard. The city wall was solid rock and immune to the flames, though tents and banners and other flammables stacked near it were twisting skeletons of orange-lipped black ash that writhed and shrank in the night.

Close by the main harbor gate stood several clusters of nervous animals. Some were in uniform, others only partially so. Behind them were several large wagons, three axled, sporting hand pumps. The rudely awakened soldiers waited and held tight to their axes and spears while handlers behind them tried frantically to control the baying, hissing lizards yoked to the wagons.

Tubes trailed like brown snakes from each wagon back through the partly opened gate and doubtless from there out into the river. It was clear that the Polastrindu fire department was equipped to fight fires, but not the black and purple-blue behemoth they could hear raging and roaring behind the wall of flame that had engulfed the barracks.

"Clothahump! Where's Clothahump?" Pog yelled as the little group raced across the cobblestones toward the gate.

The leader of one of the fire teams gazed at the bat uncomprehendingly for a moment before replying. "The wizard turtle, you mean?" He gestured indifferently to his left. Then he returned his attention to the spreading conflagration, obviously debating in his mind if it was worth the risk of attracting the dragon's attention in order to try to at least contain the vangard of the blaze.

They found Clothahump seated nearby on a low hitching bench contemplating the fire. From time to time thunderous bellows and Hephaestean threats could be heard from somewhere inside the blazing barracks.

They clustered around the motionless wizard, looked at him helplessly. He appeared to be deep in thought.

"What happened, sir?" asked Flor concernedly.

"What?" He looked around, frowned at some private thought. "Happened? Oh yes. The dragon. The dragon and I were talking pleasantly. I was doing quite well, boy." The wizard's glasses were bent and dangled precariously on his beak. His carapace was black with soot and he looked very old, Jon-Tom thought.

"I was rationalizing my end of the discussion efficiently when a pair of our guards joined us unexpectedly. They wondered where you were and I informed them you were all asleep, but they remained. I think they were attempting to prove their bravery by remaining in the dragon's presence.

"Falameezar greeted them as comrades, a word I explained to them. We all began to talk. I would have made excuses, but the dragon was enthusiastic about the chance to have a serious talk with members of the local proletariat." Despite the proximity of the blaze, a cold chill traveled down Jon-Tom's spine.

"The beast inquired about their aspirations for their huge commune and their eventual hopes for strengthening proletarian solidarity. None of that made any sense to the guards, of course, but then it doesn't make any sense to me either, so I was hard put to rationalize their replies.

"But that was not what ignited, so to speak, the problem. Soon both guards were boasting uncontrollably about their plans for leaving the army and getting rich. I tried to quiet them, but between explaining to the dragon and attempting to silence them, I got confused. I could not work any magic to shut them up.

"They went on and on about their supposedly wealthy friends, one of whom was a merchant who had a hundred and sixty people working for him, slaving away making garments for the trade. They boasted about how cheaply he paid them, how enormous his profits were, and how they hoped they would be as fortunate some day.

"I think what finally set the dragon off was the offer one of them made to employ him to work in a foundry, helping to make weapons so the local police could clear the streets of 'the pitiful beggars who infest decent neighborhoods.' That appeared to send him beyond reason. I could no longer communicate with him.

"He started raving about revolutions betrayed and capitalist moneymongers and began spewing fire in all directions. It was only by tucking my head into my shell and scrambling as fast as I could that I escaped. The two rabbit guards, I fear, exploded like torches when the dragon exhaled at them.'' He sighed heavily.

"Now he insists he will burn down the entire city. I'm afraid the only thing that has kept him from destroying more of the town thus far is his own rage. It chokes him so severely he cannot concentrate on generating fire."

"Why don't you make him stop, wizard?" Talea was leaning close to his face and practically shouting into it. "You're the all-powerful sorcerer, the great master of magic. Make him stop!"

"Stop, yes? I was trying to think." Clothahump leaned his chin on stubby fingers. "Dragon spells are as complicated as their subjects, you know. The right ingredients are required for a truly effective cast. I don't know . . ."

"You've got to do something!" She looked back at the searing blaze. Then she looked at Jon-Tom. So did everyone else.

"Now the lad's willin' and good-natured," said Mudge cautioningly, "but 'e ain't no fool. Are you, mate?" The otter was torn between common sense and the desire to save his own highly flammable skin.

But Jon-Tom already had the duar swung around against his belly and was trying to think of something to sing. He could remember several rain songs, but that might only anger the dragon and certainly wouldn't solve the problem. Falameezar might not burn Polastrindu down, but from the smashing and crunching sounds issuing from behind the flames Jon-Tom judged him quite capable of tearing it down physically.

He marched out toward the barracks, ignoring the single plea that came from Flor. None of the others tried to dissuade him. They had not the right, and they knew he had to try. They wanted him to try.

The near barracks' wall suddenly collapsed in a Niagara of flaming embers and hot coals. He shielded himself with the duar and his green cape. There was a roaring in his ears from the flames, and wood exploded from the heat ahead.

"*You*! Deviationist! Counterrevolutionary!" The epithets emerged fast and accusing from the fire, though so far without accompanying arcs of flame. Jon-Tom looked up from beneath his cape and found himself only a couple of yards away from the glowering visage of Falameezar. Red eyes burned down into his own, and plate-sized teeth gleamed in the orange light as the dragon-skull dipped down toward him. . . .

XXI

"Lies, lies, lies! You lied to me." A massive clawed foot gestured toward the inner city. "This is no commune, not even in part, but instead a virulent nest of capitalistic vice. It needs not to be reformed, for it is beyond that. It needs to be *cleansed*!"

"Now hold on a minute, Falameezar." Jon-Tom tried hard to sound righteous. "What gives you the right to decide what should happen to all these workers?"

"Workers . . . pagh!" Fire scorched the cobblestones just to Jon-Tom's right. "They have the tasks of workers, but the souls of imperialists! As for my right, I am pure of philosophy and dedicated in my aims. I can tell when a society is capable of achieving a noble state . . . or is beyond redemption! And besides," he spat a petulant burst of fire at a nearby market stall, which immediately burst into flame, "you lied to me."

Since indecision was clearly the path leading to imminent incineration, Jon-Tom replied boldly. "I did *not* lie to you, Falameezar. This is a commune-to-be, and most of the population are workers."

"It means naught if they willingly condone the system which exploits them."

"How much choice does an oppressed worker have, comrade? It is easy to speak of revolution when you're twenty times bigger than anyone else and can spit fire and destruction. You expect an awful lot of some poor worker with a family to take care of. You don't have those kinds of responsibilities, do you?''

"No, but . . ."

"Then don't condemn some poor bear for protecting his family. You're asking them to sacrifice cubs and children. And besides, they don't have your education. You're expecting revolutionary sophistication from uneducated workers. Shouldn't you try and educate them first? Then if they reject the True Path and continue to accept the capitalistic evils they live with, then it will be time for cleansing.''

And by that time, he thought hopefully, we'll be safely away from Polastrindu.

"They still willingly countenance an antibourgeois life," said Falameezar grumblingly, but with less certainty.

Meanwhile Jon-Tom was still furiously trying to recall an anti-dragon song. He didn't know any. "Puff the Magic Dragon" was pleasant but hardly restrictive. Think, man, think!

But he had no time to think of songs. He was too busy trying to tie the dragon's tale into semantic knots.

"But would it not be best for all concerned if a warning was to be given?''

Falameezar's head rose high against the glowing night. "Yes, a warning! Burn out the evil influences so that the new order can be installed. Down with the exploiting industries and the factories of the capitalists! Build the commune anew, beneath the banner of true socialism.''

"Didn't you hear what I just said?" Jon-Tom took a worried step backward. "You'll destroy the homes of the innocent, ignorant workers.''

"It will be good for them," Falameezar replied firmly. "They will have to rebuild their homes with their own hands, cooperatively, instead of living in those owned by landlords and the bosses. Yes, the people must have the opportunity to begin afresh." He turned his attention speculatively to the nearest multistoried building, considering how most efficiently to commence "cleansing" it.

"But they already hate their bosses." Jon-Tom ran parallel to the loping dragon. "There's no reason to put them out in the rain and cold. What's needed here now isn't violence but a sound revolutionary dialectic!"

Falameezar's claws scraped on the cobblestones like the wheels of a vast engine.

"Remember the workers!" He shook his fist at the unresponsive dragon. "Consider their ignorance and their personal plights." Then, without thinking, his fingers were flying over the duar, the necessary words and music having come to him abruptly and unbidden.

"Arise ye pris'ners of starvation!
Arise, ye wretched of the Earth.
For justice thunders condemnation, a better world in birth.
No more tradition's chains shall bind us.
Arise, you slaves, no more in thrall!"

At the first stirring words of the "*Internationale*," Falameezar halted as if shot. Slowly his head swung around and down to stare blankly at Jon-Tom.

"Watch 'im, mate!" sounded the faint voice of Mudge. Similar warnings came from Caz and Flor, Talea and Pog.

But the dragon was utterly mesmerized. His ears remained cocked attentively forward as the singer's voice rose and fell.

Finally the anthem was at an end. As Jon-Tom's fingers trailed a last time over the duar's strings, Falameezar slowly emerged from his stupor, nodding slowly.

"Yes, you are right, comrade. I will do what you say. For a moment I forgot what is truly important. Compassion was lost in my desire to establish proper dogma among the proletariat. I had forgotten the more important task before us in my rage at petty injustice." His head drooped low.

"I lost control of myself, and I apologize for the damage."

Jon-Tom whirled and frantically waved his arms, shouting the all-clear. Immediately the wagons of the Polastrindu fire brigade trundled forward, trailing hoses like brown slugtracks. Hands and paws were laid to pumps, and water was soon attacking the burning barracks. Thicker dark smoke filled the sky as the flames were pushed back and hot embers sizzled.

"I shall cause no more trouble," said the downcast dragon. "I will not forget again." Then the great lean skull turned to one side, and a crimson eye locked on Jon-Tom. "But before long we *will* make revolutionary progress here, and the bosses will be thrown out."

Jon-Tom nodded rapidly. "Of course. Remember that first we have to defeat the most repressive, most brutal bosses of all."

"I will remember." Falameezar sighed and a puff of smoke emerged from his mouth. Jon-Tom winced instinctively, but there was no flame. "We will strike to protect the workers." He curled up like a great cat, laid his head across his right foreleg.

"I'm very tired now. I leave the night in your hands, Comrade." With that he closed his eyes, oblivious to the activity and smoke and yelling all around him, and went peacefully to sleep.

"Thank you, Comrade Falameezar." Jon-Tom turned away. He was starting to shiver now, recalling the feel of heat on his face and the fury in the dragon's gaze when he'd first confronted him.

His friends were cautiously running to him. Their expressions were a mixture of relief and awe.

"What in hell did you sing?...What spell did you use?...How did you do it?" were some of the amazed comments.

"I don't know, I'm not sure. The words just came to me. Old studies that stick," he muttered as they walked back toward the city gate.

Clothahump was waiting there to greet him. The old turtle

solemnly offered his hand. "A feat worthy of a true wizard, whether you believe yourself that or not, my boy. I salute you. You have just saved our journey."

"I'm afraid my principal motivation was to save myself, there at the last." He couldn't meet the wizard's eyes.

"Tut, motivation! It is accomplishment and result that count. I welcome you to the brotherhood of magicians." Jon-Tom found his fingers clasped in the cool but emphatic grasp of the elderly sorcerer.

"Perhaps it would be a good thing if you were to teach me the words to that spellsong, in case something were to happen to you. My voice is not particularly melodious, but at least I would have the words. It sounded especially powerful, and may serve to control the beast another time."

"It specializes in control, for all sorts of beasts," Jon-Tom replied.

The others listened as well, but the words had no special effect on them. Across the courtyard the fire brigade was bringing the last of the blaze under control. Falameezar snored unconcernedly nearby, his rage spent, his conscience assuaged.

Possibly it was because of Falameezar's tantrum, but in any case the summons to council came the following day. A much subdued beaver informed them that the representatives they'd wished to meet were already assembled and waiting for them.

Jon-Tom had spent much of the previous night coaching Caz in socialist jargon, realizing that Clothahump could not remain behind this time. The fact that the rabbit had volunteered to remain behind and keep a watch on the still somnolent dragon pleased Jon-Tom.

The fact that Talea and Flor had decided to remain and assist him did not. So he was in a foul mood as they neared the city hall.

"My boy," Clothahump was telling him, "if ever you live to be half my age you will learn that love is a lasting thing,

while lust is but transitory. Are you so sure that you've sorted
out the degree and direction of your feelings? Because if you
are drowning in the former, then you have my wholehearted
support. If merely the latter, then I can only sympathize with
your subservience to the follies of youth, which are locked to
but physical matters.''

"It's just physical to *me*." He slammed the butt end of his
staff angrily into the road with each stride. "Anyhow, you
can't be objective about it. Aren't turtles by nature sluggish in
such matters?''

"Occasionally yes, sometimes no. What is important is
one's mental reaction, since it is the mind that makes the
separation between love and lust, not the body. You let your
gonads do your thinking, my boy, and you're no better than a
lizard.''

"That's easy for you to say. I'd imagine the internal fires
are barely simmering after two hundred and a few odd
years.''

"We are not talking about my situation but of yours."

"Well, I'm trying to control myself."

"That's the good lad. Then I suggest you stop trying to
find water beneath the street.''

Jon-Tom eased up on his staff.

Mudge strode cockily alongside the youth. He was basking
in the attention of the pedestrians who stopped on the street to
stare at them, in the curious looks of others peering down
from windows. Pog fluttered and soared majestically overhead, darting past aerial abodes with seeming indifference to
their feathered inhabitants. While Clothahump did not antici-
pate treachery, he'd still insisted the bat remain safely out of
arrow shot. Pog was their link with the unspoken dragon-
threat sleeping back by the harbor gate.

"We're here, thirth." The beaver came to a halt, and
directed them onward. They climbed a series of stone steps.
Two guards stood on either side of the arched entrance. They
snapped to attention, ceremonial armor shining in the sun and

giving evidence of much laborious polishing. Dents in the metal were testimony to other activities.

Life quickly returned to normal around the fountain that dominated the small square in front of the city hall. Jon-Tom paused to study the peaceful scene.

A young wolf bitch nursed two cubs. Young hares and muskrats played a crude variety of field hockey with sticks and the battered skull of a recent guillotine victim. Two grizzled oldsters chatted casually about weather and politics. The aged possum hung from an oak tree branch while his corpulent companion, a fat fox clad in heavy overcoat, sat beneath him on a bench. The fact that one was upside down and the other rightside up had no effect on their conversation.

A clockmaker and candleshop owner stood in their doorways and argued business in the warmth of the unusually benign winter day. A customer entered the clock shop and the proprietor, an aproned gibbon, returned reluctantly to ply his trade.

Maybe the warm day was a good omen, Jon-Tom thought as he turned away from the peaceful scene. It was hard to imagine that all who frolicked or chattered in the square might soon be dead or locked in slavery.

It looked heartbreakingly normal. He felt that if he could only blink, refocus his mind, when he opened his eyes again there would be old men sitting and talking, boys and girls running and playing. And yet they were old men, boys and girls, for all their shapes were different and they were covered with warm fur. It was the warm blood that mattered. Everything else was superficial.

He turned to gaze into the hallway before them. They would have to face and convince a hostile, suspicious Council of the danger that was imminent. Somehow he would have to master the magic inherent in his duar and in his voice. He was not going to confront a group of teachers now, not about to present a scholarly master's thesis on some obscure portion of history. Millions of lives were at stake. The future of this world and maybe his own.

Except . . . this was his world now, and the dark future forseen by Clothahump had become his future. His friends stood alongside him, ready to offer support and comfort. Flor Quintera never looked as beautiful shouting inanities beside a field of false combat. He would talk loud and hope silently.

"Let's go, and may the strength of our ancestors go with us," announced Clothahump, trundling up the last steps.

Jon-Tom could only agree, though as they passed beneath the appraising stares of the soldiers lining the hallway, he wished fervently for a little grass, and not the kind that grew in the courtyard outside.

Watch for **SPELLSINGER's** thrilling sequel, **THE HOUR OF THE GATE,** now available from Warner Books.